THE REVENGE OF THE BANKER'S DAUGHTER

T. MATT RYAN

KITSAP PUBLISHING

The Revenge of the Banker's Daughter
First edition, published 2016

By T. Matt Ryan
Cover design: Nick Johnson at CIMA Creative

Copyright © 2016, T. Matt Ryan

ISBN-13: 978-1-942661-28-3

Published by Kitsap Publishing
P.O. Box 572
Poulsbo, WA 98370
www.KitsapPublishing.com

Printed in the United States of America

TD 201701090

50-10 9 8 7 6 5 4 3 2

Acknowledgments

My wife, Pat Ryan for keeping me going; listening and being a helpful critic.

Brian Roberts for editing this manuscript.

Nick Johnson for creating the book cover.

Bob Schumacher and friends at the Café Noir for teaching me the craft of writing.

Jack Archer and Dick Mace, critics and supporters.

*Old-timers in Goodwin, Colorado, mark the day of the
annual Community Graduation Ball, Friday, May 31, 1946,
as the end of an era. Who would have believed Gloria Knight
would have been the catalyst, the cause of it all? She was
the daughter of Lyle Knight, the richest man and political
kingmaker of Goodwin County.*

CHAPTER 1
The Marriage Proposal

Senior Deputy Sheriff John Diamond rushed from the dance floor to the pay phone in the lobby of Goodwin County's National Guard Armory. A big man, John filled the phone booth to capacity. He also filled his uniform to more than capacity. His stretched shirt was barely fastened by its buttons over his huge belly so that his white undershirt appeared where it shrank back between the buttons. He scratched the top of his bald head while the number rang. After greetings he said, "Mr. Knight, Joe Caulfels just got up on the bandstand and proposed to your daughter. She said yes."

"What? John, thank you. I know you share my values. Unfortunately my daughter has been blinded by the charm of that whoremonger's son. Painful as it will be to her, there will be no marriage to that … that half-breed. I'll get my shoes on and come on down to the armory."

"Okay, but they aren't here. The reason I called is, I seen them drive off in the bootlegger's dream car."

"Left the dance early? Damn, I know what comes next. I need your help. She's seventeen and below the age of consent. Caulfels is an adult.

The Caulfels family must be driven out. They have evil genes. Arrest that gigolo for statutory rape. As for Gloria, short of criminal charges, I trust you to use your ingenuity to bring her to reality. Bring her to reality, sharply!"

"Yessir, sharply it will be. I gotta take a few minutes to get a backup and bring in an officer to take my place."

Gloria Knight, in her thirteenth year, had noticed how men's eyes were drawn to her. By the end of her senior year in high school, she was the girl who had everything: knockout beauty, brains, and the drive sufficient to be class valedictorian. She was the only child of gifted banker and financier Lyle Knight; and now, on this evening, the fiancé of the most popular boy in her class, Joe Caulfels. Tall and sensual, she could have passed as a model in an ad for a new Cadillac.

Gloria kissed Joe as he helped her into the passenger seat of his father's classic white 1928 Cadillac touring car--the "bootlegger's dream car" as the deputies called it. She pulled in the skirt of the high-fashion white strapless gown she was wearing. She touched the rhinestone choker, a graduation present from her father.

As she watched her fiancé, a dark-skinned, muscular six-footer, circle the car to the driver's side, she thought, *Yes, Joe is the handsomest boy I have ever met. That just drew me to him. Over the two years I've known him, I've never doubted his honesty or felt embarrassed by the way he treats people, as I have by my father. I like being with Joe. I pray that his belief that we must make known our love, our engagement, will be enough to overcome the hatred between our families. Tonight I enjoyed being in his arms in public on a dance floor.*

She looked back over her shoulder at the faint outline of the steel and concrete National Guard Armory, where the people standing on the front steps noted their departure. On this unseasonably warm evening, they rode with the windows down so that the breeze picked up and tossed her ringlets of thick brunette hair, while the noise from a rusted-out muffler made conversation difficult.

I'm still getting used to the idea, Gloria mused, *that this absolutely wonderful boy—no, wonderful man, has fallen in love with me. Joe could have any girl in Goodwin and he chose me! When he stood up on the podium in front of everybody and proposed, he sent a message. We're serious about ending our courtship in the shadows. Like Joe said, we'll give our families time to get used to the idea. Our job will be to bring love into hearts where there has been hate.*

Joe made a turn that put the white Cadillac on the highway out of town and up the canyon. Gloria found travel at night on the canyon highway a bit disconcerting as they wheeled through the narrow stretches. Granite and sandstone cliffs, chiseled out of the mountainside, rose from almost the road's shoulder to the sky where the tops were lighted in the semi-darkness by a moon just past full. Guardrails whizzed by on their right. Water vapor from the spring melt, tumbling over the rocks below, wafted up and was just damp enough for Joe to run the wipers and roll up the windows.

Halfway up the canyon, the walls spread apart where a sizable stream joined the river. Joe pointed to an intersecting road. "This is one of Ma's favorite stopping places on the way home from town. I learned to swim in the pond behind the little dam."

After the road turned away from the canyon and went through a loose hairpin curve to climb upward, Gloria pointed out the promontory in the park below where she and her father once had stopped to watch a freight train of flatcars loaded with U.S. Army tanks coming down the grade.

Joe said, "In the first few months after Pa came home from Leavenworth, he used to park down there and watch the trains for hours."

I'd love to get on a train with Joe and never come back, thought Gloria. She sat close by her fiancé with a hand on his right thigh. At last they turned off the highway and into a short drive that took them to an old but sturdy two-car garage and holding pens for the Caulfels' cattle. This ranch, consisting of five acres on the highway side and twenty-one acres on the railroad side, was all that remained of the family's real estate empire. A hand-powered cable car connected the parcels, replacing a bridge that had washed out. A lease on adjoining federal grazing land made the cattle rearing operation possible.

Her first hint of the trouble ahead came when Joe exclaimed, "The cable car is stuck on the other side."

She cautioned Joe to avoid soiling the tux she had rented for the graduation ball. He turned on the yard lights so that the cable and the opposite bank, some thirty yards away, were visible for the first time. After ten minutes of Joe's fussing with the apparatus, calling out, and finally honking the horn, his father, Orville Caulfels, emerged from the shadows. "Damn you, Joseph Corwin Caulfels, you lied to me. Take the Knight girl back to her slimy papa. Come on back without her and we'll talk. I can't afford for you to go off and join the Army."

Joe said to Gloria, "They found my papers for enlisting in the Army. I've been ordered to report to boot camp on the tenth of June."

Oh my God, thought Gloria, *tenth of June! The recruiter promised nothing earlier than mid-July. That doesn't give us much time together before Joe has to leave.* Gloria and Orville both asked, almost simultaneously, "Why didn't you tell me?"

Joe answered Gloria, "I'm sorry, I planned to. Once you sign the papers, you have to go when they say. I want my parents to agree to keep in touch with you while I'm away." He looked at her out of the corner of his eye.

Gloria stepped to the edge of the bank, cupped her hands around her mouth, and shouted, "I'm going to marry your son in four years. We need to talk now."

"Not with a damned Knight, I don't. Get the hell off my property."

"We're engaged. Please, let us talk with you."

"Joe, take her home before she gets you in trouble"

Gloria pressed her hands together in a prayerful posture. "Please, Mr. Caulfels, please give me five minutes."

"Pa, we will get married. I will join up on time."

"Git!" Orville turned his back and walked away.

Save for the sounds from the river, silence reigned. Joe gently pulled Gloria back from the edge. "Pa's too angry. Look at it through his eyes. He almost went back to prison because your mother turned him in for drinking. What do you think we ought to do? Go back to the dance?"

Vera jumped up from her chair on hearing Orville's angry voice as he approached the house from the river. As she made her way to the front of the cabin, she reminded herself that if her husband destroyed this door, the next one should open inward. She arrived in time to see the front door jerked open. "Orville!"

He stood with his hand on the knob of the wide-open door, his arm extended and his torso twisted. As soon as he saw her rawboned figure in the shadows, he said, "If I hadn't jammed that trolley car to keep him on the other side, I could have gotten my hands on Joe. I woulda beaten him black and blue."

She thought, *This is the man they gave me back after his time inside, with most of his self-control drained away. Look at him, whatever did our son do for him to be wound up so?* Her sharp, dark, half-Indian eyes stared him down. "Orville, enough of that talk. Don't you dare slam that door! Where is he?"

"Like I told ya, I knew something wasn't on the up and up. That boy, Ma, that boy, I'm so damned angry. After all we've done to explain that the Knights are more powerful trouble than any of us can handle! Well, in one fell swoop, he sticks it to us."

"What in blazes are you talking about? Where's Joe?"

"I locked the trolley right after I found the letter from the Army. He's leaving on the tenth. Just to rub my nose in it, he brings that Knight slut here to introduce her as his fiancée." Orville handed her the letter.

Vera took the envelope over to a table lamp, "He's enlisting like Sunny advised him to. With that Republican in the House, chances of a Congressional appointment to West Point right now are between slim and none. Sunny told Joe that if he's in the Army, he'll have to compete against a broad field for a limited number of appointments,"

"Goldang it, I need him here. At fifty-eight years, I'm not getting any younger. Joe is all we got now. Sure as God made little green apples, Sunny can't be counted on to come back home and give up his Army Air Forces career.'

"Well, Orville, I'm afraid we're in for a soap opera complete with heartaches," said Vera. "Joe knows he can't get into the Point if they're married; but announcing the engagement now makes me think she's bound and determined to hang onto him, come what may."

"She's in for a battle because her folks don't want this any more than we do. Knowing old crooked Lyle, he'll figure a way to get 'em thrown in jail."

"Oh, what kind of charges could he think up? Nothing serious, because Joe doesn't drink and is an honest, hard worker. The worst Lyle can do is some petty misdemeanor charge, long enough to get the girl out of town."

Orville vigorously rubbed his hands together. "He'll think of something--and maybe that's the answer to our prayers. Let this young man stand on his own feet and face the consequences. We'll take him back afterwards."

Once Orville unwound, he lay down in their bed and soon was snoring. Vera sat down at the table, not sleepy enough to retire and with a mind full of racing thoughts. *I couldn't think of a better way to teach Joe a lesson and send a message to Lyle that we don't want the match either,* she thought, *than to let him face the consequences.*

The word "consequences" triggered Vera's memories, stretching back to when they learned that Virginian Lyle Knight had been sent from New York, after closure of the last gold mine, to save the Goodwin National Bank. She and Orville had felt confident that whoever became the new bank president would welcome their business. Had they not in the past bought stock at full price to keep that one bank in town alive? The current manager praised Lyle for his skills in finding substantial investors for qualified projects.

Vera and Orville had a dream project, a resort hotel on the hill that overlooked Goodwin. They looked on the resort as the way they would survive if Prohibition, which was then being debated in Congress, should become the law of the land. They held an option on the water rights to the hot springs and enough acreage to build the resort. They had a hotel in town that got most of its income from its saloon, but they figured they could sell it before whiskey was outlawed.

Orville even coaxed the president of the new Rotary Club to invite Lyle to speak at their hotel on the subject of Prohibition. It was well known that Lyle was a "dry" and strongly favored it.

However, another strong attitude of Lyle's came to the fore when he arrived for his speech and met Vera for the first time. "I didn't know savages were allowed to work in drinking establishments," was his comment on seeing Vera's dark face. She introduced herself as Orville's wife and demanded an apology. Lyle looked down his nose and said in his Southern drawl, "I don't intend to lower myself by apologizing to the woman of the owner of what will soon be an outlaw establishment."

Vera was so angry that she told the waiter to fill the water pitcher on the podium with iced gin. The dry Mr. Knight was halfway through his talk when he took the first swig. He coughed and spat. He lost his voice. He took another swig. He sounded like a frog. Everybody there laughed, and he sat down.

It went downhill from there, Vera recalled ruefully. *I wish I could have undone it.* This was a turning point in their lives. The first consequence was the bank's letter informing them of a change in their credit profile. Lyle put them at the bottom end of the scales for everything and raised rates prohibitively. He made it clear that he had resolved to force the Caulfels family with their "evil genes" out of town and, if possible, out of the county. They vowed to stay.

Prohibition passed Congress and became effective in January of nineteen twenty. Prior to that date, Sheriff Brad Hanlon "invited" Orville to keep on providing strong drink for Goodwin so as to "keep out bad elements" from the other side of the Continental Divide. Truth was, the sheriff wanted to add the rake-off from illegal booze to his under-the-table income, and he didn't want outsiders muscling in on his racket. His deputies provided protection and tipped off Orville and the other local bootleggers when Prohibition agents were on the road.

Those were the good times for Orville and Vera. The sheriff kept the competition away while Orville's stills were supplying speakeasies as far away as Denver. Money flooded in. Orville and Vera used cash to build their dream house on Garfield Street, next door to the Foyle's. Instead of putting money in the bank, they loaned it to farmers, many of whom paid off the bank. Lyle's resentment grew as Orville ate into the bank's lucrative mortgage business. Unlike Lyle, Orville did not reserve the mineral rights for himself.

Vera remembered the abrupt end of the good times in the spring of nineteen twenty-eight, when they were raided by a horde of Prohibition agents. Lyle, she knew, had to be behind it with the sheriff's connivance. In hindsight, Vera felt she should have recognized the threat when forty-year-old widower Lyle wed his new bride Theodora, known as Theo. She was a beautiful twenty-three-year-old leading lady from the temperance drama stage. She brought to life the local chapter of the Women's Christian Temperance Union, which picketed the hotel, drawing attention to the cribs on the top floor and Orville's speakeasy in the alley.

That was a terrifying day for Vera. The agents rushed with submachine guns into their new house on Garfield and forced her outside. She was nursing Joe. All their accounts and real estate were seized except for a safety deposit box with five thousand dollars in it. When the dust settled, her handsome husband was locked up in Leavenworth Prison on a twenty-year sentence. Lyle Knight bought their house and properties in town, at the sheriff's auction, for a song. Vera was exiled to the ranch, the only property they had left. Lyle was so confident he had won that he offered to buy Vera a one-way ticket to Leavenworth.

It couldn't have been much worse, recalled Vera, *but there were some circumstances in our favor.* Orville's customers, to whom he had been generous to a fault, loved him and looked after her until the repeal of Prohibition brought parole for Orville after seven years. The terms of his release spelled out "no alcohol," which Vera felt saved his life. Nevertheless he fell off the wagon a few times and was reported to his parole officer by Theo and her WCTU ladies.

One more fall could return Orville to prison, Vera thought, *but he's been dry over six months. I don't have to worry about him.*

Standing by the riverbank, Gloria pondered what to do next. *Ten June, that will be it. I want him. I can't afford to lose him.* "If we go back now, my father is as stubborn as yours. I know, let's kill some time down at Promontory Park."

"Before we go, do you remember when my parents and I visited the Wind River Reservation over spring vacation? Well, it's official. I am now an enrolled member of the Northern Arapaho tribe," announced Joe.

"I wish I could have been there for the ceremony."

"Thank you, that would mean so much to me. Tribal elder Sky Wolf drove down from Wind River with the letter inviting me to join. I learned my mother has an Indian name, "Happy Eyes.""

"Happy Eyes, I'd like to get to know her," answered Gloria.

"I'd like that too. Sky Wolf said his people lived along the river valley here after the Sand Creek Massacre of eighteen sixty-four. They kept lookouts at key places to spot Army patrols and ambush settlers."

Gloria laughed, "Just like the sheriff uses the Forest Service smoke spotters along the road to the east pass to catch bank robbers. We know there are only three ways in or out of the county. The bad guys'll never learn."

"Someday they'll learn that there's really four."

"Four? Come on, you're pulling my leg."

Joe laughed. "It's four counting the new county airport—five, with the airfield the Army is abandoning."

She gave her fiancé a playful hug. "Joe, darling, let's get on down the road to the park."

"You surprise me that you aren't upset about the Army calling me up way early."

"If I'm going to be married to a man who's in the Army, I 'm going to have to learn to adjust my plans to fit the Army's. Let's go. We can take a swim."

"It'll be cold."

"It's okay, we're engaged. We'll bundle in the back seat to get warm, then dress and drive home."

Joe's smile was broad enough to be seen in the moonlight. "Are you sure you want this?"

She put her hands on his cheeks and kissed him. "I'm sure I love you and I want to be with you always. It's okay, I've got rubbers."

Thank you, God, for bringing Joe Caulfels into my life. I can't believe I'm so lucky as to be his first love. He was like a jackrabbit. He came in my hand. It's so exciting. I have the second one on him, but I don't think he's anywhere near ready. I'll just lie here on top of him.

"Listen," Joe whispered, "there's somebody out there sneaking up on us."

Gloria rose up on her knees. "There's a car right behind us. Jokers? Could it be Andy Foyle? No, this guy's too big. Shove the door open."

Joe turned the lever and shoved the door hard. The door hit someone solidly, followed by the sound of breaking glass. "Son of a bitch," said a voice from the darkness. From behind Gloria, a flashlight beam lit up the back seat of the touring car for a moment.

As Joe pulled the door shut, the passenger side door was opened. Gloria was taken by surprise to feel a powerful hand grab her right calf and pull hard. She screamed as loud as she could. She aimed a blind kick, which hit her assailant's groin. Now it was his turn to shout. He had pulled her far enough out the door that her feet were on the ground. As she turned, there was just enough light from the stars and moon that she could make out the attacker's shadowy shape. He had dropped into a squat. Gloria heard the words "law officer" mixed with profanity. She made a fist and drove it into his face. Feeling his hands on her, she twisted away. She slipped clear as a familiar voice came from the other side of the car. It was Deputy John Diamond yelling, "Joe Caulfels, you are under arrest."

Gloria ran while the other deputy screamed warnings at her. She heard Joe throw his door open a second time. Deputy John's voice wailed, "Ooww, damn, that hurts! Joe Caulfels, you're under arrest--statutory rape--possession of alcoholic beverages as a minor—assault--resisting arrest …" The voice sounded like he was on the ground.

"Rape? Resisting arrest? Who are you? You're not funny."

Deputy John inserted himself in the open door, a hulking shadow, and shouted, "Peace officer! Peace officer! Don't you move. You're under arrest. Damn you, Joe Caulfels!" He shined his flashlight on himself for a moment before turning the beam on Joe's face. "I am Deputy John Diamond. You will obey me, sit up and face forward, hands on your head. Stop resisting or I will use deadly force."

As soon as Deputy John saw that Joe was sitting up facing forward, as commanded, he punched him in the jaw hard enough to lay him on his side. With practiced moves, he pulled Joe's arms behind his back and handcuffed him.

Joe shouted, "No, no, wait a minute! Why are you doing this? Who are you?" as the fat deputy dragged him from the Caddy and toward the Hudson cruiser car. Joe pleaded, "Please stop. I've cut my foot. I think it was broken glass. I'm hurt, please stop."

Deputy John spotted the condom on the otherwise naked teenager.

He spun him around and gave him two hard punches in the stomach. "What was it, going back for seconds or thirds?"

"Why did you hit me?" Joe was doubled over.

John grabbed him by the hair. "Seconds or thirds? How many times did you screw the banker's daughter?"

A low, weak voice came out of the darkness. "John, the bitch kicked me in the balls. She's gone."

"I hope she gets away," said Joe. "This isn't right. We weren't doing anything wrong. We're getting married." He struggled to get free.

Deputy John guided Joe by the arm. "You're in serious trouble. Her father is filing charges, statutory rape. At seventeen, she's under the age of consent. Get in the cruiser."

"We're innocent. We're high school classmates. This is crazy."

Deputy Lincoln Brown appeared out of the shadows. He was out of breath and leaned against the cruiser. "The Knight bitch got away. So this is how you shoot fish in a barrel? John, we've got to do something. I repeat, the Knight girl got away."

John Diamond blinked his eyes as he looked at the deputy with the bloody nose. "Oh, shit! Linc, how could you? Marcia's going to be pissed. How'd you let that skinny little whore get away?"

"First of all, she was slippery and she *ain't* little. I couldn't get a hold on her. I didn't see it coming. The bitch kicked me in the balls. Oh my God, it hurts."

"She punched you in the nose too. How bad is it? Can you drive?"

With Linc's affirmative, John reported the situation over the radio to Marcia Hanlon, the sheriff's wife. He concluded, "Marcia, she's bare-ass except for a rhinestone choker and it's getting down into the sixties. The only way for her to go is down the highway to town."

Marcia was the unofficial undersheriff. Officially she was Sheriff Brad's gofer, but she actually did most of his work. After John's report, she radioed orders to deploy all cars to the road up the canyon, except for Linc Brown's, which would be used to transport Joe; Deputies Tom Weisner and John were to patrol the park. Then she let loose on John and Linc with a harangue, ending with a warning to Linc that he was on probation until she was satisfied he could handle arrests of adult males. Both deputies stood by the cruiser with a handcuffed Joe locked in the back seat.

Deputy Tom, who had just joined them in the park, said, "What a holy terror! If the sheriff hadn't married Marcia, she'd still be a guard in the pen at Canon City."

John said, "With Sheriff Brad being past eighty, and she's in her forties, she's more sheriff than he is. More than an undersheriff, and more than a wife. He can't get along without her. They need to convince her to work toward getting her citizenship, so she's got official clout. Might help convince banker Knight to give her some credit. He ain't sold on her yet."

"Why is that?"

"He don't like breeds in general. And Mexicans like Marcia—well, ya know, all them taco eaters are half redskin. I think he's a wise man. As for me, it was hard getting used to Sheriff Brad being married to a Mexican. But she earned my respect. Damn, she puts the fear of God into all the trash we arrest!"

CHAPTER 2
Capture of Gloria Knight

After the adrenaline rush passed, Gloria felt the pain from the twigs and sharp rocks underfoot. The flashing light atop the approaching sheriff's cruiser gave her ample time to hide. She realized there were at least three of them and one of her. She thought that since they had arrested Joe, they would take him in, but no such luck. She dreaded walking all the way home naked.

She knew and feared the fat deputy in charge, John Diamond. Diamond was known behind his back as Deputy Four Eff because he failed the physical for the military in World War II. It was generally known that he failed because of his obesity, which should have also disqualified him as a deputy, yet he stayed on and kept getting promoted. He was said to be "in" with the right people, which was said about a lot of Goodwin County's public servants in the nineteen forties.

Diamond had always been cordial to Gloria when he came to the house to deliver papers, but the way he looked at her made her skin crawl. There was the story she heard from her friend Carole Foyle, about a Mexican girl Four Eff arrested for underage drinking. The girl accepted his offer of "informal punishment" over a weekend rather than chance a year's sentence if convicted of the charge. However, Gloria told herself she had nothing serious to fear from Four Eff, in spite of what she heard about "rape" and "minor consumption" in the excitement of her escape. For starters, neither she nor Joe drank.

Gloria's resolve was waning. What began as an adrenaline-stoked race had become a painful trek through downright cold, misty night air on tender feet. The farther she walked, the darker the night, the rougher the terrain, and the more difficult to find her way. She worried about who would pick her up. She reversed course with the idea of turning herself in and facing the consequences.

She paused in the shadows just inside the tree line. The cruiser's dome light was just bright enough to see Joe in the back seat and silhouettes of the deputies. They passed a bottle back and forth. She concluded that her only chance of escape was to take the white Cadillac and hope she could get to where there were people before the deputies caught up. Gloria tiptoed back to the Caddy.

She swept Joe's tux into the passenger seat and slipped into the driver's seat. Her hands trembled. She fumbled in the dark to find the key and ignition switch while the deputies talked and drank. When she turned the key, the Caddy belched a huge backfire and a roar of exhaust through the failed muffler. Gloria was so startled that her bare foot slipped off the clutch, and the engine stalled as she tried to shift into gear. The Caddy came to a jerking halt, then began to roll toward the river.

The next moments went by in a blur. Behind her, she heard feet pounding the ground. Voices ordered her by name to stop. Deputy John, lugging close to two hundred ninety pounds, reached her first. The car had just started to roll when he opened the driver-side door. Hundred-and-ten-pound Gloria had both hands on the steering wheel and her foot on the clutch when he grabbed a handful of her hair with such force that she expected it to be pulled out by the roots. She held on because she believed her life depended on it.

Her foot slipped off the clutch again. The Caddy sputtered as if it were going to start on compression, then stalled. At that instant, another deputy on the passenger side pulled Gloria's hands off the steering wheel. Her cause was lost when he cuffed her wrists. In that distracted moment, as she paused to look at the steel bracelets, Deputy John shackled her ankles. She dropped into a sitting fetal posture. She covered her breasts with her hands.

Deputy John hunkered in front of her with an open burlap bag in hand. "Miss Knight, if you want to avoid having your hair pulled again, lean forward and touch your ankles." He slipped the bag over her head.

A deputy she had never seen before squatted behind her and took her choker off. "Miss Knight, I'm Deputy Tom Weisner. You are under arrest for assaulting a law officer, escape, indecent exposure, minor consumption of alcohol, and grand theft auto."

Gloria reached up with manacled hands to pull off the scratchy bag. It was in vain because Deputy John checked her move by holding the link between the cuffs. He pressed a thumb on the median nerve on her left arm. She screamed and tried to get away. She felt a hand holding her other arm with a finger ready to press on the other nerve. Deputy Tom closed the choker over the bag.

Oh, my God, what Carole told me is true. I can smell somebody else's perfume on the burlap bag. The Mexican girl said Four Eff's informal punishment began when a burlap bag was pulled over her head. He made her keep it on the whole time they fucked her. I've got to escape.

Rough hands spanked and pinched Gloria, who tried to crawl away with steel around her wrists and ankles. She screamed, "Stop, please stop. You win. You win. Take the bag off. I can't see."

Deputy Tom said, "Sit down and stop trying to escape custody. Blindfolds were standard procedure for handling escaped prisoners in the European Theater."

"Why are you doing this to me? All I want to do is be with Joe before he leaves for the Army."

Deputy John lectured her, "You crossed the line, Miss Gloria Knight. Your daddy has run out of patience. You let that Caulfels boy screw you in the back seat. Statutory rape for him, and who knows what the prosecutor will deal up when I'm done with you."

"No, you attacked us. Nothing happened between us. He came in my hand."

"Your daddy won't fix things for you like he did the last time, when you ran away to Denver. Cut your losses and do as I say. Relax your arms."

Gloria regretted coming back and not resisting more. With the bag blocking her sight, she expected to be raped. Yet like victims in documentaries, she followed orders to spread her knees apart. She allowed Deputy John to guide her hands between her thighs and outside her ankles. She felt the free cuff pass over her ankles and trap the other wrist. Although she couldn't see the small padlock that married the two sets of cuffs, she found her predicament uncomfortable at best. She constantly rocked from side to side to ease her discomfort. "Let me go! Get this damned bag off my head! Let me up!"

"Quiet, Miss Knight, quiet! You won't escape from Deputy John again." His voice faded as he walked back toward the sheriff's cruisers.

Gloria heard one of the cruisers drive away. She increased her rocking until she was on her side, then flopped around like a beached whale. She identified approaching footfalls as John's when he said, "Miss Knight, you've made matters worse for yourself."

"Deputy Diamond, please let me up and get dressed. I won't tell anyone what you did."

"No, Miss Knight, you tried to escape. You assaulted a deputy. You must pay." John inserted a branch between the crook of her elbows and behind her knees.

"No, no, please, I'm very uncomfortable. I'm freezing."

"Punishment, Miss Knight, punishment." John turned her so she was face down with her buns in the air and her weight borne by her knees and forearms. He slid the branch farther in. "You will remain here on your knees."

Her anger turned to panic when John made a long, penetrating touch, accompanied by his banter, "Am I hitting your button?" She knew then without a doubt that he planned to rape her.

She recognized the Cadillac's engine crank and its belching start, and heard it drive off. Then came the sound of another car, which she assumed was taking Joe to jail. When Gloria heard footfalls of what she imagined was a big man, she braced herself again, only for him to walk away. Then she heard a third car start and drive away. This cruiser had an exhaust that was almost as rusted out as the Cadillac's. The sound faded until the only thing she heard was the roaring river. She feared she had been abandoned here to be eaten by some mountain wildcat.

After what seemed like an eternity, she heard that raspy exhaust coming back again. She was shivering cold. She thought, *Deputy John Diamond is a friend of my father. He wouldn't jeopardize that. Yes, he pushes the limit with this punishment routine. He was gone long enough to ask Daddy whether he's to take me home or book me into the jail.*

The vehicle stopped close by her. A car door opened. Then, silence. Gloria called out, but no one answered.

After a while she jumped when she hear John's voice right behind her. "Miss Knight, I encourage you to express yourself as loud as you wish. I shut the gate so we can't be disturbed. To get you in the mood, let me again press your button. If that doesn't start you, I have a crank that will," bragged Deputy John as he began foreplay for his benefit.

Soon she felt John's hairy belly on her back. His full weight pushed her toward the ground. "Miss Knight, tonight the doc will report that something did happen."

She cried. She screamed. She fought with all her heart and energy, suffering cuts and bruises on her knees and down her shins, ankles, and wrists, plus pinched nerves in her limbs. She feared he would murder her after he was sated.

Instead, John lay on top of her for a long time. Finally Sheriff Hanlon's disembodied voice came from the radio and rousted the deputy from the slumber he'd fallen into. John briefed the sheriff, telling him that one deputy impounded the Cadillac and covered the dance; one delivered Joe to jail; and John had an eleven-thirty appointment for Gloria with Dr. Mundal at the jail.

When John started talking about charges against Gloria, Sheriff Hanlon cut him short. "Rape victims aren't arrested. Dr. Mundal will see her at his office for her exam."

The words resonated in Gloria's brain. Her hopes soared. They soared again when the sheriff told Deputy John that her father would be there to take her home. "Oh, shit," muttered John under his breath.

Concluding the radio transmission, the sheriff said, "Convict the Caulfels boy of rape and underage drinking. That oughta be enough to convince the Caulfels family to decamp from this county once and for all."

What a horrible fuck, the pain, the smell. I've pulled all sorts of muscles in my back. I've got muscle spasms up and down my legs. I need to see a doctor. Daddy won't let him get away with this. If I live to testify, he will go to prison. As pissed as I am, I can't give him any reason to murder me. Oh, my God, he's back again.

"Good, you still respond to my touch. I'm sorry, Miss Knight, there isn't time for another round. I'll honor your father's wishes. I won't file charges against you unless I can change his mind."

"Please let me get up and get dressed."

"The question is, are you going to cooperate?"

Gloria agreed. Even then, the gyves around her ankles and the bag over her head remained in place. After John zipped her up into her formal gown, he cuffed her hands behind her back.

During her ride into Goodwin, she recalled the other time she rode in the back of a police car. She had been arrested in Denver's Union Station as a fifteen-year-old runaway. She was famished and exhausted, yet still hungry for her first "true love." Her lover and companion, Private Paul Bixler, had left her there two days earlier, promising to wire her money for a train ride home. That was the last she heard of Paul until a month later, when he bragged of his conquest on "Kilroy was here" postcards mailed to all his friends. The nose of the Kilroy face on the card resembled an erect penis.

That time, her father had greeted her with a warm hug, but immediately shifted to anger that lasted all the way home. He then shut down all her social life except for visits to the trusted neighbors, Andy Foyle and his family, who lived next door. Gloria pulled herself inside a shell and stayed away from boys. Instead of dates, she tagged along with her father to his meetings and appointments.

She did see one boy during that period: Joe, when he visited the Foyles to do chores with Andy and take a bath every Wednesday. However, her father didn't know that at the time, and she believed that after close to two years, there was a fairly good father-daughter relationship.

She told herself that one word to her father and this sick bastard of a deputy would be arrested.

Deputy John removed the burlap bag, giving Gloria back the use of her eyes. She saw the familiar sandstone siding and glass front door at the office of her family doctor, Dr. Mundal, and this gave her hope that the ordeal was all but over. "Deputy Four Eff, you're going to prison for what you did," Gloria blurted out.

John spoke in a warm and fatherly voice. "Trust me, no one will believe you when you carry on like this. I've tried to comfort you. You should have tried to enjoy receiving the evidence. For Joe's sake, I'm warning you not to make any noise about tonight. Terrible things happen to uncooperative prisoners at the jail."

"Don't you dare. You're crazy! You raped me, you bastard!"

"I'm warning you, keep carrying on like this and you'll exchange that gown for a straitjacket and a room with padded walls. Let me help you inside."

Gloria had no alternative because she was still handcuffed. She held her breath to avoid another dose of John's foul odor, a mixture of sweat, onions, garlic, and stale beer. Seething within, she feared she would never enjoy the touch of any man after suffering John's unwanted caresses, mixed with his endless banter.

She managed to contain her rage until she was just inside the doctor's waiting room and saw her father sitting between Doctor Mundal and Sheriff Hanlon. Lyle jumped up upon seeing his daughter enter. She had seen that expression before. Her father was very angry. She spat out, "Help me, Daddy, this fat son of a bitch raped me!" She then watched in shock as her father's look turned to disgust. He backed away and sat down. *Can't he see? No, he can't.*

Lyle brushed unseen lint off his suit coat. *I've seen him do that before. He's there, but he doesn't care.* She screamed, "Daddy, you ought to be ashamed. Look at me, father!" Lyle didn't respond.

"Take the cuffs off her, John," ordered the sheriff. "This isn't the way we treat rape victims."

While John was feeding the key into the first cuff, he looked at his boss. "Sheriff, I've had to keep her in restraints for her own good. She's been hysterical since we found the Caulfels kid on top of her. It was her screaming that brought us to her rescue. She's in emotional shock and suffering from some kind of delusions."

"Liar, liar! Sheriff Hanlon, your stinking fat animal raped me. Arrest him now! "

John gave Gloria a serious look. "I'm sorry, Miss Knight. Keep calm, you were out of your mind when we found you. The doctor has medicine to calm your nerves."

"Calm my nerves, bullcrap! You raped me!"

"No, you're confused, Miss Knight."

Doctor Mundal pointed toward the examining room. "Gloria, honey, don't be afraid, you're safe here. Come with me. I need for you to climb up on the examining table."

"No, I'm not confused! Four Eff, you lying son of a bitch!" Gloria shouted. "Daddy, look at me. I'm talking to you. Help me or I'll never forgive you." *My God, I even smell like Four Eff. It's horrible.* Gloria spun out of her captor's grip with one handcuff still locked around her right wrist. She drove the fist into John's eye, and the open cuff nicked his forehead. "Confused, hell, you lying skunk, Four Eff! You raped me! "

The deputy and the doctor pounced on Gloria. By the time the struggle was over, enough pain had been dealt her that she allowed them to lock her hands behind her back. They lifted her to her feet. Her strapless gown was down far enough to reveal both breasts.

Lyle arose again from his seat. He yanked up the top, then brushed her hair back. Gloria spat in his face. He tilted his head back and looked down his nose at his daughter. While she fought to free herself of John's and the doctor's grip, her father leisurely unfolded the handkerchief from his breast pocket and wiped his face. "Rape indeed, don't sully this fine man's reputation. Thanks to your unrestrained theatrics at the armory, everyone knows who you were lying with. I have the will and the means to put an end to your rebellion."

Deputy John said, "Doc, give her the knockout drops, then I'll help you move her into the examining room."

Gloria watched the doctor squirt the needle and felt the instant jab. "Please, Doctor, you don't need to do this. I'll go, I'll go. Get this fat skunk out of here, he raped me. Please don't ...." Her voice trailed off as she slumped into a stupor.

CHAPTER 3
Joe Caulfels in Custody

Handcuffed, naked, and locked in the back seat of the Hudson cruiser, Joe Caulfels had shouted until his voice croaked ever since Gloria tried to drive off in the Cadillac. He was shocked to watch Deputy Diamond manhandle Gloria and leave her sitting on the ground, naked, hooded, and fettered hand and foot.

When all was quiet save for the roar of the nearby river, Deputy Linc Brown got in, introduced himself, started the Hudson, and put it in gear. Joe said, "You saw that deputy go overboard with Gloria. Why didn't you stop him?"

Deputy Linc steered the cruiser out of the deserted parking lot before he made eye contact via the rear view mirror. "She resisted arrest. Now why should I stop him? It was my balls she kicked and my nose she punched. Force is all she understands. I'm lookin' forward to seeing her with one of Marcia's jailhouse haircuts after she sweats it out down in the hole."

"Why did you attack us? Did Mr. Knight hire you?"

The deputy glanced into the mirror again and smirked. "Ain't that Knight broad a prime piece of ass?"

Joe blushed and looked down. *I fear for Gloria in that jail. God, please help her.*

Linc continued, "Hell, boy! You ain't the first. She has a reputation, you know."

"Stop, enough! Gloria Knight is my fiancée. If you're man enough to admit you're wrong, I'll accept your apology."

"Me, apologize? You, marry her? So that's how you got her to fall on her back bare-assed. Old man Knight will run you out of town on a rail before he'd let that happen."

"We were just together in the back seat. I'm planning to give her father plenty of time to get used to the idea. We aren't going to get married until after I graduate from West Point."

"Bare-assed in the back seat! West Point? Well, kiss that goodbye. You just collected yourself a record. They don't take people who screw up."

"But we didn't do anything to anyone. We were just together."

"If the minor possession of alcohol doesn't get you, the statutory rape will."

Joe raised his voice. "Minor possession? That's a bunch of crap! Neither of us drinks."

"I suppose that whiskey smell all around your dad's car was your shaving lotion."

Joe glared at the rear vision mirror. *There was a boozy smell outside and I cut my foot. It would be like Pa to stash a bottle in a door pocket. It doesn't make sense. He's facing a return to prison for breaking parole if he's caught one more time. If he goes back to prison, he'll die there. I dare not say anything.* He watched the driver's eyes, which frequently glanced his way, but Linc looked back at the road whenever Joe's eyes met his.

At the jail, Linc took Joe straight to the interrogation room. He patted the seat of a three-legged stool on the far side of the table. "Sit here."

"Please take the handcuffs off. Don't they give clothes to people here?"

"Deputy John will decide when they come off, Mister Tough Guy." Linc settled in a comfortable, well-padded office chair. He lifted a black rubber hose from beside him and placed it on his lap. "We're allowed to use restraints to protect ourselves."

Joe was worried. *Don't provoke this little guy. He could do some damage since my hands are bound behind my back.*

The deputy stretched out and put his feet up on the table. Joe noted that the wiry man's uniform was dirty and one of his pockets was ripped off. His face was scratched, and his nose was bruised and bloodied. *Look at him. My fiancée beat the crap out of him. Maybe she's tough enough to handle living on the ranch.*

Joe watched Deputy Linc fight sleep and finally nod off. Joe stood and stretched. As he sat back down, the young deputy awoke with a start. He jumped to his feet and took a position between Joe and the door, with the rubber hose at the ready. "What the hell are you up to, Caulfels?"

"I was looking for a place to piss. It's wrong, plain wrong, not to give me something to wear, even if it's just black and white stripes."

Linc menaced Joe with the rubber hose. "You're a real smart ass. Just you wait for Deputy John."

"Come on, this place is cooling off. How about it?" Joe implored. "Have you given Gloria her clothes back?"

"Ask Deputy John."

Later Deputy Tom, who relieved Linc, said, "Deputy John will be in here shortly. Think about what you did. Be prepared to give a clear statement. You don't want to mess with Deputy John. He is not one to tolerate games and stalling tactics, like asking for a lawyer."

Back at the armory, the band played the last notes of "Good Night, Sweetheart" and the overhead lights swept away the shadows, instantly turning the dance hall ambience back into a drill hall. Like others present, attorney Ray Tudbury squinted and smiled at his partner for the evening, Melanie Johnson, one of the parent volunteer chaperons.

From their place on the bandstand, they watched Tillie, the piano player, rise from the bench and pick up the last full shot glass from a row of them that lined the top of the piano. She tilted her head back and downed it. She carefully placed the glass at the end of the row, then called out, "Congratulations, Melanie, Ray, we had a good peaceful evening." Tillie hugged Melanie and continued, "I was a bit worried because there were no deputies here for most of the time, but we made it, thanks to you and your two partners. That horse's ass of a banker, Knight, set the room on edge while making a fool of himself. But everybody else was well behaved. You and the other chaperons ought to get a medal for that."

"Thank you," said Melanie, "I wish I could feel so good. I'm a widow with a teenage daughter. I'm afraid I'll be losing my teaching position. Mr. Knight told me I'm as good as fired," she lamented.

Tillie lifted her cheroot out of the ashtray and brought it back to life with the aid of a Zippo and a few good puffs. "You two have guts to stand up to that petty tyrant after that tirade he put on. He comes down hard on anybody that takes up a position on the Caulfels' side."

Ray said, "I might have said more to Lyle, but Melanie beat me to it when she made it clear she wasn't here to be a referee or, worse yet, be a scapegoat in this vendetta between families."

"I shouldn't have reminded him what everybody else in town knows: that Joe and Gloria have been an item since New Year's," confessed Melanie.

Tillie said, "Melanie, I'll call the principal tomorrow. You didn't deserve that. He's the one that ought to be horsewhipped and run out of town on a rail."

"A phone call is good," said Ray, "but letters are better. Pen your letter to the school board."

Tillie waved her cheroot at Ray. "Well, Mr. Tudbury, you may have to kiss the politics goodbye. If you're looking for His Majesty's blessing for running for office, I don't think you made a good impression. Didn't I hear him say, 'Just what this town needs is another smart-ass attorney?'"

Melanie turned and looked at Ray. "Yes, what's this about running for office? Are you serious about running for county prosecutor? And unseating Jim Gulette?"

"Darn it, this local bar association can't be trusted to keep their mouths shut. Tillie, who told you?"

"My little brother, Byron Haskins. I don't think Mr. Knight took kindly to you tonight."

Ray nodded and said nothing more; Byron was his campaign manager. However, his mind continued to dwell on his encounter that evening with Knight, the political kingmaker of Goodwin County. Ray combined that experience with his dialogue over the past weeks with other lawyers. It left him with the conclusion Knight and Gulette rely on each other. Knight wouldn't abandon Gulette. Chances of success in the Republican primary would be slim to none under the circumstances. What running as a Democrat buys is time to convince Republican supporters in the bar association, especially those who'd had their fill of Gulette's shady shenanigans, times would change. If they didn't, one of them could run next time under the Knight umbrella.

Then Melanie's worries interrupted his reverie. "Do you think Banker Knight can really get me fired?"

Ray shrugged his shoulders. "I don't know. It depends on what kind of a hold he has on the school board. After watching this bully in action, I've made up my mind: I'm going after Jim Gulette come November as a Democrat."

"Really! A Democrat? The last Democrat to file against Gulette died in an auto accident."

"I've played in bigger leagues. From late 1939 until I was recruited into the OSS, I worked in the U. S. Attorney's office in Chicago. Most cases involved prosecuting tax frauds by what is now called Organized Crime." Ray raised his index finger and touched his nose. "During those years I became very familiar with the smell of public corruption. The stench here in this beautiful county isn't so strong that it burns your eyes. It pokes out like pockets of maggots in a side of hanging beef--slot machines openly played in a state where gambling is illegal; public officials whose standard of living is well above what their salaries support; and too many older inmates dying in the county jail of 'natural causes.' I mean to make people aware."

"Where do you think Lyle Knight fits in this?" asked Melanie.

"I don't know for sure. One example: land for the new post office. How were Lyle Knight and his cronies able to buy a parcel of land for back taxes just in time to sell it for a handsome profit?"

Melanie said, "I wish you well, but what we really need is a new sheriff. Part of the reason I'm here tonight is to watch the deputies. I've learned of some rather bizarre conduct by some of them."

"Here's what I've seen too often," echoed Tillie, "minors caught drinking are hit with a year's detention at Buena Vista by Judge Costi. Prosecutor Gulette's charging papers name adults who supplied the booze as sources, but he doesn't bring any charges against any of them."

"Is there a particular arresting officer who brings these minors in?" asked Melanie.

Ray answered her. "No, but very often it's Deputy Diamond—who, by the way, was supposed to be here for the evening but seems to have cut out early."

Tillie said, "Diamond is dirty, Ray, and he's part of the establishment. You'll be one man against them all. Other than the county treasurer, who's a friend of Lyle's, all the offices are filled by Republicans. That's been true as long as anybody can remember. There's a good reason. Run as a Democrat and by election night your house and business could have been torched in an accidental fire; you could be facing felony charges; or you could miss a turn and hit a tree. Democrats, who even come close to winning, either immediately leave town alive after losing the election or later in a box. Is that what you want?"

"Republican, Democrat, I don't care," said Ray. "I have no political affiliation now. The man I worked for in Chicago was a Democrat. My father, a Republican. I only pick Democrat for strategic reasons, and I'll watch my back, don't worry. After a war where I had to deal with the intrigues of Italian politics--the Mafia, the Fascists, and the Communists—I think I can dodge whatever these Keystone Cops want to throw at me."

Tillie stabbed out her cheroot. "My brother Byron mentioned your wartime experience in the OSS, whatever that is. He said it makes you well qualified to run for office. What does OSS stand for?"

"OSS is Office of Strategic Services," Ray replied. "The Central Intelligence Agency grew out it. I spent from late forty-two to forty-five behind enemy lines in Italy. I was primarily involved in hush-hush operations with any Italians who wanted German control ended."

"Sounds like all kinds of fun," said Tillie ironically. "Whose choice was that? Yours or the Army's?"

"I never was in the Army," answered Ray. "In the fall of forty-one, after I demonstrated that I could speak fluent Italian, I was invited to attend a spy school in Canada. Our family name was Teobaldi until my grandfather got tired of the petty discrimination. That fluency also got me my first job out of law school, working for the U.S. Attorney in Chicago, because I could speak the mobsters' lingo. *I don't think any of them has a clue about what went on in Italy,* he thought. *It was far more hair-raising than this can be. Well before November, I want them to know I can mount a winning campaign here too.*

Ray stood outside by the front door while Melanie and the other chaperons made one last sweep of the building. He saw Andy Foyle and Inez Farley standing beneath the only light in an otherwise darkened parking lot near the place where the Caddy had been parked. In the shadows on the opposite side of the street, a lone sheriff's patrol car was parked. Andy hunched his shoulders forward and walked with Inez toward the entrance.

Ray asked, "Why are you still here, Andy?"

"Waiting for Joe and Gloria. They promised to be back before midnight. I'm really worried about them. Something must be wrong. Maybe they had an accident."

"From observing what went on here tonight … maybe they were arrested."

Inez asked, "Why? What's wrong with wanting to marry and settle down?"

Ray shook his head. "Didn't you hear Gloria's father ranting about them?"

"Yeah," said Andy, "I heard Mr. Knight tonight. I didn't like what he said." Then he fell silent. For a while they stood in the clear, cool night, each wrapped up in his own thoughts. Andy folded his arms across his chest and rubbed his biceps. "Heard you're going to run against Mr. Gulette. I think he's an arrogant asshole."

"Why's that?"

"Well, take Vienna Woods. Vienna's soldier boyfriend feeds her spiked drinks. She throws up in the train station. He goes overseas; she gets a year at Buena Vista. This is typical of Gulette's selective justice. What did he do that gets you wound up?"

"Wow, you amaze me. Adults here don't cut to the chase like you just did."

Andy pointed out to the empty lot where the white Cadillac had been parked. "If Mr. Knight did get them arrested, Gulette will find something to charge them with. Gulette is his enforcer. Tell me why you'd be different."

"I won't be owned by Lyle Knight. I am an experienced prosecutor. I spent over two years living and fighting in a Fascist hell. I know the difference between right and wrong."

Melanie stole up beside Ray and took his arm. "Andy," she asked, "why are you still here? Waiting for Joe and Gloria?"

"Yes, ma'am."

Melanie turned to Inez. "I saw your mother come and get you earlier. What are you doing back here again?"

Inez blushed and looked at Andy, then said, "I came back because I wanted Andy to take me home."

Melanie arched an eyebrow. "Really? I seem to recall your mother telling me she was working the midnight shift at the phone company tonight. Come on, it's past time for you to be home. Ray, let's give them a ride."

Andy shook his head. "We're all right. We can walk."

Melanie nodded toward the parked sheriff's cruiser. "Please, I'll sleep far better knowing you got home safely."

Ray put a hand on Andy's shoulder and began walking him toward the car. He whispered, "Don't even *think* of asking us to let you off at Inez's house."

Andy took Inez's hand and held it as they silently walked to the car together.

Melanie's daughter Lisa and her date waited in the back seat of Ray's car. There had been a rustling of crinolines and much movement as the foursome approached. All Ray could see in the darkness were two pairs of bright eyes and two rather embarrassed smiles.

Ray's was the last car out of the lot. As they approached the cruiser, the deputy turned on his headlights and drove off. In the center of Goodwin, Ray waited for traffic to make a right turn onto Main Street behind a new Ford Super Deluxe Tudor Club Coupe with a Denver license plate. The Ford stopped in mid-block to let another car clear a parking place in front of the Crown Prince Hotel, the oldest and largest hotel in town. A pair of young women, who were sitting on a seat on the porch, stood up and watched the new Ford pull into the parking place.

Melanie pointed at the pair as Ray drove by. "I hope that if you and Larry get elected, you'll do something to enforce the law on prostitution. It's been on the books since nineteen thirty-seven."

Ray glanced at the young women as he drove by. "How do you know they're prostitutes?"

"This is a small town. You have to be blind to miss it. The mobster in that fancy car comes over every Friday, bringing new girls. On Monday, some ride back and some stay. I lost a student a year ago last winter. She was above average, but came from a terrible home. When she turned eighteen, she began working at the Crown Prince on weekends. Come summer, she went to Denver and got arrested. I talked to her after she came home and found out her father was living off her."

"Did you talk to the sheriff?"

"Now there's a waste of time. Everybody knows he collects a 'crib tax.'"

"Why hasn't anyone complained?"

"That's a question to ask the *Goodwin Globe*. Turn right at the next intersection. Inez's is the third house on the right."

After dropping off Andy, his last rider, Ray drove slowly through the warm, peaceful summer night over streets empty of traffic. Yes, he savored moments like these; a night with a sky full of stars; a night he could enjoy without fearing what lurked in the shadows and could expect to awaken tomorrow without the specter of death around him.

Ray looked forward to a cool morning when he could cast a line for a rainbow trout. He needed time to come to grips with the dreams and nightmares accumulated during his service in Italy. Most of all, he needed time to heal from losing his wife, Gisela. It was good to be home again, even if it was the calm before the storm.

Ray chose a familiar way home that took him by the courthouse. He needed time to think before he was ready to sleep. He parked and looked across the courthouse commons at the substantial marble building in the shadows. He recalled the tales his father, the former Judge Tudbury, had spun about his role in its design and construction.

Yet this evening had been very unsettling. He realized that this wasn't a newly born problem and certainly influenced his father's decision to return to Italy as much as his refusal to live under Prohibition after he retired from the bench.. There was a question he wanted to ask his father, *Padre, how did you let such a beautiful place become so corrupt? Today I saw the men coming from Denver to service the illegal slot machines. Was it just a coincidence I saw one of them giving that fat Deputy Diamond an envelope? I don't want Colorado to become another Italy with its Mafia and a justice system on the take.*

What a contrast it was to compare his father and the prospector Jabez Goodwin, for whom the county was named, to the banker Lyle Knight and his cronies. Through Jabez's generosity and leadership, the county had raised the money to build the resplendent courthouse on the town commons, along with that wonderful gazebo where in summer months Ray had listened to everything from country to classical music.

Ray remembered Lyle's behavior earlier that night. He was still smarting over letting Lyle run roughshod over his date. *The corrupt power of that man is immense if he can reach into the public school system and get a teacher fired because she didn't break up a match of his white daughter with a handsome half-breed.*

This had been the week he seriously began his run for the office of county prosecutor by asking for endorsements and contributions from businesses. "You need to run on someone else's money," seasoned politicians had told him, "because if you can't find enough people willing to put money behind your name, you shouldn't run." So far, every businessman Ray spoke to had balked at going public with support for him, pending Lyle Knight's approval. Just like the attorneys. What surprised Ray, though, was the number of business owners who wouldn't endorse him yet were willing to empty a wallet anonymously into his campaign.

Such wasn't the case for the one land owner Ray contacted, who became an endorsing volunteer. There would be many more, if what he was told was true. During the hard times before the war, just about every farm and ranch had been foreclosed upon. Prosecutor Gulette had recommended to Judge Costi, his father's successor, that the mineral rights be separated from the fee simple. When the farmers renegotiated their mortgages with the bank, Lyle kept the mineral rights. A recent public relations piece in the *Goodwin Globe* about Shell Oil's plans to drill an exploratory well gave immediacy to this situation.

If oil is found, thought Ray, *who owns it? Lyle Knight, of course— all of it. I made the decision tonight to run on the Democratic ticket, something I may regret. Yes, my opponent on the ballot will be James Gulette. There is no doubt: Lyle Knight pulls the strings on these pup-*

pets. He's about as close as you can get to a Mussolini and still fly the red, white, and blue. Wound banker Knight, and you wound the Republican ticket. It looks like I'll be on familiar turf.

pets. He's about as close as you can get to a Mussolini and still fly the red, white, and blue. Wound banker Knight, and you wound the Republican ticket. It looks like I'll be on familiar turf.

CHAPTER 4
Saturday Morning Before Dawn

What seemed like half the night later, Deputy John Diamond pushed the interrogation room door open and stood in the threshold with his hands on his hips. He sniffed the air. "Isn't that fragrance sweet, Mr. Caulfels? Take a deep breath and savor Miss Knight's scent, because tonight is the last time you will ever be close enough to smell traces of her perfume."

Joe was slumped over on the stool. *What is it with this fat guy? Why does he have it in for me?* His hands were still locked behind his back. "I'm cold. Give me clothes and get these handcuffs off. I need to use a restroom."

John dragged a straightback chair around the table and placed it with its back facing Joe, no more than two feet away from him. The deputy sat on it with his fat belly pressing against the vertical wooden bars and laid his beefy arms on the top piece. He studied Joe's face. "Does that jaw hurt?"

"Yes, it does. Why'd you hit me?"

John pushed a cigarette into his mouth and lighted it using a Zippo with a Goodwin County Sheriff emblem on it. "Mouth off to Deputy John again and I'll pop you again."

Joe studied the deputy's face, which sported a weeping black eye, a cut on the forehead, and a swollen upper lip. "Did you arrest Gloria too?"

"Let's say she hasn't been arrested, yet."

"Why not? She worked you over, didn't she?"

"The sheriff says we don't lock up rape victims." John blew exhaled smoke into Joe's face. "Caulfels, we have you cold for statutory rape; possession of alcohol as a minor; resisting arrest; assaulting peace officers; and contributing to the delinquency of a minor. You can make it easy on all of us or make it difficult. The courts look favorably on people who admit their mistakes."

"We weren't drinking. If you don't let me go to the bathroom, I'm going to pee on the floor."

"Okay, I'll take you. But before we break, let me show you the evidence. Here is the label from a broken pint bottle of Four Roses bourbon. Here are two used condoms, one from the back seat, one off of you. The doctor will testify that Gloria Knight had sexual relations tonight. Think it over while I type up your statement."

John took Joe to a holding cell with a toilet. *Pa warned me about ways they'd use me to get him. The letter from the parole guy made it clear there'd be no booze, period. Besides covering for Pa, I've got to make things right for Gloria.*

Some time later John brought his naked prisoner back to the interrogation room and locked his left wrist to the table. All Joe thought about was going to bed and sleeping. The first time he fell asleep, he found out why John kept him naked. John poured a small stream of ice cubes down his back. Joe jumped to a full upright position. "Oh, my God, why did you do that?"

The deputy checked Joe's upward motion with a hand firmly pushing him back on the stool. "If you want to go to bed, sign your statement."

Joe surprised himself with his reaction of anger and rage. Like hell he was going to sign it! He was getting to better understand his father. John put a pen in Joe's right hand and told him to sign the typed statement. Joe felt he was crossing over from being a manipulated prisoner to an angry, resistant captive. He held the pen inside a closed fist that he shook at the deputy. "Screw you! I'm not signing." Joe placed the pen back in its inkwell, unused.

Deputy John made a show of lifting the pen out of the inkwell. He waved it in the air and repeated his demand. Joe watched and said nothing. The deputy returned to his comfortable chair with the pen in hand. He lectured about "the wye in Joe's road" and pleaded with him to avoid going to trial. He alluded to Joe's damaging statements to Deputies Linc and Tom, most of which Joe didn't remember. Joe said, "I'm not signing any statement that puts hard stuff in Pa's car."

John then shifted tack and questioned Joe about how he and his father got along. He demanded to know when his father struck him last. Joe refused to answer.

At last Joe saw the first light of his first day in jail through a small barred window high in the wall. He stood and pointed toward the window. "You've kept me up all night. How many times do I have to tell you I haven't done anything? I don't drink. My father is a law-abiding man. I want to go home."

John dipped the pen into the inkwell. With great care, he handed it to Joe. "Sign here that you don't drink and you don't know nothing about where the Four Roses came from. That's enough progress to call an end to today's session. Jailer Stokings ought to have you outfitted and assigned in time for reveille."

Joe held the pen over the paper. "This sure has a lot of writing on it."

"Sign the damn statement, Caulfels."

Joe turned the sheet over and wrote, "I was attacked by Deputy John Diamond while doing nothing wrong. Like my fiancé, Gloria Knight, I do not drink alcoholic beverages. There was no bottle of Four Roses in the car. We are innocent."

Joe handed the pen back.

"Nothing wrong? Innocent? You're a real wise guy. This isn't in the form the prosecutor can use. I'm running out of patience with you, Caulfels." John took the pen and drove it into the sheet Joe had just signed. Residual ink spread out in a radial pattern on the paper.

Four Eff can barely control his temper. I want this over with. Joe picked the pen up off the table. "Mr. Deputy John, sir, you ruined the nib on this pen. I think we're both too tired to continue."

John leaned over close to Joe. "You're a damn fool, Caulfels. My recommendations carry weight. Prosecutor Gulette doesn't suffer fools gladly."

Joe awoke ten minutes later when he felt his wrist being freed. He blinked his eyes to see a familiar face, but couldn't remember who it was. The middle-aged man in the uniform said, "Leo Stokings, Joe. Give me your other wrist."

"Hi, Mr. Stokings. Still helping Mae Blackmon?"

"Not since the deputies elbowed in last fall after we baled her hay. You are about the last boy in town I expected to be one of my charges. Before I take you back, have you had your phone call?"

Joe shook his head. "Ma and Pa don't have a phone. I was hoping they'd come to town to ask about the Caddy."

"Do you have a friend who could go out to the ranch?"

"Andy Foyle, I guess. Where is Gloria locked up?"

"She's not."

"Good, I'll cover for her."

Stokings leaned close to Joe and spoke low out of the corner of his mouth. "Gloria is a Knight. The one you need to cover for is your father for his drinking. John is bragging he's got your father for violating his parole and that you'll provide the evidence. I brought you a uniform and a cup of coffee. Where are your clothes?"

"In Pa's Caddy, rented from Kahn's Department Store."

"I'll notify Mr. Kahn. No spreading the word that I told you anything. I could lose my job."

CHAPTER 5
Later on Saturday

Joe rested his head on his left arm, which was handcuffed to the metal table in the interrogation room. Prosecutor Jim Gulette strolled in and banged a notebook on the table. Joe was still wiping sleep from his eyes when Gulette finished introducing himself. Joe studied him, never having seen him before. Gulette had streaks of gray hair in his brown sideburns. He wore a blue and white seersucker suit with a red, white, and blue bow tie. *Kind of garish*, thought Joe. *Is he advertising his patriotism?*

The prisoner was still stretching and yawning when Gulette said, "Deputy John told me you haven't been cooperative."

Joe frowned and raised his free hand. "Excuse me, Mr. Gulette, what do you do?"

"I am the Goodwin County Prosecutor. Look, Caulfels, I don't want to play games with you." The prosecutor opened a folder and held up a handwritten sheet. He scanned it before he laid it on the table. "These are the charges against you."

Joe took a sip from his cup of coffee, which had grown cold, and read down the list. *They're going to send me away. That Deputy Linc is right, I'll never be a pilot like my brother. I don't want to add to Gloria's hurt, and I don't want to be the one who gives them cause to throw Pa in prison. What do I do? Do I dare do what I prayed about? Pa talked about how he bargained.*

Gulette said, "Well, Caulfels, are you going to stand tall and accept responsibility for what you did?"

"There was no drinking and no Four Roses. You left out at least one charge, where I kicked that Brown guy in the nuts and punched him in the nose." Joe handed the sheet back to the prosecutor, who studied it.

Gulette stared at Joe through the thick lenses of his eyeglasses. "What's your game?"

"I don't have any money to pay a lawyer. Pa won't talk to me. I'll plead guilty to everything on that list except the ones involving under-age drinking. You'll agree not to charge Gloria or Pa for anything. As I recall, Pa said to have you put it in writing."

"Here's what I'll offer: all charges dropped *except* acknowledging the Four Roses and pleading guilty for the rape, with jail time until next May. No contact with Miss Knight."

"Mr. Prosecutor, the only reason I'm fighting you is I love two people too much. If I hadn't given in to Gloria's magnetism, we would be going our way together."

"Magnetism?"

"I love Gloria so much I'd die for her. She is the smartest, brightest, sexiest girl I ever met. She looks at a page and she's got it." Joe snapped his fingers. "A year inside could break her spirit. I don't want her to lose that gift like what they did to Pa."

Gulette opened the file folder and made a show of laying his fountain pen and a ruler atop the charging sheet. "You surprise me. From the arresting officer's report, I expected an entirely different response. Did someone set you up?"

"If you're referring to that fat, drunken deputy waving a Four Roses label, yes. If you're talking about attempting to make a deal, I had ample time to think and pray while I spent the night sitting naked on this stool."

Gulette stared at the open folder for almost a minute before he said, "Okay, Caulfels, I'll agree to your offer because you've given me an out for the Knight girl."

The next thing Gloria remembered after she watched the doctor empty the syringe into her arm was awakening in the guest bedroom at home. Dim light colored the thin window curtain enough that she knew it was close to dawn. She felt groggy--much like a hangover, she thought, from the descriptions she'd heard. Her head hurt. In fact, her whole body hurt, inside and out, especially along the nerves the deputy had pressed. The pinched nerve in her left arm was acting up. When she turned over to relieve the pain, she realized she was naked except for bandages around her wrists and ankles, where she had fought her restraints.

As consciousness flooded in, so did the memories of the night before. With them came anger and shame like she had never felt before: anger for what her father had set in motion against both her and Joe in the name of race; and shame for failing to realize to what ends her father would go.

Gloria remembered this room as the one her father had marched her to from the dinner table last fall, when she announced that Joe was her date for the harvest ball. She got up to dress, but found the closet and drawers bare. *He's out of his mind. This is worse than last fall. At least he left me something he to wear back then. I'll try my own closet.*

The door to her room was locked with a hasp and padlock. *What's he up to? He threatened to have me committed last time. This is the middle of the twentieth century, for crying out loud.* She found one of her father's cotton bathrobes, along with a bra and panties, lying in a basket next to the new washing machine. She put them on and slipped out the back door. As much as she wanted to run to the Foyles', she limped along. Each step sent fireballs of pain down her calves and thighs.

Gloria was surprised to find Andy and his mother sitting around the kitchen table so early in the morning. Andy jumped to his feet and opened the door for her. "Where are your clothes?"

"I'm scared. You've got to help me. Daddy put a padlock on my door like last fall. They could come and get me anytime. Deputy Four Eff raped me. Awful, awful … I kicked that new deputy in the balls and punched him in the nose … escaped for a little while. They attacked us without warning. Joe and I …."

Celeste Foyle cut her off. "Where are your clothes? What were you thinking?" Celeste's response reflected what she had heard from Lyle Knight the night before.

Andy said, "If you had come over fifteen minutes earlier, you could have talked to Joe."

"What? How is he?" Gloria asked.

"We were his one call. Joe sounded tired. Deputy Four Eff kept him up all night, questioning him. They're taking him over for the preliminary hearing. He wants me to drive out and tell his father he's in jail. Besides sex with you, there are charges for underage drinking because they found a bottle of Four Roses his Pa left in the car. He said to tell you to go on with your life without him."

"No, I won't give him up. None of that is true. When is this preliminary hearing?"

"I'm not sure," Andy responded. "I think it's the first thing this morning."

"Why me?" Gloria sank into a kitchen chair and bawled.

Over breakfast followed by coffee, Gloria told the Foyles about her father's reaction when she told him she had been raped by Deputy Four Eff, and how her father had put her in the guest room without anything to wear. She spilled her heart about her love for Joe. She sensed the Foyles' reactions of surprise and shock to the rape; but Andy blamed her for Joe's arrest.

Gloria asked if she could sleep on the couch until graduation. "After that, I plan to take a train to Denver and get a job."

Carole, who had been listening but saying nothing, said, "Before you run away to Denver, I need you to show me exactly where this happened."

"Why?"

"To help Joe and get Deputy Four Eff. I'm sure our archaeology team would drop what they're doing. You see, we were scheduled to be on the road to New Mexico with our advisor, Dr. Finlay, but he's been called to Europe instead. All the equipment and supplies we assembled for our big dig are ready. All we have to do is see who can come out on short notice."

Celeste put up a hand. "Wait a minute, young lady. Just what are you proposing?"

Carole explained how Dr. Finlay had taught them techniques that were transferrable from archaeological work to criminal investigations. She concluded, "It's Gloria's word against theirs unless she has evidence to confirm it. We'll find out who's telling the truth."

Gloria agreed to put off her departure until the team was done. However, Celeste pointed out that running would play into their hands because Gloria would appear to be a fugitive hiding from the law. Gloria then agreed reluctantly to give up entirely the idea of going to Denver.

Celeste insisted that Gloria had to go home, and Gloria voiced her fear of her father committing her. The discussion was cut short by a call from Gloria's frantic mother, Theodora (Theo for short), who asked if she was there. Celeste agreed to take Gloria home and talk with the Knights to work out an agreement both sides could live with.

Celeste felt the negotiations went as well as possible. Theo quickly granted Gloria access to her room and her clothes. It was another matter when it came to Gloria and Joe. Celeste was stonewalled when she tried to help Gloria describe what actually happened. Theo stiffened when the Caulfels family was mentioned, and Gloria knew what that meant: she had long known that her mother was in complete sympathy with Lyle's bitter racism.

Theo sat tall with the subdued elegance of the professional performer she once had been. Her voice was silky smooth and her diction nearly perfect, making her points as if she were on stage. She brushed her silver hair back as she said, "Your father showed me a copy of the police report. I don't want to soil my mind with stories from fornicators."

"Mother, look at the bottom of the report," said Gloria. "Who wrote it?"

"It's signed, Deputy John Diamond."

"Right. It's his story, it's not the truth. Mother, Joe did not rape me. Four Eff raped me."

"Gloria, you're trying to cover for that opportunistic young gigolo who seduced you."

"No, if anything, I seduced him. I was his first. But he never got that far; he came in my hand. Look at my bruises. Look at my wrists and ankles. Joe wouldn't have roughed me up like this. Deputy Four Eff raped me."

Theo shook her head. "I am so disappointed that my own daughter would use such a despicable tactic as a counter to avoid taking responsibility for her own underage drinking. As your father pointed out,

John Diamond is a respected elder of his church ... a married man with two daughters."

Gloria rose out of her chair. "You taught me the reasons to avoid strong drink. Why do you think I would start drinking, out of the blue, with a boy who, like me, has never tasted a drop?"

"What your father and I seek is your commitment to end your liaison with this half-breed Caulfels crook and put an end to your alley-cat morals."

Lyle nodded his agreement from his easy chair. "An end to all contact with the Caulfels."

Celeste cut in. "Lyle, I don't believe there's time or a means to settle the dispute between your family and the Caulfels family. You have a brilliant, beautiful daughter who is on the verge of packing her bags and catching the next train with a one-way ticket. That's the last thing either you or Theo wants. I suggest an agreement with commitments by both sides."

Gloria was surprised how quickly the negotiations went after that. Her anguish over being locked out was met with an apology from her father, hugs from her mother, and a promise that it wouldn't happen again. As to events around the graduation ball, she agreed not to use the name Caulfels in her parents' presence. Lyle wished for her to commit to being a paid summer intern at the bank, working a minimum of half-time for the internal auditor. When she accepted that, Lyle committed to giving her a clothing allowance. Gloria agreed to act like an adult, with no drinking and no affairs, and they agreed to treat her as an adult. For safety's sake, she would keep them informed of her comings and goings.

While they were ironing out the last details of their agreement, Carole called. She said that Dr. Finlay and a team of five other teenagers had volunteered to come to the aid of her fiancé. Gloria's presence was needed as early as possible, as their adult mentor had much to do before catching the Monday morning train.

By late Saturday afternoon, the number of volunteers had swollen from seven, including Gloria, to twelve. All the evidentiary objects found were cataloged, such as Trojan rubber wrappers, the Four Roses bottle neck, and the bottle top. The team's archaeological grid of stakes and connecting colored strings covered an area from the water's edge of the reservoir to the far side of the parking lot. All that was left was to finish recording the findings in the logbook and taking photos of important objects. Soon there would be too little light to take pictures, because they didn't have flashbulbs.

Carole, a petite blonde, was decked out in a blue cotton tank suit and men's work boots. The other girls were dressed about the same, which was appropriate for working at a dig. Gloria, however, chose to wear non-work clothing: a nylon blouse, plaid cotton skirt, and saddle shoes. She covered the wounds around her ankles and wrists with bandages. If anyone asked about the bandages, she was at the ready to tell all about Joe and the gross Deputy Four Eff.

Gloria took a break to watch a pair of big steam engines work a freight train up the canyon. Returning to the site, she heard raised voices and screams. She wanted to throw up as soon as she saw Deputy John sitting in his patrol car. He had driven far enough into the lot to break the outer string and loosen two of the stakes holding the cross-strings.

John rolled down his window. He stuck his head out far enough that his black eye and bandaged forehead were visible. "What in the Sam Hill are you up to?"

The student who had been left in charge by the professor gave the deputy the cover story they had all agreed on. "We're Dr. Finlay's group, just practicing procedures for when he gets back from Europe."

Gloria ran around the edge of the marked area toward the deputy with anger boiling. "Four Eff, get your fat ass out of here and leave us alone!"

John stuck his left arm out the window and pointed his index finger at her. "That's no way to talk to a law officer. If it weren't for your daddy, you'd be in jail right now."

Standing a few squares away from John, Gloria made fists of her hands, then drew them together as if ready to be handcuffed. "Go ahead, arrest me. I dare you. I'll have your badge. I'll have your uniform. I'll have your ass!"

John opened the driver's door slightly, then closed it. He smiled through gritted teeth and cast swift glances to those working in the squares before he looked back at Gloria. "Girl, you're baiting me. Deputy John is no fool. I will only act on a complaint from a citizen about your interference with the right to park in this public lot. Then you all will be arrested."

John put the cruiser in reverse and spun his tires, spraying sand and gravel. While he was shifting gears, Carole said, "You didn't have to break up my markers like that. We'll be finished and out of here before dark."

He paused, snapped open his Zippo, and relit his cigarette. "Tell your hot-tempered friend to relay to her daddy that we caught that sucker fish, gutted him, and put him on ice."

When Four Eff's patrol car was out of sight, Carole worked her way close to Gloria, carefully avoiding the grid strings. "Whatever possessed you to act and talk like that? He could have thrown you in jail."

"He knows what we're doing. Did you see him sweating? He's scared. He knows that if he arrests us, everything we've found will have to be looked at. As for the language, it's what he understands."

"I have to admit that everything we've found today--footprints, tire tread markings--backs up what you told us. Then there's the bag with the receipt for the thirty-first from the liquor store, which was caught on the sticker bush. If Joe didn't buy it, then who did?"

"The receipt has a time stamp. Maybe we can find out that way. We were out of town at that hour." Gloria gave Carole a hug. "You are a genius to think of coming out here and cataloging everything."

"If they can do this sort of thing to hang those Nazis, we ought to be able to help Joe when his trial comes up. Gloria, I overheard you talking to Andy about not giving the valedictorian speech. Are you sure you want to pass that up?"

"I don't deserve the honor. Because of what I did, my fiancé can't be there. I'll call the principal tomorrow. Your brother Andy will do a good job. We have until Wednesday afternoon to get ready."

Carole said, "Isn't it ironic that the one boy who tutored both the number one and two in the class in algebra and trig won't even graduate?"

"I know, I owe him the rest of my life."

Late in the morning on Sunday, Celeste Foyle worked at the kitchen counter preparing lunch. Carole looked up from a newspaper spread out on the kitchen table. "More Goodwin news. The English teacher, Mrs. Johnson? Her boyfriend is going to run for county prosecutor."

"Who?"

"It says here that 'Ray Tudbury, former federal prosecutor and OSS agent in the Italian theater, has announced his intention to run for county prosecutor on the Democratic ticket.'"

Celeste walked across the room and looked over her daughter's shoulder. "The obituary page, that's a fitting place for his announcement. None of the Republicans will vote for him because he's a Democrat, and none of the Democrats will because his father was a Republican."

Through the screen door came Lyle Knight's hearty laughter. "That was perfect, Celeste. You have a good way with words. May we come in for a short visit?"

"Lyle, Theo, certainly. How's Gloria?"

They stepped inside the back door just enough for the screen to close. Lyle said, "We can't stay but a minute. We're on our way home from church."

Theo smiled. "We are so relieved. Gloria has taken the terms of the agreement seriously. Without a word from Lyle or me, she called Herb Kahn to come over. She has changed her wardrobe to a far more modest style than most girls her age wear. We came by to thank you for being the wonderful neighbor you are. Carole, I'm surprised to see you here. Weren't you excused early from school to help on the archaeological expedition down in New Mexico?"

"It's been canceled because Dr. Finlay's leaving for Europe to work with the Nuremberg Commission," responded Carole.

"What a disappointment for you. The Lord often intercedes to place us where we are needed most. Being Gloria's best friend, I'm sure you'll help pull her up from where she has fallen."

"Where we are needed most," how coincidental, thought Celeste. *Volunteer schoolmates are ringing our phone off the wall, wanting*

to help Joe, ever since Carole organized last Friday's dig at the river park.

Lyle picked up the paper from in front of Carole. He turned it so the front page was visible. The banner headline read, SON OF NOTORIOUS BOOTLEGGER CONFESSES RAPE.

Lyle read aloud, "'Joe Caulfels, the son of convicted tax evader and bootlegger, Orville Caulfels, confessed to sexual relations with a local juvenile ….' That pretty much seals it. He's following in his father's footsteps right into the penitentiary."

Celeste thought, *Poor Joe, how could they pass a law that would throw an unworldly eighteen-year-old in prison for sex with a sexually active and voluptuous seventeen-year-old? It seems the only one in that family to have a conscience is the daughter.* She said, "Yes, we read it. Lyle, Theo, wake up! You're destroying the Caulfels' son with these charges. Joe is a good boy. When Gloria tells her story in court, you will be embarrassed. Don't you see the depth of the hurt and her feelings of guilt? Please listen to me. You are losing your only daughter."

Lyle took his time to return the paper to the obituary page and place it in front of Carole. "My daughter got over the last one. She'll get over this half-breed scum."

"At least hear Gloria's version. I'm convinced that Diamond or Deputy Four Eff, as the kids call him, is ..."

Lyle waved his hands as if he were calling a runner out at home. "This isn't the kind of subject that your daughter ought to be hearing. John Diamond is a respected elder of his church ... a married man. I was so ashamed last night! The first thing Gloria did was to punch him right in the eye. She makes the mistake of thinking that if she sullies this fine man, it will divert attention from her opportunistic gigolo. There will be a very short trial. He has confessed."

"We must be going," said Theo nervously. "I have a special dinner cooking. Thank you for giving us hope." She hugged Celeste and patted Carole on the shoulder.

Carole asked, "What are you having, that sucker fish that Deputy John gutted and put on ice?"

Theo looked puzzled. "No dear, where did you hear that?"

“Didn't Gloria relay the message from the deputy, ‘We caught that suckerfish, gutted him, and put him on ice’?”

Celeste drew her hand across her throat. “Carole!“

Lyle's face turned red as he guided Theo out the door.

46 | The Revenge of the Banker's Daughter

“Didn't Gloria relay the message from the deputy, ‘We caught that suckerfish, gutted him, and put him on ice’?”

Celeste drew her hand across her throat. “Carole!“

Lyle's face turned red as he guided Theo out the door.

CHAPTER 6
From a Butterfly into a Scorpion

Andy watched the "new" Gloria stride past their house. She wore low-heeled leather shoes and unflattering brown hosiery. Her skirt was so long that only her bandaged ankles were visible. Her hair was piled in a bun that had two black needles through it. Enough locks hung down to give her a slightly disheveled look. She hid her eyes behind aviator-style sunglasses with reflective lenses. "There's Gloria going out. It looks like she's finally come out of her cocoon now that graduation is past. I liked the old Gloria far better, with the sexy dresses and overdoses of French perfume."

Carole chimed in, "She's becoming a colossal bore. I went over yesterday after dinner and she told me she was too busy to talk. She showed me the stack of books she has to read. Who cares about how checks are cleared or what you use for cattle-er-all for a loan?"

"That's 'collateral.' She's all business."

Celeste strolled across the room to join her children as they watched Gloria walk up Garfield Street. "Take a careful look at her. I believe we are witnessing the first known metamorphosis of a butterfly into a scorpion."

Gloria's path took her from home to the town's business district. She stepped into a phone booth and dialed the county prosecutor's number. The secretary's message was short and clear. "I'm sorry, Mr. Gulette is not available to talk to you." Here it was Thursday morning and no calls had been returned. As she had done before, she left her phone number. *That slimy son of a bitch can eat the steaks my mother broils, but he can't return my call.*

They didn't read from the same script in the sheriff's office. There, they passed the phone to Deputy Four Eff, but all he would say was that she should stop harassing him. The clerk in the office of Judge Costi turned her away too.

Only one call resulted in an appointment: not at the courthouse, but at Price's Drugs. Arriving there, Gloria looked around the store, which was empty of people except for the soda jerk and one clerk. *Good old Price's Drugs,* she mused, a *marble-topped soda fountain, white tile floor, round marble-topped tables. I remember when I slid into that back booth with Paul Bixler and believed his worthless promises.*

She chose a table along the back wall facing the door. She seated herself in a chair with a circular caned seat and curved wire back. No sooner had she checked her watch than the bells on the door jangled. Ray Tudbury came just inside the door and stood, scanning the eating area. His eyes did not light on her. Gloria thought maybe he passed her over because he didn't want to see her. He looked at his watch, turned toward the door, then looked back over his shoulder as he placed his hand on the doorknob.

Gloria waved a gloved hand. "Mr. Tudbury, Mr. Raymond Tudbury! Thank you for coming here to meet with me. You said you could give me at least fifteen minutes."

Ray turned around. He squinted unbelieving eyes in her direction. Gloria rose and extended her hand. "Mr. Tudbury, I'm Gloria Knight. We met at the graduation ball. I want to work in your campaign, to make sure you beat Jim Gulette."

Ray appeared surprised. He looked up at her as she rose to her full height. "Gloria? The girl at the graduation ball? You are certainly a master of disguise. Please take that as a compliment from a professional. But why all the secrecy?"

Gloria was confused. *Doesn't he know what happened to me?* "Secrecy? I ... I'm not trying to be secretive. Nobody else has been willing to listen to me. I'm surprised you didn't recognize me. I thought you had been personally assigned to keep an eye on us that evening. You certainly stared at me enough."

"Yes, I suppose I did. I'm sorry if I made you uncomfortable. You remind me of my late wife, Gisela. She was young, vivacious ... nineteen when we married. I lost her in a bombing raid in September of nineteen forty-three."

"I'm sorry. I didn't know." Gloria made a prayerful gesture with her hands.

"Yes, some of the Allied bombers missed their target ..." Ray's voice broke in midsentence. "I'll always be grateful for the four months of happiness we shared."

"Nineteen! And you were how old ... over thirty?" *Watch out for him, he's a cradle robber.*

Ray nodded agreement, but she saw him squirm in his chair.

"What sort of justice is this? You married a woman more than ten years younger than you, but I want to marry a man just eleven months older than I and they throw him in jail."

"There must have been something more ..."

Gloria pushed the sunglasses down her nose so Ray wouldn't miss her cold eyes flashing anger. "Something more! Something more! You bet!" She held her bandaged wrists together. "I was shackled with my hands bound to my feet ... totally helpless. Deputy John Diamond, Deputy Four Eff, raped me. Nobody will even give me the time of day ... not my parents ... not the sheriff! The stinking fat animal came out to my house today. He tried to get me to sign a damned statement that's a pack of lies. The prosecutor won't return my phone calls, either. They won't even let me see my fiancé."

Ray raised a hand. "Gloria, I don't believe this is the appropriate place to discuss this. Would you be willing to come to my office ?"

"Do I still have fifteen minutes?"

"At least. Later I will have a meeting with a member of my campaign committee. I want to hear all you have to say, especially about Jim Gulette and that deputy."

Gloria sat on the padded seat below the law office's open window. In front of her on the frosted glass of the office door were the gold leaf letters, RAYMOND TUDBURY - ATTORNEY AT LAW. A cooling late afternoon breeze whisked around her and spread through the early-nineteen-hundreds vintage office building.

The promised fifteen minutes turned into forty-five. She felt good about how thorough and fair-minded Ray was. He went over her story twice. He told her about his chasing down gangsters in pre-war Chicago and vignettes of his exploits in Italy. She didn't have much understanding of the law, but she sensed that Ray Tudbury put ethics above all else. She recalled the times Jim Gulette had allowed himself to be compromised over dinner by her father.

She heard Ray's campaign manager well before he pushed the office door open. He walked with a measured gait to compensate for his wooden appendage to replace the leg he lost in the war. "Miss Knight," said Ray, "I'd like to introduce the manager of my campaign committee, Byron Haskins. In fact, he's my *whole* campaign committee as yet unless he has some news for me. Byron, Miss Gloria Knight."

Byron was a barrel of a man whose red face and light brown hair fringed a balding dome, giving him a monkish look. He talked slowly and with such a nasal twang that Gloria's first impression was that, if he was an attorney, any hayseed could pass the bar.

Byron extended his right hand. "Miss Gloria Knight, the banker's daughter? Are you really the mystery woman who called Ray?"

Gloria stood up and smiled. She took his hand in both of hers. "Yes, Ray is a wonderful man. He took the time to hear my side of the story. I had the opportunity to learn about his history, from his days in Chicago bringing hoodlums to justice to his very exciting exploits behind the lines in Italy, fighting with the partisans. He is a giant compared to Jim Gulette, who won't even return my calls. I will give my all for Ray. Just tell me what you want me to do."

Ray said, "Gloria, we'll be in touch. I'll leave the messages with Carole Foyle as you asked."

Gloria nodded toward Ray in acknowledgment. As she released Byron's hand, she spoke in a soft, husky voice, "It has been a pleasure to meet you, Mr. Haskins. You certainly are not like the man Jim Gulette described to my father over dinner."

"How's that?"

"I was expecting someone like Captain Hook. He kept calling you

'Peg Leg.'"

Byron laughed. "Peg Leg! In what context?"

"Both he and Daddy were very upset that you somehow used a legal loophole to save Mrs. Smith from going to the women's prison."

"Smith? That was in the news back in October," volunteered Ray.

Byron smiled. "It was a victory that I had mixed feelings over. Mrs. Smith embezzled so much money that her employer went bankrupt. She admitted it and was willing to plead guilty, but Jim wouldn't budge from going for the maximum. The loophole was that the prosecutor didn't do his job. He didn't submit evidence to substantiate each and every element of the indictment. Besides, the woman didn't spend the money on fur coats. She used it to get her kinfolk out of a displaced persons' camp."

"Daddy was very angry," said Gloria, "because the bank had to eat the loss when the company went bankrupt. Ray told me you were an Army Air Forces pilot. And you lost your leg on the very first day of the war. Gulette should hold you up as a hero. He doesn't deserve to be in office. I will work very hard, I promise. Goodbye, Mr. Haskins … Ray."

Ray watched his friend amble across the office and heavily drop his weight into one of his new chairs. "What do you think about her?"

"This is a high school girl? You could fool me. She's sophisticated and articulate. Knowing the way this crowd operates, I don't trust her. They don't play by the rules."

"In the OSS, nobody played by the rules. I learned an awful lot about people. She is smart, very, very smart. And very, very angry. If I hadn't seen firsthand how women reacted to Gestapo interrogations, I think, I too, would be inclined to keep clear of her. The physical change to disguise her beauty and, most important, the rage that came across in her voice and gestures are all too familiar. More than one of those women became extremely effective fighters. I'm going to take a chance with her."

"Okay," Byron sighed, "it's your call. I guess I don't have to tell you to be cautious when dealing with Knights." He pulled a pair of envelopes from his inside coat pocket. "I've been following up with the bar association. Add up the contents of those two envelopes and you will find eight hundred dollars cash."

"Eight-hundred, who ...?'

"The esteemed law firm of Anon, Eee, and Muss. They are so brave that I've been instructed not to reveal their names to you. Of the twelve-odd members of the local bar, I now have one hundred percent moral support. To a one, they all agree they want Gulette gone, but they're still afraid to stick their necks out. I also spoke to the families of some of the people who were convicted in the last four years. By contrast, none of them are asking for anonymity."

"Eight hundred bucks, a good start!" Ray exclaimed. "What about the families? I don't expect they have money to spare, but have any of them volunteered for your courthouse project?" *I imagine Jim looks at Byron as a one-man wrecking crew. Wait until he sees Byron showing these kids where to snoop at the courthouse.*

Byron continued, "I've found two volunteers. Both of them are recently mustered-out veterans. One is a sailor, who has a bone to pick with the prosecutor. The second is his friend. Neither of them knows much about anything. The sailor was a Navy storekeeper. He has agreed to be your treasurer. His friend, Charlie Lang, was in the infantry."

"I know Larry's family. It's a good start."

"I was in the clerk's office today at the courthouse, but I didn't want to say anything while the Knight girl was here. Trevor Lyman has been appointed to defend Joe Caulfels."

Ray winced. "Ouch! You couldn't pick a worse attorney from any county on this side of the Divide. This is part of the scheme to railroad Joe. Diamond tried to get Gloria to sign some statement this afternoon and when she didn't, he promised that Judge Costi would throw the book at him. Nobody from Gulette's office has even contacted her. The earlier the trial and sentencing, the better for our campaign."

"Is there any way you can help the Caulfels kid?"

"I have to make hard choices. Save him or save the county."

Gloria was one step behind Mary MacBride as they entered Price's Drugs the next day. She knew little about Mary other than that she had graduated from high school a year ago, that she delivered meat to Theo, and that she seemed eager to work for Ray. They went toward the back, to the soda fountain--the town's teenage hangout. Most of the patrons were footloose teenage males enjoying the beginning of summer vacation. For the first time since Gloria made a commitment to herself to wear a plain wardrobe, she saw the difference in the reactions of the opposite sex. Male eyes tended to glaze over when regarding a female figure in a shapeless dull gray suit and low-heeled leather shoes, versus a figure in clinging white dress with black polka dots, nylons, and high heels. *As long as I dress like this, boys will leave me alone. It makes it easier to keep my promise to Joe.*

Byron was there to meet Mary and give her an assignment. Gloria noted that even Byron couldn't take his eyes off her. Mary was a well-scrubbed blonde with broad shoulders and an ample bosom, who seemed to know someone at each table. Several of them asked her about her father, Cody, who owned the local meat market, MacBride Meats.

Byron sat in the big booth in the back, along with a couple of Gloria's schoolmates and Andy and Carole Foyle. Even after the introductions were made and everyone was seated, Byron was still staring at Mary. *Come on, Byron,* thought Gloria, *eyes front! We're here to help Ray.*

Almost as if he heard Gloria's thought, Byron broke off his stare and asked Mary and the two schoolmates some questions about their feelings and motivations. Gloria thought her schoolmates were there for the right reasons. Mary, however, gave vague answers. Gloria wondered if she was holding something back.

Byron leaned across the table and said in a soft voice, "Ray demands a wartime level of security. It is critical to minimize opportunities for the establishment to compromise our strategy and tactics. Past experience shows they will try anything. For example, the phone company's daytime operator is the sheriff's niece. She's a nice spinster lady, but she listens in."

Byron pulled a stack of mimeographed sheets from his briefcase. "I want you to read these so you know how we will use technology to dig up what they've been doing all these years. They are complacent because they know we don't have time before the election to go the usual route of hand copying everything. Here is the list of documents in court files that I want you to check. There'll be some hand copying, but mostly we will be using our secret weapon."

While he created two teams and gave instructions, Gloria studied the handouts. *I've got some better documents than what's in these court files.*

Byron asked if there were any questions. Andy broke the silence. "Mr. Haskins, thank you for laying out the work for my neighbors and dear friends. We're ready. Let's go."

Byron stretched a hand toward Andy and nodded at Carole. "Thank you, I do tend to get too windy. There is a ton of work to be done. I'll get your Cokes and we'll walk on over to the courthouse. I'll show you how the system works and where to look. Here are the legal pads. It's going to be hard work. You'll have to copy everything down just like it is recorded. Don't leave anything behind. Remember--your work doesn't involve confrontation."

"If we're not going to get in their hair, what are we doing this for?" queried Carole.

Gloria said, "We're providing the raw information. Ray will get in their hair. We don't elect people to office so they can get rich on our money. Ray will pin the tail on the elephant, so to speak."

CHAPTER 7

Digging for Dirt

Joe Caulfels frog-stepped his way to the table in the jail lunchroom, where his mother, Vera Caulfels, and his father, Orville Caulfels, sat. *It's good to see Ma and Pa. I thought they had abandoned me.*

Deputy Leo Stokings said, "Okay, Caulfels, give me your right hand."

Ma's dark, weatherworn Arapaho face added a frown to the many care lines etched on it as she watched her youngest son being shackled to the table. "Leo, why is this necessary?"

"He resisted arrest, injured two deputies."

"This is what they do when you confess to serious crimes, isn't that right, Pa?" Joe asked.   Orville squinted at his son through bitter, cold brown eyes that had the haunted look of an ex-convict. "They never did that to me. What the hell got into you, son? You've never been one to pick fights."

Joe kept running the fingers of his free hand over the cuff locked around his wrist. He remained silent. *I'm the one in the snare. Look at him, Pa would never survive. Prison would ruin both him and Gloria.*

Ma reached across the table and held Joe's other hand. "It's not like you to not respond. Are they mistreating you?"

"They? How about you? For seven empty days I've waited alone in a cell for my father and mother to visit. I made a deal with the law, a plea bargain, to keep two people I love out of prison and maybe save your ranch. I have to ask Pa, why did you hide the Four Roses in the back door pocket?"

Joe watched the red in Orville's face rise up to the top of his bald head. "Wha--what? Everybody knows I haven't touched a drop of anything--no wine, no beer, and nothing hard since that Knight woman made a stink."

"I don't understand. That fat son of a bitch said it fell out of the door when I swung it open hard."

Orville pounded a fist on the table. "It wasn't mine!"

"Well, I'm guilty of all the rest. Statutory rape because Gloria's under eighteen. Then I took the credit that belongs to her for kicking Deputy Linc Brown in the balls."

Pa leaned close across the table; Joe could see the ruptured blood vessels in his cheeks and nose, the signs of years of heavy drinking. He shook his large, powerful hand under his son's nose. "I'm so damn mad that you lied, went behind my back, not listening to me, and bedded the banker's bitch. I counted on you."

"I counted on you too, Pa, to be man enough to release that cable car and meet the woman I love. I had a dream of following Sunny into the Air Force. You're getting your wishes. I'm not on the way to the Army and West Point. I'm not marrying Gloria. But I am getting one wish—I won't be spending my life herding your damned cattle. Did you get your white Cadillac back?"

"Yeah, the back seat was a mess. Blood on the floor, a little on the seat. Nothing I couldn't clean up."

"Blood?" *Whose blood? What did they do to Gloria?*

Ma pulled a book up from her lap. "Enough of this talk. You sound just like your father did, full of anger and disappointment. Son, they're going to take you away. You will be alone. This Bible is your father's. Remember, no two objects can occupy the same space at the same time. It's up to you: love or hate."

"I apologize, Pa. My tongue was a bit sharp. Thanks, Ma. I hope they let me keep it. I wish you could have met Gloria. She's a ball of fire. Please see if she's all right."

"I'll talk to Leo," said Ma. "Speaking of fire … that reminds me, there was one quotation from Roger de Rabutin that helped see me through those years your father was in Leavenworth. 'Absence is to love what wind is to fire; it extinguishes the small, it enkindles the great.' You'll have to wait to find out what sort of fire burns in her heart."

Except for her green eyeshade, Gloria was dressed for bed, with a silk robe over her pajamas. She gave Lyle a perfunctory hug. He in turn lifted the eyeshade and kissed her on the forehead. "Gloria, I am so proud of you. It pleases me very much that you would value staying here to work, study, and gain practical experience, over the seminars and fine dining at the bankers' convention."

She pulled down the eyeshade as far as it would go, till she looked a little like a Marine recruit. "Daddy, counting travel time, the convention will be eleven days, which is a big chunk of time for me to take away from learning the business." *Eleven days to find out where he buries the bodies.*

Lyle pulled his gold pocket watch out of his vest pocket. "It's kind of late for you to be staying up."

"No school in the summer, Daddy. I wanted to see you off and then spend some time with this accounting text. That's what the eyeshade is for. Have a safe trip."

Gloria returned to her seat on the living room chair with textbook in hand until after the family car turned off Garfield Street in the direction of the train station. She arose and did some mental calculations as she watched the taillights disappear. *Let's see. He's off to Omaha for the convention, leaving here a few minutes after midnight Saturday so he can ride all the way without a change of train in Denver. He leaves Omaha Friday night and arrives here too late for dinner Saturday night. To be safe, give yourself a week to get everything copied. Mother always stays at the station until the train is out of sight. I've got maybe half an hour to gather up those papers from the den.*

In the courthouse, Byron Haskins sat in the county clerk's basement storage room with his arm around the waist of his new heartthrob, the fascinating Mary MacBride. For the moment, however, his attention was riveted on the document she was transcribing in longhand on the yellow legal pad. It was another suspicious real estate purchase and subsequent sale, one of many Byron's crew were finding in the files. But this one got his special attention because it involved Judge Costi.

The crew of mainly eighteen- to nineteen-year-olds were working close by. They never got too far from Byron's end of the table because the only light fixture for the room was a single naked bulb hanging there from the ceiling. At the other end, some light shone down into a small tray on the tabletop. That came from their copying setup, which looked like a worn leather briefcase mounted on sturdy legs. Inside the case were two high-intensity bulbs and the "secret weapon"--a small stainless-steel German Minox camera. The Minox, the infamous subminiature "spy camera," was not generally available in the United States, but Ray had taken this one from a Waffen SS major. Ray got film for it from a prewar stash that had been kept in a photo retailer's refrigerator in Denver. Photographing the documents took only a small fraction of the time required to hand copy, and the resulting exact image could not be challenged.

Each document to be copied was carefully positioned on the tray before it was memorialized on one of the thirty-six shots on the film roll. One person fed the documents in on the left, another clicked the shutter, and a third swept them away on the right. The room was quiet save for the sounds of paper being processed through the queue. That made it easy for Andy to notice the now familiar "squeak, squeak," like a failing bearing on some cheap machine, echoing across the open space from the hall. It grew louder with every footfall as Prosecutor Jim Gulette entered the room. Andy leaned across the table to whisper to Byron, "The prosecutor's here again."

Oh, shit, thought Byron, *he's down here checking on us. Thank goodness we're not copying bank papers too.*

Byron turned, and his eyes searched the shadows. There, close by the wall, he saw Gulette standing in his shirtsleeves, rocking back on his heels. Physically he was inconspicuous, but if his purpose was to hide, he had compromised himself with every rocking footfall of his rubber-soled shoes. If that weren't enough, he popped the gum he was chewing. *Sheesh! How that man got reelected without an opponent, I'll never understand.*

Byron mentally focused on what Mary had written on the legal pad. He was amazed by how much material his crew of teenagers had identified in the space of eight working days. *Jim would crap his pants if he saw the implications.* There was a pattern emerging. Gloria's father was the general partner and banker for the real estate purchases. Cash magically turned into equity, which paid an income free of taint. Thus laundered and held long enough, the property sold at a deep discount in an illiquid market, resulting in favorable tax treatment. Banker Knight reaped the rewards and presumably—although there was no paper trail—passed on part of them to his co-conspirators.

Byron couldn't swear to it, but each of these sales seemed to surface not long after Gloria brought another ledger out or, as she was doing now, delivered legal-size accordion files. He wondered how this high school girl knew where to look and what to look for. *In truth, all I have to go on are the candidate's suspicions and the transactions this angry girl is coming up with. No time now to pore over them. After we're done here and I analyze them, I'll know what to do.*

What Byron needed most was for Jim Gulette to go back upstairs and do the work the people were paying him to do. He turned toward his visitor in the shadows, holding a hand over his eyes to keep out the glare of the bulb overhead. "Mr. Prosecutor," he drawled, "is this how you prepare for your next day in court, here in the basement, rocking back and forth in the shadows just enough to make your shoes squeak?"

The wiry prosecutor bolted from his place along the wall. His bright orange bow tie bobbed up and down as he shouted, "What the dickens are you up to, Counselor? The clerk said you are on an Easter egg hunt. What the heck is this funny-looking briefcase thing with the lights shining down?"

"Jim, you need to break your habit of asking a second question in front of a judge before the first question was answered. I borrowed this field photostat device from Ray. It's much cheaper and quicker to develop the images at home."

"What are you doing with these high school students?"

Mary shook her head and waved her index finger back and forth. "Correction, sir. The majority are high school graduates. We are Mr. Tudbury's campaign workers."

A middle-aged woman in a tan dress looked up from shuffling papers. "Thank you, Mr. Prosecutor, don't I wish I had that much life to look forward to! You know me, I'm Madge from the clerk's office. I assure you nothing has been changed, added, deleted, or removed."

Byron gave his crew a hand signal to rise. "Mr. Gulette, you are largely correct to observe the youth and inexperience of my team. These youngsters are learning how local government works in this county. Since we'll be rubbing elbows over the next few months, let me introduce them to you. Hey, boys and girls, this is Mr. Gulette, Goodwin County's prosecutor."

Andy Foyle extended his hand and announced his name, followed by his sister. Jim brushed past them and made an impromptu fan of a stack of folders, "Dooforthe ranch… Wildcat Groceries… Aspen Meadows… hey, these are all mine! Haskins, cut the BS."

"Just showing these kids how public records work in this county. Might get a candidate or two for law school, never can tell."

"Law school, hell! Two of these kids are female. You have them going through everything I've ever invested in. What's your game?"

Byron slipped his lined pad farther under the papers as Gulette stepped closer. "If we find anything, I'm sure you'll know by November. You'd better hope and pray Gloria Knight doesn't get the law bug, because if she does, she'll have you for breakfast."

Gloria was standing nearby. Gulette pulled his glasses off and glared at her while she adjusted her green eyeshade, studiously avoiding eye contact with him. He looked down at Byron. "Mr. Haskins, I'll tell you what was on my mind: your attitude, which is apparently unchanged since the Smith case. I was sorely tried by the way you skirted through the shadows of legal precedents to blindside the prosecution and confuse the judge. Are you …"

Byron interrupted. "That's a wordy way of saying you screwed up. Now if you will excuse me, sir, I need to get back to Carole Foyle. She's a real experienced hand in digging up old skeletons."

Gulette turned his attention toward Gloria. "Miss Knight, you must be aware of your father's strong feelings regarding partisan matters. I will call the bank. You might miss the national banking convention in Omaha."

"No, Mr. Gulette, the convention's already started. Daddy left Saturday on the overnight train. We at the Goodwin Bank have to earn our spurs before we qualify for travel. I only have this summer to learn how the bank's and the county's systems work. More important, I must be in court when my fiancé appears."

Gulette stood tall with a hand held out, as if he were a policeman directing traffic. "He's confessed. We have damning evidence."

Gloria's eyes were a cold blue as she sought his. "Confess? Confess to what? Mr. Gulette, listen to me, since you haven't returned my phone calls. Joe Caulfels is innocent. Deputy John Diamond raped me."

Gulette looked past her as if she were invisible. "I have the doctor's statement. Don't make an issue of this. Heed your father's judgment. In time, you'll come to understand."

Byron thought, *"Come to understand," you bastard. You're so deep into her father's pocket that you don't think the law can touch you. Just keep thinking that way.* He turned to Gloria. "Gloria, darling, as much you want justice for your fiancé, we can't spend campaign time arguing with Ray's opponent today. Could you focus on our work here?" He gave Prosecutor Gulette a nod of the head plus a hand signal to leave.

Gulette took the hint and ambled out of the room, squeaking all the way.

At the courthouse's closing time, Gloria was curious about who had made Byron's short list. She stole a look at his legal pad, where he had listed projects, names, dates, and dollar amounts. Printed in caps were: BRAD HANLON, MARCIA HANLON, CODY MACBRIDE, LYLE KNIGHT, and RONALD COSTI.

CHAPTER 8
The Private Stash

Gloria and Byron met on the street and walked into Price's Drugs together. They moved past two tables with customers to the booth against the back wall. After they ordered a lemonade for her and a coffee for him, the rotund attorney and the banker's daughter exchanged briefcases. Byron asked, "What's in here?"

"Daddy's private records on all the deals. There are dollar amounts, when paid, and by whom. He even noted denominations and serial numbers when they paid in cash."

Byron grimaced. "Why didn't you take pictures like we asked?"

"I'm out of film. There are way too many. You have access to a photostat machine I think you'll need these to unravel the stuff we collected in the courthouse.

"Cash … who buys real estate for cash?"

Gloria smiled and whispered, "If you work at the courthouse, it's the only way to buy. Doc Mundal and Cody MacBride did it the same way. Oh, yes! And included in there is the list of people who have pricey Cadillac, Buick, and Oldsmobile autos on order, along with their down payments. Too pricey to match their declared incomes."

The attorney's eyes bulged. "Gloria, where in blazes did you get that?"

"I made a copy from the dealers' loan documents. I learned something else at the bank. John Diamond wrote a check at Canyon Liquors for the exact amount on the receipt for the last day of May that I found at the arrest site. It's date and time stamped for after we left the dance."

"You can't dig through people's records like that. It's against the law. The courts won't accept it as evidence."

Gloria threw her hands up and gave Byron a disgusted look. "I don't know why I put all this stuff together if it can't be used. As best as I can tell, these files are full of dirt. You have until Friday afternoon to decide which of them you want copied. Mother goes out to lunch Friday, followed by getting together with some friends from church. Afterward she shops at the grocery. She'll get home at the earliest four forty-five, and at the latest five fifty."

"Okay, I'll pick you up on the commons at three p.m.. By then I will have read the whole file. It can only go downhill from him calling you a no-good whore."

Gloria no longer attempted to keep her voice down. "This isn't about me. It's about Joe! We were set up. Leon Hopewell told me he overheard Deputy Four Eff on the pay phone at the armory with my father, engineering the whole damn thing! I want to get Daddy's attention so he'll never think it's worth his while to interfere in my life again."

Byron made gestures with his hands to hold her voice down, then shook his head. "I don't know what to say. Ray mentioned that they could track which Nazi was interrogating people by the methods they used. If even one more person could be turned up who was bound the way you were, it would go a long way toward erasing the doubt of your word against his."

"Interesting."

Thursday afternoon, the newly installed electric-bells on the front door of Kahn's Department Store jangled. On hearing them, Herb Kahn rose from his office chair on the mezzanine. He looked down to see a brunette with her hair down, wearing reflectorized sunglasses, walk up to the front counter. He was halfway down the stairs when she took off the sunglasses and moved her hair back from her ears. *Gloria Knight, wow! Whatever happened to that girl since she rented the tux? She was growing into one of the most beautiful women I've ever seen. Look at her now. She's working at making herself unattractive.*

He sped down the steps. He was proud of Kahn's, which was a rural emporium. If what you wanted wasn't somewhere in the basement, on the main floor, the mezzanine, or the second floor, Herb knew where he could order it. "I'll be right there. I'm short of help this afternoon."

"Good afternoon, Mr. Kahn," Gloria called out, "did you get Joe's tuxedo back okay? Did my deposit cover the cleaning?"

Herb, a vigorous middle-aged man who dressed and looked more like a successful rancher than a merchant, smiled, gave her a thumbs-up, and greeted her in the New York accent he still hadn't lost in twenty years. "Thank you for coming in, Gloria. I didn't recognize you at foist. Such a waste, you hiding your tremendous beauty undah that gray tent. I owe you an apology for selling you that suit. Show off that *shaynkeit*. Too soon it's gone."

She teared up, and her voice came out in a croak. "I can't do that. I made the commitment to marry Joe Caulfels, and no one else will do. I'm sorry, I cry too much."

"Theah, theah, Gloria, you've been put through hell." Herb pressed keys on the cash register until the drawer rolled open. He pulled out a single five-dollar bill and held it up for a visual examination before he handed it to her. "Yes, da tux was in mint condition, so here's your deposit back. I have a few questions about it, but foist, you're here to pick up da custom holster for that Smith & Wesson revolver?"

"Yes, what questions?"

While he reached under the counter and pulled a box out, she opened her purse and laid the S&W .38 caliber revolver on the counter. Herb said, "I went over to da jail to pick up da tux. Natchally I asked to see Joe, but they said no."

"Who said no?" asked Gloria.

"Deputy John. But too many things don't ring true. If you don't feel comftable talking about that night, I'll understand. Da papers say it was sex with a minor, but now you come in here and order a wardrobe of business tents. To top it off, you, a minor, order an S&W thoity-eight custom holster."

Gloria shrugged her shoulders and looked annoyed at his comments. "So? The revolver is my father's. I'm the only banker's daughter, and I work at his bank." She slipped the belt around her waist. "I brought it with me to make sure this fits."

He leaned across the counter and dropped his voice to a confidential level. "That boy … theah's a sparkle in your eyes whenevah you mention him. Why is he treated like a violent prisoner? What happened to you?"

"I am so sorry. Joe proposed to me in front of everybody at the graduation ball. After his father wouldn't see us, I seduced Joe, but he never got in." Gloria got through maybe two more sentences of telling her misadventure before tears overflowed and she was in his arms where she completed her story, implicating her father and Deputy John.

So the S&W is her father's, and he is out of town on business. She gives good reasons why a seventeen-year-old city girl should carry a gun, but I have my reservations. Herb pointed to the revolver. "Do you plan to get even with that gun?"

He would long remember those cold blue eyes. "Get even? You mean … shoot them?" asked Gloria. She vigorously shook her head no and continued, "No, I'm not going to shoot to get even. There are better ways. Why am I packing? That's to stay alive so Joe won't be forgotten. Why I'm dressing this way … to keep boys away so I won't be tempted. I'll marry him if he'll have me."

Herb busied himself writing up the receipt, including express shipping charges. *The smartest thing this girl can do is leave and never look back. She's saucy enough to believe she can beat them alone. Here I worry about injustice on the far side of the world, and it's going on under my feet. Diamond did something terrible to her, and her father did nothing! I never had much use for either of them.*

He picked up the revolver and spun the cylinder. "Empty. Very good. How much experience have you had shooting this gun?"

"I've been shooting since I was thirteen. I don't miss very often. Since I'm working on the Tudbury and Shyflinski campaigns, I'll practice every week."

"Tudbury? Shyflinski? Who are they?"

"They're running for prosecutor and sheriff, as Democrats."

"Democrats! Lotsa luck! How do you live in da same house with your Republican fadda, especially having da knowledge of what he did to Joe?"

"How do I live?" Gloria picked up the thirty-eight and began feeding rounds from her pocket into the cylinders. After she spun the loaded cylinder, she said, "With caution. I would have been gone from home, and from Goodwin, if it were not for my neighbor. She convinced us to work out an agreement for the summer. I would be disappointed if Daddy denied me this means of defending myself."

Gloria counted out the bills and handed them to Herb. "Oh, one last thing, Mr. Kahn. The last time I was here, you said you and some of the veterans don't like to see the German Iron Cross on the high school uniforms. If you're willing to raise the money, I have a suggestion. Change the name to the 'Goodwin Bootleggers.'"

"Da veterans want to get a music program started. How does that fit in?"

"Offer to dress the band in nineteen-twenties attire. Have them play jazz. Sew straw boaters on the football uniforms. Go to the school board with the idea."

"Why Bootleggahs?"

"Our local war ace, Colonel Sunny Caulfels—Joe's big brother--his plane is the 'Bootleg Lady.' Remember the bootleg passes that were so effective for the team last season? And Daddy says Goodwin stayed alive through the twenties by making moonshine."

"The iron crosses were all your fadda's idea. What do you think his reaction will be?"

Gloria looked Herb in the eye."He'll bounce off the walls. It will bring out the Women's Christian Temperance Union. But in the end, my father will end up putting up the dollars to remove the crosses."

"Oh, yeah, those sanctimonious old ladies in the WCTU will surely object." Herb gently rested his hands on her shoulders as he spoke in a gentle manner. "I'll pass your ideas to da veterans. They're pretty much fed up with the status quo."

Herb searched around the counter for a clean piece of paper. He began writing while he was talking. "I've lived here long enough to understand how those in power stay in power. I should fault myself for not having courage. What you must do now is get on da train to New York. Take this, it's my cousin's address and phone number. I'll tell him you're coming. He has contacts to open doors in high-fashion modeling. Leave now, put it all behind you. I'm worried about what might happen if you use that gun. Life in prison starting at eighteen is about as long as you can get."

She shook her head. "I can't desert my fiancé. I know what happens to people here. The thirty-eight is for protection."

"All right, you take it for later on. I'll pass your idea along. No shootouts, you understand?"

On the hot Friday afternoon before Lyle's return from the convention, Gloria walked leisurely across the commons in front of the courthouse carrying an empty briefcase. She looked around for Byron's car, but she didn't see it. *If he doesn't show, I don't know how I'll get those files back in the drawers. Come on, Byron, where are you?*

She mounted the steps of the large octagonal gazebo that was set up for the Goodwin Concert Band that would start playing an hour or so after sunset. It was just past the time the thermometer began its daily descent. Gloria carefully picked a chair in the shade that gave her visibility to see approaching traffic and feel a cooling breeze. She loosened her necktie and unbuttoned the top button, but that didn't cool her much. She reached around to her back and felt the pistol grip. She practiced releasing the leather strap and pulling the weapon out far enough to release the safety.

Ray pulled up ten minutes later in his nineteen-forty Ford coupe. He waved for her to get into the car, leaned across, and unlatched the door. "Sorry I'm late, the last of the copies were run today. Get in, I'll give you a ride to Garfield Street."

As she climbed into the passenger seat, Gloria said, "Thank you, I must have these files back before my mother gets home. What's going on here? Where's Byron?"

"He's busy with Mary." Ray gave her a slight smile and a nod as he put the car in gear. Once he was up to speed, he said, "I checked it. Everything is back in the briefcase and in the correct folder. Don't bring us any more."

Gloria tapped the empty briefcase in her lap. "I think I got it all. Any obvious holes?"

"You've actually brought too much. Let's say we've got a ways to go. Both Byron and I are having a hard time getting our arms around the extent and depth of corruption. Please, no more."

"Good, then there's enough to bring my stinking father down?"

"I don't know. What we see in those papers is evidence of corruption in government and the community. He's their banker. However, there's no law on the books today that keeps him from fashioning purchases and sales of real estate as a way of wiping away the taint of corrupt origins."

"All this work for nothing? I'm so disappointed."

"No! It wasn't for nothing. He's going to have to testify. The way those partnerships are set up is, they get pennies on the dollar on an early out to pay defense costs, and he gets the properties. He'll still be rich, but he'll be hated."

They rode for another block in silence. "Ray, a couple of times you've alluded to something between you and Gulette that sparked your decision to run. Care to tell me?"

Ray caught her eye for a moment. "You're earned your spurs, young lady. If I can't convince a majority that change is in order based on what you and your friends dredged up, I don't deserve to serve. Yes, there was an incident."

Ray began, "My first court case after the war came when my father's friends asked me to defend their grandson, who'd been arrested for passing two bad checks. He was twenty years old and freshly home from the Merchant Marine. He had made a mistake recording a deposit. By the time he realized his error, the car dealer had complained. He made good on the checks, and the dealer was no longer interested in pressing charges. It was at this point that they came to me. Seeing no intent to defraud, I agreed to take the case for a hundred dollars, figuring it would involve no more than a meeting with the prosecutor. Was I ever wrong! He refused to listen to reason and pressed for a felony conviction."

Tears welled up in Gloria's blue eyes. *I've always thought Jim Gulette was some sort of weasel from the way my father treated him.* "Felony conviction …" her voice showed the strain of her ordeal, "that's what Deputy Four Eff says they'll hang around Joe's neck. Why hasn't he had a hearing yet?"

"I suspect Trevor Lyman is hoping to stall his way into a lighter sentence."

"Who's Trevor Lyman?"

"Joe's lawyer. He was appointed by the court."

"Why hasn't he contacted me?"

"Good question. Probably incompetent representation. Grounds to ask for a new trial."

After Ray pulled up to the curb, Gloria asked, "Did you get your client off?"

Ray nodded, and a satisfied smile colored his face. "Yes, that was the easy part. Out of the blue, I found myself facing a Kafka-like bill of charges from the Bar Association Ethics Committee about my work with the OSS in Italy. They were going after my license, under pressure from Jim. Seems he'd found that I 'cut some ethical corners' in my activities, such as confiscating property, like the Minox--never mind that we executed its owner—or like not allowing prisoners to have counsel, not disclosing who else I was interrogating, et cetera. They alleged that I should have followed legal ethics even though I was making war, not practicing law, at the time."

"How did you stop them?"

"The U.S. Attorney's Office in Chicago and Allen Dulles, who was my OSS control, weighed in. The Ethics Committee caved in and cleared me with full apologies. Jim was livid."

Gloria applauded. "Wow, you beat them! Congratulations. How did Jim dig up dirt on you?"

"I'm not sure. Maybe he eavesdropped when I told my war stories. What I found from talking with members of the local bar is that there is a pattern of intimidating counsel, either in court or through complaints like this. Byron is about the only one who's not afraid of Jim." He looked her in the eye. "Byron feels that what you've done is too good to be true. That's why I'm personally returning this briefcase of your father's papers."

"Too good to be true? I don't understand. You and Byron taught me. Am I on your team or aren't I?"

"Byron can't visualize any father treating his daughter as he has you. Nor does he understand why you stay."

"You just told me I had earned my spurs, then you evaded me. I need a real answer. Am I on your team? Yes or no?"

Ray's eyes opened wide. "Gloria, I apologize. Yes, you are. Let me qualify that with a real answer. I don't know what the Internal Revenue Service will do with all you've unearthed. I suspect they'll go after the low-hanging fruit plus the politicians in the news. What will it do to your family if they go after your father?"

"In his own way, my father loves me. So you too are afraid of him?" Gloria pursed her lips and stared at him.

Ray didn't answer directly. "Your father won't be so fearsome after all this information breaks. Talk to Byron, he's got some good ideas. But please, please, get those files back before your mother gets home."

CHAPTER 9

Adjudicating Joe Caulfels

A jovial Deputy John delivered the news with breakfast. "Joe, today, Thursday, 27 June 1946, is your big day. Hurry up and eat. Judge Costi had a cancellation in his calendar. Your case will be the first on the docket."

"Thank you, Deputy John. You're talking sheriff talk again. What time does the judge get started? I want to get the word to my parents."

Jailer Leo Stokings got Joe ready, took him to the prisoners' waiting room, and assured him he would call his friend Andy Foyle. Unlike Joe's cell, there was a ticking clock on the wall. Joe sat there in a fresh county jail uniform plus walking chains. *Here I am sitting in a room with a noisy clock. Let's see. Leo locked me in here at seven thirty. That minute hand's gonna travel one-and-a-half times around the clock or five hundred forty degrees before the thing starts. Listen to that clock, ticking away my life.*

At eight fifty-five he heard the key in the lock. His court-appointed attorney Trevor Lyman, a slightly built man in his late forties, was the first through the door. He carried Joe's folder like a football and stiff-armed the door. Behind him rushed in Prosecutor Jim Gulette and Deputy John Diamond.

Joe was surprised to see the others with Lyman, whose eyes seemed to bulge just a little more than usual. He slid onto the chair across from his client, opened the folder, and turned it to face Joe in one motion. "Joe, I need your initials where there's a line in the margins. This is necessary in the agreement so it matches the evidence. It's a technical matter." He put a fountain pen into Joe's hand. "Hurry, initial it, court goes into session in five minutes."

"Why are you so late? I've been waiting so long, I thought you'd decided not to show up."

Gulette answered him in a voice reeking with contempt, "Look, Caulfels, I'm taking heat for ignoring that booze bottle. Either you agree now or I put these two warrants in John's hands. They're your father's and your girlfriend's."

Deputy John had taken a position off to one side, where he stood tall. He repeatedly struck his right hand into the palm of his left with such force that his belly rippled.

Joe looked at the typed document, but he couldn't tell what had been changed. He put his initials on each of the typed lines. *I don't like what they are doing or the way they're doing it. I'll have to trust this Trevor Lyman guy with his Goodwill wardrobe. He's never answered my questions. I don't think he could tell the difference between beans and bullfoot.*

Lyman closed the folder and handed it to Gulette, who made a cursory examination of the page on his way across the room. He pounded on the door while John returned Joe's wrists to the walking chains.

Lyman leaned forward in his chair. "I'm sorry to be so late. With the change in schedule, I had to get this offer changed this morning."

"I don't understand what's going on. Are you representing me or not?"

Lyman's Adam's apple stood out below his receding chin as he replied, "Of course, what made you make such a hurtful comment? It's no easy task cleaning up after the mess you made."

Deputy John started to apply a gentle pressure to Joe's lower back. Joe said, "You're still sitting there and the deputy is dragging me into the courtroom. Did you tell Andy so he can tell my folks?"

Lyman rose slowly and stretched his arms. "The prosecutor told me not to because anything I tell him, Gloria hears."

Joe said, "You never mentioned these changes before, either. You're a useless son of a bitch." *That's what you get for nothing--nothing. I'm screwed. What was so important that it had to be changed at the last minute?*

Joe stepped into a fully staffed courtroom with a bailiff on one arm and John on the other. Jim Gulette stood at his table staring at the back of the room. Joe's heart sank when he saw that the only spectator was Lyle Knight. *I need Ma and Pa to give me the strength to get through this. I'll be damned if this Trevor Lyman hasn't turned his chair around so he can sit with his back toward me.*

Joe had almost screwed up enough courage to ask his counsel to stop tapping a pencil at an impatient beat on the tabletop when the bailiff called out, "All rise, the Honorable Ronald Costi presiding. Hear we now the case of The People versus Joseph Corwin Caulfels."

Jim Gulette's sneering voice carried to the back of the nearly empty room. "On your feet, pervert, and be quick about it."

Joe's eyes started to tear. He wiped them with shaking hands as he stood up. Lyman wrinkled his nose and moved away from him. On orders of the bailiff, they sat down again. Gulette, as was his practice, moved his chair as close to the defense table as he could while still sitting behind the prosecutor's table. His voice was barely above a whisper. "Caulfels, be a man, admit you're guilty as sin."

Judge Costi wiped back his curly silver locks and lifted himself off the seat to adjust his robe. All the while, he stared at the second visitor to enter the gallery, the buxom Mary MacBride. She was on her way to a seat immediately behind Joe. The courtroom routine proceeded until the Judge said, "Clerk, let's hear the reading of the charges."

Lyman bounced to his feet. "Your Honor, the defense asks to dispense with a reading of the charges and agrees to a plea of guilty on all charges and counts." He took a swallow from the glass on his table and wiped sweat from his forehead.

Mary leaned over the railing and gently touched Joe's back. "Joe ... Talk to Gloria. Don't let them railroad you."

Joe sat up as if her fingers were charged with electricity. *Talk to Gloria? I can't. That lying Diamond tricked me, and this fool, who passes himself off for a lawyer, either can't or won't help. I'm screwed.*

Lyman shook an index finger at Mary. "Shut your damned mouth before you screw things up for this boy."

Judge Costi pounded his gavel. "Young lady, you sit in this courtroom at my pleasure. I will not tolerate disruptions. An accurate record cannot be made in a bedlam. Any more from you, Miss MacBride, and you will be ejected." He then said in fatherly tones, "Mr. Caulfels, please stand. Is it true you are willingly pleading guilty to ..."

Mary screamed, "Don't say it! You didn't do anything wrong!"

Joe flinched, but went ahead with what he had planned to say. His voice could barely be heard. "Yes, Your Honor. I know what I did. I am guilty."

"No, you're innocent and they know it!"

"Order, order in the court!" Judge Costi pounded the gavel loud and long. "Mary, behave yourself, young lady! I'll have no more of your outbursts. I have reviewed the files, and compelling evidence supports the young man's confession. Bailiff, remove Mary MacBride from the courtroom."

Lyle's voice boomed, "Please, Your Honor, grant my wish to put an end to this affair."

Judge Costi nodded toward Lyle. He flipped through the pages of his calendar, then cleared his throat. "I will issue an order barring any contact between Gloria Knight and the Caulfels family. In light of the heinous nature of Mr. Caulfels' crimes, I don't know why she would want to contact him. Let me look at the calendar for July for a good sentencing date.

CHAPTER 10
Sheriff Brad Hanlon

Sheriff Brad Hanlon perused the walls of his office. *This has been a rewarding career,* he mused. *Every item on these walls is a happy memory or reward for a job well done as sheriff.* He had been there so long that there was hardly a space for another plaque or framed photograph of Hanlon with Republican presidents, starting with Teddy Roosevelt, whom Hanlon went hunting with after being sworn into office. *As for the other Roosevelt,* thought Hanlon, *thank God he never visited Goodwin or I'd have to decide between him and an honorable Republican president.* His gaze lingered over the wedding picture of himself and Marcia some six years earlier. *Former prison guard and Mexican national or not, that was the wisest move I ever made. She brought order to my life and this department. Without her, I would never have agreed with Lyle Knight's notion that I ought to run for another term.*

Marcia Hanlon, a powerfully built woman in her late forties, came through the door. She dropped into the upholstered leather chair at the side of the rolltop desk. "We're over the first hurdle with the Caulfels kid. The guilty plea for forcible rape makes it a clean case."

Brad pointed to the headline. "Wait, I don't know why the *Globe* didn't get it right. They say 'statutory rape,' but the charge was forcible rape. Maybe ..."

"Let sleeping dogs lie. The paper got it wrong. Old Lyle has put us a hair's breadth away from a disaster in an election year. How John brought this all together was nothing short of a miracle. We'll have only one more chance for screw-ups: the sentencing. I hope the judge uses some sense."

The sheriff leaned back in his swivel chair far enough to make the springs protest. "I admire the way Lyle can get small favors out of our judge. When he asked to be present for each court appearance, the judge delayed the arraignment to yesterday because Lyle was out of town at a bankers' convention. The boy will be forgotten before the year's out. As for his no-good father, we'll turn over the broken whiskey bottle to Orville's parole officer as soon as the boy is in the pen. Without any menfolk to help the old lady, she'll have to sell out. Lyle will be ecstatic."

Marcia shook her head. "Let's wait on the bottle until after Goodwin's war ace, Colonel Sunny Caulfels, goes back to his Army post. It'd be bad timing to put his father behind bars while the town is celebrating him as a favorite son."

Brad had time enough to light a cigarette, inhale, and place it in one of the burned spots along the edges of his rolltop before Deputy John rushed through the door holding up a red, white, and blue brochure. "I've got a double dose of bad news. Gloria Knight is out at the counter. She's demanding to see the blotter. And she gave me this brochure. You've got a Democrat running against you."

Marcia stood up and took the brochure. "Who's this Shyflinski?"

"The son of that Polish guy who worked for the oil company before the war."

"It says here that Larry Shyflinski was a major in the military police," Marcia said, "He looks like some movie star in that picture."

The sheriff took the brochure from his wife. He held it almost at arm's length to read it through the bottom half of his bifocals. "Military police, a pretty nobody. The people of this county aren't stupid. They've been putting me into office every election since nineteen ought six. As for Lyle Knight's spoiled brat, it's time I go out there and give her a piece of fatherly advice."

Hobbled by arthritic knees, Sheriff Brad shuffled slowly from the door toward the counter past a prisoner swabbing the floor. The prisoner, a young Hispanic, wore striped blue and white pants with leg irons clamped over the cuffs. The sheriff stopped inside the counter opposite

Gloria. He pushed his upper plate in with his thumb, then he smiled. "Gloria, I don't see you that I'm not reminded of the day your mother stepped off the train into your father's arms. What a stunning beauty she was. She gave up a career on the New York stage to marry that good man and raise you up."

"Actually, Sheriff, she starved on Broadway. Please, I came here to look at the blotter."

Brad waived the Shyflinski brochure under Gloria's nose. "Countless times I've broken bread with you and your momma and daddy. Like them, I care for you. I'm worried about the crowd you run with. There is nothing more you can do for Joe Caulfels. He's on his way to prison."

With her index finger extended, she thrust out her hand toward Sheriff Brad, who retreated a step. She glared at him with cold blue eyes. Gloria's voice was angry. "Sheriff Hanlon, you and I know Joe is innocent! Section four-one-five, paragraph twenty-seven point two, requires that your blotter be open to public inspection. Do I get it now, or do I come back with a court order and a reporter? Perhaps today would be a good time to tell the press you are retiring, throwing your support to Major Shyflinski."

"Retire? I'm not retiring. He's a damned Democrat."

"The blotter, sir. I have no time to waste."

Sheriff Brad pulled the blotter notebook from under the counter and slammed it down in front of Gloria. She opened the ledger, and her fingers began turning pages. She barely smiled and spoke with a low velvet tone in her voice, "Thank you, Sheriff Hanlon."

He stood looking at her for a full minute before sucking in a lungful of cigarette smoke. *Lyle Knight's daughter or not, no damned brat talks to me like that and gets away with it.* He blew it in her face, then coughed.

Gloria took a couple of steps back from the counter and waved her hand to disperse the smoke. As Sheriff Brad reached for the blotter, she called out, "Please, Sheriff, I'm not done with that blotter."

The sheriff had no sooner closed the notebook than Gloria turned and announced to jail guard Leo Stokings, "You're my witness that he wouldn't let me finish. What's your name?"

Leo, who had watched the interplay between his boss and Gloria from his blocking position by the outside door, said, "Leo Stokings. My job is to watch prisoners. Chico here," pointing to the Hispanic, "is just about done with the lobby."

The sheriff reopened the blotter notebook and laid it on the counter.

Joe Caulfels heard the door opening at the end of his cell block. He heard the now-familiar sound of the metal wheels on the water buckets squeak as first one and then the other were pushed through the door and into the otherwise empty cell block. Joe listened carefully to the sounds, as his father had taught him when they went out hunting. There were two sets of feet out there, and one set was hobbled. He recognized his father's friend's voice. Leo Stokings was all right, Joe concluded. He felt lucky that Leo was on duty. After coming down to inspect the prisoner's work, Leo slammed the cell block door behind him and locked it.

Another empty day, sighed Joe. But soon he'd see a human being, the prisoner who was mopping the floor. The prisoner swabbed his way past empty cells, the hobbling chain clinking on the cement floor as he proceeded. He continued his mopping past more empty cells until he came to the last cell, where Joe was sitting on a bunk holding a Zane Grey novel.

As Chico swept the mop close to the bars, he said in a guarded voice, "Hey, Joe, your girl is out front giving the old man a hard time. She said you're innocent."

Joe sat up and closed the book. "Gloria, here? The judge told her to stay away. She could get in serious trouble." He shook his head and laughed. "Innocent, oh, how I wish! It's over. All that's left for me is to do the time. Pa figured they might have given me probation if I hadn't hurt the deputy's ribs and fessed up to kicking the other guy in the balls."

"You'd better pray the judge gives you enough time to send you to Canon City. You don't wanna stay in this jail with the sheriff's *mujer* running it. She is *mas loco*. She put leg irons on me just to mop down the place. Pray that she never puts you down in the hole in the basement."

"Hole? What hole?"

"It is *mas* terrible. It's hot and it stinks."

"Thanks, pal, for talking to me. It's terribly lonely back here all by myself."

Chico looked back toward the door and nodded as he maneuvered the mop back up the other side.

Some minutes later, Joe returned to the book. Turning the pages, he found and cautiously lifted out a sheet of pastel stationery headed "To Joe Caulfels." *That's Gloria's handwriting!* His hands shook as he unfolded the sheet. He read:

"My Dearest Joe, I love you. Each day that you are in jail deepens the guilt I must bear for leading you into this trouble. I ask your forgiveness. Please give me one chance to make up for all the anguish you must endure. I want to devote the rest of my life to making this right to you. If you still want me, I will wait for you for however long. I hold you in my heart and pray for your safe return to my arms. I will remain true to you, my fiancé. All my love, Gloria."

Tears filled his eyes and his lips barely moved as he reread the last line, "'I will remain true to you, my fiancé. All my love, Gloria.'" *That's her hand, I'd recognize it anywhere. Is she crazy sending this ... or are they trying to set me up?*

He crumpled the sheet into a ball. "*It would be like those bastards to slip this in so they can go after Pa.* He changed his mind and smoothed it out. *No, no, it was no coincidence I found this on the same day Gloria was out front. The Lord has given me a sign so I can have the strength.* He folded it up and put it in his shoe.

<hr>

Gloria answered the phone while seated at the well-polished writing stand next to the antique coat and umbrella rack. "The Knight residence, hello."

"You spoiled little bitch! I don't like the vile rumors you're spreading about me. I'm thinking about contacting an attorney." She heard what sounded like a truck in the background.

"Oh, hello, Deputy Four Eff. The truth hurts, doesn't it? May I recommend Trevor Lyman? He'll give you the representation you deserve."

"Don't smart-mouth me. I'm keeping track. I know who's asking questions. Deputy John never forgets. Sooner or later there will be payback time for each of you."

"Does Sheriff Hanlon put you up to this crap?"

"The sheriff is sick and tired of all the unsolicited phone calls about Caulfels. The more the sheriff hears, the more difficult Caulfels becomes. With the record he's building here, coupled with the serious conviction for forcible rape, I guarantee he'll start out in maximum security. Listen to your daddy and forget him. You'll be a grandmother by the time he's out."

"Forcible rape? That's bullshit! The papers said statutory ..."

John laughed. "The papers got it wrong! You'll be all dried up and ready to blow away before he's done his time."

Gloria slammed the phone down hard on the receiver. *Forcible? All the force came from him!*

Shortly afterward, Lyle burst into the room. "Was the phone for me?"

She stood by the phone with her hands balled into fists. She spit the words out of her mouth, "No, Mr. Knight. The call was for me on a subject you don't want to hear about. But I'm positive you ..."

Lyle cut his daughter off in midsentence. "Get control of your temper. Remember we pay for that phone when you break it. And stop calling me by my last name outside the bank. What's going on with you? Brad Hanlon warned me, he has had enough of your contempt. What have you done now?"

"I asked to look at the blotter, sir."

"Look at the blotter? I can't help you if you break the law and end up in jail. Gloria, I'm your father."

"Your memorandum was quite clear. You're my employer. When at work, employees are to address the president as 'Mr. Knight.' I listened to the Ford and Chevy dealers' concerns last week. I will be working on the bank's auto loan policy after dinner, sir."

Lyle paused and smiled at Gloria. "Okay, okay. But I'm Dad or Daddy at home. We've gone through some rocky times since that graduation ball. There are moments when you make me proud. Like tonight, when I saw your preliminary numbers. You didn't waste time while I was away. You're right, there has been too much leakage of money out of our community into those big banks."

"Thank you, Daddy."

"Speaking of autos, there was a fellow from the FBI in today. He wanted the dealers' lists from the commercial loan papers. It seems there is a national program to catch people who stayed home from the war and got rich cheating on their taxes."

"And you just gave them the information?" She was wide-eyed as she asked the question.

Lyle held his hands out, palm up, and dipped his head. "We always fully cooperate with the IRS and law enforcement. Gloria, one last thing … I got a phone call from the president of the school board that they will be discussing changing the name of the Goodwin Knights because Herb Kahn and some veterans object to the German influence. It ought to be easy enough to remove the Teutonic cross from the breastplate of the mascot costume, don't you think?"

Gloria smirked. "Do you mean that stupid walking potbellied stove? Get rid of it! It looks like something out of the Depression."

"That's a keen insight. You're right, that suit of armor is a relic of the Depression. We've sponsored the same mascot by default ever since the school district ran out of money in thirty-four. Maybe it's time for a brand new knight."

He doesn't get it, she thought. *I'm saying change the name to something that has nothing to do with knights … or Knights.*

CHAPTER 11
Injustice in Goodwin

"Deputy John, what brings you back here?" Joe was standing, holding onto the bars of his cell.

"It's the presentencing meeting with your lawyer and the prosecutor."

"Mr. Lyman said I had a month."

"Summer vacations, I guess. Usually the judge takes a month to have the sentencing hearing. Didn't your attorney tell you yours will be Thursday?"

"Yeah, but he didn't say which Thursday."

"I'll walk you down."

Joe was surprised he wasn't shackled before he was led into the same room he had been in before the preliminary hearing. As before, he took the seat next to Trevor Lyman and opposite Prosecutor Gulette. Lyman moved his chair down the table away from Joe as he seated himself. Joe asked, "Did you get probation for me?"

Lyman shook his head and looked at Gulette. The prosecutor opened a manila legal folder and laid the top sheet on the table in front of Joe. Gulette managed a weak smile as he said, "So there won't be any surprises next Thursday, our recommendation to the court will be twenty years to life for the counts of forcible rape, aggravated assault on a peace officer, and resisting arrest."

Joe stood up and shouted, "Twenty years! Stop right now! I never confessed to raping Gloria. Mr. Gulette, you said that if I confessed to having sex with her, they wouldn't say anything about Pa's booze. I love her. I'm not doing twenty years for something I didn't do!"

The prosecutor smiled like a stand-up comic who had just pulled another trick on his straight man. "Sit down, Caulfels. We amended the charges after we got the doctor's report. Look, you initialed right down there."

"Wait a minute! The two of you came into the room five minutes before court opened and had me initial the paper. You lied to me, Mr. Lyman. You told me this was just a technical correction. I would never hurt Gloria. I love her. She loves me. Tell the judge I'm not going to go through with this deal. I've talked to Pa. Diamond lied. Pa's a dry and if there was booze, it was planted. No, not twenty years!"

Gulette leaned across the table as if he were going to grab the defense lawyer's arm. "Trevor, this is your deal."

Lyman turned toward Joe. "Oh, no, you don't. This case is open and shut. You admitted screwing the girl. I saw the report. Her father, the sheriff, and Deputy Diamond signed statements that she was hysterical. The doctor will testify that she had vaginal injuries. He will say that she told him you raped her. There is the rubber with your sperm on it ..."

"If she was hysterical, it wasn't because of anything I did. She escaped, but they caught her trying to start the Caddy. The last I saw of her, Diamond had handcuffed both of her wrists and ankles. What did Gloria say when you talked to her?"

Lyman steepled his hands, then said, "There was no need to traumatize her further. You confessed."

"Not to this, I didn't!" Joe pounded his fist in the palm of his hand. "Tell the judge you screwed up. Change my plea."

Lyman shook his head and replied in a disgusted tone, "I screwed up? You perverts are all alike. You can hand it out, but you can't take it. I got you a better deal than you deserve. We were going to leave for Wyoming Thursday. But no, I had to wait an extra whole day to hold your hand. I'm not canceling my fishing trip because you have a case of cold feet. Jim, how come he isn't chained up? Guard!"

Deputy John moved toward the door to let the guard in.

Joe yelled, "Now I know what Mary MacBride was trying to tell me. You, Prosecutor Gulette, Mr. Lyman, how can you sleep at night? That wasn't a technical correction. It was a lie. Why? What have I ever done to you?"

Joe moved toward the door just as John released the latch. Before he could relatch it, Joe swung it open with John leaning on it. The fat deputy stumbled and, before he regained his balance, Joe spun him around. John hit the far wall, back first. Joe drove his forearm hard across John's neck. "Confess, Four Eff, you raped my fiancé!"

John gurgled. Lyman ran out the door yelling, "Help, help, the pervert is trying to escape!"

Gulette hit Joe on the back and the neck, while John swung glancing blows. John struggled ineffectively while Joe's chokehold remained in place. Gulette tried to pry John free. Only after Deputy Tom Weisner entered, swinging a nightstick, did Joe's hold loosen. Weisner struck Joe mostly across the back. Marcia Hanlon followed in his wake.

John croaked out the first words. "Easy, Tom, easy with that nightstick. We don't need to have the doc examine him."

Marcia snagged one wrist with a handcuff, then the other. "Okay, Caulfels, I exact a high price on anyone who injures an officer of this department. You're going in the hole. It's going to be hell."

"Marcia, don't get carried away now," ordered Gulette.

"Don't worry, Jim, the Caulfel's kid will be meek as a lamb by sentencing."

The other prisoners craned their necks as they saw the victors, Marcia Hanlon and Deputy Tom, push their charge toward the hole. They recognized the dreaded sound of hinges scraping, metal on metal, signaling that another poor slob was about pass through the steel door and take the stairs down to that den of what the jailers liked to call "penitence."

Joe was blindfolded and locked into walking chains. As he lurched down the creaking stairs, he thought, *I've never found it necessary to fight, but for those few moments I think Pa would have been proud of me. I blackened that damned Gulette's left eye. That fat Deputy John is moaning about his neck. I'm sorry I didn't break it. The man is pure evil.*

Joe was nearly gagged by a fetid smell that rose up the stairs during the frightening descent. Once at the bottom, Marcia used pokes from a cattle prod to direct him toward the punishment cell. Still blindfolded and terrorized by the cattle prod, he didn't resist the exchange of his prison uniform for a straitjacket and hobbles on his ankles. The heat hit him like a wave; his body was covered with a sheen of sweat by the time Marcia tightened the jacket's straps. When she whipped off the blindfold, he found himself in a room about four feet by eight. He spotted a dripping faucet on the back wall.

Marcia rechecked the straps on the straitjacket. "Caulfels, you're gonna come out of here a changed man."

"Where's the toilet? I've got to go."

"Toilet? Hah! Squat on the floor. A trusty will hose it down tomorrow." She walked out and shut the door.

Joe heard bolts being thrown and the turn of a key in a lock. Seconds later, the one dim light went out. Just like in his cell above, he was totally alone. But unlike his cell, where the light was always on, he was plunged into darkness. It was relieved only by a finger of light that stretched from a crack between the door and the jamb to the faucet on the back wall. Joe watched drops of water swell, catching the light, then fall one by one into the darkness. This was the only noise beyond the white noise of the boiler in the next room.

Through what seemed like endless hours, Joe drifted in and out of wakefulness. When he sat up, he was dizzy and felt like he was going to vomit. He curled into a ball in a vain attempt to ease the cramping in his arms, legs, and abdomen.

Then the light snapped on. Joe pleaded, "Help, help, please ... somebody ... let me up. Thirsty, cramps ... Please."

He counted the three bolts being thrown and the key working the lock. Joe looked up to see Deputy John standing just outside the door. He was wearing a neck brace and holding a hose. "Okay, Caulfels, Mr. Tough Guy. You took the bait, now suffer, you son of a bitch. It doesn't matter if the rape conviction is tossed. You attempted to murder a peace officer."

"Terrible pain ... Please let me up ... I have to go ..."

John laughed as he squeezed the lever on the hose nozzle. "It's your first day in hell. Squat and crap on the floor. This is a preview of life in the Big House."

The blast of icy water caught Joe by surprise. Without free arms to help him stand, the most he could do was sit while John kept the stream aimed at his face. Joe fought to free himself from the confining straitjacket by rolling back and forth until well after the stream was directed onto the floor. John stood over Joe, who rolled away until he was against the wall. John kicked him in the ribs. "Drink all you can," said John as he turned the hose on Joe's head.

From the door, John said, "It's time to go home and enjoy an evening with family. Oh, yeah, Caulfels, if you think last night was bad, just wait until Marcia Hanlon gets done with you tonight."

"Please don't leave me here. It's too hot. I feel sick."

The door slammed. The bolts were thrown. The key turned. The dripping continued. Joe was returned to sweating in the dark.

Gloria didn't sleep the night before Joe's sentencing. She had just finished glancing at the Thursday morning headline, JOE CAULFELS FACES 20 YEARS - SENTENCING TODAY, when Andy called at breakfast time to tell her he had a phone call from jailer Leo Stokings. The message was to tell Joe's parents that he had been moved from a punishment cell to a two-man cell. Neither Andy nor Gloria knew what that meant: they had never heard about punishment cells. Andy told her he had called everyone in the graduating class to be at the sentencing.

Gloria's mind was on what they planned to do to create some head-lines during the sentencing phase of the trial. She and Andy had the briefest of conversations on holding a rally for Ray Tudbury before Lyle walked in and announced, "We're got to get down to the bank. There's been some problems with one of the tellers' drawers."

I laid out the day so we could have an orderly demonstration. He's trying to keep me out of the courtroom if he can. Gloria shook her head. "I can't. I have to be there for Joe's sentencing at nine a.m."

Lyle had not slept well either. Before going to bed, he had discovered that the file drawer in his study at home was out of order. He stayed up late to confirm that nothing was missing. Then he awoke in the wee hours with an answer as to why the IRS agents had been asking pointed questions about his good friend, Judge Ron Costi.

He had gone as far as Gloria's door, intent on awakening her, but changed his mind. She had met every goal he had set. She was the fastest learner and hardest worker in the bank. Yes, he could see her being capable of running the bank.

The next morning he had shared his suspicions with Theo over the pillow. Her reply was, "If she informed on Ron, it's because you taught her to be honest. Please keep this to yourself. I don't want to lose her."

Honest? thought Lyle. *Two of those bribes came out of my wallet.*

They arrived at the bank to find it in a state of turmoil. One of the senior tellers was supposedly one hundred fifty dollars short on the previous Friday, the last day she had worked. She was outraged because, she claimed, all was in balance Friday when she left. Lyle handed Gloria the ledger, "This is yours to correct. It will be a good education."

He gave the order with the full expectation that she would obey. Instead, without any hesitation, she handed it back to him. "It's your bank. It's your problem. I'm going to the courthouse."

"Gloria Knight, you gave me your word. You know I can't tolerate disobedience."

She looked him in the eye. "Fire me if you must, Mr. Knight, sir. I'll be back after my fiancé's sentencing."

Lyle shook his finger under his daughter's nose. "Don't do something stupid. You could spend the fall in jail."

"Nothing like the twenty years you arranged for Joe. If anyone should be going to prison, it's me." She ran for the bank's door.

Lyle followed Gloria out the door and onto the sidewalk. He had never considered her athletic, yet there she was, sprinting like a marathon runner. He muttered, "I'll be damned, look at her run. I'll never catch her."

The teller said, "Go on, Mr. Knight. Go after her. We'll keep track of every transaction without fail until you or Gloria decides what to do."

Lyle's first hint that Joe's sentencing was getting attention was that all the parking places near the courthouse were full. The closest spot he could find was across the block-wide commons that the county buildings fronted. He met Sheriff Hanlon outside the door. "Morning, Sheriff, is this crowd here for sentencing the Caulfels kid?"

"Yes, Deputy John suggested I come over. He told me Judge Costi wasn't accepting calls because he was in a meeting. I don't see what the problem is. All he has to do is drop the gavel and order the court cleared. I have the day shift on its way as backup."

"I hope there isn't any trouble. My daughter left work against my wishes. Why she'd do this defies imagination after what he did to her."

Sheriff Hanlon placed a fatherly hand on the banker's shoulder. "Lyle, as long as Gloria or Joe don't go off the track today, the game is over for the Caulfels boy. Starting today, you'll have to convince her that it'll take time for her to heal. Be gentle with her."

Their feet echoed off the marble floor of an otherwise empty lobby. Sheriff Hanlon said, "I don't think there is another county in Colorado that has as elegant a courthouse. I marvel at the high ceilings, the marble columns, all financed by the gold rush. It couldn't be replaced today. This lobby is where I was sworn in back in nineteen ought six."

"Yes, what's that--ten terms?

"Yep, and that's forty years that no one has successfully robbed your bank, banker Knight."

"You've had help from our geography. With only one east-west highway and that miserable pass to the south, your boys can always head them off. Say, Brad, what the hell is going on in there? I've never heard noise from the courtroom out here on the stairs."

Lyle slowed his pace to stay with the sheriff, who didn't answer the question. The sheriff was fully engaged physically and mentally to climb the steps and walk down the hall. A deputy opened the hearing room door. "Sheriff, Mr. Knight, welcome, the judge is late so you haven't missed a thing. As you asked, we've held a seat in the last row for you."

"Fine," queried the sheriff, "where's Deputy John and the two deputies I assigned?"

"John's down in the first row, a couple of seats from the Knight girl. I heard him give her the warning from the judge that she would be arrested if she disrupted the sentencing. The bailiff has the other two deputies posted by the fire doors. Unfortunately, Mr. Knight, I know your daughter was the victim and I apologize, but there are no more seats unless someone yields."

"I'm fine, please don't. I have to get back to the bank." Lyle paced back and forth along the back wall. *There's Vera and Orville Caulfels. Should I offer them just short of a fair market value in cash or wait to pick up their ranch on the courthouse steps after the old man goes back to the pen?* He waved to Herb Kahn, one of the bank's big customers, and was surprised by the angry expression on his face. *I'd like to understand what powers this little man. Why does he think it's good business to go out of his way to dump the Goodwin Knights for "Bootleggers"?*

Lyle recognized most of the people in the audience. He didn't find Gloria until she stood up in her front row seat to confront the defense attorney Lyman as he walked through the barrier. He felt she had a way of projecting her voice while maintaining a soothing, feminine quality, much like her actress mother. "Excuse me, Mr. Lyman, why is it you never return my calls? I wanted to name the rapist and tell you Joe Caulfels never raped me."

Lyman ignored Gloria's question. The room fell quiet. Mary Mac-Bride called out, "Lawyer Lyman, Gloria Knight asked you a question. I also want to know why." Orville and Vera Caulfels, from their front row seats behind the defense table, joined a rising chorus. Gloria repeated the question. Lyman's bulging brown eyes skittered around the room behind his bifocals rather than address the question.

The prosecutor came to his rescue. He leaned over and whispered, "However slight." At this, Lyman brightened and smiled at Gloria. "Under the law, Miss Knight, any penetration, however slight, is sufficient to constitute rape. He confessed, didn't he?"

The side door opened, and the clink of chains preceded the prisoner. The gallery fell silent as they watched a gaunt Joe Caulfels shuffle toward the defense table. He was wearing the blue and white striped jail uniform and was shackled into walking irons with his hands locked to a chain around his waist.

Lyle was shocked at how bad he looked. *What the hell did they do to that kid? If that guard wasn't half-carrying the Caulfels boy along, he'd fall down. I've only seen real old men walk along bent over at the waist like that. Serves him right for thinking a half-breed could have my daughter.*

CHAPTER 12
Judge Costi Presiding

The Honorable Ronald Costi opened the door to see a packed court-room. Nearly all eyes were on Joe, so few noticed when the judge stopped short of the bench with his eyes on the stationery imprinted with a DEPARTMENT OF THE TREASURY letterhead. His hands shook so much he couldn't reinsert the stationery in the envelope.

The judge hadn't recovered from what happened at eight o'clock that morning. Internal Revenue agents with gold badges, special agents from the Criminal Investigation Division, had shown up at his chambers and served him with papers. The papers declared that five thousand eight hundred dollars in income was missing from the judge's tax returns. A quick call to the judge's accountant had been no help; the accountant said the income had to be disclosed, even if it was bribes.

The Judge slowly sank into his seat, thinking, *Why here? Why now? I'm ruined. I hate to think all they'll find when they go back eight years. Thank God, it's only sentencing on my docket today and not a full-blown trial.*

Then a commotion in the courtroom pulled him to attention. *What is all that noise? What the hell is going on? What does Deputy John hope to accomplish, bringing all these people in? There are more kids here than on a civics day. Every graduating senior must be here with their parents. There's Lyle Knight coming in late. He'll have to stand to hear me sentence Caulfels.*

The judge wondered if this was Lyle Knight's way of making it known that there would be no mixing of races in Goodwin. *He sure made it clear to me at church yesterday that we were to show no mercy to the Caulfels boy.*

By the time the clerk finished his call to order, the room was silent save for the clattering chains echoing across the silent courtroom when Joe collapsed into his chair at the defense table.

Judge Costi slapped the envelope and letter in his hand against the top of the bench and took up his gavel. He struck the bench with the gavel and shouted, "Prisoners in my court stand on their feet when I pass sentence on them. Mr. Lyman, of all attorneys coming before me, you ought to know that." *That useless Trevor Lyman,* thought the judge, *how he passed the bar I'll never know. Why doesn't he get the Caulfels boy up on his feet?*

"On your feet, dammit." Lyman gave Joe a nudge, then held onto his arm. Slowly Joe pulled himself up onto his feet. All the while he grunted and made guttural sounds. He remained bent over at the waist, with his gaze now on the table in front of him. The courtroom fell silent, with everyone's eyes on the prisoner.

Judge Costi's hands were still shaking as he opened the folder. After more sorting through sheets, he said, "Mr. Lyman, I have the recommendations from the prosecutor, but nothing in writing from you."

"Judge Costi, you can see that this is just a young man. This is his first brush with the law. I hope you take this into account."

The Judge scowled as he hit his opposite palm with the freshly opened envelope at the end of each sentence. "First brush? He's blackened eyes; John Diamond is on light duty with an injured neck; Tom Weisner is just getting over two bruised ribs; and Lincoln Brown is still on light duty with a groin injury. On top of that, we have forcible rape of a juvenile."

With the reading of each charge came more and more jeers and comments from the spectators. *I'm losing it,* thought the judge, *I need to finish this and get out of here.* Judge Costi picked up his gavel and pounded as he read, "Joseph Corwin Caulfels, I hereby direct that you be taken to the place of confinement at Canon City and that you serve a sentence of not less than twenty years nor longer than life."

Before the judge finished calling out the sentence, pandemonium broke loose. The entire spectator body began shouting and screaming.

Gloria leaped over the barrier, not far enough ahead of Deputy John Diamond to avoid his hand, which snagged the sleeve of her baggy jacket for a moment. He checked her motion but lost his balance. She twisted away and left the jacket in his hand. Gloria's voice was loud and anguished. "Don't die! Please don't die. Stay with me, Joe. Stay, stay! Joe, Joe, I love you! Please don't die."

John was left sitting on the floor close by the rail. "Halt! Halt! You're under arrest, Gloria Knight. Oh, my neck. Do as I say!"

"Clear the court!" yelled the judge, who was quickly losing his composure. "Bailiffs, call the sheriff for backup!" As he spoke, the audience began surging forward and leaping the barrier. Joe's frame shook as he again sank down into the chair. Gloria dashed past the prosecution's table to Joe as he sat slumped over with his head on the defense table.

Judge Costi banged the gavel and shouted, "Miss Knight! Miss Knight! No theatrics in my courtroom. I hold you in contempt. Bailiff, seize her!"

Gloria stood and pointed at the judge with her right hand and at her father with the left. "For shame! I hold you both responsible. Look at him! He belongs in a hospital, not a prison."

Prosecutor Gulette, from behind her, grabbed her hair in a loose grip. "Gloria Knight, get back to your daddy and stop making more trouble for yourself." In a single motion, Gloria stood up, twisted, and kneed him in the groin. He lost his grip and doubled over. "Damn you, damn you, Gloria Knight! I won't forget this. You bitch!"

"Joe is innocent and you know it." She punched him in the left eye.

He scurried in retreat to the prosecution table. "Your daddy won't save your skinny little ass this time."

Gloria moved aside so Vera Caulfels could take her place at Joe's side. Vera touched her son's forehead. "My Lord, Joe, you're hotter than ....Watch out, Gloria!"

At the warning, Gloria saw the bailiff coming for her with handcuffs. She danced away from him, holding her fists up like a boxer. As she threw a left jab, Lyman came from behind and drove his shoulder low into her back. Gloria lost her balance, stumbled, and fell with her arm extended, missing the bailiff with her jab. As he pulled her right arm behind her back and cuffed her, Gloria screamed at Lyman, "What is my father paying you? Or are you actually this stupid? Joe is innocent!"

Lyle stood as if frozen, incredulous that his daughter could be responsible for causing such an uproar. He watched in confusion as his formerly trusted neighbor Andy Foyle and the youngsters with him crowded between the judge's bench and the bailiff.

What in hell are they trying to accomplish? thought Judge Costi, who continued to pound his gavel. "Bailiff, bailiff, seize every one of these demonstrators. They're all in contempt!"

At this point, to his amazement, the demonstrators broke into song—a combination protest and campaign chant. First the single female voice of Mary MacBride sang it through, then the voices swelled as they all repeated it, "Set Joe free! .... Vet Gulette! ... Ray is the way! ....." The chant continued as the sheriff's patrol cars began to pull up outside the courthouse.

Sheriff Brad Hanlon stood halfway up the visitors' gallery, imperially surveying the courtroom that he and his deputies had just pacified. His uniform, as usual, was resplendent with stars and ribbons designed to make him look like some tin-pot general reviewing his troops. In truth, however, his wife Marcia had barked most of the orders that cleared the courtroom. Marcia had hauled off eight prisoners who kept on chanting after the deputies blocked the doors. .

Lyle walked over to confer with Hanlon. The sheriff nodded toward Gloria and Vera Caulfels, who both stood across the room near Joe. Both were handcuffed. "Deputy John is writing charges against those two for instigating this rebellion and resisting arrest. I had no idea your daughter was capable of such upheaval. Do you really believe you can trust her in the bank?"

The banker stared at the sheriff, then at his daughter. "She had help from that Communist, Tudbury. How much is her doing is for you to find out. I've never met a man or woman with the ability to absorb as much knowledge in such a short time as she has in the few weeks she's been at the bank. Unfortunately, we're embroiled in a father-daughter war."

"Terminate her before she does you real harm," intoned Sheriff Hanlon as he shook his head.

"With great sadness, I agree." Lyle lowered his voice. "There is one victory. With the boy at Canon City and the old man soon to go back to Leavenworth, that squaw of his can't hang onto the ranch. As for Gloria, I don't see much harm she can do if we keep her busy. She is her mother's daughter. Put them in a department store and give 'em time to fill out a season's wardrobe, and they'll both come home happy women. I'll send them down to Denver before Labor Day. Then it's off to Bryn Mawr for Gloria."

"Your daughter is too damned willful; she instigated this rebellion. I'll solve your problem with some serious time in my jail. Marcia will straighten her out."

"Might be a good idea, except Theo has her heart set on sending her to her alma mater. I'll see if I can talk Ron into giving her a get-out-of-jail-free card."

Lyle walked across the room to his handcuffed daughter. "Gloria, I can no longer ignore this fixation of yours. Don't expect me to bail you out this time. You are on unpaid administrative leave from the bank until you extricate yourself from this mess."

She turned around and stared, then nodded. "Thank you, Mr. Knight."

Lyle looked down at Joe. *John came through,* he thought. *Who is this Joe Caulfels, anyway, that he can command such a following?*

Lyle decided to call Judge Costi after dinner to seek mercy for Gloria. *Let her spend tonight stewing about tomorrow.* He concluded that the judge would never achieve reelection after this day's performance. *He seemed more concerned about the letter in his hand than the high jinks disrupting his court. If it weren't for Marcia Hanlon's strong authoritarian voice, those agitators would still be spewing all sorts of hogwash.*

⸺ ⸺

John came to the defense table where Joe sat, still slumped over. "Caulfels, on your feet, you scum. The quicker you're safely locked away in Canon City, the better."

Vera Caulfels called out, "Leo! Leo! I've never seen Joe so sick. You've got to do something."

John dragged Joe to his feet. As he pushed his manacled prisoner toward the exit, jailer Leo Stokings stood between them and the door. "Stop him, Judge Costi. This man is too sick to travel."

"Sick, nothing," John protested, "He's been sentenced. He's the state's problem now. I have the car gassed up and ready to go."

"Stop, what's wrong with him?" asked Judge Costi.

Stokings grabbed Joe's arm. "Please hear me out, Your Honor. He has heat exhaustion from a day in the hole. Look, the kid's in rotten shape. My job is to keep 'em in jail, not execute 'em!"

John faced off the jailer. "What makes you such an expert? Doc Mundal gave him a clean bill."

"Two years in the Pacific theater. Caulfels should have gone to the hospital when I dragged him out of the hole Wednesday morning. I told that quack the boy was suffering from a heat stroke. Judge, this man is in a bad way."

"What do you propose?" asked the judge.

"Get him stabilized and then move him to Canon City."

Gloria didn't understand why Marcia Hanlon was "expediting her processing" until she took her intro an empty holding cell, backed her up to a pole, and locked Gloria's hands around it. Marcia then passed a rope over the link between the manacles and through an eye welded to the pole at shoulder level, and tightened it. Gloria watched as one after another of her fellow arrestees were freed from their handcuffs. While they were allowed to at least sit on a bench or on the floor, she had to remain standing. When Deputy Linc came for another prisoner, she asked for the cuffs to be removed.

His face lighted into a smile as he said, "Now ain't that a coincidence. The tall, skinny girl who kicked me and prosecutor Gulette in the balls and escaped my custody is asking me to remove her handcuffs. Then today you punched the prosecutor in the eye just after you delivered one below the belt. You're such a bad girl, even your daddy cut you loose! Here's your plan for today, Miss Knight. Stand right where you are. Hold one hand in the other behind your back. You're last. Only after you're safely in your cell, then the cuffs will come off."

As much as she wanted to cuss him out, she remained silent. *For what I did that put Joe in prison, I deserve the hard time.*

Two hours later, Gloria moaned when a lunch tray was placed on the floor in front of her, out of her reach. She was hungry and thirsty and aching from standing so long. Much to her surprise, the first person to talk to her was Joe's mother, Vera. With a warm smile, she held a plastic cup to Gloria's mouth. "Drink this. I can't believe they left you cuffed and bound to that pole. This is a first--a Knight treated like a Caulfels."

"Maybe it's because I want to be a Caulfels. I deserve whatever punishment's handed down for what's happened to Joe."

"Well, I think it may have something to do with your resisting arrest or punching Jim Gulette in the eye. But what about what that young deputy said, that you kicked him in the balls? My son confessed to that."

"No, I did it, all right. Joe made that confession to take the blame off me. I love him."

Then Vera held up a sandwich for her. She had taken just two bites when Deputy Linc came over and pulled Vera's hand away. "What in blazes are you doing, talkin' to her? The judge ordered you two separated."

Vera retorted, "Listen to her. You railroaded my boy."

"Don't go down that road. Your son confessed. Be good, and my guess is you'll be home for supper."

"We need to talk," were Vera's last words to Gloria before the deputy pulled her away.

CHAPTER 13
Vera and Gloria

Gloria was left in the intake cell alone for what seemed like hours after the last of her friends and classmates were taken away. She was fuming from the clothing change, when she'd had to stand naked and witness the male deputies from both day and night shifts flip coins to determine who would inspect her for contraband. While she endured the indignity of the inspection, Deputy John hovered behind the winner, acting as "witness," chortling all the while.

Jailer Stokings took charge of her for the rest of the in-processing. When she was finally led past the cells where the others sat, she was hungry, hot, and exhausted, with aching shoulders. They were all in street clothes, but she had been put into a scratchy jail uniform and was still handcuffed. He walked her past the one empty cell to the last cell. No sooner had he put the key in the lock than she recognized the woman inside as Vera Caulfels. Gloria was pleased to be greeted with a happy voice. "Hello, Gloria, this is an answered prayer."

"It had better be, because the day shift is going to see I put her in the wrong cell," said Stokings as he removed Gloria's handcuffs. "I knew you wanted to talk with her, so I left her to be processed last."

"Thank you, Leo," said Vera. "This isn't something that could cost you your job, is it?"

"Only if you and Gloria try to escape. Vera, after the last couple of days, I'm not sure I want to admit I'm part of this department."

Vera pressed against the cell bars. "Tell me, how is my son?"

"He's stabilizing. Thank God, he has the resilience of youth."

"Why is Gloria in a jail uniform?"

Stokings moved closer to the bars and lowered his voice. "Madame Undersheriff wants to even the score because Gloria injured deputies. Gloria is paying the price for her outburst."

The women stood looking at one another while the jailer's footfalls became fainter. Gloria rubbed her wrists, then ran her fingers like combs through her long, damp tresses that hung down in a tumble. Vera eased herself onto her jail bed. "I can't get over what you said, 'I want to be a Caulfels.' Are you prepared for a life like this?"

"I didn't mean to, but I've ruined Joe's life. I'm in jail where I belong. I'm so afraid Joe is going to die, and it's all my fault. Do you hate me for what I did to him? Please forgive me."

Vera patted the thin, hard mattress next to her and made signals with her eyes for Gloria to sit. "Forgiveness … that's what I taught Joe, to meet hate with love. Little did I realize, he listened to me. We were wrong not to meet you the night of the dance. We should explore how we can set that aright."

Gloria brushed her long locks back from her eyes as she eased herself onto the cot. "I'd like that."

The two women sat silently for a while. At last Gloria cleared her throat and realized Vera was looking at her. She hesitated, then blurted out what was on her mind, "Why didn't you visit Joe?"

"I am ashamed. We were so goldarned mad at that boy for lyin', we didn't visit him for over a whole week."

"Nobody, including both Mr. Gulette and Mr. Lyman, listened or talked to me either. How can they throw the book at him for what we never did?"

"That's not what he says." Vera arched her eyebrows and studied her cellmate.

Gloria held her index finger and thumb to make an O. "His organ was throbbing in my hand while I rolled up the rubber. He never made it; he came in my hand."

Vera looked confused. "I read the doctor's report. It said you had vaginal injuries … If not my son … then who …?"

"Believe me, Mrs. Caulfels, if Joe had been the one, there wouldn't have been any injuries. It's not like it was my first time. I must admit to you … I'm not a virgin."

Vera laughed and lightly slapped Gloria's thigh. "Gloria, everybody in town knows that!" At that, Gloria's face blushed a fiery red. "But if not my son … then who did it?"

"Deputy Four Eff, John Diamond."

"The fat, lyin' son of a bitch! That explains why Joe attacked him. I'm worried about my son being in his power. Too many people have been dying in this jail."

"Who?" asked Gloria. *I never heard of anybody dying.*

"Mae Blackmon's husband is one that comes to mind. Thank God that Leo Stokings got hired on as a jail guard. I believe he saved my son's life. I hope he can keep him safe."

Gloria echoed her concern. As they sat together, she described all the gritty details about John's Four Roses purchase at Canyon Liquors the night of the dance. Vera told Gloria how prison changed Orville from a respected businessman to a fugitive alcoholic, and how a loose circle of friends pitched in while Orville was behind bars. "They saved the ranch," she said, "doing everything from chores to rounding up cattle. Orville, bless his heart, has tried his best to return the favors."

Gloria told Vera how she first connected with Joe. "I lived for Wednesdays, when he came to visit the Foyles. Joe told me he liked to come there because they let him take a real bath with hot water. I didn't want him to go into the Army. I was afraid he'd be killed like Mr. Foyle was. I was going to wait while he did his time at West Point and be there for him when he got out."

Vera opened her arms wide. "Come here, child. How can I hate the girl that won't stop loving my son? Gloria, you have more grit than common sense. I should have been the one screaming at the judge. I'll talk some sense into Orville and we're going to get this untangled somehow. Let's pray for Joe together."

They both bowed their heads and recited the Lord's Prayer together. After praying, Gloria rested her head on Vera's shoulder. *No wonder Joe is so wonderful. I really like his mother.* Gloria told Vera of her strong commitment to the campaign to elect a new prosecutor, Ray Tudbury, and a new sheriff, Larry Shyflinski.

"They're Democrats, and I'm a Democrat too," said Vera, "but you surprise me. Your family and all the other high muck-a-mucks in this county are dyed-in-the-wool Republicans. Why are you, a Knight, changing into a Democrat?"

"I didn't know I was changing into anything," Gloria replied. "I've sat through more meals than I care to remember when these guys have sat there sucking up to my father. They wanted his money, his endorsement, and then after the election, deals to enrich themselves. Well, I want to bring them down." Gloria shared some of the deals she'd uncovered in her quest by matching public records with bank transactions and the minutes of commissioners' meetings.

Vera was incredulous. "What, they didn't cover their tracks? Seems foolish to let all this dirt be written in the public records."

Gloria paused and smiled. "Well, most of it was there. Of course I had the advantage of listening to them talk to Daddy over the years. I'm sure they thought I wasn't paying any attention."

"Or that a little girl wouldn't remember it ...." Vera rubbed her hands together in expectation. "What are you going to do with all this incriminating information?"

"That's up to By and Ray--Byron Hankins and Ray Tudbury."

"I'll tell you what I'd do. I'd put it together like a book, in chapters, and pass it on to a top reporter, one installment at a time."

Gloria shook her head. "Forget the *Goodwin Globe*. The reporter took down everything I said about the rape, then--no story was ever printed. When I asked him why he wouldn't print my story, he said the editor didn't feel it was the 'sort of thing to go into a family newspaper.'"

"Nobody in Goodwin County dares offend the Knights. 'Family newspaper,' my foot! They still print Harriet Woodward's columns, don't they?"

"Yes, but I hardly ever read her. Isn't she way over on the other side of the state?"

"Yes, her column is carried all over because she digs up the dirt in the capital. But she doesn't write about this county—or hasn't up to now anyway--and that's why they feel safe printing her, 'family newspaper' or not. You ought to read her." Vera gave a strong thumbs-up salute. "She's a muckraker and doesn't pull any punches. She's fearless, a real news hound, one that's not afraid to give 'em hell. She doesn't care whether they're Democrat or Republican. About Ray Tudbury, you say he's a real Democrat?"

"Real? I don't know. He never asked for my father's blessing, so I guess he is. Ray recruited Larry to run for sheriff, and Larry has no political history that I know of." Gloria recalled the spirited conversations at home. *How prepared are they to deal with real dirty tricks? Daddy and his friends talked about terrible things that have happened to people who ran as Democrats. I don't think either Ray or Larry knows what can be done to them.*

Vera rose from the bunk and looked up and down an empty corridor before coming back and whispering, "My first chore on getting out of here will be to volunteer to run Ray's campaign."

"You? What experience do you have?"

"Thirty-two Congressional race, managed the Western Slope and won. For the Democrats."

"Can you risk it? Daddy wants to chase you out of Goodwin."

"Gloria, we've never courted trouble, but it's found us. In the end, it's always been the same. First Pa and now Joe ... Get them in jail and throw the book at them! We have no choice but to fight."

The next morning, as Judge Ronald Costi settled into his posh seat in his courtroom, he knew he was putting off the inevitable. The two IRS agents from the Denver office, with the power to arrest, were there again. He pulled out the letter from the IRS and reread it. *Do I admit I should have reported another fifty-eight hundred in income? Damn, I can't answer "yes" without implying I took a bribe. How did the IRS find out about this anyway? I should have listened to Lyle and had an accountant do my taxes and finesse those gratuities from the Caddy dealer.*

He looked out and saw chubby Norm Nadau, the editor of the *Goodwin Globe*, sitting in the front row. *What the hell is going on? I asked Norm for a reporter to be here because I wanted the* Globe *to have a story about Tudbury being served humble pie. There he is sitting in the front row. He's the damned editor, why did he come in person? Why didn't he send a reporter? My God, there's my attorney talking to the IRS guys. Why here and not his office? It's all over if Norm recognizes them. Good, they're still sitting up in back.*

A thumping sound came from outside the closed courtroom doors. *Ah, here comes Byron Haskins now. I'd recognize that thump anywhere.*

The slow, steady beat of Byron's leg on the marble floor grew louder until the door opened. He walked through the spectators' seats toward the front of the courtroom with the steely expression of a man going to face a firing squad. He held up that day's *Goodwin Globe* and started to open it. "Your Honor, may I approach the bench?"

Judge Costi waved him forward. "Certainly, Counselor, if it will take just a moment." *Byron ought to stick to the law and stay out of politics. He will have to eat a whole batch of humble pie now, thanks to those kids.* He reached out for the paper Byron handed him.

The judge then read today's headlines for the first time: "TUDBURY TEENS DISRUPT CAULFELS SENTENCING," with a subhead "Compounding Judge Costi's troubles was the arrest of Vera Caulfels, mother of Joe Caulfels, for seeking medical care for her son."

The judge's feelings of frustration and embarrassment washed over him again as he realized this slanted headline was how people would remember him. *Now I know why Nadau is here. They're turning him against me.* He tapped the newsprint. "Counselor, the impact of this … this charade will be the first item I deal with on today's calendar."

"Your Honor, this story and especially this headline came as a complete surprise to both Mr. Tudbury and me. Mr. Tudbury wishes to extend his sincere apologies and promises that he won't sanction such acts as part of his campaign."

"I certainly hope not. Or you'll be campaigning from inside the county jail." Judge Costi's lenses were all the way down his nose. "Are you admitting the paper is wrong about Vera Caulfels? She has a well-established reputation as a troublemaker. I hear you are bringing her on board in your campaign." *They could do a lot worse,* he grudgingly admitted to himself, *Vera does know how to manage a campaign.*

Byron shifted his weight from one leg to the other and back again. "Who are these juvenile demonstrators? The papers didn't identify anyone by name other than Mrs. Caulfels. By the way, I'm running Ray's campaign and I've never met the woman."

"Don't put me on, Mr. Haskins," snarled the judge. "This is a small town, and your juvenile storm troopers are no secret. Don't try to tell me they are not the same ones who have been all over the courthouse copying records. In all my years on the bench, I have never experienced such an open contempt for authority. Because you are an officer of the court, however, I will take your word that this was spontaneous. Please step back, Counselor." He signaled the bailiff. "Bring in this morning's daisy chain."

The bailiff led in the prisoners from the side door. They shuffled in, single file, in a chain like a slave coffle, each joined to the next by handcuffs. Herb Kahn and five older males led off, followed by seven teenage males and nine females, with Gloria and Vera on the end. They all looked as if they had slept in their clothes. Scared eyes searched the empty benches. Even Gloria, the only one in a jail uniform, looked subdued. The bailiff led them to the space between the counsel tables and the bench.

Judge Costi pondered whether to give them any more punishment beyond the night they had spent in jail. *If I show them mercy, will the feds do the same for me? As for Gloria Knight, I'll let her assault on Gulette slip through unless he's here to make an issue of it.*

The judge scowled and slowly looked down the row at each one. *I had these kids' parents on the line all evening, literally begging for mercy. Then there was Lyle Knight, worrying about my next election in forty-eight. That's the least of my worries.*

The judge spoke slowly and solemnly to the line of frightened young miscreants. "I know each of your parents. In their phone calls, they have shared my disappointment in your judgment when you disrupted the decorum of my court with a political demonstration. I hope that the night you have spent in jail has been enough to teach each of you a necessary lesson."

The prisoners, some of whom couldn't stand the gaze of the judge, looked at one another in puzzlement and disbelief.

Judge Costi shuffled the sheets in his folder. "Mrs. Caulfels, my apologies. On reflection this morning, I realized I acted precipitously by not giving you the latitude for acting on a mother's instinct. Your son's collapse was ..."

"Joe! Joe, how is my son?"

The judge said, "I don't have good news. Superintendent Carberry from Canon City called this morning. Your son is in critical condition. It's so bad that they have granted permission for you and your husband to visit him in the hospital. Andrew Foyle is driving out to fetch Orville. Once he comes into town, I urge you to make every effort to speed your way to Canon City. I'm sorry to bring you this news."

Vera tugged on the handcuffs. "When will you let me go?"

"Shortly." He paused and shifted his gaze to the others. "I have been given sincere apologies and assurances by Mr. Byron Haskins that this demonstration was spontaneous and will not happen again. Do I have the understanding that he was speaking for all of you?"

He allowed enough time to pass for the affirmations and thank yous to trail off before he ordered, "With Joseph Caulfels' departure, I declare this affair over. Bailiff, release Mrs. Caulfels and the prisoners who are under twenty-one."

Gloria was the first one released, followed by Vera. The banker's daughter stepped forward and swept her long locks back over her shoulder. "Judge Costi, is what I say here on the record?"

"Gloria, he's letting you go. Be quiet!!" ordered Vera.

The three men in the back of the room stopped talking and listened. The judge looked puzzled. "Yes, Miss Knight."

Gloria pulled away from Vera and halted in front of the bench. "Yesterday you took away twenty years to life from me, so it matters little to me whether I'm in jail or out. I bear the pain because of what I did. I destroyed my fiancé's future, and now his very life teeters on the brink. If I hadn't kicked that drunken deputy in the balls and escaped, there would have been no fight. It's all my fault."

Judge Costi looked exasperated. "After your earlier outburst, I thoroughly reviewed the files and spoke with the prosecutor. There is no doubt that you are suffering from delusions. Joseph Caulfels is a violent criminal."

Gloria pulled up the sleeves on her jail jumper. She held up her arms to show fresh scars on her wrists. "Delusions? You never asked me. Prosecutor Gulette never asked me. Deputy John Diamond raped me. Why do you think I fought the handcuffs? Joe never entered my body."

Judge Costi frowned. "Both of you naked? What about the used condom?"

"I put my rubber on him after we agreed to marry. I undressed him, but he couldn't wait. He was still in my hand when he came. Everybody in town who will listen to me knows this. Why won't you believe me?"

Oh, crap, thought the judge, *what possessed Lyle to sic John on his own daughter? Pray that the boy survives, look at the fire in her eye* ... Judge Costi was so flustered that he only sputtered out two words, "Your father ...," before Gloria cut him off.

"Judge Costi, I didn't sleep worrying that my fiancé would die. None of this would have happened if Lyle Knight were not my father. I beg you, please allow me to go to Joe's side."

Vera joined Gloria, putting her arm around her. "Your Honor, Judge Costi, the bad blood is between the adults, not the children. Joe's feelings were so strong for her, he couldn't stand to have her testify in court. Can't you admit you made a mistake giving him the twenty years? At least let her visit with us."

"That is beyond my scope of authority. I'd like to put to rest the charges against the remaining defendants." Judge Costi sat tall in his chair. "Herb Kahn and the five who had worn the VFW hats, you should know better! I find you guilty of contempt of court. I fine you each one hundred dollars and sentence you to time served."

Herb Kahn raised his hand. His New York accent couldn't be hidden. "Judge Costi, please let me speak a few sentences for the bennie you just levied on me."

"Bennie?"

"Yeah, Benjamin Franklin, he's on the hundred. I shudda known betta, you say. Let me tell you what I know. Ten years ago, I had a big family in Germany. They're all dead now. And for what? The bigot running the country hated Jews. What's been done to Joe Caulfels is criminal. No finah young man cudda been found in Goodwin. He cudda died. And it's because you got a bigot banker who hates half-breeds. Please call the supe."

The judge shrugged his shoulders. "It's beyond my authority."

"Please call. Da woist he can say is no."

Judge Costi struggled to keep from looking at the men in the back of the courtroom. *What can I do to keep Norm busy writing notes so he doesn't talk to the IRS agents? I know, but it'll piss Lyle off. I'll give Gloria what she wants and pray.* He raised his voice in hopes the editor would hear it. "I am lifting the restraining order against Miss Knight. I will include visitation privileges. As for the sentence, I need to do some research. Your son did enter a guilty plea, Mrs. Caulfels. I'll reschedule my calendar and confer with the prosecutor and Mr. Lyman before the end of next week."

Gloria asked, "Can I have the same visiting privileges as Joe's family?"

"I will spell it out in my instructions lifting the restraining order. This doesn't guarantee that you will be able to see him. Prison regulations must be followed." Judge Costi watched a transformation flash across Gloria's face, then fade. *Look at her. I spent all that time thinking Tudbury and Haskins were behind yesterday's high jinks. She used them all. I'll be damned if I'm going to haul Lyle's water again. His goose will be cooked too if they question my nineteen forty-four return.*

As Gloria, Vera, and the others filed out, editor Nadau approached the bench from across the room. "Judge, without jamming your schedule for the rest of the day, when could you give me a briefing on the import of what you will accomplish during your meeting with the IRS?"

CHAPTER 14
Joe in Prison

Gloria was excited as she wiped yet another layer of sweat onto her skirt. She had just parked the white Cadillac in the visitor's lot of the Colorado Men's Penitentiary. *I did it. Pa Caulfels let me drive most of the way. Best not to tell anyone. The less Daddy knows, the better.* She smiled at "Pa," Orville Caulfels, her attentive instructor, who sat next to her in the passenger seat. "Pa, thank you for letting me drive this wonderful car almost all the way to Canon City."

Vera, from her place in the back seat, said, "Orville darling, this has been a smooth ride back here. What's your impression of Gloria's driving abilities?"

"Ma, she's still a bit green, but she has the fundamentals down. What I like best is, she is cautious. When are you going to take the test, girl, and get that driver's license?"

"Thank you, Pa. It would be a waste of time until I'm on my own. My father told me, after I accepted Joe as my date to last fall's dance, that there would be no driver's license. He'd just take it away. Thank you for trusting me with the Cadillac."

Vera pointed across the lot. "There's a phone booth right by the door."

Orville looked at his watch, "Don't go yammering on the phone now. We're cutting it close for seeing Joe today."

"I'll make it brief, Pa. Byron asked me to call Ray Tudbury when we got here. He seemed relieved when I made my offer to manage the campaign. He's clearing it with Ray at their afternoon meeting. I'm going to promise Ray to give it my full time right up to electionday."

Orville watched his wife make the call, then said, "I like this Ray fella. They're gonna learn the hard way there is a high price to pay for doing harm to my innocent boy."

Ten minutes later, Vera emerged from the booth. She hugged Gloria. "Ray has accepted me to manage his campaign. More importantly, I followed up on his call to Harriet Woodward. She's open to meeting at Twin Lakes. We'll swing by there on the way home tomorrow. I have the makings of her first exposé about Goodwin County."

Orville stepped off at a swift pace, holding Vera's hand and almost dragging her behind him. "I never thought I'd see the day when I'd be in a hurry to get inside these walls. Come on, Ma, Gloria, you can walk faster than that."

Orville barely got his name out of his mouth at the gate when the guard replied, "Prison Superintendent Carberry is expecting you, please follow me." Their path took them through the first security screening. Gloria watched Orville stiffen and brace his shoulders on hearing the sliding steel door slam shut behind them. She thought, *So sorry, Pa, for what I did. You shouldn't have had to come back here.*

Superintendent Hugh Carberry, with his broad shoulders, bull neck, and shaven head, reminded Gloria of Orphan Annie's Daddy Warbucks. After greetings and refreshments, he said, "You made excellent time from Goodwin. I thought you'd be here tomorrow. We normally don't permit visits during the first two months while the prisoner is making the adjustments necessary to life at the penitentiary. However, given Joe Caulfels' critical condition on arrival, the medical staff recommended a waiver for family visits. Miss Knight, my staff raised questions about whether you are eligible for visitation."

Gloria blurted out, "Wait a minute. Please, if my fiancé dies, I'll never see him again."

Carberry pondered her words. "That's true." Then he pointed to the newspaper on his desk. "By the way, folks, do you read *The Denver Post*? There was a wonderful article yesterday about your son, Sunny. You must be proud of him--West Point graduate, ace fighter pilot with over twenty-one kills, promoted to bird colonel, one of Colorado's true heroes. Here's a picture of him next to his P-51, 'Bootleg Lady.'"

Vera stood tall and grinned. "Yes, he'll be home on leave in late

September."

Carberry handed the front section to Orville. "My kid brother flew B-17 bombers. He has the greatest respect for those pee-fifty-ones. They saved his bacon numerous times." He turned to Gloria and asked, "In all my years in corrections, no victim of a violent rape ever willingly married her attacker. What draws you to him?"

Gloria thought, *Boy, he doesn't mince words. What can I say to convince him?* "Mr. Carberry, Joe is innocent. I was raped by Deputy John Diamond. I love Joe, pure and simple. When he was taken from my arms, he was innocent in every way. He was the nicest, gentlest boy in my class. He has a way of making me feel good about myself."

"Was Diamond not the arresting officer?"

Orville, his voice bouncing up an octave, interjected. "Yes, but it's true, Diamond raped her. He tried to murder Joe to cover his trail. Give them a Goodwin County uniform and a badge, there isn't a crime that can't be written off!"

Look at the top of Mr. Carberry's head turn red. What can I do? I'll give him my speech. Gloria stood up and faced the superintendent. "We're not here about Goodwin County, Mr. Carberry, sir. We're here to see the man who almost died. All the way down here, I thought about what I'd do if you turned me down. I'd tell myself I got what I deserved because I seduced the sweetest boy and out of ignorance, set him up. I'd cry because during his last minutes on Earth, I wasn't there to give him the comfort he deserved. Please grant Joe one visit with me."

Orville began to tear up. "I blame myself. I let my hatred of her father cloud my judgment. Joe is a decent boy who doesn't belong inside these walls. This young woman belongs in his arms, not waiting for visiting days."

Gloria asked, "If it's possible to marry a convict, when is the earliest you allow them to marry?"

Carberry reached into a drawer and handed her a mimeographed booklet. "Here is your copy of the rules. Everything you need to know about marrying a convict is right there. Is there an urgency? Are you … pregnant?"

"There's an urgency, yes, but that's not it." Gloria handed an envelope to the superintendent. "Here's the letter from the judge." *Please,*

Mr. Carberry, please.

Carberry cycled his bushy eyebrows up and down and tossed the unopened envelope on his desk. "I'm not making this exception because of any argument I've heard today. I'm making the exception because his brother is a genuine American hero. If Joseph Caulfels doesn't survive, I want to be able to look Colonel Sunny Caulfels in the eye and tell him we did everything we could to keep him alive. Now, in light of the lateness of the hour and your very valid concern for your son's health, I grant an exception to allow one brief visit for everyone here. My staff physician feels that Joe Caulfels remains in critical condition. Only time will tell if he has suffered permanent damage."

"Thank you, sir. Can you help us by alerting somebody about Goodwin County?" pleaded Vera. "Don't you have a policy to investigate someone who mistreats prisoners? My son could have died."

"If there's an indication that it happened, I rely heavily on my staff to determine an appropriate response. Where we have a situation entangled with local politics, as we have in Goodwin with the town's banker in a snit about his daughter being seduced by criminals with 'evil genes'--I tread carefully."

Gloria thought, *That's Daddy for sure. He'll stifle any investigation.*

While they were talking, the medical orderly entered and stood by the door. His name, PANO KARGOLIS, was stenciled above his breast pocket. Lean and thirtyish, Pano had a Mediterranean complexion, with dark hair and eyes. His white coat hid his prison uniform, but his nearly dead eyes and "prison pallor" betrayed his true status.

The superintendent was visibly relieved to see the orderly. "Ah, good, your escort is here. Kargolis, this is the Caulfels family and Miss Knight, the boy's fiancé. Here are their passes. Their visit will be short. Have them at Control no later than six o'clock."

"Yes, Mr. Carberry."

Gloria was surprised how empty the well-kept corridors were until the guard accompanying them volunteered that all prisoners in this section were on lockdown. As they approached Joe's room, she was still trying to classify Pano's accent. He sounded like an educated Englishman one sentence and the next, like someone from South Boston with a foreign accent.

Pano said, "Your son arrived in desperate condition early this morning. It was touch and go all day until less than an hour ago. I don't know which helped most, the IV that rehydrated him or the news that his fiancé would be here. He was sitting up and eating when I left him."

Gloria had never seen anyone with a complexion so gaunt as Joe's. The broad smile she beamed was met with tear-filled eyes and lips that quavered. Joe's voice broke as he spoke. "My life is over. Why don't you just go on with yours?"

"I can't do that. I love you."

"Joe, this beautiful young woman loves you. Don't you quit on me now," Vera pleaded.

He stared at the ceiling until Gloria spoke up again. "I don't deserve happiness until I'm in your arms. I read in this booklet that it is possible for us to marry. Please don't reject me. To have you in prison with me unable to communicate would be the worst of all worlds."

Joe stared at the ceiling with blank eyes. "Pano, tell them how long I have to stay here on a twenty-to-life term."

Pano tilted his head, calculating. "A twenty-to-life ticket translates into the earliest visit to the parole board at, maybe, ten years. If he's lucky, maybe he'll actually get parole at twelve or fourteen years. I'm getting pretty short here myself. Gloria, I understand we have something in common, an interest in banks."

"What?"

Pano smiled. "I had a successful run in front of the teller's cage." He gave her a wink. "It kept me away from the nastiness over in Europe. Now with the big war over, they're shipping me back to my home soil on an early parole. So I can be Greece's problem instead of America's."

"In front of the teller's cage? Oh, I get it. You were a bank robber?" Gloria eyed Pano up and down with renewed interest. He was nodding his head. After a pregnant pause, she said, "Well, Mr. Kargolis, I hope you have a good trip home. You probably wouldn't want to stick around and rob my Daddy's bank … even though security is lax because no one who did it ever got past the county line." She winked back at him, as if daring him to try it. He raised his eyebrows.

She turned around and barely touched Joe's face. "Darling, however long you're here, I'm serving this sentence too. You must appeal. That is our only hope. But before that, right away, let's get married. The man running for county prosecutor says the courts will favorably weigh the fact that we are married. And so will the parole board if the appeal fails."

Joe gritted his teeth and shook his head. "Gloria, please let it go. Mr. Lyman and Mr. Gulette explained it to me. There is no appeal when you plead guilty."

Orville paced up and down by the foot of the bed. "Lyman is an incompetent. The prosecutor never talked to Gloria. That deputy faked the evidence. Like I said, I didn't have a pint stashed in the back door pocket. They flimflammed you all the way. We're gonna move heaven and hell to get this reversed."

"I'm sorry to cut this short, but we have to go," Pano announced from his place by the door.

Gloria rose from her chair and bent over her intended. "We're not giving up. I love you." She gave him a passionate kiss.

Joe rose up on his elbows. "I won't forget you, or your kisses."

Gloria cried all the way to the Caddy. She took one of the back seats next to Vera. Between sobs, she lamented, "Ma, I'm so scared I'll lose him. How did you ever keep Pa's love alive through seven long years?"

Ma Caulfels put her arms around Gloria. "Just by doing plenty more of what you did today. Believe in him ... and let him know that by writing him and visiting as much as you can. I never said it before, but that one note you hid in the Zane Grey novel gave him the will to survive."

"You mean one of them got through?"

Orville's thumbs-up affirmed his wife's assertion. "I was sure it was just another nasty Knight trick to make it look like we'd violated the restraining order. I was suspicious of everything connected with you. I'm sorry now for all the bad thoughts I had about you."

Vera looked at her watch. "If we don't dawdle too much, we can be in Twin Peaks in time for a late dinner. I told Harriet Woodward we'd buy her an apple pie and coffee on our way home. Gloria, what's your pleasure? Stay at a motel and get an early start in the morning? Or drive straight back after dinner at Twin Lakes?"

"If you aren't too tired," replied Gloria, "let's drive straight through to your spread. The judge gave us four days. I want to spend that time doing whatever kind of work you need done. Then I want to go home, sweaty and dirty, to take a real hot-water bath."

At her doorstep, Gloria turned and watched the white Cadillac drive away. She was exhausted from the many hours she had pushed herself at the Caulfels ranch. She moved as quietly as she could up the front steps and through the front door. She stopped to look at herself in the mirror. *I am looking forward to a short dip in the tub, then dinner, and I'll go back again to soak. Oh, my gosh, my white blouse is ruined. Look at all the blueberry stains. I have to clean my shoes. They are terribly muddy. Mother hasn't ever seen me this dirty.*

Gloria eased the front door closed, but the spring-loaded latch snapped with a loud report that echoed. The only other sound was the rattle of plates from the dining room. Theo Knight's voice carried in, loud and clear, "Lyle, is that you, dear?"

"No mother, it's me. I'm home. Dinner sure smells good."

Theo entered the foyer carrying a dinner plate. "Gloria Knight! Whatever possessed you? I've been worried sick these last four days."

"I sent you a night letter from Canon City."

"It arrived the next day, and your father called the superintendent. He said you were only there a very short time with those dreadful people. Your father let the superintendent know, in no uncertain terms, that you have paid your last visit to the penitentiary. Now where have you been the rest of the time?" Theo's face turned red as she shouted the last two sentences.

Gloria let a tear run down her cheek and in a soft, sad voice replied, "Mother, 'those dreadful people' have a son who is starting a twenty-year sentence in the infirmary. He's there because of me. I was out at their place working and doing what little I could to try to make up for the harm I've caused them. They are not dreadful, they are decent people. I am so ashamed."

Gloria watched her mother break eye contract to look at the floor, then look back at her and smile. *I think I got through to her for the first time.*

Theo opened her arms wide and stepped forward. "Dear Gloria, you denied me the chance to say I forgive you. You've embarrassed us by going against our family values, and I hope that you've seen the error of your ways. You are no longer my little girl, but a grown woman who must learn to recognize the consequences of her actions. Come into my arms."

Heavy footfalls on the porch carried into the house. After the key slid into the lock, Lyle pushed the door wide open. Gloria pulled away from her mother and glared at Lyle. His first words were rich in his Southern accent and in the baritone she remembered always used to precede a spanking. "Young woman, where have you been? Look at you! Why, you look like you've been sleeping in that suit."

Gloria took a stance like a boxer, with her fists up, and spoke through clenched teeth. "Mr. Knight, you know where I've been. I am keeping my end of the bargain."

"I get neither respect nor gratitude from you. When I taught you the rudiments of boxing, I never intended for you and me to fight. What are you trying to prove?"

"That I'm not going down without a fight."

"It's over, Gloria. I paid my attorney to sit outside Judge Costi's chambers to make things right after your insane conduct. Before the judge went back into conference, as a special favor to me, he expunged everything--the contempt, your theatrics Tuesday morning. Everything."

Gloria rolled her eyes and dropped her arms to her sides. "Everything? Do you mean he is ignoring my statement about John Diamond?"

"Someday, when you're trying to make something of yourself, you'll thank me. You have a clean record. He said it's like it never happened."

"He can't do that! Four Eff tried to murder Joe in the bowels of the jail. I've got to talk to the judge."

Theo stepped up and put a caressing hand on Gloria's shoulder. "I'm sorry to have to tell you this," she said gently, "Judge Costi committed suicide late Wednesday night. He called me about seven, looking for Father ... but it was your father's night for lodge."

"No ... no ... no ... it can't be. Why did he do that?" exclaimed Gloria.

Theo said, "The *Globe* said it had to do with his taxes and not reporting his bribes."

Gloria recalled that the judge was on the list she sent the IRS of people who preordered Cadillacs. *Oh, my gosh, those IRS guys don't waste any time. They'll come after you too, Daddy.*

Lyle stood tall and brushed some imaginary lint from his sleeve. *Uh-oh,* thought Gloria, *that's his gesture when he's going to put me down.*

"It's time consuming and frustrating," said Lyle, "to chase down a judge riding a circuit. I just came back from Buckeye with Jim Gulette. The judge there has reinstated and extended the restraining order. If any of the Caulfels family have any contact with you, they'll go to jail. Stay away from them! They have criminal genes. Young lady, I've never seen you look or smell like this before. You smell like a pig!"

She brushed back a lock of hair and stuck out her chin while holding her hands up, palms toward Lyle. "You have a keen nose, Mr. Knight, sir. I was shoveling manure this afternoon."

"You can stop calling me Mr. Knight. I fired you when you didn't show up to work."

She maintained her stance. "I've been doing real work. See the blisters and the dirt? I feel better today than I have since back in May. I made a very small down payment on a terrible debt we owe. Daddy, I want this insane feuding to end."

"So do I. The sooner the last of them decamps, the sooner ..."

Theo interrupted. "Gloria, your friend Mary MacBride called. She was very upset because her father just got arrested for running a huge black-market meat ring during the war."

Gloria studied her father. *Mister MacBride was on that Caddy list. Then there were the trucks he bought with undeclared income. Oh, Daddy, I hope you're starting to sweat.* "Please reconsider this court stuff," she said to Lyle. "The Caulfels are decent hard-working people, who worry every minute that their son won't survive. He's in prison, not because he was bad, but because he was good. He feared for his father's freedom. He worried about me."

Lyle studied the cufflink his fingers idly played with. "About the Caulfels boy, you should remember him for his one decent act, like Sidney Carton in *A Tale of Two Cities.* His conviction spared you from spending the next year behind bars for unlawful fornication and underage drinking. The superintendent told me that most likely he won't even serve twenty years. By then ..."

Gloria's face reddened and her eyes flashed with anger. "Let me tell you why I lured him into the back seat. I was afraid he'd go to West Point and I'd lose him to some prettier girl back east. Well, he's not going to West Point and there are no pretty girls in the Canon City pen. I will proudly take his name and wait. And if he dies, you will never meet your grandchildren."

"Marry that mongrel and I will disinherit you and whatever litter of curbstone sitters you produce!" Lyle advanced toward Gloria.

"No, don't go there," exclaimed Theo, her eyes filling with tears. She reached for Lyle as he stormed past Gloria and up the stairs.

CHAPTER 15
The Blackmon Ranch

Gloria walked toward Byron Haskins, who was sitting on one of the side benches of the large gazebo on the courthouse commons. As she mounted the steps, Mary approached from the opposite direction, saying, "Hi, By, darling. I'm sure glad the weather's cooperating today. They're forecasting a high in the low eighties." She kissed him on the mouth.

Byron said, "Hi, sweetheart. Hi, Gloria. Thank goodness we've got some relief with the middle of August. I wish I could offer an air-conditioned space to assemble the Labor Day fundraiser, but all I have is my conference room. It'll be toasty until the equinox time of year. I picked up the brochures and envelopes from the printers yesterday.

Mary took the key he offered. "There's a total of six of us working today. I convinced them to start by nine so we can get done before it gets too hot. We'll be doorbelling the tracts that Mrs. Caulfels mapped out with the veterans working for Larry."

Byron turned to Gloria. "Gloria, Ray asked me to give you a great big thank you for steering Vera Caulfels to his campaign. We have the most organized effort of any races. She's working him and Larry from before breakfast to after dinner. He thinks Vera has committed to memory every voter who would even consider him. She and Ray found some Mexican families who have enough of a hate for both the sheriff and the prosecutor to get registered to vote. When is Harriet going to start writing?"

"Soon, I hope," Gloria said as she handed him a stack of folders.

"Here are the first four folders for her. Larry will like this photo from the first one--the sheriff playing the illegal slot machine at the Hangman's Creek resort. It's a twofer."

"Oh, my," exclaimed Byron, "with his right hand pulling the lever and the Goodwin County shoulder patch front and center. He looks like a raccoon caught in the headlights just before being hit by a gravel truck. How is it a twofer?"

"Because Prosecutor Gulette chose to ignore it. A copy has been sent to the Colorado attorney general."

"Bravo," replied Byron. "The AG can't ignore it." He turned to Mary again. "Speaking of prosecution … what's happening with your dad?"

Mary's voice broke as she said, "By, I've got some bad news. Finally my father is facing reality. His attorney called home today to tell us he's accepting the plea deal. Other than we're losing our house and the store for taxes and penalties, we don't know the details."

"Is he turning over his list of those who bought black-market meat?" asked Gloria. *If he fingers Daddy, great.* Gloria rubbed her hands together, then stopped on seeing the disgusted look on Mary's face. *Uh-oh, maybe she knows I was the one who told the IRS about all that money her dad didn't report.*

"I don't know. I guess so," Mary replied glumly, staring at Gloria.

Gloria quickly changed the subject. "Did we get any more stuff on Diamond?"

"For a few brief moments," replied Mary, "I thought we had Diamond. I talked to a seventeen-year-old girl Four Eff caught drinking a couple of years ago. She was with an older man. Get this: after they agreed to accept 'informal punishment,' he told the man to pay her fifty dollars in advance. She had to lock her own hands behind her back. Then he put a hood over her head so she couldn't see or hear. He and his buddies kept her drunk and used her from dinnertime Friday till early Saturday morning." Mary paused and looked down.

"What an ordeal!" said Gloria. "Wait, by 'he,' do you mean Four Eff or the older man?"

Mary hesitated and looked away, shrugging her shoulders. "Four Eff, I think. She wasn't clear about that."

"It's sounds like he made her a real whore, taking money and all," said Byron. "When can I see her?"

"Well, that's the problem. I promised not to tell you or anyone her name. That's why we can't go after Diamond for this. She's engaged to a serviceman, and what decent man would marry a woman who sold herself like that?"

"Who was the older man?" asked Gloria, excited.

Byron interrupted. "Don't expect cooperation there. They've got this guy coming and going, sex with a minor and prostitution, so he would never give us any evidence. We'll have to consider it water over the dam and keep looking for a better case. Ray suggested you talk to old Mae Blackmon. She has scars on her wrists and ankles that he thinks look like yours."

"She is also on another short list," noted Mary. "Her husband Danny died in the Goodwin County Jail while awaiting trial. Her son was born just over ten months after he died. She's still living on her folks' old spread about five miles south of town."

"I have to talk with her," Gloria said.

"Slow down, Andy," shouted Gloria. "We've got all day." Each time she bounced off the passenger door, she was thankful the door latch held on the Foyles' green Buick. Andy slowed a bit, enough that she no longer thought she'd be bouncing off the ceiling when he hit the next chuckhole. It wasn't enough, though, to end the kaleidoscope-like patterns of sun and shadow on the forested hillside. Soon they came to a clearing where a large barn and a small log cabin stood close to the center of hay fields. Beyond was forest and, in the distance, snow-capped peaks.

Andy said, "This place looks like a dump. I hope we're not wasting our time here."

"Yeah, I don't know. But I brought along a voter registration packet too, so at least today won't be a total waste. For what it's worth, I think Ray and Mae Blackmon went to school together."

The pair got out of the car and rolled back the gate, which groaned and squeaked as it trundled on failed bearings. They walked toward the cabin, only to be greeted from the barn by a large-boned woman wearing faded, dirty mechanic's overalls. She wiped her hands with a rag. "Hello, I'm Mae Blackmon, what brings you out my way?"

"Hello, I'm Gloria Knight. This is my friend Andy Foyle. He drove me out here because I don't have a driver's license yet. Ray Tudbury said I could talk to you about Deputy Four Eff, er, Deputy John Diamond." *Pheew, she smells like yesterday's eggs and her face is smudged with grease. Her hands are so dirty I wouldn't want to touch them. How could she be Ray's classmate? She looks like she's sixty.*

Mae smiled. "Yes, Ray told me about all the ruckus you're raising. I figured you'd be out here sooner or later. Ever overhaul an engine?"

Gloria and Andy shook their heads. *Unh-unh,* thought Gloria, *not in my business suit. I already ruined one blouse at the Caulfels'.*

Mae sounded proud. "I'll do all the dirty work. All I need is for hands to man the chain falls. Come on, I'll chat afterward."

The inside of the barn looked more like a truck repair shop than a place for farm animals. What caught Gloria's attention first were the happy sounds of a child. Mae pointed toward an early-nineteen-hundreds vintage staked flatbed truck. "That's my son, Daniel. He's my pride and joy. I put a playpen where he can be safe and I have him nearby. Gloria, here's a pair of gloves. Climb up here and take a look at Daniel. Then I'll show you how to operate the chain fall."

"Um … I'm not dressed for dirty work. My mother is still upset over the silk blouse I soiled."

"What do you do with the trucks?" asked Andy.

"Cement work. My late husband, Danny, was a talented cement mason. He designed and built this rig you see on the flatbed, from the mortar mixer bolted to the frame on the back end to that overhead rail and the chain fall for lifting pallets of bricks and mortar. Unfortunately the engine blew in the pickup, and the flatbed is my only transportation until I replace it. But it's a gas hog. I can't afford to drive it everywhere with gas costing over twenty-one cents a gallon."

Gloria visually followed the chain from the chain fall on the flatbed to where it disappeared into a tank about six feet long, three feet wide, and five feet deep. A second chain dangled into the tank from another chain fall fixed to a reinforced rafter.

"What's this?" Gloria pointed at the tank. She would have satisfied her curiosity and looked into the tank had the outer sides not been dirty and soaked with oil.

"We call this a gunk tank," said Mae. "I like to work on a clean engine, so I dip it in solvent, then scrub it with a wire brush to remove gunk, caked dirt, and grease. This here used replacement engine has a pair of burnt valves. I think it will be easier to fix those after I install it in the pickup. How about it, Andy, can you handle the fall hangin' from the rafter?"

After Andy agreed, Mae manned the chain fall on the flatbed. Gloria was impressed with the skill with which Mae coached Andy so that the engine, clean and dripping with solvent, came out of the tank and was positioned and lowered into the engine compartment of the pickup.

Mae climbed down from the flatbed. "Before they took Dan from me, the hard part was fixin' the engine. He'd park so you'd lower it and everything lined up. I have to do a bunch of jiggerin' to make them align."

"They took your husband?" said Gloria. "Who took him? How?"

"I'll tell you about it after I bolt this engine in place. If you can climb up there, all you have to do is pull that chain the little bit it takes to align the bolt holes. If it takes too long, I won't have time because I have other chores."

Gloria looked at Andy, thinking, *I've never done anything like this. Here it is the middle of August and I'm no closer to getting Deputy Four Eff than I was on the first of June. Mae is the first person who's even hinted she would talk about what happened.*

She picked up the gloves. Andy said, "Go on up, Gloria. Pulling a chain isn't that hard."

"There's really nothin' to it," explained Mae as she took her place by the pickup. "All you have to do is pull the chains. It's called mechanical advantage. Gloria, please take my place up on the truck. Andy, are you ready? I'll guide it in and put on the bolts."

Okay, I'll do this for Joe. Gloria put on the gloves and climbed up on the flatbed. She was amazed that this device made it possible to lift and reposition something as big and heavy as the pickup's engine.

Sooner than she expected, she heard Mae say, "That's the hard part, all done, thank you both. I'll finish puttin' it together tomorrow. Gloria, would you pick up little Daniel and hand him down to me/? I'll run in and clean up and change him. Andy, please use the sink over there to clean up. Could you entertain yourself outside? What I have to talk over with Gloria is very personal in nature."

—~—

Gloria waited in Mae's one-room cabin while Mae breast-fed Daniel. It was large but sparely furnished. They sat at a square table, on two of the four chairs in the cabin. Gloria faced the door and an unmade brass bed. To one side was a wood stove on sheet metal flooring. There was running water but no electricity, which reminded her of the Caulfels place. She told herself that if Joe were to say this was home, she would find a way to be happy here.

Soon Daniel was asleep in Mae's arms. She gave Gloria a knowing smile. "Ray said he'd send you up, but you popped up on my doorstep far quicker than I expected. He and I go all the way back to grammar school."

Grammar school? thought Gloria. *So it's true, they are the same age. But she looks old enough to be his mother.*

"Regarding John," Mae drew a hand across her throat, "I don't care to relive the memory."

"I'm sure it's difficult," said Gloria sympathetically. "if it's anything like what he did to us. He ruined us and almost killed my Joe. Nobody believes me! I need you to back up my story." Gloria held her scarred wrist alongside Mae's.

"Wow, the scars match!" said Mae. She took Gloria's arm and ran her fingers along the scar. "I can't take any chances for Daniel's sake. I'm barely hangin' on here now. The money from the state and Social Security ain't enough if I don't have this land to live on. You have all the high cards. Just play them."

Now she's chickening out. "What cards? Without strong evidence, how will I ever convince a jury to set my man free?"

"Convince his wife. The rest will fall into place."

She's out of her mind.

"Think about his pillow talk. Did he ask, 'Does that make you want to turn over?' or 'Am I hitting your button?'"

Gloria felt herself getting angry. "Yes! What a stupid question to ask after he hogtied me! He never stopped talking. I hate the son of a bitch!"

Mae gave a wink. "So do I. They're his style, his habits. I've been doing John since I worked over in Falcon, back when it was legal. He's as predictable as the sunrise."

"You let him tie you up? And handcuff you? Is that how you got the scars?"

"I've done everythin' for money. Don't you tell Ray, but John was one of my first payin' customers when I started in the business."

Paying customers? Gloria couldn't picture it. *Who'd pay money for sex with her?*

"I was young. It was legal then. But enough about me. Men are creatures of habit. You know what I'd do? Go up to his wife in public and offer to give evidence about his adultery when she divorces him."

"You mean ... tell her?' *Whatever did Mrs. Diamond do to me?*

Mae clapped her hands together. "Hell, yes! Describe his techniques in detail in front of her friends. Think of what he did and said. Plainly tell her. Why try to convince twelve strangers, when all you have to do is convince one woman who knows him? Think back to the way he stroked your legs and the details of his technique. Or do you remember?"

I can't forget. He just kept saying and doing the same things over and over. The pain was so terrible that the last thing I wanted to think about was sex. I have nightmares all the time.

"You do that, and you'll put that woman in a real bad place. This is a small town. She has to keep her self-respect. You watch, she'll have to dump him. The sheriff will have to do somethin', too. There will be too many rumors."

Gloria sat and looked at Mae. "I don't know ...."

"Do it, you ain't got nothin' to lose. Afterward, if you have a brain, you'll get on that train and never come back. Wait till old Lyle croaks, stay long enough to sell everythin', and live happily ever after."

"I don't want his money."

Mae laughed and laid her heavy, dirty arm on Gloria's shoulder. "Then you tell ol' Lyle to write me into his will. By the way, your girl friend, who was with Ray, really has it in for John. Did he get her too?"

Gloria stiffened. "Who? What did she say?"

"Don't remember her name ... Mary somethin'? I seen her around. She didn't have to say nothin', I can tell." Mae's arm dropped down enough that she felt Gloria's holster in the small of her back. "Are you packin' a gun?'

"Yes, a Smith and Wesson. I'm not going to give them a second chance with me." She fumbled to reach her pistol.

"You gotta draw faster than that." Mae reached up to her hair, which was gathered in a bun, and pulled out a long, slim rat-tail file with a wooden handle. She handed it to Gloria. "Here, Danny ground down the end of this file for me. Take this as a present for helpin' me out of a jam today. Always keep it in your hair until you feel safe."

Gloria returned the pistol to its holster. She hefted the file and examined it. "It's heavier than it looks. The point is sharp. How would I use it?"

"Wear it as a hatpin, or you could style it in a French twist. Here's a holder to slip around your neck."

"Thank you, Mae."

"You gotta practice with both weapons. The file's as dreadful a weapon as a woman can carry. Push it in right in the gut on the left side and twist up with all your strength. You can kill, just like that!" Mae snapped her fingers.

"I don't think I could ..."

"You damn well better! After what you've started, don't for a minute think that bein' Lyle Knight's daughter gives you a bye. It's either you or them. How good is your aim with that piece tucked in the middle of your back?"

She may be an old hooker, but she sure knows what questions to ask. Gloria shook her head. "I've been out plinking tin cans."

"Let's spend the next hour, a half-hour on each, doin' some serious trainin'."

Gloria was among the first to exit the Sunday eleven o'clock service at Goodwin's Peace Lutheran Church on Labor Day weekend. Around her was a small crowd of happy children who scampered to a table with cookies and glasses brim full of pink lemonade. Within the church, the full tones of a mighty pipe organ were still playing through the last chords of a musical postlude.

Added to her uniform of an ill-fitting business suit, Gloria wore reflective sunglasses and a very feminine straw hat with a large floppy brim. The rat-tail file's handle was sticking up above the hat. She walked at a marching pace across the lawn toward Chloe Diamond, John's wife, whom Andy had pointed out to her during the service. Mrs. Diamond, plump and in her thirties, was talking with three church ladies who each had a round of coffee from a silver carafe. Her two small daughters played nearby.

Gloria extended her hand. "Mrs. Diamond, I'm Gloria Knight, Joe Caulfels' fiancé. I don't think we've ever met."

Chloe smoothed her print dress that was stretched over her girdle before taking Gloria's hand. "Gloria Knight, the banker's daughter? I don't believe I've ever seen you at our church before. What brings you to Peace Lutheran today?"

"I felt like I needed to come because I no longer feel welcome in my church. My pastor calls me a fornicator and adulterer." Gloria held Chloe's hand until she jerked it away.

Chloe struggled to regain her balance. She looked toward one of the other ladies and shifted uneasily from one foot to the other. "Miss Knight, I'm absolutely shocked by your admission."

"Mrs. Diamond, I am willing to testify on your behalf at your divorce trial that your husband committed adultery with me."

Chloe's face reddened and her jaw dropped. "What … what … You've got your nerve! Here! After church! What sort of proof do you have? More emotional rantings, like you carried on at the courthouse? You should have been committed, like my husband said!"

Chloe pulled her arm back as if winding up to slap Gloria. She spilled some of her coffee, making oval stains on her white dress.

Gloria raised an arm into a blocking position and held it as she went on. Her voice was flat, with little emotion. "Here are specifics, Mrs. Diamond. Your husband likes to start foreplay by long, gentle stroking of the inner thigh and then lightly running his fingers across the pubic hair. Surely you've heard him say, 'Let me press your button, darling. If that doesn't start you, I have a crank that will' or 'Am I hitting your button?'"

Chloe threw the rest of the cup of coffee at Gloria. The other women's faces reddened like beets and they turned away, but not so far as to be out of hearing. Most people standing in the background turned their attention toward Gloria and moved somewhat closer.

Gloria wiped the coffee from her face and continued, "He nips on a bottle of vodka on patrol. The dinner you fed him the night he attacked me was cooked with onions and garlic. He knows how … Shall I continue?

Chloe maintained eye contact as her face turned pale. "Shut up! I've never been so embarrassed … humiliated. Damn, you certainly don't talk like a juvenile! Gloria Knight, whatever else you have accomplished here today, you certainly ruined your reputation."

Gloria held her arms up with the palms toward Chloe. The sleeves on the suit jacket slid down, revealing the fresh twin scars left by her struggles against the handcuffs. "Mrs. Diamond, I have no reputation left. My fiancé rots in prison for a rape committed by your husband. He attempted to murder my Joe. These scars are part of what he did to me."

Gloria looked around to find herself in the center of a crowd of embarrassed churchgoers. For a moment she saw Andy trying to work his way toward her. She felt triumphant until she looked back at Chloe. Tears formed in the corner of Chloe's eyes, and her mouth was twisted into a pattern of anguish. Her free hand touched the wet brown stains down the front of her dress. As she began to turn away, Gloria pressed a piece of paper into her hand. "I'm sorry to have done this to you. Here is my address at Bryn Mawr."

"Sorry, hell, you whore!" Chloe wiped the stained dress with the paper, crumpling it as she did. She threw the paper at Gloria, but it fell short.

Gloria scooped it up. "You know there were others before me. The nerves in my arms still hurt. If you do nothing, what girl in this county will be next? Maybe your own daughters. Think about it." Gloria handed the Bryn Mawr address to one of the church ladies. "Please pass this along to Mrs. Diamond."

Andy grabbed Gloria's arm and pulled her through a break in the dispersing crowd. "Gloria, what possessed you? I can't believe you'd stoop to do such a thing. You've gone over the edge with this stunt. I'm through playing chauffeur. Goodbye!"

Gloria pushed her sunglasses down her nose and grinned. "Mission accomplished. I saw the look. She knows I told the truth. She believes!"

Sheriff Brad Hanlon was sitting at his desk in his office, but not in his usual posture--leaning back in his chair with his feet up in the air. Instead he sat bolt upright with both feet on the floor. With his bifocals on, he reread the headline of the political cartoon on the opinion page of the *Goodwin Globe*: "Sheriff Brad Hanlon, Goodwin County, stays home to play the slots." *How can this be?* Below was a sketch of the photo of him feeding coins into a slot machine. *Damn, this is old news. That freelance clown caught me feeding my change from dinner into a slot back in July. Such originality. So the muckraking columnist thinks I oughta retire and move to Las Vegas. Well, Harriet Woodward, you can go to hell.*

He read the rest of the column, which was mostly about Jim Gulette and the late Judge Conti. *Why did that son-of-a-bitch editor hang my picture over these sorry tales of incompetence? Damn, damn, damn!*

Brad looked up from the newspaper he'd been staring at to see Deputy John standing right outside the door to his office. "Come on in, John. What's this I heard about the Knight girl at church Sunday?"

"Sheriff, I don't know where that Knight bitch got the idea to involve my wife. She came up to her at coffee hour right after the late service. She's claiming I had an affair with her. Now I can't talk with my dear wife. Chloe kicked me out. Please, could I bunk in the standby room until the end of the month?"

"That's terrible! I'll drop by and talk with Chloe. Sure, I can give you a place to lay your head."

"Thank you, Sheriff. Where did she get the idea?" John flopped into one of the office chairs.

"That Knight girl may be book smart," said the sheriff, "but she ain't that clever. John, in this election we're dealing with the most evil and diabolical bunch this county has ever seen. It can't be a coincidence that on Sunday you're attacked and on Thursday, I am pilloried in today's *Globe*. That cartoonist fellow is a damn hypocrite. I've seen him out there sucking up. He'd be drawing up a storm if I shut down the only place you can buy a porterhouse for under two dollars. I was ambushed. We have to lie low for the time being."

"You sound worried."

The sheriff nodded. "I am. John, I got a call from the State attorney general's office about the Caulfels boy. I convinced the AG to hold off until after the election so as not to muddy our waters. But I'm sorry, I can't ignore this."

"Sheriff, what are you trying to say?" John's voice squeaked in a high octave.

"I'm saying that the night this all started, the girl's story looked believable at first--until her daddy acted like he did in Doc Mundal's office. That destroyed her credibility because certainly, you'd think, a father oughta know his own daughter. But she's persisting in trying to destroy his reputation. It took her a while to build up a full head of steam. John, I've known her since she was a brat. She's stubborn and spoiled, and she ain't gonna quit. She's a loose cannon. If Lyle's reputation goes, so does yours. Take this." He handed John a yellow legal pad.

John whined, "I done exactly what Lyle Knight told me to. I got results. The breed is out of her life permanently and the Caulfels family will be gone by spring." He read what was written on the pad. "Wait! I done too many jobs for you to be dumped like this."

"Now don't get your dander up, John. You and I go way back. I ain't been sheriff in this county for forty years by not being loyal to the people who made that success possible. I have always counted on you."

"I'm sure glad you remember, but … but …"

The sheriff put on a face of concern. "I worry for you, my friend. You have to deal with a state investigation on one hand and marital turmoil on the other. That ain't fair. I want you to write up a request for administrative leave, like what I wrote on the pad. I will keep you on the payroll. And as a backstop, I suggest you also draft a resignation and keep it handy."

"But, Sheriff … Why?"

"John, if I ain't reelected as your sheriff, your problems will multiply. The Knight girl leaves for college Saturday afternoon. I'll give you until Saturday to come up with some sort of permanent fix to your problem. Talk to Marcia, she may have some ideas. John, we're under siege until November. You've always come through for me before. I know I can count on you."

Sheriff Hanlon watched his deputy turn and leave his office. *Oh, John, oh, John, what can be done to turn this around before election day?*

CHAPTER 16
Gloria Seeks Independence

Gloria and her mother were in the kitchen after finishing the main course. Theo said, "You have a whole closet full of fashionable frocks. I wish you would choose one of them for evening wear over that drab business suit."

"Mother, this will be my uniform until my fiancé is set free."

"Please, dear, the martyr's role gets tiresome. You could at least hang up the jacket in the evening."

Gloria paused in her chores. "Come sunset, it cools off. I feel more comfortable the way I am." *This jacket nicely covers my holster, thank you.*

As she had done since she was twelve years old, she poured coffee into the silver carafe and went to the dining room where she poured her father's cup first. *This is the last cup I pour for you, Daddy.*

"Dear," Theo announced to Lyle, "I baked your favorite strawberry-rhubarb pie." She served slices, one-quarter to Lyle and one-eighth each to herself and Gloria.

"Thank you, Theo," said Lyle. "You are my dream come true. I have to wait until I come home to dinner for something to go right. This pie is one of your best." Lyle's eyes were swollen, and he looked tired.

"Thank you, dear husband. Celeste Foyle brought over mail for Gloria. She was presented with three offers to apply for scholarships. I never knew they searched people out just because they had good grades."

Lyle frowned at Gloria. "Your mail comes here, young lady. Tell them, no, thanks. I have the means to send you anywhere you choose.

Scholarships are for those of modest means."

I'm breaking out, daddy. There's nothing you can do to stop me. Gloria ate a bite of pie, followed by a generous sip of coffee to wash it down. "Daddy, I need a topnotch education without fear of retaliation. After what I've endured this summer, I can't risk being under your thumb."

Lyle reddened and his hands shook so that he placed his coffee cup back on its saucer. "You ... you ... What's this, piling on in the end zone? I can't believe I've ever had as tumultuous a day since the run on the bank in thirty-two."

'What happened, dear?" asked Theo.

"Four IRS agents are working in little Goodwin County. All of them descended on me at once. All demanded information immediately. All of them are warning about penalties. One of them is the most overbearing son of a gun I have met in years. In addition, I had to have my attorney draft a letter to the Office of the Attorney General in Washington, who has demanded to know about our meat consumption in nineteen forty-four. How the devil should I know that?"

"Oh, dear," said Theo, "I hope I didn't get you in trouble. Back then, Cody MacBride put aside a side of beef for me. He said it was surplus so I didn't need to use any ration stamps."

"A whole side? Good grief!" Lyle pushed a piece of pie around his plate. "There's more. The president of the school board called to tell me it's final. They changed the name of the team from the Goodwin Knights to the 'Bootleggers.'"

Theo bristled. "Bootleggers! I will call the ladies of our chapter. We will not stand for glamorizing that kind of evil, especially around our children! How quick they are to forget our generosity to the district when they weren't getting money during the Depression."

Gloria stifled a smile. *I don't know if this will help Joe's family, but it will sure rub Daddy the wrong way every football season.* "Mom, there's a football play called the bootleg pass, and we scored at least a touchdown in every game last year using it. There are more meanings. Besides, Prohibition has been repealed."

Lyle stood with his napkin in hand. "Gloria, you're behind all of this, aren't you?"

Can I cause enough pain to force him back from going after Joe and the Caulfels? She shoveled a man-sized bite of pie into her mouth and took her time chewing and swallowing before she asked, "Behind what, Daddy?"

"Behind what, I'll start with this 'Bootleggers' razzmatazz."

"Oh, that. Well, you knew that Mr. Kahn and the vets didn't like seeing Iron Crosses. Mr. Kahn lost his whole family to the gas ovens in Germany. When I checked to make sure Joe's tux was back, I told him everything. Diamond all but pushed him out the door when he tried to visit Joe. We talked to the head of the American Legion and the Veterans of Foreign Wars. The veterans were particularly displeased that the little brother of Goodwin's most decorated war hero was railroaded on your say-so. Mr. Haskins and the veterans took it to the school board. It's more than just a mascot, though. Mr. Kahn and the Legion post are outfitting the band and the cheerleaders under a Roaring Twenties theme."

"Just wait until the next hard times hit Goodwin and see how much Herb Kahn has to bail them out with. What upsets me most are all the inquiries by the IRS and federal prosecutors that will end up with me testifying against my best customers."

"Since you've always cooperated with the IRS, why should it be a problem? Or is it?"

"One last thing, you aren't old enough to vote. Must you so openly support these two renegade Democrats?"

"Daddy, as Mr. Tudbury said, I cut my political teeth around this table. You could have told the sheriff he is too old and feeble. And the prosecutor is crooked."

Lyle broke eye contact. "I'm flabbergasted. Compared to you, Judas was a saint."

Theo had risen from her place at the table and was organizing dishes for the trip to the kitchen. "Lyle, dear, we agreed to talk with Gloria about Deputy John. As much as I'd like to put it off, tomorrow night is our farewell before she leaves Saturday."

Gloria asked, "What about Deputy John?" She looked her father in the eye and saw the same cold anger she had seen in forty-four when he picked her up at the Denver Juvie. That old fear of what he could do next made her swallow hard, even though he hadn't spanked her since she was ten. *Daddy may be mad enough to shoot me, but I needn't worry because I have his pistol.*

Theo said, "Lyle, dear, I had no idea I added to your woes today. For that, I apologize. But Gloria, I am still in shock over what you did Sunday. Did you know Mrs. Diamond's daughters were within earshot?"

"No, I didn't see them. She's kicked Four Eff out."

"Yes, I believe every Lutheran in town has called. What shocked them was Chloe's reaction," said Theo. "Your father and I have had one of the very few arguments we've had over the years of our marriage. I feel we owe you an apology."

Gloria began helping her mother clear the table. "'We'? Did you say 'we'? Mother, Daddy, you finally believe me? Now will you help me get my Joe out of that terrible prison?"

Lyle's voice dripped sincerity and forgiveness. "I should have temporarily looked past your criminal affair to realize the hurt done to you."

There he is brushing lint off his sleeve. I don't trust a word he says. Gloria threw a napkin down on the table. "Criminal affair?"

"Miscegenation is against the law in Virginia, and it certainly should be here as well. By the time he's eligible for parole, his blood will have cooled and you will have matured."

Like hell, I'm marrying him as soon as possible. "Nothing happened! How many times do I have to repeat it? Joe is innocent!"

"Good, if nothing happened, that should make it easier for you to end the relationship," Lyle preached.

Theo held up her right hand in a theatrical gesture as if quoting from on high. "This is one place where your father and I are of one mind. This country cannot remain great if it mongrelizes the races. We will join in efforts to reduce the boy's sentence, provided you agree never to see him again."

"That does it! You knew all along I'd been raped! I can't believe the two of you are actually my parents! I'll be on the noon train east tomorrow, thank you." Gloria threw her folded napkin on the table and stomped out of the room. *If I don't get out of this house and cool off, I'll pull this gun and shoot them both.*

Lyle and Theo stood at their places and looked at the closed door through which their only daughter had stormed. Gloria's footfalls on the stairs broke the silence. Then the door to her room slammed.

"I thought I'd never say this," Lyle said, "but I'm looking forward to Saturday when that train leaves the station. She has been a one-girl wrecking crew."

Theo said, "We've got to use restraint. If we don't, she will leave and never return."

He gave her a hug. "Not to worry, my love. Like a homing pigeon, she'll be back here come Christmas."

"I wish I could be so optimistic, dear. What I hear is that John Diamond's threats are on everyone's lips."

"Who …?"

"The central telephone operator warned me that Gloria's life is in danger and we need to keep her close to home."

Just then, the front door slammed.

"Central operator?" demanded Lyle. "You mean that war widow that hooks up all the local calls? I don't believe it. I saw John in the bank today. He cashed a large paycheck and closed his accounts. He was subdued, calm as a cucumber. But Gloria's fire feeds on itself. She's in full rebellion. Let her walk it off."

"Full rebellion, dressing like a middle-aged spinster and shunning makeup? We goaded her tonight. She had every right to get angry. Lyle, please humor me. If she leaves tomorrow as threatened, what do we tell our friends?"

"After her performance tonight, celebrate."

"Go after her, please, Lyle. Between now and then, both of us will have to hold our tongues and give her reason to return home."

Lyle looked out the window to see his daughter walk toward the Foyle house. "She's going next door. Don't worry. She'll come home again just like she did the time before, contrite and begging forgiveness."

Gloria stood on the darkened porch of the Foyle house watching the lights within, from kitchen to hallway, go dark while Celeste Foyle's rejection rang in her ears. Celeste hadn't wanted to hear her side as she had that first night. She had allowed the door to be opened a crack long enough to give her the one-sentence decision: "I'm sorry, Gloria, you aren't welcome here after what you said to my friend Chloe Diamond at the Sunday coffee hour."

They've cut me loose. The best thing I can do is move up my departure by a day. I'll have to walk down to the station tonight to change it.

She reached up under her suit jacket and touched the holster of the S&W, then feinted lifting the rat-tail file from behind her head. *Given how my parents feel, I'm as much at risk there as on the street.*

The clear blue sky had darkened to a shade or two short of the black of night, sprinkled with bright stars, by the time Gloria walked into the train station. It was just before closing. She asked if she could change the day and also trade the Pullman seat for a roomette. The clerk advised her to pick up her tickets the next morning if she wanted to upgrade to a roomette.

As much as she wished to spend the night at the station, she needed to go home and pack. As her feet echoed off the sidewalk along an empty street, she heard noises coming from the bushes just ahead. Suddenly a stray dog bolted out across the sidewalk and into the darkness. Gloria jumped back, then laughed.

In spite of all that had happened earlier that evening, she was relieved to see the bright porch light of the Knight house cut through the darkness. Above, the gentle rustling sound of leaves in the evening breeze, mixed with subdued big band music, allowed her to feel relaxed for the first time since she left home. She recognized Eddy Howard playing his current hit, "To Each His Own." For that three minutes she was again in Joe's arms. Just short of the final notes, Gloria identified the car parked in the shadows on the other side of the street as a nineteen-thirties Hudson like the ones the sheriff used. At the same moment, she heard heavy footfalls rapidly coming up on the lawn behind her. Now it was too late to go for Daddy's thirty-eight; her attacker lifted off her feet.

She started to turn and reach up for the rat-tail file. All she accomplished was to get her right hand trapped behind her head while her attacker's large hand reached around and closed her nostrils. The other hand forced a gag into her mouth. Gloria's scream was so short, it was like the yip of a dog. The familiar, unwelcome essence of stale sweat, cheap whiskey, and pungent onions told her that her attacker was Deputy John.

She lost all chance to use the rat-tail file when John knocked it from its holder. Then she saw that the trunk door was open and he was pulling her toward it. *I can't let him put me in his trunk.*

She exploded in a frantic fight, trying to reach the file on the ground, while her assailant used both hands, pulling on the gag strap like reins to keep her away from it. John won the next maneuver when he buckled the gag strap behind her head. She refused to accept that she had no moves left until she heard the permanent sound of the gag's lock snapping shut.

John had a firm grip on her arm. He pulled it straight and twisted it hard. She heard the sound of handcuffs coming out of a leather pouch. During a brief moment in her struggles, she made out, in the shadows, the Goodwin County Sheriff's insignia on the car door. Gloria energized her struggle with a kick to that place her father told her always got a male's attention, the groin. Her aim was off, but close enough to distract John so he dropped the handcuffs. She surprised herself at her strength and the amount of pain she endured as she twisted to kick the handcuffs down the sidewalk.

Gloria exhaled through both nose and mouth, but could only inhale through her nose. Her lungs screamed for more air as if she were drowning. She used her free hand to try to tear the gag off her face. This distraction gave John an opening to pull his captive to the patrol car. The open trunk ahead looked like some hungry animal that John was feeding her to. She felt light-headed and off balance for a moment as she was bent over with her head and upper torso in the trunk and her shins against the bumper. Then the oversize deputy drove his shoulder into her thighs, and she made a hard head-first landing as John, in one swift motion, folded her legs inside. She heard the clunk of the revolver beneath her just before John slammed the trunk lid shut.

Desperate for air, she forced her hand down her cheek to break the seal and inhaled. Minutes passed until her body's supply of oxygen matched its demand. Only then did she begin her search for the revolver. She found it, and turned so her head was against the back seat and her legs spread, with her feet at the sides of the trunk door.

Gloria fully expected John to drive away, but he didn't. With gun in hand, she began to kick the trunk lid. It didn't take long for her to find she needed to stop to get her wind. The lid hadn't budged. The feeling of oxygen starvation wasn't going away; the gag snapped back tight on her mouth once her hand was removed. Her body craved more air than she could get through her nostrils.

Some minutes later, she heard John return and open the driver's door. She laid the revolver on her belly and pulled and clawed at the heavy leather gag. The lock held it firmly in place, and the gag was too strong to rip apart. The most she could do was get a temporary path open to pull air into her mouth.

Then came John's voice. He was standing close by the trunk. With his first whispered words, she reached for the revolver and thought, *I'll have to wait to shoot until he opens the trunk because I can't get out otherwise.*

"Well, Miss Gloria Knight, we meet again," he whispered. How ya doin', bitch? Oh, I forgot, you're wearin' a gag with a special lock, and I have the key. Just lay still and relax so you don't need much air. Oh, yeah, I found Mae's rat-tail file in your hair. I know how you got it. Mae told me everything. You're next. I'll teach you for fuckin' with Deputy John."

Then he got in the car and drove off. For the first part of the trip, Gloria felt confident that she had a fair chance. She went over in her mind the tips Mae had given her. She imagined where he would be standing and practiced clicking the safety on and off.

The longer they drove, the more she feared that, even armed, she would be no match for him because she simply wasn't getting enough air through her nostrils. Those first miles, she lay there awake and alert, but the adrenaline wore off. She knew she was drifting off, much in the way a student sleeps in class. She called on every bit of willpower she had to try to stay alert.

Suddenly the ride became so rough that she was bounced around the trunk like a stuffed doll in a clothes dryer. It felt like the road on the way to Mae Blackmon's, but John didn't slow down.

After a punishing ride, she felt the car stopping. It wasn't until John shut off the engine that Gloria realized the revolver was no longer on her stomach. He opened the car door. "Ready for a good fuckin'?"

Where is the S&W? Dear God, help me! She began feeling around in the dark. His footfalls grew fainter until they were faint crunches of his big shoes compressing the gravelly soil. Her panic subsided and she listened closely. There were disquieting sounds of groaning metal as a gate was dragged open. She imagined all sorts of medieval torture devices being dragged into place. *It sounds like Mae's gate! Why would he bring me here?*

The sound of John's footsteps coming back toward the patrol car gave her a shot of adrenaline that swept away the cobwebs. She had to lay her hands on that revolver. He started the engine without saying a word. Soon the exhaust echoed off walls, telling Gloria they were inside a building. The engine stopped. Gloria felt her stomach churn on hearing the car door open. *How could something as big as a gun disappear in a place like this? Please, God, I can't die now. Please help me. Who'd be left to fight for Joe?*

The fates must be with me, thought Deputy John, because he had nabbed Gloria before Sheriff Brad's deadline. *This is cutting it close, but I'll make it. Good thing I was watching the house when she took off by herself.* He took his foot off the gas and came to a rolling stop by Mae's darkened cabin. There was just enough moonlight to catch fingers of smoke curling up around the eaves. *Plenty of time. I'll come back and take them out to the gunk tank after I finish fucking the banker's brat.*

John gunned the engine enough to roll to a stop short of the barn. He opened the doors and turned on the lights. He backed the patrol car inside the barn so the rear bumper was about four feet from the gunk tank

John lifted his pint bottle, still in its brown paper bag, and took a long swallow. Remaining behind the steering wheel, he turned his head to the side. There were faint sounds of Gloria's breathing, along with sounds of her moving about. John thought, *Good, she's starting to get anxious. She'll be tight as anything after I give her a good whipping. Time to put her in the right mind.*

John shouted, "You can't fight Deputy John for long with your mouth sealed shut, wearin' Marcia Hanlon's special gag. Exhale all you want. It's the inhalin' through those two tiny nostrils that gets you. I bet your lungs are cryin' for air. Yeah, you're right to worry about gettin' enough air to breathe."

John sat still and listened while he looked through a large bank envelope. *Good, she's still moving around. I want her awake and screaming when I drop her in the tank.* He thumbed the bills, then dropped the envelope back onto the seat. *So that's what a bundle of hundreds looks like. I'm so glad I set up those extra accounts at the bank now that Chloe kicked me out.*

He waited until there were only the sounds of night insects and Gloria's breathing. He took another nip and got out of the patrol car. He pulled a cigarette out of his breast pocket and lit it. John faced toward the Hudson's trunk and scratched his belly. "I could just as easy have snapped your neck back in town, but after what you done to me and men I respect, that was too good for you. If you think it hurt the last time, you're in for a surprise. I won't be hearin' your damn insults or your beggin' Deputy John to end your misery."

John took off his uniform and undershirt. He didn't want to have to patch or scrub another stain from his uniform or explain them away. He neatly folded the clothes, so carefully that they could have passed inspection, and put them on the back seat. He stood still and listened, then walked up to the gunk tank.

The mason's truck was still parked close by the gunk tank, as it had been for many months. John made ready for Gloria by running the chain fall attached to the rafters all the way out and tying a rope to the hook. Then he used the mixer on the truck to make a slurry of sand, lye, and cement, and dumped it into the gunk tank. He left the mixer running because when empty it made a clattering, banging noise that he felt would annoy his captive even more.

He walked to the far wall of the barn to get the coiled bullwhip. He uncoiled the whip and tested it by making it snap over the car. *If I hang her by her wrists, she'll jerk at the sound, just like when I wrap it around her.*

He stopped by the trunk. "Ya hear that, bitch? That's the last thing you're gonna hear because when I'm done with you, I'm buryin' you alive in cement. You and Mae and her little crotch fruit. Yeah, ol' John knew how to make Mae confess how she helped you break up my marriage. At the end, she begged me to end her misery. Well, she's gettin' her wish."

He chuckled. "Just think of lookin' down at the wet mud gettin' deeper and deeper. Then I'll trip the chain fall. Every place the whip has marked will burn doubly from the wet cement. But you won't be able to move because Deputy John has you stretched right and proper in a hog tie. There won't be any animals diggin' you out either. And that tough guy of yours will rot for the next twenty years!" *Good, building up acid in the tummy, are we?*

There was more movement in the trunk. John thought he heard her try to talk. He walked outside the barn and snapped the whip again and again. Each time it popped, followed by echoes, he imagined Gloria hanging by her heels looking down into a pool of lye. He tossed his cigarette butt into the darkness, returned inside, and latched the barn doors shut behind him. He walked softly away from the car and swung the whip so it popped right above it. "Do you hear that? I'm gonna whip the clothes right off your back till you're buck naked."

John was sure the inside of the trunk lid was taking a beating from Gloria kicking it. A slight smile curved his mouth. *She's getting panicked. I can hardly wait. She ain't some dumb whore like Mae, but a real looker.* John opened the car's back door. He tilted his head back to get the last drop from his bottle, then tossed it on the floor.

He stripped down further until he was wearing nothing but his socks. "It's gonna be different tonight, darlin'. I'm not gonna have a uniform on so you can tear the pocket or dirty my pants. And I'm not gonna be wearin' a raincoat. But don't you worry, I guarantee you won't have a baby." Gloria's feet pounded the trunk lid.

With the whip in his strong right hand and the keys in his left, John decided he had done enough terrorizing. Now it was time for some fun. His first two attempts to unlock the trunk should have warned John he'd had too much to drink, because he missed the lock both times. On the third try his key slid into the lock, but his fingers slipped off it. John swore, and the kicking stopped.

The naked deputy carefully grasped the key again. *It didn't turn. Damn, I thought that was the one.*

There was a muffled, unintelligible voice accompanied by the sound of Gloria's feet pushing on the trunk lid. He selected another key. It went partway into the lock and hung up. *What in the blazes? Let me see. It has to be one or the other.*

He studied the keys in the light, then tried the other key with his right hand. He missed the hole once, then carefully slid it home. *Now pick up the whip, easy now, turn the key. Yes, the tumblers aligned, turn the lever.*

The trunk lid flew open.

CHAPTER 17
Deputy John's Comeuppance

The naked John Diamond filled Gloria's view as the trunk popped open. He held the bullwhip in one hand while his wide, round eyes were still on the other hand that was holding the key in the trunk lid. She pointed the revolver with both hands and squeezed the trigger. Nothing happened. *OhmyGod, the safety is on!*

"Don't try to fool Deputy John. Lay down your toy."

As she moved her trigger finger to the safety, John swung his whip arm back. The whip slipped out of his drunken hand and sailed into the gunk tank, handle first. He bent forward, groping for the pistol. Gloria saw his open hand in front of the muzzle as if to stop the first bullet. She found the safety and fired. The palm of his hand exploded in a cone of flesh and blood. He screamed and stood straight up. She fired two more rounds.

John fell back against the gunk tank. Three wounds on his naked torso registered on her mind. For a blink of an eye, they looked like a trio of red buttons. John held his wounded hand over a hole in his chest close by his breastbone. Blood squirted around his fingers. There was a terrified look on his face. "You done it now! ... I'm a peace ... offa....sir."

Gloria jumped out of the trunk, fearing he would fall forward and trap her inside. *Why aren't you dead, you lousy raping bastard?*

He took a half-step before his legs buckled. "Help me, dear Jesus. Help me." John fell to his knees with his good hand swatting at the pistol. She fired a fourth round into his chest. He fell forward, grabbing at her ankle. She toppled over backward to sit on the car's rear bumper, stretching her arms to the sides to keep from falling back into the trunk. She lost her grip on the revolver and saw it strike the sloping side of the trunk and ricochet off the bumper to land between them. John reached out toward the revolver with his wounded hand. She saw his anger and determination staring her down until his eyes glazed and blood oozed out of his mouth. Scooping up her weapon, she heard a sound that was new to her: a death rattle. John's bloody, dead hand was less than an inch from the revolver. *I did it. I did it. The fucking fat pig is dead.*

Some minutes later, Gloria used the deputy's key ring to release the lock that held her gag. She sucked in that first heady lungful of air and tossed the gag into the back seat. She went back to where John lay and sat down with her back against the gunk tank. With each breath, her head cleared more. She felt the enormity of what she had just done. *Those two little girls will never see their father again, which might not be such a bad thing. What about me? They'll railroad me just like they did Joe. Never mind that he kidnapped me, Four Eff is revered by important people in Goodwin.* She remembered Vera's words, *We've never courted trouble.... It's found us ... In the end, it's always been the same ... First Pa and now Joe ... Get them in jail and throw the book at them ....*

She stood atop a stool to get a vantage point and peered down into the gunk tank. *Look at the way that stuff in the bottom of the tank is attacking the whip. My God, he was really going to bury me alive in that stuff!*

Now Gloria thought, *What's he done to Mae?* She shouted, "Mae! Mae!" as she trotted toward the door. It took all her strength to open the barn doors. She stopped and reloaded the Smith & Wesson. She used the dead deputy's flashlight to find her way to the cabin. A burst of stinking, smoke-laden air engulfed her at the door. She turned on the light to find Mae and her baby son dead inside. Mae lay in the bed, covered with soot, one wrist handcuffed to the center of the metal headboard. Her face was covered with cuts, bruises, and blood. Baby Daniel lay on the floor by the side of the bed.

Gloria found the source of the acrid smoke that filled the cabin. It rose from the smoldering remains of a used tire placed on the sheet metal flooring. Someone had stuffed it with coal and wood and set it on fire. Fearful of succumbing to the noxious fumes, she ran outside.

Now I know why Mae "told him everything." He tortured her and set the fire, and the smoke killed them both. Marcia was in on this--he said she made the gag he used. They kill everybody who gets in their way.

She sank to the ground and looked herself over. *His blood's all over my blouse! I'm on my own now. What will I do? Think, think! I have his car keys, so I can be at the station by six. That gives me over eight hours.*

When Gloria opened the driver's door of the Hudson, she spotted a large, heavy-duty Goodwin National Bank envelope lying on the passenger seat next to her purse and the rat-tail file. She slid into the driver's seat to examine it. Reaching in, she pulled out a bundle of hundred-dollar bills. *Wow, twelve thousand plus change. So that's what I'm worth! Daddy must have called him as soon as I went out the door; that's why Four Eff was there when I came back.* She reached for some of the loose bills, then halted. *Wait, girl, don't be tempted. Daddy no doubt has the serial number of every one of these bills.* She put the cash back in the envelope.

What have we here? Under the envelope she saw a yellow legal pad. Handwritten, it read,

For good of the Goodwin County Sheriff's Department, I resign. Always have been a loyal officer, but I can't stop the lies destroying my marriage and spotless reputation.

No signature. So after he killed the people who could testify against him, he was planning to run. And look at the sheet under it.

The next sheet read,

This is official request for paid administrative leave. I feel that this is all in the best interests of both the department and this loyal officer. Due to circumstances beyond my control, slanderous statements have been made which have put my happy marriage in jeopardy. Also, I need to devote full attention to the false allegations of abuse of the powers of my position.

Neither statement was signed.

Gloria started hatching a plan. *Why, if this unsigned resignation, his pistol, and badge were found in this car, people would think he ran away. Dear God, maybe I can stay out of jail long enough to free Joe. I can't waste any more time. I can bury him in the gunk tank. If I use the chain fall, he couldn't be much heavier than an engine. I can do it. I've shoveled more manure in a day at the Caulfels'.*

Gloria stripped to her panties and bra. She washed her blouse, spot-cleaned her suit, and hung them up to dry. With her usual amount of drive, she put on the work gloves and went to work on John. First she handcuffed him so she could hoist him by the wrists. Then, with help from the rope extending the main chain of the chain hoist, she dragged him back and hoisted him up high enough to get him into the tank. With help from the second chain fall, a handcuffed Deputy John Diamond was put to rest in the gunk tank.

She started making batches in the mixer. The first ones were too soupy, but they flowed nicely around the late deputy. Her original plan was to cover him with cement, but his hands floated. By the time she got those out of sight, she had hit a rhythm. She worked until she ran out of cement with another eight inches to fill. Then she shoveled sand until she ran out of that. She finished leveling it with a rake just before five a.m.

The engine was slow to start, and for a time she thought she would have to walk out of there. When it finally kicked over, she drove out of the barn and stopped to look back. Both her tire tracks and her footprints were there on the barn floor. She got out, raked the area around the gunk tank, then pushed the barn doors closed and turned out the lights.

As she drove past the cabin, she silently said her goodbyes to Mae and Daniel. *How could he do this to you and Daniel? I'll never forget you, Mae, you gave your life for me.*

She turned the patrol car toward Goodwin with a head full of worries. Through the night she had dwelled on what to do about John's money. She decided to take the loose change and the smaller bills because she believed they were from the teller's till and therefore unlisted. That gave her about twenty-four hundred dollars. She decided the best use for the rest would be to leave the envelope where his wife could find it.

To deliver the big envelope to the Diamond house, she drove down the alley to avoid being seen. Behind the house she found an unattached garage with its doors open. It was an easy matter to roll down the window and toss the envelope with its bundle into the open garage. The loud exhaust noise reverberated in the alley and set her pulse to racing. *The car's too loud, I can't leave it at the jail, they'll hear it inside. I need another place to ditch it.*

She worried that it had gotten light enough that someone could see her driving the deputy's patrol car. She wore John's hat just in case, but what if a car got close enough to see her face? She was the only one on the street until she saw a pickup truck headed her way and thought she'd better turn off. The closest turnoff was a rail crossing, and she went for it. She drove along the track with her right wheels on the roadbed and her left bouncing over the ties. The track sloped downhill on a gentle curve where, once out of sight, she parked between two buildings. She stayed in the car long enough to stuff her bra with bills. She hoped there wouldn't be a train on those tracks before noon. All that was left was to walk alleys and back streets until she was close to the station.

Gloria breathed a sigh of relief to find the door to the waiting room was unlocked. However, her wish to use the ladies' room to clean up was dashed when she saw her mother. Theo rose from the bench facing the ticket window. "Gloria! You worry me sleepless. Your father and I have been up all night looking for you. Where have you been?"

Gloria rushed to her mother. They hugged. Theo repeated, "Where have you been?"

"Waiting for the window to open."

The smile that had lighted Theo's face turned to a scowl. "Not here, you haven't. I've been worried sick, waiting up all hours. Are you in trouble? What are those marks on your cheeks?"

Gloria felt her cheeks where the top of the mask had been, then pushed her hands up her cheeks as she folded her fingers. *Am I in trouble? No, only after they catch me.* She pulled her hands down as if she was forcing them inside invisible material. "I can't talk about them. They're just scratches. Where's Daddy?"

"Looking for you. I don't know where exactly. I have never seen your nails this dirty. Were you out at the Caulfels'? What happened? Please tell me."

"No, don't you go after Ma and Pa. They're not involved."

"Please, Gloria."

"Nothing happened to me that I care to talk about."

"Herb Kahn dropped by last night. He was all excited about the prospect of you becoming a model. You are still planning to go to Bryn Mawr, aren't you?"

"Absolutely. But I'd like to have a source of pin money that doesn't require a license or working regular hours at minimum wage. Oh, there's the stationmaster."

"It's not that easy. The competition is ferocious. I want you to cancel this change of schedule. Take tomorrow's train and I'll go with you."

"No, mother, I can't."

Theo followed her daughter to the ticket window. "What you're doing is such an embarrassment. Tonight is your sendoff, and everyone will be there."

"Everyone? Mrs. Foyle won't. Will my fiancé be freed?"

Theo pleaded for Gloria to change her mind until, minutes later, Gloria walked away with a fresh set of tickets. "I can hardly wait until this afternoon when I can sleep," said Gloria.

"Then I'd like to go on the train with you. I don't want to face all those people."

Gloria shook her head. "Up until last night, I would have welcomed you. After last night … please stay home and keep Daddy company. He needs all the love you can give him."

"Please Gloria, I'm trying hard not to be argumentative."

"Then let's go home so I can be back down here in time for the noon train east."

⁂

The hour was fast approaching the time when Gloria would be boarding the train. Although she had secreted Diamond's money without either parent finding out, the morning had been strong on confrontation from the moment Lyle stepped through the front door. She froze when her father hugged her, the first time he had done this since sometime in the spring. When he said,"Thank God, you're home safe. You scared the devil out of me," she thought, *Good.* But she replied, "There's no need to worry, Daddy. You've raised me up well."

The next time she saw Lyle, he was dressed for work in a light blue wool business suit. He saw that she was cleaning his S&W. "Why are you using the Hoppe's #9 on my gun?"

She thought, *It's what you taught me, to clean after every shooting,* then said, "Daddy, I thought you'd given it to me. Having it in my holster gives me the peace of mind that I can defend myself."

"I gave you permission to use it for target practice. I know of no college that permits its students to go about ... Have you been carrying this gun concealed?"

Gloria felt like she was falling into a trap as she struggled with how to answer. "Daddy, I'm too tired to spar with you. I'm sorry you haven't noticed I've been living here scared out of my wits. That's why I wanted my own gun and went out target shooting. You're right, I shouldn't carry on campus."

"Gloria, there's something different about you today. You're distant, cold."

Something different? I shot a man four times. He's dead. If I say word one about the twelve thousand bucks Four Eff had or ask if that wad was his down payment, I'll be implicating myself.

Lyle sat down next to her. She finished cleaning the gun while he watched. Once done, he put an arm around her. "You are very meticulous, thank you."

As he reached for the revolver, she found her hands shaking. Her father said, "It's okay, darling. Just relax. You're safe here with me. I love you."

If I hand him the gun, would he kill me himself? If he really wants me dead, it would be so easy to say the gun went off while being cleaned. Don't a lot of "accidental" shootings happen that way? No one would suspect him.

Well, it's his S&W. I'll give him his one chance to do the deed himself. She put the gun in his hand. She watched him load six bullets. He spun the cylinder once. She held her breath.

Lyle leaned over and put the gun away in a drawer. "If you feel so threatened back east, I'll reconsider Bryn Mawr."

Gloria let out her breath. "No Daddy, please. I'll be safe back there. Mother will be crushed if I don't go." *There, that wasn't so bad. I think he's mellowing on me.* She did her best to give him a genuine smile, accompanied by a hug. "Thank you, Daddy, for paying my way to Bryn Mawr even though we disagree."

He held her loosely in his arms. "As much as your mother wants to accompany you to the East Coast, I respect your desire to make the trip alone. As for what has created this disagreement, I expect that by the time you graduate, you will have matured. God bless you, Gloria."

The last of the prearrangements fell into place with Theo's phone call to Celeste Foyle. Andy agreed to drive Gloria to the train station. While she dressed in a fresh suit, she worried that someone was out there waiting to collect a bounty on her and she should have taken the gun anyway. She looked in the mirror in the foyer to see a face she hardly recognized, with rings around her bloodshot eyes. Heavy make-up did cover the fingernail scratch marks on her cheeks, but it was far too white. *I've seen more color on the corpse at a funeral.* She hid her eyes behind reflectorized sunglasses. The long, silky black hair was piled on her head in a little worse than its usual disorder. The rat-tail file was in its usual place. She wore leather gloves to hide the abrasions from burying John Diamond in concrete.

One suitcase was closed and waiting by the door. The other was open, and Theo knelt by it to put in a black swimsuit. "I can't believe this is all you're taking with you to college. You have a whole closet full of beautiful formals and party dresses. I'll have them shipped ..."

"Please, Mother, leave them here. I won't have the time or opportunity to wear them. I've already shipped the ones Mr. Kahn recommended."

Theo said, "I am completely undone by your unwillingness to make your trip as planned. I saw a real thawing in your father. Another twenty-four hours could make a difference."

Gloria's voice was cold. "I've said the last words I care to say to him."

Theo stood in front of her daughter and waggled her finger. "That is not the attitude that will get you anywhere. Your father was quite upset--no, shocked--this morning over your wanting to take his gun without his permission. My word to you is for you to open your eyes. Your father loves you unconditionally. The next time you come home, give him love in return."

No, Mother, it's too late in more ways than you know. There never can be a next time. Gloria gave her mother a big hug. Tears streaked down her cheeks. "I'm really sorry I've made such a mess of things. If there were some way I could go back and change what happened last May, I would. Well, there's Andy. I'll be okay. Goodbye, I love you."

The new diesel engines, which the railroad had bought to haul troops, throbbed at the head of the passenger train while Andy struggled up the steps and into the passenger car with Gloria's bags. She turned and slowly looked at the town and the hills beyond. Andy's voice betrayed impatience. "Come on, Gloria, you've got to get to your compartment before the train leaves."

There was a wistful quality to Gloria's voice. "I just wanted to get one last good look at Goodwin. If I'm lucky, I'll never see this place again."

"Come on, Glor, this is the third time you've said that. We'll all be home for Christmas and have some big stories to tell about the fall term."

"Joe can't--and I won't."

Once in the roomette, Andy stowed Gloria's luggage. "Are you sure you're all right? You look even worse than the morning after the graduation ball. Those are nasty marks on your cheeks. Glor, those sunglasses can't hide your eyes. What really happened?"

She took off her sunglasses. "It's nothing. I'll be better after some sleep. I had a very bad night. Joe is on my conscience. Did you get a letter this week?"

"No, but Ma did. She said he's okay. He lives for your letters, so don't you forget to write. I've got to go. Conductor's called, 'All aboard.'"

Gloria pulled the pins out of her hair and let it fall free. "I'll write him. Thanks, Andy, you've been like a wonderful brother to me. I'll miss you and Carole and your mom very much. Goodbye." She hugged Andy, who dashed for an exit. He stepped onto the platform from a barely moving train.

Gloria watched Andy run alongside and wave all the way to the end of the platform. By the time he reached the end, she was laughing at his antics. Across the street, Sheriff Hanlon began jaywalking from where he had stood by his patrol car toward the moving train until he was almost to the curb. As the car Gloria was in passed him, he began waving. She waved back. He stopped waving and watched the train while he licked a freshly rolled cigarette. *What's on his mind?* she wondered. *Does he know something?*

She heard the engines throb when the engineer opened the throttle. Soon she watched the canyon go by with only late summer's low water in the river. On the highway she spotted the white Cadillac with Vera and Ray as they rushed toward Goodwin to canvass for votes.

Later, it tore her heart to see the rocky promontory come into view where she and Joe had parked on that May night. A couple in a convertible broke from a clinch to watch the train pull up the canyon. Gloria closed her eyes and heard again in her mind Eddy Howard singing "To Each His Own": "... For a rose must remain, through the sun and the rain, or its lovely promise won't come true ...." She wanted to go back and hold that May moment forever and never live beyond it. Instead she cried until she fell deeply asleep, to awaken just short of Chicago. She lay in her bed listening to the sounds of the train, from the steady staccato click of the wheels passing over rail joints, to the Doppler shift of the crossing gate bells and the less frequent roar of a passing train. *Don't ever kid yourself, Gloria. The only difference between you and those desperadoes on the post office wall is that the law has pictures of them for the "Wanted" posters.*

CHAPTER 18
Deputy John Is Missing

Marcia Hanlon sat in the top of the line upholstered sheriff's chair in his well-decorated office with the phone to her ear when her husband Brad stepped through the door. She stood and gestured for the sheriff to take his accustomed seat. Her face grew redder while she listened to her caller until she threw a fist above her head and vocally exploded, "No, Mr. Stokings, you listen! No way am I going to keep an employee who openly supports the sheriff's opponent. I have fired you." She took a deep breath. "You should have thought this through before you opened your yap. It's going to be tough getting any kind of a job in Goodwin County carrying a Brad Hanlon blackball. Before you go passing out Pretty Boy's literature, empty your locker and turn in your gear. Good day, sir!"

She firmly placed the receiver in its cradle on the sheriff's desk. "I've just fired Stokings for double dealing."

"Stokings out? Too bad. I like Leo. For what, specifically?"

"He betrayed your trust. I confronted him about the Shyflinski literature in his car. He gave me some line that he could be loyal to Goodwin County, but he couldn't support you. He's still upset because I reprimanded him for putting the Knight girl and Vera Caulfels in the same cell."

Brad thought, *She sure can give people hell when they need it. Marcia has taken a part of the job I never liked and done it well.* "Well, you're right, that had to be done. By the way, I don't know if this is good news or bad. Gloria Knight climbed on the afternoon eastbound a day early."

"What? Are you sure?"

Brad sat down. He pursed his lips as he nodded. "Young Andy Foyle delivered her and carried the bags."

"Hmmm, it may be bad, I don't know. Can't think about it right now. We've got another problem, a bigger problem. John clocked in early, like I suggested, but he never clocked out. Your deputy and the nineteen thirty-eight Hudson are missing."

Brad pounded a fist on his desk. "That does it! When he comes in, he will, in writing, ask for administrative leave. And if he doesn't, I'll fire him myself. I brought that man up from nothing!"

The office settled into its usual routine. Marcia and the staff took care of the details for the sheriff. Marcia carefully wiped his bifocals and set a fresh cup of coffee on his desk. While she and a young clerk laid out the weekly reports in the proper order, faint sounds of the railroad leaked in from outside the building through the windows and doors. Such noises were inescapable because this was a railroad town set in a mountain valley. Thus the faint squeal of brakes being applied to a string of cars could easily be tuned out. But then came a sound that couldn't be ignored: a sickening metallic screech followed by a thump, more squealing, then a resonating silence.

Everyone in the office looked at one another except for the sheriff, who was getting hard of hearing. While the voices rose, asking one another essentially "What was that?" Brad pulled open the lower drawer on his large oak roll-top desk and put a worn, dirty piece of plywood over the opening. He winced as he eased his handcrafted cowboy boots onto the surface.

Marcia asked, "Brad, did you hear that?"

Brad was still getting comfortable. He looked puzzled. "Hear what, darling?"

There followed multiple short blasts of a steam engine's whistle. Brad looked confused. "What's all the fuss about at the rail yard? Accident, maybe?"

Marcia got on the departmental radio to find out what happened. She was still sending her message when Deputy Tom Weisner called in, "There was a collision between an auto and a boxcar. I'll make my report orally. There were no injuries."

Within twenty minutes, Deputy Tom pushed the door open and laid a pile of items on Brad's desk: three empty pint bottles in brown bags, the leather gag, gun, badge, and a sheet of yellow scratch paper on top. "You ain't gonna like this one bit, Sheriff. They were in John's patrol car's front seat. He left it parked way back in the right of way by the co-op loading dock. I heard it hit."

"You heard it hit what?" said Brad.

"You can't go blame the railroad none. The track curves around so when they cut loose a string of boxcars, the engineer fellow couldn't see the Hudson. When I left, there was a photographer from the *Globe* snapping pictures."

The Sheriff gripped the armrests. *Damn, I'm ruined! Could that Polack Shyflinski have engineered this? That damned Diamond set me up. What the hell was he doing on the tracks? Three bottles, the drunken son of a bitch!* Brad examined the badge and gun. *No John in the car. He's on the run, probably caught any one of the morning trains. Ho, wait, what is this?* Brad held up the leather gag. "Marcia, please tell me this ain't the gag you bought for disruptive witnesses."

Marcia abruptly got up and made a shooing gesture. "¡*Fuera de aqui!* ¡*Avante!* Everybody out of the office! Close the door." After she shut the door, she said, "Brad, you told John to ice the banker's daughter."

"Why the gag?"

"He asked me, could he borrow it. He said you told him, take time off and take care of Gloria, shut her up before she left on Saturday. Yes, I loaned him the gag. It wasn't the solution I would have chose, but county politics, especially your elections, have always been high-stakes games."

Brad leaned back in his chair, seating himself on his lower back. "Yes, I suggested it to John as much to cut his losses as I did to limit our damages and Lyle's damages. Lyle should have had her committed, that would have got rid of her and she wouldn't have been digging around in his desk. Did John spell out his plans for Gloria?"

"He only said he had a place where she wouldn't be found."

Brad held his head in his hands. "This obviously didn't just happen. I warned John to be prepared to stand down, either temporarily on paid status, or resign. The bastard! Why did he take this way out? Two months before the election! Damn you, John!"

"There is one outcome you haven't considered. Maybe Gloria got the better of him," opined Marcia.

I don't even want to think about that. John's been my go-to man. Brad shook his head vigorously. "I can't visualize John having trouble with that skinny teenager."

"Why do you think he's not shown his face around here? That skinny teenager, as you call her, is a dead shot. I watched her shoot early this summer."

Dead shot? Horseshit! Wait until she comes home on vacation.

Marcia opened the door and waved in Deputy Tom. Brad asked him, "How bad is the patrol car? Is there any sign of foul play?"

"Totaled. The coupler punched a hole in the trunk. That old thirty-eight Hudson should have gone to the junkyard years ago. Don't know about foul play. His uniform was folded in the back seat."

"Tom, with the war and all, that Hudson was among the newer cruisers." Brad handed him the keys to his own vehicle. "Be careful, or we'll all be walking. Take over John's duties. Your first job is to find him. Bring him in! He's made a fool of this department."

Later, the phone on the sheriff's desk rang. Marcia answered, "Hello, Chloe … yes, we just heard. It was John's car. ... No, it was empty. Do you know where he is? .... The girls must be disappointed ... She found how much, when? ... *Santa Maria!* That much! .... I don't know .... We must talk to him too ... Thank you, Chloe, 'bye."

Marcia twirled the leather gag absent-mindedly. "Chloe's oldest found ten thousand dollars in a Goodwin Bank envelope on the floor of their garage."

"Ten thousand!" exclaimed Deputy Tom, bouncing to his feet. "When John started here in forty-one, he said he was flat broke. Where did he get that kind of money?" Tom directed his question toward the sheriff.

Brad looked down. "I don't know how he accumulated that sum. See the world through his eyes. Wife left him ... fired from his job ... the state after him ... He probably took his own life." *At least I hope he did.* "He was a decent man in the end, caring for his family. I was always able to depend on him."

"Dead or alive, I want him found." Marcia took a pose like a matador and made a thrust as if she had a sword in her hand. "If he's alive, that fat slob will wish he stayed in that patrol car!"

Ray Tudbury felt relaxed, almost pampered, in his seat behind Vera Caulfels in her white Cadillac touring car with its top down. Today Ma, as everyone in the campaign called her, would drive him to the voters' doors so he didn't have to walk block after block. Here it was the middle of September, and his feet hurt from all the miles he had walked handing out "slim jims," the term for a piece of campaign literature about the size of a folded letter. Yes, he felt good about having Ma as his campaign manager; she knew what was what. The slim jims were an example: he now saw the worth of going all the way to a union shop, some distance from Goodwin, to have them printed. Just this morning, he'd gained the support of the railroad unions only after the business agents made a point of finding the printers' union "bug" on the slim jims.

Fellow candidate Larry Shyflinski, running for county sheriff, climbed up and sat next to him. After Ray exchanged greetings with Larry, Ma turned and shook his hand. "I've got some good news. Over breakfast we met with business agents of the three rail locals serving the Western Slope. Each will be mailing a hundred dollars to both your campaign and Ray's."

"Three hundred dollars! That's my biggest contribution!" exclaimed Larry.

Ray commented, "Larry, I've been across the table from some skillful wheelers and dealers, but Ma, this woman in the sheepskin jacket, is a force to be reckoned with. She could have been setting me up for a run for Congress."

Vera pulled her sweat-stained straw cowboy hat farther down her forehead and winked. "In due time, all in due time. I sold them on an investment in the future. Larry, how did the face-off with Brad Hanlon go at the Chamber of Commerce meeting?"

Larry shrugged his shoulders and pulled the chinstrap down on his "Smokey the Bear" campaign hat. "I don't know. On one level, I feel sorry for the man. His faculties are failing him. Twice he forgot the question while answering it. He mounts the steps to the platform one at a time like there's a hangman awaiting him. He's going deaf."

Ma asked, "What kind of applause did he get?"

"More on arrival; less at the end. He's counting on the sympathy vote; in almost every answer he gave, he kept repeating how many times he's been reelected. But he now has to overcome the scandals about Deputy John Diamond, who seems to have become his personal albatross. Mary MacBride asked why he didn't arrest John for rape when Gloria reported it, and he responded that the point of the question was to slander him. That brought out some boos. Then the reporter for the *Globe* nailed him about the patrol car getting destroyed on the tracks. He claimed that John did that out of spite before hopping a train out of town. The whole room laughed. Ma, where are you taking us?"

"Calvin Bohl's spread. He's a good friend of my husband's. Cal's a widower raisin' up two fine boys."

They headed out of town toward roads that neither candidate knew existed. After a kidney-punishing trek over a rutted trail, Ma pulled up in front of a modest ranch house. She jumped down from the car and bellowed, "Cal! Cal Bohl, get on out here! I've got two fine young men for you to meet."

The old man smiled, showing them a mouth full of yellow teeth whose crowns had rotted into hollows. "Vera, what you doin' out traipsin' around the countryside this time of year? Don't tell me you left Orville to git ready for winter all by hisself."

"Don't you worry about Orville. I want you to meet Ray Tudbury. He's a Democrat running for prosecutor. He's honest and fair minded. He's not afraid to go after corruption. He knows how to put the crooks in jail because he did it in Chicago before the war."

The old man extended a sunburned hand that Ray found was as rough as sharkskin when he wrapped it around Ray's in a crushing grip. "Ray Tudbury, eh? The old judge's son. You're takin' on a tough bunch in the courthouse. If Vera says you're okay, you've got my vote." Putting a hand on Ma's shoulder, Cal said, "I thought you gave up the political game. Bein' an active Democrat in this county can be dangerous to your health."

"What else can they do to me? They took my boy away to prison. They almost murdered him."

"He should've stayed away from that Knight bitch," replied Cal. "She's bad news."

"Don't judge her by her father. I'd be pleased to have her in my family. She's as much a victim as is Joe."

"That may be. Speakin' of her father, that greedy SOB had some slick guy out here not long ago, tryin' to buy up the mineral rights to the north forty."

Hugging Ma, he continued, "There ain't a time when we give our thanks to the Almighty that we don't say a word for Orville. I'll never forget back in twenty-six when he bought the place at the foreclosure sale. He deeded it back over to me free and clear in exchange for the mineral rights. Then when the feds were takin' everythin' he had, he told them I had an option to buy them back. We only had enough money for forty acres. Lyle got the rest. I'm one of the fortunate ones. At least I don't rent from the bastard."

After Ma drew Larry into the conversation, Cal asked, "What are you gonna do to bring justice for poor Mae Blackmon?"

Ray said, "Mae, my classmate in grammar school? I haven't seen anything in the paper. What did she do this time?"

Cal kicked the hard ground with the toe of his cowboy boot, then looked up at his guests. "Ain't what she done, I'm talkin' about how she died. No, Mae, the retired whore, whose husband was murdered in that damn jail, deserved more than a fine-print public notice in the *Globe*. If ever there was a suspicious death that deserved front page news, that was it. Instead they're beatin' a dead horse speculatin' about Deputy John's whereabouts."

Larry asked, "How did she die?"

"I think it was from breathin' too much smoke from a fire set in the cut-up tire she used to store coal for the cookstove."

Ray asked, "How terrible! How could they miss such a story?"

"Dunno. You need to look into it." Cal rubbed his chin. "I was talkin' to the hunter who discovered the bodies. He said she was handcuffed to the headboard. Her baby boy, Daniel, passed too. It just ain't right. I looked through the cabin and I didn't see no handcuffs, but there was scratches on the horizontal pipe goin' across the top of the headboard. There's nothin' about handcuffs in the coroner's report. When I asked that Deputy Brown about it, he acted like he had somethin' to hide."

Larry and Ray promised Cal that Mae wouldn't be forgotten. They climbed back into the Caddy and headed to another obscure white clapboard house, and yet another, until they blended into a blur. They followed threshing crews as they went from place to place. Ma had the knack of pulling up at a general store just after the postmistress had finished sorting the day's mail and had a crowd waiting to pick it up. They shook hands until they couldn't hold a pencil.

As they drove down the long country roads to the next stop, the men had ample time to chat with this ageless woman. On one of the first days, Ray asked her how the vendetta with the Knights began.

Ma took a long sip from her coffee cup. She replied, "I don't think it was two months after old Lyle got in town that we were hosting a service club dinner at the saloon. The regular fellow who supervised the dining room took sick, and Orville asked me to help out. Lyle walked through the door like he owned the place." She then recounted what Lyle had said to her about "savages" and how she retaliated with the iced gin.

Larry laughed. "So … he tried to get even for that, did he?"

"Yes, he sure did. I wasn't raised that way," she mused, "but we've been sparring back and forth ever since. There was a month or two back in thirty-two that I had him on the ropes, when I organized a run on his bank. He's won every round since, but the next rounds will be mine."

Ray put a hand on her shoulder. "Wait, Ma, pull over, we've got to talk. Byron heard there are federal bank examiners scheduled to visit Lyle's bank. Are you involved in that? I'm not going to let you use this campaign to keep this feud alive."

Ma reached inside her blouse and pulled out a letter. "I won't. Gloria is the instigator, and she's settled in at Bryn Mawr until after the election. Then she wants to spend Christmas in Canon City. She's intent on marrying Joe, and I'd love to have her as my daughter."

CHAPTER 19

Bryn Mawr

Gloria opened her off-campus mailbox in the nearby post office, reached in, and took out a pair of envelopes. The one that made her heart skip a beat was small, with a five-digit number in the upper left corner where the sender's name should be.

She pulled out the big envelope, which had Mary MacBride's return address. This was the package containing the substantiating facsimiles she was to organize and mail to Harriet Woodward. Harriet had said she needed verification before she would print the article about the timing of the groundless condemnation and quiet title suits filed by Prosecutor Gulette. The filing of the suits caused the properties in question to lose value drastically, and that was when Lyle bought them at fire sale prices. Then, as if by magic, Gulette dismissed the cases, the values rebounded, and Lyle found buyers at full price.

Gloria's dormitory roommate, Jenny Vaughan, was with her. "Well, you're finally getting your money's worth," she said, "for the rent you're paying on that box." She knew this was the first mail Gloria had received in the box.

Soon Gloria and Jenny strolled back onto the campus from town through the long shadows of late afternoon. Fellow freshman Jenny, a blonde of medium height with a boyish figure, wore a modest nautical-style sundress. Willowy Gloria wore one of her ill-fitting suits and the low-heeled shoes she had worn in Goodwin. Unlike other days when she returned empty handed, she found herself smiling as she felt the single small envelope in her hand. *I have a letter from Joe! I have a letter from Joe!*

Gloria said, "Thank you for keeping me company on this walk to the post office."

"It's the least I could do after all the help you gave me by going over that English homework. What happened to that poker face? You're walking faster and smiling. Somebody special in Goodwin write?"

Gloria took a few steps before she held up the large stuffed envelope. "Yes, I've got some work to do. I have to send this back out as quick as I can."

"And they insist you rent a mailbox? Interesting."

"My idea. I want the privacy for things like modeling too." Gloria nodded. *Best not to talk about Byron giving me money for a year's box rent. I'm not sure I need a larger box, except this does give me the assurance that snoops can't track what's been received.*

About half a block onto campus, two girls blocked their way. The taller of the two was an inch or two shorter than Gloria and had a much bigger frame. "What is it with you, Salvation Army girl? Who died? Yes, you in the widow's weeds. Why'd they let you in?"

"I'll wear what I want. My mother graduated from here with a BS in performing arts. I graduated valedictorian at Goodwin High."

Jenny stepped between them. "What business is it of yours what she wears?"

The shorter girl said, "Your skinny friend looks like hell wearing that dumb suit. Doesn't she have any decent clothes?"

Widow's weeds, I like that. Thanks, that's exactly how I want to look. Gloria eased Jenny out of where she stood between Gloria and the taller girl. "No trouble, please. I'm dressed to learn. I don't want distractions."

"Distractions?" said the taller girl. "Can't you afford any more?"

"Thanks for your concern. I have a whole closet full at home. There is a very personal reason for what I choose as my wardrobe," said Gloria in a testy voice.

"Please, no offense," replied the girl, "I wanted to let you know there's some money left in the special needs scholarship fund." Gloria took the business card she offered.

They walked back to the dorm before Gloria broke the silence.

"Thank you for sticking up for me." *I like this girl. Jenny may be little, but she has guts.*

"You're right. It's no business of theirs what you wear. Look, it's the last weekend in September. The weather this weekend is going to be like summer. I want you to come home with me. It'll be the last time we can swim until next May or June. I owe you so much for all the help. I don't want any ifs, ands, or buts."

Gloria pondered the invitation and then said yes. Mentally she returned to the large envelope. *I have to have this in the mail before the weekend. This is the one where Daddy got outbid for the resort hotel, then picked it up cheap after Gulette filed a lawsuit. His dirty hands are all over it. I wish I had Byron to check my work. If I don't get these references right, Harriet Woodward won't write the story.*

Back in her dorm room, Gloria opened the letter from Joe. The envelope was small, roughly three-and-a-half by six inches. She read,

Dear Gloria,

Each morning I say a prayer of thanks that another day has been added to my life, a day closer to you. Ma filled me in on what all you and she have done. You doing the articles and Ma helping Mr. Tudbury and Mr. Shyflinski. Thank you. I love you. It's a hard life here, but I try. Ma and Pa say it's important to fill my heart with love so there'll be no room for hate. I've been talking to a chaplain, Father Covell. He has been a great help to me. I would like for you to meet him. Be of good cheer.

Love, Joe.

She re-read the letter, then thought of the others she had received in the school mailbox. Andy was homesick at the university in Boulder. Ray and Larry filled in the news of the political campaign where Ma left off. Ray praised Gloria's research skills. *No news is good news,* she thought. *How could they have investigated Mae and Daniel Blackmon's deaths and not looked at the gunk tank filled with cement? If they'd looked inside and found Four Eff, they'd know this was a homicide.*

Friday afternoon found Gloria in the swimming pool at the Vaughan estate, nestled on a five-acre parcel in Upper Darby, Pennsylvania. Refreshed, she broached the water and climbed out onto the surrounding deck. She had taken a half-dozen quick, short steps across the sun-heated tile toward her deck chair when a wolf whistle stopped her in her tracks. She felt herself blushing. *Oh my gosh, why on earth did I ever let Herb Kahn sell me this knit swimsuit? When it's wet, I might as well be naked.*

She turned, fully expecting it to be somebody Jenny had invited over. Instead she was surprised that it was Jenny's handsome, silver-haired father, Henry Vaughan. He rose from his poolside chair and held up a terry cloth robe. "Gloria, I apologize for embarrassing you. You are obviously unaware that you have been given a rare gift of beauty and grace. It is very refreshing to meet a young woman so unaffected."

Unaffected, my ass. She covered her breasts with her hands and walked to where she allowed him to put the robe over her shoulders. Gloria stammered, "My fault. The suit wasn't transparent when I tried it on last May. I apologize. This is the first time I've worn it."

"Interesting. Where did you buy the suit?"

"Kahn's Department Store in Goodwin, Colorado."

"Gloria, your suit is more provocative than the French bikinis I bought for the girls at the Paris show. But don't worry. There are places around here where the police will arrest you for wearing a bikini--but not your swimsuit."

"You're kidding, why?" Gloria wrapped the robe around herself.

"Because your navel is covered. Let me share what I would tell Jenny if she were in your shoes with the ambition to model. Go for it. Those blue eyes … you have a look, a style that's in demand. Don't hide that light under a basket."

"Thank you, Mr. Vaughan. Back in Goodwin, Mr. Kahn encouraged me too. He owns the department store there. He set me up with a fashion photographer in New York before school started. I skipped out of class at noon last week to sign up with the agencies Mr. Kahn referred me to, but I got bad news. None of them would even look at my portfolio because I'm not eighteen. I feel cheated."

"All you need is a parental consent form."

Gloria sucked in a lungful of air between her teeth. "Parental consent? I didn't leave home on the best of terms."

He leaned forward. "I don't know what Jenny has told you about us.

I'm the vice-president for marketing at Wanamaker's. Let me introduce you to our ad agency. Here's what I'd like to tell your parents: that I sense in you a fire, a competitive spirit that could go right through the camera and give life to the prints. If you're embarrassed by that swimsuit, I'll treat you to a new, more modest suit when you come by the store--provided you pose in it for us."

Wow, he's so eloquent. "Thank you, Mr. Vaughan." She chose to sit in the chair next to him. *I wonder if he'd be so generous once he hears Daddy's side. Maybe I could steer him to Mother.* "Oh, I just remembered I was supposed to call home collect this afternoon." *I don't want to, but I should call. Hopefully Daddy will have gone fishing and I can talk to Mother.*

While they were talking, Jenny came around the house wearing a sea-green bikini. *She has good clothes sense,* thought Gloria. *I can learn from her. Like now, she chooses something that accents those striking green eyes. She does all those exercises. Her tummy is flat. I don't know how I'd look with my hair bobbed and bleached blonde like hers. I'll go back to serving my time with Joe before dinner. I'll wear my "widow's weeds" and sweat.*

Henry put the cigarette he had just lit into the ashtray. "One last question before I call. Are you planning to drop out of college and go into modeling full time?"

"Father," interjected Jenny, "don't worry about that. She needs something to keep busy." Jenny snapped her fingers. "She reads it once and she's got it."

Gloria responded, "Modeling is pin money. My goal is to graduate early with honors, so I'm taking the maximum credits allowed."

Henry replied, "I'm glad Jenny talked you into coming. From my daughter's description, I thought you'd be different. She told me you plan to be an attorney. That's quite an ambition for a girl."

'Yes, sir. I did legal research for a wonderful man this summer. He is running for county prosecutor. I've never found anything as fascinating."

"Ah-hah, you're full of good ideals. Legal research is certainly a safe place for a woman."

To gain eye contact, Gloria looked over top of the sunglasses with the reflectorized lenses. She smiled ever so slightly. "No, sir, I mean to be a trial lawyer. As to where safety lies … I'll leave that to the judge and jury."

"This is classic Gloria," said Jenny. "She's seventeen going on thirty-five. Come on, roomie, let's get in the pool before it cools down."

While Gloria was taking off the robe, Jenny whispered, 'That swimsuit, now I see why my father whistled. You are full of surprises."

"He encouraged me to model."

"Fantastic! You're the first friend of mine that he has noticed."

Once in the water, Gloria swam laps with Jenny until she tired. She floated for a while with her eyes closed. She relived her moment of truth with Deputy Four Eff, from his diatribe and the whip cracking to burying him and watching his hands disappear under the cement. *It's only a matter of time until they come for me with handcuffs. I can't just lie back. I have to keep working.* She swam another couple of laps, making no attempt to keep up with Jenny.

Chapter 20

Campaign Trail 1946

A tired candidate, Ray Tudbury eased himself into his seat in the conference room at the *Goodwin Globe*. Ma Caulfels took her place in the front row of the spectator seats. *How good it feels to be off my feet,* thought Ray. *Here on the third Saturday in October, the end of the campaign is in sight. That is, if I survive today.*

Ray considered this his campaigning "day from hell" for it had not started well. It began with a breakfast face-off with Prosecutor Gulette sponsored by Goodwin's KMOO and the Women's Christian Temperance Union. Ray came prepared to talk about drunk driving and minors, but instead Theo Knight pressed him on banning tobacco. Then she unloaded all over him when he inquired about Gloria. *She blames me for their rift. I shouldn't have said there's something wrong in that family. That was broadcast on KMOO over an open mike.*

After eating the box lunch that Ma fixed, Ray studied his schedule for the rest of the day. One o'clock: a debate sponsored by the *Globe*. Four o'clock: Goodwin High School homecoming parade and kickoff. Four forty-five: football game. Eight o'clock: first student dance at the armory. Half-past eleven: the last dance. He expected to be dead on his feet by then.

Ma had yesterday's paper, and she chuckled as she read Harriet Woodward's column. "Mister Gulette will be a case of spontaneous combustion by the time he finishes this. It says, 'Judge Costi granted a series of Gulette's injunctions, which were regarded by the local community as frivolous. It was enough to scare away potential developers.' Goshalmighty!" She continued, "'The owner's appeal was never heard because banker Knight bought mortgages on the properties and foreclosed. His holding company took possession. Its proposal for a retail center was copied, drawing for drawing, from earlier work. Scenarios like this happened time after time while Judge Costi was in office.'"

Ray said, "Good, although I don't think the average voter understands what happened with these real estate shenanigans. But Jim doing nothing after those deaths in jail--that resonates. I'm going to pound on that."

From just outside the room came Prosecutor Jim Gulette's voice. "You son of a bitch, Tudbury. It resonates with the bar association. I spend all my time fighting these bogus charges, and you get a free ride." He entered the room pointing a folded newspaper like it was a knife or a stick. "Is it you, Vera Caulfels, who's feeding Harriet this stuff?"

Ma pulled the brim up on her sweat-stained cowboy hat and saluted Jim with her right hand. "Well, Counselor Gulette, you're not the first to ask. As I always say, I'm just a simple rancher's wife and don't much know about high finance and low dealing."

Close to one o'clock, an audience started coming in for the debate. Ray shook hands with *Globe* editor Norm Nadau, who was going to be the moderator. *I don't think Norm realized Vera was sandbagging Gulette this morning with questions directly from the audience.* Mary MacBride arrived, and Ray waved to her. *Mary is one very hard worker for both Larry and me.*

Nadau brought the room to order. At this point in the campaign, those who had followed it could conclude this was a rehearsed play that began with a handshake between opponents and the flip of a coin to decide who went first. Each candidate gave the same speech he had given at every other forum. The moderator opened the floor for questions.

The first questioner asked, "Mr. Gulette, the Denver papers make Goodwin County look like a seamy pulp novel. Your name and that dead judge's name keep croppin' up in what looks like some pretty shady deals. What have you to say for that?"

"My office is the equivalent of the law firm that handles civil matters for the county. You will notice that in not one of these cases have they said I broke the law."

"Yeah, but yesterday's article in the *Globe* ..."

Gulette's face reddened as he interrupted, "I'll be glad to meet with you after this meeting to go over these complex legal issues. Next question."

Ray stood up. "Please, Mr. Prosecutor. I haven't had a chance to respond. This columnist has a reputation for telling it like it is. I ask the people to vote for me, and if it hasn't changed in four years, fire me."

Ray's response brought the small audience to life. Eyes that had been reading or dozing were now on him. More hands waved for attention. The next questioner pointed at the prosecutor. "Mr. Gulette, is it true you're under investigation by both the IRS and the U.S. Attorney's Office?"

There was a pause, in which the room was totally quiet. Gulette turned pale and stared at the young man asking the question. Then he turned angrily to Ray and whispered, "Tudbury, what are you up to? You and your damned Gestapo."

Ray rose to his feet again. "Mr. Nadau, this is my question to answer. No one from either the IRS or the U.S. Attorney's Office has contacted me. In fairness, let's drop this matter. One of the basic tenets of our justice system is that every citizen accused of a crime is innocent until proved guilty. If my opponent is under suspicion, I ask that it not be an issue until such time as a jury decides there is guilt beyond a reasonable doubt."

Gulette scanned the audience, then glared at Ray. Gulette's voice barely carried as he whispered through clenched teeth, "You rotten son of a bitch. You set me up."

"Mister Prosecutor, I sense your strong feelings. Please join me in making this disclaimer before each debate. Let's lift up the process so the voters make their decision based on where we stand."

Gulette held his position with clenched fists. "Strong feelings! Process!" He turned to the audience. "Listen to the slick talk about fairness. He spent the war throwing our tax dollars away while rubbing elbows with Communist murderers and Nazi war criminals."

Ray held his bemedaled cap over his heart. "War makes strange bedfellows, especially when fighting behind enemy lines. I paid a high price for this Distinguished Service Cross. I lost my wife. I'm proud of what I did in service to the United States of America to help bring the light of freedom back to Italy. Certainly you have intimate understanding of the term 'strange bedfellows,' Mr. Gulette?"

Gulette was halfway out of his chair with his arm drawn back as Nadau pounded his gavel. "Please, please, gentlemen! One more question."

Ray shifted to a defensive position. *Does this fool know that if he swings at me, I'll lay him out on the floor?*

"Calm down, Jim. You don't want to commit an assault," warned Nadau. "There will be one more question."

Both candidates took their seats. Mary MacBride asked, "Mister Gulette, knowing what you know now, would you have prosecuted Joe Caulfels and asked for twenty years to life?"

"He pleaded guilty, Mary, just like your father is in the process of doing. He made an agreement just like your father is doing."

Ray turned and looked out over the audience. "I believe young Joe Caulfels' conviction will be overturned on grounds of prosecutorial misconduct. Police powers and prosecution are separated to provide a check. As your prosecutor, I will be vigilant. When a rape victim or any citizen calls, I will listen, investigate, and take action as necessary. Had the prosecutor returned just one of Gloria Knight's phone calls, Joe Caulfels would be a free man. And John Diamond would not be a fugitive."

Ray was indoctrinated by Vera to work the crowd wherever circumstance or plan created an opportunity. At the homecoming, he or a volunteer greeted and thanked every marcher in the parade while they stood in place before it started. He offered red buttons to them. Other volunteers passed out red slim jims to those headed for the stands.

Look at Gulette standing there by himself, waving at the crowd from the back of that truck. He has no organization. Between Ma and Mary MacBride, I think we're got every active Democrat in the county who can walk, giving out literature.

Goodwin was a town that loved parades but lacked the numbers to satisfy the need, so they held their parades on the track around the football field and circled it twice. While the paraders were circling on the far side, the teams made their entry and began warmups.

The focal point, the reviewing stand at the fifty-yard line, was demarked by red, white, and blue streamers beneath a bright blue banner with the iridescent red letters BOOTLEGGERS 1946 HOMECOMING. Within the stadium, the three front rows were filled with decorated or wounded men in uniform. All the remaining seats were jammed with other spectators.

Ray felt pleased as he looked over the crowd. Three-quarters of the non-uniformed spectators either wore red buttons or had a red slim jim sticking out of a pocket--or had both. Close to half of the male spectators were in military uniforms. He spotted a few red buttons among those, and noted that most were carrying slim jims.

As the parade came around for the second time, led by the white Cadillac with its top down, all the people in the bleachers applauded and whistled, just as they had the first time around. Sitting between the queen and her court, in his Army Air Forces uniform with the silver oak leaf insignia of a lieutenant colonel and a chest full of ribbons, was the grand marshal, Goodwin County's most decorated hero, Sunny Caulfels. The dark, handsome six-plus-footer waved to the crowd. Orville was at the wheel. In a white suit and a straw boater, he looked like an extra from the cast of *The Great Gatsby*. Ma sat beside him in a red dress and a nineteen-twenties vintage hat. Surrounding them were girl cheerleaders in twenties-style red and blue flapper dresses with short skirts, wearing cowboy boots and waving pom-poms.

Those in the stands gave Sunny Caulfels a standing applause.

Soon the cheerleaders were on the ground performing their first routine around the next unit, a nineteen forty-six Ford patrol car driven by Deputy Tom Weisner. Sheriff Brad Hanlon sat in the front passenger seat. Behind them was a small marching band. The girls in the band were attired in modest blue and red flapper dresses, and the boys wore red and white striped blazers and white trousers.

When his car reached the reviewing stand, Sheriff Brad slowly and painfully lifted himself out with help from his deputy and mounted the stairs to take his place among the reviewing officials. He stumbled on the first step and would have fallen had the deputy not caught him. The parade waited until he shuffled step by step to his first-row seat.

The announcer gave the sheriff a spirited buildup. "Bring your hands together for a man honored eight times as grand marshal, a distinguished alumnus who hasn't missed a homecoming since graduating in eighteen eighty-four, Goodwin County's Sheriff Bradley Hanlon. Welcome and God bless you, Sheriff!" Despite this accolade, Ray felt the response was tepid.

Herb Kahn joined Ray and shook his hand. "Ray, why on earth did the sheriff come out today?"

"You heard the announcer, he's never missed a parade. Larry will be elected anyway. Herb, I believe we have you to thank for a different spirit, an uplifting spirit, here today. Thank you for your generosity in outfitting the kids with uniforms. What an idea!"

"Give credit where it's due--Gloria Knight." He reached into his pocket and removed an envelope. "Speaking of Gloria, she sent me her Wanamaker's ads for a swimsuit and lingerie. She says she's keeping up with her studies. My friend, tell Byron to come by the store. I have more contributions."

Ray saw Andy Foyle and Inez Farley in a gathering of their classmates. "How's college, Andy?"

Andy smiled and shrugged his shoulders. "It's not as tough as I expected, except for freshman algebra. I sure do miss having Joe explaining what the teacher is really saying. By the way, what's happening with Joe? Why haven't they let him out pending the appeal?"

"They never do that. Sunny just came back from Canon City, and he says it's hard for Joe, but he's adjusting. The good news is that Joe is now a high school graduate. He scored very high on his GED test."

"Why didn't he get a diploma from here?" asked Andy.

"A call and a letter from Lyle Knight to the school board."

"I might have known. But what surprises me is that after all I did for Joe last summer, Lyle was downright warm today, real fatherly like."

Thus went the conversations of the class of forty-six about themselves and those who didn't attend, especially Joe and Gloria. Early on, Andy climbed up on a chair. With his nonalcoholic drink held high, he proposed a toast. "To Joe and Gloria, may this year bring them happiness! May they find their way home in time for next year's homecoming!"

Still dressed for a cold November day, Gloria entered the dorm room ahead of her roommate after dinner. She pointed at the dozen roses sitting on the small table between their beds. "Jenny, oh, Jenny, you hit the jackpot last weekend. My oh my, one dozen red roses! What are you gonna do?"

"I don't know. Nobody ever sent me flowers before, let alone a dozen red roses. Maybe my date is trying to make amends for Sunday afternoon. It's Wednesday, he'll call tonight." Jenny grinned and her green eyes sparkled as she peeled off her wool trench coat and her scarf.

"Don't give him the time of the day."

"Why?" asked a surprised Jenny.

"Remember what you said Sunday, that all he wanted was a fuck. You're worth more than a dozen roses."

"Gloria, you're gross. You act so tough, so cold toward men, then cry yourself to sleep. You're going to miss out if you ..." Jenny took the card out of the little envelope. "Hey! These roses aren't for me, they're for you!"

"No, you're kidding." Gloria came around behind her and looked over her shoulder.

Jenny read from the card, "'Thanks. I couldn't have done it without you. You're one hell of a campaigner. I owe you one, Ray.' Who is Ray? Or should I even ask?" Jenny handed the card to her roommate.

Gloria's blue eyes came to life, then quickly overflowed with tears. She took the card from Jenny and held it to her breast. *He won! He won. Joe, Joe.*

"So you had an affair with a married man and he's lonely? Is Ray's divorce final?" gibed Jenny.

Gloria shook her head. "No, nothing like that. Ray Tudbury is the man I worked for last summer. He just won the November election. Thank God! Yes, thank God, maybe my Joe ..." She paused and looked at her roommate, "Jenny, can I trust you? I mean *really* trust you to keep a confidence even if it's something that really offends you?"

Jenny sat on her bed facing her friend. She reached out for Gloria's hands. "You are a bit quirky, but all in all, a wonderful roommate. I'm here to listen, and you should know me well enough by now to know I can keep my mouth shut. Tell me what makes you the mystery woman who gets the roses."

Gloria began, "I'm not the good girl you think I am. I'll go back to the beginning. The first boy I ever seduced was a camp counselor during the summer of forty-two. I was thirteen." She told Jenny about her soldier lover, Paul Bixler, who had humiliated her with his postcards. She waxed long about her true love, Joe, and his unjust treatment. She wove in her father's role and how everything was riding on Ray Tudbury's following through to free her fiancé. She concluded, "I only deserve two letters a month after what I did. The worst part of the pain is bracing myself for when Joe realizes that he deserves far better than me. I dread the day when all I will have ahead will be emptiness until I die. At least now, I have hope. I have Ray's promise."

"But Gloria, you've lived ... you've had adventure. Look at me, why, I'm close to nineteen and I'm still a virgin. For the first time, you've made me feel like I missed something."

"Hold onto it, Jenny. Keep yourself whole. With every new man, you leave a bit of you behind. Don't be fooled into letting yourself be used."

"You've said it far more convincingly than Mother. Come home with me this weekend. My father has contacts. He can get you the help Joe needs."

The two victorious Democratic candidates turned at the sound of the door to Ray's law suite opening. Byron Haskins came through the door with his right hand wrapped in an elastic bandage. Ray asked, "What happened to your hand?"

"I got so mad, I hit the wall. If I ever get my hands on Diamond, I'll kill the fat pig."

Larry asked, "Where is he and what did he do?"

"I don't know where he disappeared to. Do you remember that little tale Mary told about the seventeen-year-old whom Diamond put through an ordeal and then paid her fifty bucks?"

"Vaguely."

"That was Mary! And the older man was our town sawbones, Dr. Mundal! I really messed up. After what I know about what Diamond did to Gloria, I simply blew up. Mary's probably still scared out of her wits."

"How did you find out?" Larry pulled a notepad out of his pocket.

"When I asked her to marry me, she said there was a secret she had to tell because it might change my mind. What I should have done, what I want to do, is take her in my arms and tell her that no one will ever harm her as long as I breathe."

Ray was excited. "This is the missing piece in the puzzle regarding Joe Caulfels. John was holding this over the doc's head. When the dust settles, we will have a case of subornation against the doctor."

"You're in line behind the feds," said Byron. "I just came from the courthouse, and the county commissioners are in a dither. We are now short a sheriff, prosecutor, and county treasurer."

Larry said, "I don't understand. What does this have to do with the sawbones?"

"Criminal tax evasion. The IRS has been investigating our local hoi polloi, and they cast the net wide enough to draw in Dr. Mundal. Seems he was being paid in cash under the table. But he'd been reporting payment in firewood and produce since the lean times of the thirties, and he just kept on doing that. So today Dr. Mundal and some of the other notable and notorious of this county, including the prosecutor and treasurer, were seen boarding the afternoon train in handcuffs."

"Wow!" said Larry, "I'd like to have seen that. But you mentioned the sheriff. Did they take him too?"

"Unfortunately Sheriff Hanlon was not among them. He had a stroke while they were questioning him. He's in the hospital and, for now at least, incapacitated."

Ray was already on his feet, lifting his new Stetson hat off the hat rack and reaching for his wool topcoat with a fur collar. "Arrested? Hospitalized? This gives a whole new meaning to the term 'lame ducks.' Come on, Larry! Let's go meet with the commissioners and see if we can start our terms early."

Larry shook his head. "First things first. We don't leave a soldier out in the field. Let's get over to Mary's and put in some good words for Byron. I can't think of a finer couple in Goodwin County."

CHAPTER 21
Christmas 1946

While riding west with a classmate for Christmas vacation, Andy mulled over the weeks of news stories in the Denver papers about Goodwin County's scandals. There were plenty of charges besides tax evasion or non-filing of tax returns with the feds. The state attorney general's office was questioning sources of income well beyond salaries as evidence of malfeasance in office. The sheriff's office was under investigation for payoffs to a Denver crime family boss, deaths of county jail prisoners, and falsification of vouchers. Much to Andy's surprise, Gloria and Lyle Knight's names were conspicuously absent from the drama spelled out in the papers. He was sure Gloria was the instigator who got the wheels turning. He was also sure that Lyle was as guilty as any of them.

It wasn't until his friend turned onto Garfield Street that he saw the natural beauty of the Christmas season. The wind had whipped lines of high-country powder snow into ever-changing, exotically shaped drifts. Above, the late afternoon sunlight passed through ice frozen on branches of leafless trees as if they had been decorated with diamonds. There ahead was the Foyles' modest house overshadowed by the Knight mansion. The single Christmas wreath, threadbare of needles, on the Foyles' door was the same one his father had hung in December nineteen forty-one before he went to war. Andy contrasted it to the Knights' display, where lights were strung along the eaves, augmented by a larger wreath lighted in mid-afternoon and a big, well-lighted tree that filled a front room window.

After Andy was greeted and hugged by his mother Celeste and sister Carole, he joined them in the kitchen. He lifted the lid off a pot and sniffed. "Boy, it sure smells good! I can't tell you the times in Boulder that I've looked down at a plate of what was supposed to be fit for human consumption and thought of being right here in this kitchen."

Carole chimed in. "Do I hear a touch of homesickness? I can't believe my ears."

"Just you wait, Sis. Your time will come." Andy looked out the window. "Do you know when Gloria is coming home?"

"No idea, we're out of touch. She's written me only two one-page notes," Carole replied.

Celeste looked up from her bowl. "I've tried my best to be a good neighbor to Mrs. Knight. Hardly anyone speaks to her outside her WCTU circle at her church. I've learned not to ask if they've heard from Gloria. As best as I can tell, they've heard nothing. I must say that the splitting of that family has produced almost as much fallout as the A-bomb at Bikini."

"Do you think Mr. Knight will go to jail?" said Andy.

Carole shrugged her shoulders. "Ray Tudbury told me that if they ever catch Deputy Four Eff and he talks, he'll tie Mr. Knight to the framing of Joe. It's called suborning of perjury. Andy, do you remember the search grid we set up by the river?"

"Yes, what about it?"

"Ray said it is key evidence in the appeal and in the charges against the deputies. He said to give everyone a pat on the back."

"More important than Gloria's and her father's bad blood," Celeste commented, "our county government is in shambles. Sheriff Hanlon passed away, and most of his deputies are either in jail or in hiding. His wife and John Diamond are both fugitives. The Republican Board of Commissioners appointed a Republican to serve out the term as sheriff. Larry thought he could start his term early, but they said no way."

Andy asked, "What about prosecutor?"

"That has been our local soap opera. The canvassing board certified Larry and Ray as winners after Sheriff Hanlon died and Jim Gulette was arrested. Everything was going according to the law. The county commissioners declared the offices vacant and solicited applicants."

"Why do that when you have certified winners?"

"Politics, simply politics. Mr. Gulette negotiated with the federal prosecutor to resign immediately in exchange for a shorter prison sentence. The Republican Party chair nominated Trevor Lyman as interim prosecutor. Vera told the board why she felt Lyman was unfit and asked them to stop stalling."

"Joe's mother has good reason to say that."

"The result was, Goodwin County was without a prosecutor from just before Thanksgiving until the commissioners held a special meeting and appointed Ray on Christmas Eve. At the same meeting, the treasurer's clerk informed them that, due to legal expenses, the county is broke until January tax proceeds are booked. On top of that, I'm afraid the local economy may collapse because the IRS has been grabbing so many people's money and seizing what they own."

It doesn't surprise me, thought Andy. *The county was rotten all the way through.* He asked, "Mom, how about Mr. Knight?"

Celeste gave a wry little laugh. "It's amazing how much trouble you can avoid with a platoon of good lawyers. Now I know how Moses crossed the Red Sea. He sent a phalanx of lawyers ahead and arrived on the far shore with dry feet."

That's easy for her to say. I saw all those papers Gloria had when I worked with Byron Haskins. Mr. Knight is in shit up to his eyeballs. What goes around will eventually come around.

Celeste put her arm around her son's shoulder. "I know how you feel. The Knights are going through a terrible crisis. It would be very easy for me to give in to emotion and join the crowd. But they are our neighbors, and Lyle Knight, for all his faults, has been wonderful to this family. Since your father died, we have always celebrated Christmas Eve together. We'll do it again this year, and for the right reason. We are celebrating the birth of our Savior."

"What do you want me to do?"

"Thank you, Andy, I want you to take over this stack of presents. Be sensitive, especially to Mrs. Knight. Today is Gloria's birthday. She should have arrived on the morning train."

While Andy was placing the Christmas presents under the Knights' tree, Lyle answered the front door. His commanding Southern accent boomed through the house, "Like hell she did! Of all the inconsiderate damned nerve!"

He walked into the living room and handed his wife a telegram. "This explains why she wasn't on the train."

Theo's hands were shaking as she read the telegram out loud, "'PULLMAN TICKETS ORIGINATING BRYN MAWR PENNSYL-VANIA VIA CHICAGO AND DENVER TO GOODWIN COLORA-DO EXCHANGED FOR ROUND TRIP COACH TO CANON CITY COLORADO.' Oh, my stars! How could she do this?"

Andy spoke up. "I guess she really meant it. On her way out of town, time and again she said that if she were lucky, she'd never see Goodwin again."

Theo tossed the telegram on the table. "Why didn't you say something?"

He shrugged his shoulders. "I thought you knew."

Theo said, "We bought her a round trip ticket in September. Looking back on it, I guess she has been sending us this message. We have not heard one word, not one postcard even, since she left, except the time she was required to answer the phone in the provost's office."

"Isn't there a court order forbidding her from seeing Joe?" asked Andy.

"It expires today on her eighteenth birthday," answered Lyle. "The out-of-town judge ignored the fact that she is still a minor, still our child. The state attorney general stuck his oar in. He said she is a conscientious citizen who has reached the age of consent for marriage. Why don't they mind their own business and stay down there in Denver?" He swept the telegram into a wastebasket,

On Christmas Eve, Lyle ushered the Foyle family into his spacious living room. "Thank you all for coming and helping us celebrate the holidays. You are truly good neighbors." He seated Celeste, Carole, and Andy on the oversized couch that faced the warmth of the fireplace.

One chair was empty. Lyle looked at it and mused, *Gloria should be sitting there. Theo warned me about how she changed. I marveled so much at my own daughter's skills, her encyclopedic mind, and her hard work that I ignored what she was up to.* The banker stoked his fireplace. *I must keep a door open. She is my only child.*

He tweaked the dial on his new Philco console radio. *Now that's my kind of music. Too bad about that accountant who bought our own station KMOO. He should have known better than to cheat on his taxes. If Gloria hadn't given the IRS his name, he would have slipped through unseen. I'll have the station back through foreclosure before he gets that TV license he applied for.*

Theo came in with a tray of hot cider and bowls of cookies, nuts, and dates rolled in powdered sugar. "Lyle, dear, a toast."

Lyle held up his cup of hot cider. "Here is to a merry Christmas to the most wonderful friends and neighbors, the Foyles. Without you, there would be no joy in this house. God bless you all." He paused and took a sip. *There was a time when my little girl hung onto every word. I miss Gloria.*

While her husband sat staring out the window, Theo went to the tree and hefted a small but weighty package. "I'm so excited. Gloria didn't forget us after all. I can hardly wait to see what's in her package. Lyle, would you like to do the honors?"

Hell, no. Isn't it enough that she chose not to come home? Lyle wrinkled his nose, then smiled. "No, dear, I'll not take away from your pleasure."

All in the room watched Theo's shaking hands as she went to work on the present. After the ribbon fell and the paper was torn, a sheet of red-hued typing paper was revealed. A small trail of brick dust sifted out and down. "What on earth is this?" The brick came fully into view as the sheet of paper fell to the table.

Theo held up the brick with one hand and turned the sheet over with the other. Even before she had time to read a paragraph, her hands began to shake. She never let her eyes move from the paper during her walk to the nearest chair. "Oh my stars ... we've lost her forever. Listen to this. 'No matter the outcome, I have decided that I don't want to be related to you. If a parent can disinherit a child, it follows that a child can break the ties as well. You cut me too deep ...'" Theo's voice trailed off.

Lyle took the letter and brick from his wife. "What has she done now?"

The tendons in Lyle's jaw worked as he walked in a circle, reading. His eyes scanned to the last sentence before he read, "The children, if they come, will be told that their grandparents are dead." At that he crumpled the letter into a ball and threw it toward the fire burning in the hearth. Instead the crumpled letter flew up almost to the ceiling and fell not far from his feet.

A short, cynical laugh escaped his lips. *That look Theo gave me. Oh, I've done it now.* He kicked the scrunched-up paper. All eyes followed its bouncing, curved path that left it just short of the hearth.

Theo stood and held her head with both hands. "Lyle, how can you be so heartless?"

He paused and looked at his wife. "This is a bluff. I have no one else to leave my estate to. They're all dead!"

Celeste walked to the fallen paper. She smoothed it. "I'm afraid this is not a bluff. The second letter Carole got from Gloria asked for addresses for a list of people. It was mid-November, and I thought she was compiling addresses for cards. See, it says here, 'Copy to' and it's followed by the names she asked for. She's announcing this to everyone she knows."

"She used me," said Carole. "I didn't know. I am so sorry. We'll talk with her. Hopefully she'll change her mind."

What have I raised up, a monster? Lyle drew his arm back and pitched the brick through the living room window. "Damn you! Damn you, Gloria MacAfee Knight. Damn you to eternal damnation!"

The glass had just fallen when Theo pulled him away. "Look at what you've done now! Not to see my own grandchildren? Gloria has been the light of my life. You planted the seed when you threatened to disinherit her ..."

The banker's voice had lost its theatrical power. "Theo, please don't."

"What could I have done to keep her from being an alley cat?" wailed his wife.

"I thought she had learned something after that Bixler boy." Lyle opened his arms. "Come, dear, let's not ruin Christmas for everyone. It's the time of thanksgiving and good cheer."

"Not ruin Christmas for everyone? You baited her. Now you lost your temper. You threw the brick through the window. It'll drop well below freezing tonight."

Gloria, in a plain long-sleeved dress, couldn't keep her eyes off Joe as he made his way across the crowded prison dining room to the square table where she sat with his parents. The boy she remembered from high school was now a man in prison uniform, who exuded a sense of calm acceptance. Instead of a kiss, however brief, he held her hands ever so briefly before greeting his parents as if he had walked in the door from work.

He took his seat opposite Gloria and extended his arms toward his parents. "We can't dawdle because they will be setting up for Christmas dinners until six. Come, let us pray that we may honor the Lord on his birthday."

All four held hands with their heads bowed. Orville asked his son to lead the blessing. Joe began, "Heavenly Father, we thank thee that thou hast brought us together that we may celebrate thy birthday. We ask thee to bless this food which we are about to eat. We ask thee to teach us forgiveness that our cup may be emptied of the bile of hate and be filled with the nectar of thy love. In Christ's name we pray, amen."

Gloria held onto Vera's and Orville's hands. "Thank you for allowing me to be part of your Christmas."

She had to lean forward to place her hands between Joe's. She was very much aware of how rough and strong his hands had become. "The sound of your voice, your words, the touch of your hand all make me feel at peace. My insides have been tied in knots since they took you from me. Nothing good has come of this ..."

"Nothing good? Just a minute, Ma, Pa, do you think I ought to marry this girl?"

Vera placed her hand atop theirs. "If you don't, Joe Caulfels, I'll be sorely disappointed. She is as fine and brave a woman as I have ever met."

Joe smiled and motioned toward Orville and Vera. "See? Something good came of it. You have won over two of the most hard-headed people in Goodwin County. When I get out, it will be my turn to change hearts."

Gloria pulled her hands back. "That won't be necessary. I disowned my parents."

"Have you lost all love for them? I've been here long enough to learn that the cons who are really burned out did it to themselves with hate." Joe touched his chest. "The only place I have to call my own is my heart. I've found it isn't big enough to hold both hate and love."

Gloria's eyes filled with tears, and she shook her head. "I can't go back, ever. I burned every bridge behind me. And how will Mother ever forgive me if Daddy goes to prison?"

"I forgave you. I've forgiven them all."

She lowered her eyes. "For me to be good, I need you at my side. What should I do, write them to apologize?"

Orville said, "No, don't do a damn thing. Your father never was arrested. He's too rich and slippery to get caught. Mark my words, when all the dust has settled, he'll be a richer and more powerful man than he was when it all started."

Joe tried to interject, "Pa ..."

"Don't take a step until you have something they want," continued Orville, "like to see their first grandchild. Of course, if he sends you any signals, you could change your mind."

Gloria unfolded a letter from her pocket and held it so Joe could read it. "Thanks, Pa, you made my day. Joe, you will be contacted by Mr. Simon Dadoun and Mr. Felix Frankman. They are attorneys for the American Civil Liberties Union."

"That's the damn outfit that was started by the Communists," fumed Orville.

"Pa, I know that, but they do some good stuff," said Gloria, "and we are betting the best years of Joe's life on one appeal. Frankman is a top constitutional lawyer and the ACLU is paying for everything--that is, Joe, if you will accept him. Please say yes."

Joe nodded yes.

Gloria ate and listened to Joe. Between her own thoughts of love and desire, she felt his inner calm and strength as he talked about finding purpose in his life, one day at a time, and how his faith was seeing him through. He described the satisfaction he had from teaching basic algebra to other inmates. The minutes swiftly passed until she only had time to tell in the briefest terms that she had been granted a full-ride scholarship plus a modest stipend. She added that she had a part-time job two days a week in addition to periodic modeling assignments. She didn't say where the job was. With other inmates within earshot, she didn't think it wise to mention that her job was working in the Montgomery County Sheriff's Department as a file clerk, or that they agreed to let her use the firing range one day a week.

On the ringing of the bell, all the guests arose and moved toward the exit door. Joe and the other prisoners remain seated. Gloria bent over and took Joe's face in both hands. She said, "Yes, I will marry you, Joseph Corwin Caulfels." She kissed him squarely on the mouth. He stiffened for a moment, then accepted her advance. Gloria walked away, rolling her hips in the best runway style she knew, then turned at the door and blew him a kiss. *I love you, Joe. However long it takes, I will wait.*

The day after Christmas, Gloria stood tall in a pay phone booth at the nearly empty Denver Union Station. She smiled on hearing the other end pick up. "Thank goodness, I finally caught you in the office."

"Well, Gloria! Good to hear from you. Where in blazes are you?" asked Ray.

"Denver, and it's almost time to board my train east. They only let me spend an hour with my Joe."

"Was it worth all that travel for an hour?"

"Yes! I've gotten to know Ma and Pa. We had Christmas dinner together with Joe. Those were the happiest minutes I've had since last spring. Ray, Joe still loves me. We want to get married as soon as we can."

"Gloria, with him in prison ... that's a tough way to start life ..."

"I don't want it any other way. I made my commitment last May. I know there is no guarantee that the appeals court will let him go. And if they don't, I'm going to stick by him no matter how long it takes. Right now, I'm counting the minutes until his appeal is heard."

"Who's representing Joe?"

"Simon Dadoun and Felix Frankman. They're from Philadelphia."

"Where are you and the Caulfels going to get that kind of money?"

"The ACLU is taking the case."

Ray replied, "Congratulations, you continue to amaze me. Joe is a very lucky man to have you."

"He'd be a lot luckier if he wasn't serving time because of me."

"That letter you wrapped around that brick is the talk of the town. How will you ever finish college?"

"Thanks to you, I have a full four-year scholarship through the Carnegie Foundation, with a hundred dollars a month spending money. The prison regulations say that only the court that convicted Joe can object to the marriage. Who's the judge since Judge Costi croaked?"

"He hasn't been replaced. We're serviced by circuit riding judges, so we get a different one about every month. Some are retired judges acting *pro tem*, and others may come from across the Divide. So none of them will know your history. Before acting, though, the court will pass the marriage request to my office for comment."

Gloria crossed her fingers. "Thank you very much, Ray. What's happened to the Sheriff's Department?"

"Charges have been filed against four deputies and all the jailers except Stokings."

"I thought you'd take office in January."

"Officially, yes, Gulette is history. He took the plea deal that included his resignation. I was sworn in on Christmas Eve."

"How about that creep, Diamond?" She crossed her fingers.

"He and Marcia Hanlon are fugitives. There have been no leads." Ray cleared his throat. "Without Diamond, I don't have sufficient evidence to try your father."

They haven't found him yet. Thank you, Lord. Maybe Ma's prayers are working. It's only a matter of time, though, until they come for me. "Ray, we're planning to get married this June after my spring term. May I ask one more favor?"

"What's that?

"You're the kind of man I wish my father had been. Would you please give me away?"

"Gloria, that would be really awkward. I would hope you attempt a reconciliation with your parents."

"You sound just like Joe. He's not pleased either with what I did to them. Oh, there's the 'All aboard,' I have to run, 'bye."

CHAPTER 22
The Long Winter

The Christmas holidays had been islets of pleasant memories. Gloria's life settled into a frantic routine that on the surface changed little with the season until the school year ended in late May. Jenny came to expect her roommate to put in eighteen- to twenty-hour days. Her hallmarks on campus were her drab, oversized suits. She made time to write Joe and to enjoy a weekend a month at the Vaughans'. The Montgomery County sheriff was impressed with this Bryn Mawr student, who was as accurate on the tactical firing range as his own deputies.

Those who saw her on the train, or somewhere else in public, came away impressed by her beauty and poise, as well as how studious she was. She picked up a New York agent in mid-January, a cousin of Herb Kahn. By Easter he had her booked to the limit she felt comfortable with.

Spring break was devoted to giving depositions regarding Joe's appeal. In the early segments, she felt the hostility and disbelief of the Pennsylvania AG attorneys who were standing in for Colorado's AG office. By day's end, however, she sensed there had been a turning point. Questions were parsed in ways that made her feel the lawyers had become uncomfortable with representing Goodwin County. Both of Joe's attorneys said that what happened to Joe wouldn't be allowed to occur in Pennsylvania. Just short of noon on the second day, the session ended. The older counsel representing Colorado and Goodwin County expressed his disgust with Joe and Gloria's treatment.

In early May, Gloria got a letter from the prison giving tentative approval, provided Gloria attend counseling sessions prior to the ceremony.

Letters from friends back in Goodwin told her they recognized her as the new model whose poses graced several half- and full-page ads showing manufacturers' spring and Easter fashions. Gloria learned from Herb Kahn that there was a chill in the Knight household over a scrapbook Theo assembled of those ads. Lyle had torn it up. Herb made a new one. Lyle let Theo keep it, provided she kept it out of sight.

While Gloria's portfolio grew, her collection of *Goodwin Globe* headlines also grew:

January 4: QUESTIONS RAISED ABOUT FIRE DEATHS ON BLACKMON SPREAD

January 16: AG ASSUMES CAULFELS APPEAL: COUNTY WILL PAY

January 24: COMMISSIONERS BLAME PROSECUTOR TUDBURY FOR SHORTFALL

February 9: EX-TREASURER SAYS HE'S SORRY

March 16: FOUL PLAY SUSPECTED IN KEY WITNESS'S DISAPPEARANCE

April 6: BANKER NOT CHARGED BUT WILL TESTIFY

April 20: TUDBURY CHARGES GULETTE WITH SUBORNATION OF PERJURY

April 21: PUBLIC DEFENDER LYMAN WILL FIGHT DISBARMENT FOR INCOMPETENCE

May 17: GOODWIN WITHOUT DOCTOR; MUNDAL SENT TO LEAVENWORTH

May 31: CONFESSED RAPIST TO MARRY VICTIM

Joe left the dining room that Christmas to step back into a routine that was the same endless circle of bars, guards, lines, menial janitorial work, meetings with a chaplain wearing clerical garb, and tutoring other prisoners in math. He met with the ACLU attorneys, who gave him every impression that they were ready to step into the ring and come out swinging in his behalf. What Joe lived for was the day when he would reach up to place his fingers on the screen in the visiting room to match Gloria's.

The wish to see her intended was in Gloria's heart as well. However, the day she arrived wasn't a visiting day, so she got started on her high-priority goal to line up a summer job in Canon City. She had applied to work at every bank within a hundred miles of the pen, but there wasn't that much interest in part-time tellers. The first bank she chose for an interview was the one closest to the prison. At the end of the interview, she was invited into the president's office. She was surprised to be offered a position as his assistant to perform an internal audit. He wanted her to follow the same checklist she used at her father's bank. She accepted with the understanding that she would have the audit completed by the end of July. Her modeling assignments were fully booked for August and well into September.

Joe had warned her, both in letters and during visits, about the one man he felt was his nemesis, Mr. Russell Karkian, counselor. She had to book her visits with Joe through him. She was annoyed at his response when she tried to change the time for her appointment. "Look here, Miss Knight, don't expect us to make it easy to meet requirements. Miss or be late for your one fifteen-minute window in June and you make it easy for me. I'll reschedule for the second week in September."

When she came for the fifteen-minute conference, she was surprised that a man so short could have so commanding a voice over the phone. Dressed in a cream-colored cotton suit and a black leather bow tie, the fortyish counselor reminded her of men she had seen reduced to tears by her father. He directed her to a hard, wobbly wooden chair. Beyond greetings when she came in, he said nothing. His eyes focused on a two-inch-thick folder with her name on it and roamed to stare at her figure. His activity was to thumb through her file and place three-by-five cards on different pages. She recognized some of them as green-bordered stationery from her father's bank. *What's this? Does my father have a stooge even here, three counties away?*

Well before Karkian completed his leisurely review of the file, the fifteen minutes came and went. The smell of men confined--a mixture of sweat, human waste, and the products used to clean them up--wasn't as strong as in the visiting area, but gradually started to stifle Gloria. She felt annoyed but waited in silence, while in her mind she was sure her every garment would have to be sanitized.

Once that task was completed, Karkian rose from his chair to use the pencil sharpener across the room. She felt his eyes undress her both on the way out and the way back. As much as she wanted to speak up, she remained quiet.

Karkian smiled while he made a few scratches on the pad in front of him. "I can understand what would draw any man, in here or outside, to commit to nuptials even without the prospect of consummation. You are one hot-looking piece of ass."

Hot-looking what? What a demeaning asshole! He thinks I'll break off the interview. Gloria still sat in silence.

He rolled a cigarette along his full lower lip before lighting it, then blew a lungful of smoke in her face. "Just because those high-powered ACLU attorneys can intimidate some circuit-riding mountain judge into a tentative approval, doesn't mean you will marry this year or at all."

Gloria waved the cloud of tobacco smoke away from her face. *Hold your temper. Superintendent Carberry didn't talk like this.* "What possible objection would you have?"

"Immaturity. They granted approval for this very ill-advised marriage over my very vehement objections. Your father, both personally and through his attorneys, very strongly disapproves of this marriage. Noting that you are still a minor ..."

She recalled what Ray had told her. "Mr. Karkian, the state code specifically gives me the freedom to marry whomever I choose now that I have passed my eighteenth birthday. My father's opinions are none of your business."

"He is your guardian in a legal sense."

"He may *want* to be, but I have disowned him. I am financially independent of him to the extent that he can no longer claim me as a dependent on his tax return. Once I'm married to Joe, Daddy can whistle 'Dixie.'"

"I have here your request to use a police firing range. Are you carrying a firearm?"

"What's this all about? I'm an employee of the Montgomery County Sheriff's Department."

"Never heard of Montgomery County. Your father says you were intent on stealing his gun."

"My bigoted father hates Joe's guts. Come off it."

"Tell me what went on between you and number eight-four-two-six-three that got him twenty years to life."

"Me and *who*?"

"Joseph Caulfels' convict number is eight-four-two-six-three."

"I resent that kind of reference. Call my man by his name."

"You'd better commit that number to memory, because that is how we identify felons. You still haven't answered my question, Miss Knight."

"Nothing went on but corruption, prejudice, and incompetence on the part of the county. That's why it's being appealed."

"Come on, kid. You two were bare assed ..."

"Mr. Karkian, I am prepared to report to the superintendent that you are among the most insensitive and obscene boors I have met ..."

"This counseling session ..."

"End our meeting without approval and I must react. This marriage is my way of making a terrible wrong right. Do I have to arrange for counsel to be present?"

"That won't be necessary, Miss Knight."

"Fine. Let's get this over with."

"You do have the gun, a Smith and Wesson?"

"Mr. Karkian, I am a citizen of the United States. Based on my part-time reserve position with Montgomery County, Pennsylvania, I submitted a request to use the local range concurrent with my purchase of an S&W. I can't see what this has to do with Joe and me." *Maybe it was a mistake to buy that revolver, especially if they find Four Eff's body this summer. Daddy must have put him up to this.*

She watched him shake the point of his pencil at her. "Perhaps you plan to assist in his escape."

"Knowing Joe as I do, I don't think he'd run if you left the front door open."

"Then why carry?"

"I was raped by the same man that they let get away with the attempted murder of my fiancé. He's out there somewhere."

Karkian went through his laundry list of all the reasons why she shouldn't marry Joe in a monotone voice while she drummed her nails on his desk. He turned his attention to the pad, on which he began scribbling. "My recommendation to Superintendent Carberry will be to delay this very ill-advised marriage until you can accept the counseling necessary. I feel that you are rushing into this match ..."

Joe needs me to be his wife before his appeal is heard. "Mr. Karkian, are you familiar with the discovery phase of civil litigation?"

He signed the sheet, ripped it free of the pad, and held it out for her to take. "Planning to sue? Miss Knight, that was absolutely the dumbest tactic. I take that as a threat."

She replied, "Like I said, I lead an exemplary life. The question that will have to be answered is ... Do you? I have extensive knowledge of how my father makes discreet payoffs. You will have to answer whether you have a sweetheart mortgage or have made investments that are just too good to be true. If my attorneys discover evidence of wrongdoing, such as tax fraud, it will be turned over to the appropriate authorities."

She watched the color drain from his face as she concluded, "I'll only do battle if I can't marry Joe."

The balding man stared at her through his thick glasses, then pulled some mimeographed forms from a file and fed carbon paper between them. "A fine young woman of your background; tying up with a convicted half-breed criminal. These prison marriages seldom work out. It's my job to get you to face reality."

Once he was done, he pushed a mimeographed form across the desk for her signature. "I thought when I read your file that I'd be talking with an impressionable teenager, who was marrying her boyfriend because she thought she'd be doing the right thing. Instead I found myself at sword's point with as tough a young cookie as I've met in quite a while. I think you will even the score with anybody who gets in your way. Be careful, or by the time Joe Caulfels is out, you'll be in ... and in for good."

Do they know about Four Eff? Gloria nodded. "Have you ever been raped?"

"No. Of course not."

"Then get off my back and sign the form. Now where is this Father Covell?"

A middle-aged prison guard escorted Gloria to the chaplain's office, where an Episcopalian priest warmly greeted her. "I am so pleased to meet you, Miss Knight. I'm Father Covell. Please come in and have a seat. I just brewed a fresh pot of coffee, would you care for a cup?"

Minutes later Gloria sat forward on her chair with elbows on her knees and holding the coffee cup with both hands. Mentally she braced herself for another hazing like the one she endured with Karkian. Instead the priest chatted about the un-springlike weather across the West and his concern about the effects of the atom bombs tested at Bikini. He segued so smoothly from the weather to how she and Joe met, that she felt the tension of her last session vanish.

He opened a dog-eared copy of the Book of Common Prayer. Soon Gloria found herself unable to stop crying, overwhelmed by feelings of grief and blame. She confessed her fear that she wasn't good enough to be Joe's wife.

Yet she found herself clinging to every word, for this priest was counseling her as if she and Joe would step out into the world following the ceremony. He probed her feelings about her commitment to Joe. He very gently let her know what kind of job opportunities her future husband would have. He made her aware of the emotional problems Joe would face in adjusting to the outside world.

A knock on the door interrupted the briefing. She jumped to her feet. Her heart was pounding at the sight of Joe. The guard stepped between them. As long as he was present, they stood and looked at each other. When the latch clicked shut, Father Covell said, "Go ahead, hug your fiancé."

As the seconds ticked off, Gloria put her arms around Joe so she could feel the muscles in his back. She pressed hard against him. She wanted a second, third, and even a fourth and fifth kiss. She became aware of his warm brown eyes when he held her at arm's length. *I know I should say something, anything. All I can think about is what I can't have.*

Joe guided her to a chair in front of the chaplain's desk. "It's not like you to be so quiet. Has the cat got your tongue?"

She smiled. "I'll be okay. I'll be good."

"That Karkian, what did he do? What did he say?"

She shook her head vigorously. "A lot less than my father or the pastor back home. He finally signed off, so I can't complain."

Father Covell looked quizzical. "I'm surprised he signed off after he talked to your father. He swore he wouldn't."

If he hadn't talked to my father, he never would have signed, Gloria thought.

Joe said to Gloria, "With your acceptance, I want to marry following the liturgy of the Episcopal Church."

She picked up the little red prayer book. *As long as they don't call me names because I was raped.* She thought of the reaction of the Knight family's preacher a year earlier when she told him about what happened. The preacher's words, "fornicator, adulterer," now came to her mind whenever the word "church" was spoken. Since then she had only gone through the motions of prayer or religious services. *I was pretending when I prayed with the Caulfels family at Christmas. But Joe embraces religion enough that he could be a preacher himself.*

She thumbed through a number of pages, then placed the book back on the table as it were made of glass. "Joe, what's important to me is that I want to be part of your family. I have no preference."

"Father Covell is Episcopalian. I would like for him to bless us with words from the Book of Common Prayer."

Her impression of Father Covell was positive. She was convinced that he and Joe were on very good terms as he went through the marriage vows with them. During the discussions on their meaning, Joe did most of the talking. She had no doubts about whose word would be final. If Joe was using marriage to her as a get-out-of-jail-free card, she didn't see it. She worried about the hurt Joe would feel when they arrested her for Four Eff's murder.

The chaplain wound up the meeting after he explained, step by step, how the marriage ceremony would take place and signed off on the form. His last words weren't a blessing, but a warning that her soon-to-be husband would be called back into the daily routine a half-hour after the ceremony was over.

On the way to the front guard post, Father Covell said, "I know the two of you are expecting the court to throw out the conviction, but let me give you another slant. In the ten years I've been at this prison, seldom have I found an individual who so plainly should not be on the wrong side of the wall. Yet that's where the Lord has placed him. If this appeal comes out wrong, I'm sure he'll land on his feet and carry on doing good in here. My last question to you, Gloria, is, what is your contingency plan?"

Gloria felt them staring at her. *The odds are I'll be in prison for life*, were the words that swirled through her mind. Then she said, "If I'm alive and free, I'll be there for him."

CHAPTER 23
Gloria and Joe Marry

Gloria gathered up the skirts of her classic, figure-hugging white wedding dress as Ray Tudbury aided her to get into the passenger seat of the white Cadillac touring car. Orville, who was driving, remarked, "My goodness, girl, where did you get that fancy dress?"

"I modeled the Francheska line in March. They made me a deal. I'll get the two hundred dollars back if they can use my wedding pictures." Gloria turned around. "Ma, did you remember to bring everything, the ring and the camera bag with the flashbulbs?"

From his seat behind her, Ray said, "I have the ring and the forms."

Vera, who was wearing the same red dress she had worn to last fall's homecoming, held up the camera bag. "How can you afford such a fancy camera?"

"I borrowed the Leica from my agent for the trip. They'll buy the shots they can use."

Gloria thought it was a perfect day for a wedding. The morning air was clean and cool. There were still little droplets of dew on the grass. Gloria was sure this white Cadillac that brought back so many terrible memories would be different today. She had helped Orville wash and wax it so that it looked new.

As they were turning off the highway toward the parking lot, Vera said, "I hope we don't have a repeat of yesterday morning when Lyle tried to get an injunction to stop the wedding. Thank the Lord we have an attorney here."

Ray said, "That was my first civil action since I was back in Chicago before the war. I do hope that after yesterday, he will forever hold his peace. Gloria, did you say you're going to work this afternoon?"

"Yes, and thank you for the recommendation. I've got a dream job working for the president at Canon City National."

They walked into the visitor's lobby, which was filled with a crowd of young people, all from Goodwin. Gloria said, "Andy, Byron, Mary, what are you doing here? Joe is forbidden to have guests beyond the preapproved wedding party."

Andy said, "We drove all the way from Goodwin and spent the night here because the ceremony is so early. Now you say we can't see the ceremony. What kind of a deal is this, anyway?"

"Joe and I had to sign a letter promising we wouldn't do a list of things. Otherwise--no wedding. Tops on the list is inviting extra people. You are all dear friends and I thank you for coming all the way to Canon City, but I must ..."

Superintendent Carberry burst into the room. "Miss Knight, there will be no wedding. Your letter of instructions was very clear: no guests beyond the wedding party."

I knew it. I knew it. It was too good to be true. Daddy must be laughing up his sleeve. Gloria took a half-dozen steps so she was in front of the superintendent. "You can't do this. I didn't invite them."

"They're here, aren't they?"

Byron said, "Wait a minute, sir. Gloria's right, she didn't invite us. The *Goodwin Globe* ran an article giving the time and place. We're all Joe Caulfels' friends and supporters. Please don't screw up their lives any more just because people care about them."

"It's a safety issue. You're disrupting the regular visitors' accommodations. We can't have civilians mingling inside the walls. Rules here are to be obeyed, or there are consequences."

From the crowd stepped Norm Nadau holding up a press card and the press release. "Consequences? Hugh, you old stinker, you haven't changed a bit. This young man and his family don't deserve this. This press release arrived at my office courtesy of Western Union."

Superintendent Carberry vigorously shook the editor's hand. "Norm, I haven't seen you since you left Canon City years ago. What the hell are you doing covering this? You're the editor of the *Goodwin Globe* now, aren't you?"

"Yes, I made the excuse of a need to come back to the old stomping grounds. The truth of it is, I have a story that needs to be told of a young woman. She turned her back on wealth beyond belief to marry, in prison, the boy of her dreams. That press release was a good follow-on to a feature we printed a week ago last Sunday."

Carberry took the release and read it with care. "It sounds like an invitation to attend the infamous banker's daughter's wedding. Interesting, it originated right here in Canon City. Norm, you know better. Why didn't you give me a call?"

"Hugh, I'm glad you asked that question. Her father asked me not to call, so I found out who sent the telegram--Russell Karkian. Does that ring a bell?"

Carberry rolled his eyes and took a deep breath. "Whatever possessed the man?" He crossed the room and extended his hand to Gloria. "Please accept my apologies. Perhaps I was hasty. The wedding can go on, but it has to be the authorized wedding party only inside the facility."

After Gloria gathered the group outside, she said, "Joe and I are honored that you came. I wish our wedding could be a normal one. Superintendent Carberry bent the rules to allow our marriage so soon. They have given us an hour to complete the ceremony. Then Joe has to go back to his routine. I have missed seeing you. Could you meet us at the Arkansas River Grill up the road about ten thirty?"

Minutes later, the wedding party was brought through the entry process. With Gloria in the lead, they passed through heavy powered gates into a hall that was warm and smelled of sweat and bleach. Two guards, who accompanied them, spread the few prisoners along the walls. Gloria heard the tapping of her heels on the ceramic tile floor, mixed with a few low wolf calls.

She saw Joe standing next to the priest on the far side of the room. For those precious moments his smile and his warm brown eyes were the center of her universe. She was barely aware of his clean prison dungarees and freshly shaved head. Gloria was vaguely aware of taking Ray's arm and walking with him between rows of empty tables with chairs on top of them. *Joe, I am so sorry for what horrible things you must endure. Your appeal has to work. I don't know why they haven't found Four Eff's body. When they do, it will be over for me.*

Vera assumed the role of cameraman and took the first of many pictures, each accompanied by the momentary bright punctuation of a flashbulb.

Gloria listened carefully as Father Covell called out the words that began, "Dearly beloved, we are gathered together here in the sight of God and in the face of this company to join this man and this woman in holy matrimony ..."

She held Joe's hand. It was cool and damp. After the priest had spoken and each of them said the right words and made the right responses, Gloria reminded herself, *These weren't just words, but promises, promises to one another for a lifetime.* As she kissed her new husband, she couldn't ignore what she saw and felt. *Joe is pale and feels clammy. His brow's covered with sweat. What can I do?*

It wasn't until after the kiss and Father Covell's announcement, "May I present to you Mr. and Mrs. Joseph Caulfels," that Gloria put her hand on her husband's cheek. "Are you all right? You feel clammy."

Joe shrugged his shoulders. "I always sweat a lot down here. It's when I stop sweating and my temperature goes up that I really have trouble. I'll be okay. How about some pictures with me kissing the bride?"

Minutes later, Gloria looked out at the small audience through eyes that saw the fading dots of numerous flashes. *I'll always want to be in his arms. I'll bet Joe will make a good lover. How I wish we could do it right now.*

Through a mental fog, with Joe at her side, she watched Ray Tudbury take pictures of Joe's parents. Joe said, "Please, may I have a copy of this picture? I've never seen Ma and Pa so alive and devoted to one another."

Ray put his hand on Joe's shoulder. "Joe, I am very pleased to meet you at last. There was a whole lobby full of people who drove down from Goodwin to witness your marriage. I cannot find the words to express my frustration with the slow pace your case has taken."

"Mr. Prosecutor Tudbury, I have people on my side who have been working at overturning injustice for more than ten years, and they have yet to be heard in court. Thank you for all you are doing. I tell myself every day that the Lord works his will in his own ways. Yet I don't want life to pass me by. I want to graduate from college and be a father. I have the faith that the scales will fall from the appellate judges' eyes. After surviving the Goodwin County jail, I believe in the power of prayer. Please pray for us and especially for the Knights."

Right on the dot at thirty minutes after the ceremony, a third guard entered the room. The lead guard said, "Caulfels, you'll have to take a rain check for the reception and wedding night. Come on, Joe, it's time to get back into the line."

Gloria held the camera out toward the newly arrived guard. "Could you take one picture with all of us and another with Joe and me and the other guards?"

"Why us?" said the lead guard.

"Please, you were witnesses to our vows."

"Sure, be glad to."

Gloria sat next to Ray Tudbury in the largest corner booth at the Arkansas River Grill. Gone was the expensive high-fashion wedding gown and in its place was her shapeless, oversized business suit. The Goodwin contingent had either left or coalesced into small groups. Like the others, she and Ray had ordered lunch.

The front door of the grill banged against the old-fashioned hat rack, sending cowboy hats flying from the conical array of hooks. Ray paused in his answer to questions, causing Gloria to come back out of her dream state to see Prison Counselor Karkian.

Gloria thought, *Look at this guy standing there, mad as hell, with one hand inside his jacket like he's armed. My piece sits in a locker in Montgomery County. I'm blocked in. What to do?* She said, "Ray, what do we do? I don't have a gun. Do you think Karkian's armed?"

"You know this thug?"

"Yes, Russell Karkian, the prison counselor who sent the bogus invite."

"Damn you, Gloria Knight, you cost me my job." He headed for their table with a trio of the wait staff surrounding him.

She remained in her place. "Please sir, call me Mrs. Caulfels. Why would I want you fired?"

Ray said, "Easy, man, easy, don't go off the deep end. Can you answer her question?"

Karkian whispered, "Mrs. Caulfels, you could wait and marry him later. As it stands, I feel you set me up with your disclosure about the press release."

Gloria laid a hand on Ray's forearm. "No, Mr. Karkian, let me guess, you had your eye on Daddy's promised prizes for anyone who delayed or spiked our marriage. He demanded results, and nothing you did worked. So you scripted a press release that was easily mistaken for an invitation and would cause Mr. Carberry to stop the wedding. Well, it didn't work. Please relay to Daddy that it's over."

Russell Karkian shook his head. "No, Mrs. Caulfels, it's not over until your daddy says it's over."

CHAPTER 24
The Bank Holdup

Late on the last Thursday afternoon in September, Theo Knight thumbed back through the news magazine for the fifth time to the page that had the pictures of Gloria's wedding. *What a talented daughter I have. She turned that prison wedding into a fashion shoot. I would have given my last dollar to see her marry that boy.*

She was still rereading the article when the new electric door chimes sounded. *Who could that be? Lyle's going directly to lodge from work.*

She opened the door to see two men wearing tan tank suits with INTERMOUNTAIN embroidered on the right chest. Both wore work gloves. The one with the papers, a short, swarthy man with a full mustache and a straw cowboy hat, smiled. "Mrs. Knight? I have your shipment from Daniels and Fisher."

Behind him the second man wheeled a large packing case on a dolly. She thought he looked nervous, and the way he stared made her nervous. She was about to take a step backward and close the door when she saw a freshly painted step van, blazoned with the words INTER-MOUNTAIN DELIVERY, parked at the curb.

"But I didn't order anything from Denver."

The first man looked at the invoice. "Ordered by Mr. Lyle Knight, it says."

Theo stared at the huge box on the dolly. *I know Lyle can't undo what's happened with Gloria, but he's trying his best to keep our marriage alive.*

"That man! What nice surprise is it this time? Yes, please bring it in."

The second man pushed the dolly in, and she shut the door and followed him. After the crate was in the parlor, the first man suddenly drew a pistol and turned around. "I'm sorry, Mrs. Knight, but I'm going to have to take you hostage. Please place your hands behind your back, palm to palm."

This has to be a joke of some kind. Theo stood tall and pointed at the door. "You cad, sir! How dare you point a gun at me in my own home. Leave at once or I shall scream!"

He moved close enough for her to see up the barrel. "Enough of the theatrics. The gun is for real. Put your hands behind your back, palm against palm. Please, we mean you no harm, we just need your cooperation, ma'am."

Do I take him at his word when he points a gun at me and says he means no harm? After the brick at Christmas, could this be something Gloria thought up? Theo raised her hands and began to slowly retreat. She went toward the kitchen door because the big box blocked her way out the front. "You dare not discharge a gun in town. It will bring the sheriff."

"Please, Mrs. Knight, this is no rehearsal, stop and put your hands behind your back or else."

Suddenly the lid on the crate popped opened and a third man's head appeared. Theo began to run. He shouted, "Pano, she's getting away!"

In the melee, Theo slipped through the arm tackle of the second man and was free for a fleeting moment. She made it across the kitchen and had her hands on the back door lock. In quick order, three pairs of hands grabbed her.

Theo had promised herself she would fight to the finish. The finish came swiftly, however, after she landed on her stomach on the hard floor. Her head was spinning. She drew in a lungful of air, with an intent to scream, when a cloth gag was forced into her mouth. She shook her head back and forth and screamed anyway, for all the good it did. Muffled, the scream came out no louder than her speaking voice.

Arms and hands far stronger than hers bound her hands, palm against palm, behind her back with fingers interlaced as if in prayer. Cords were knotted around her wrists, then woven around her hands so she couldn't move them. More turns of cord were wrapped around her arms at the elbows, drawing her shoulders back and forcing her to keep her arms straight. When that was done, they bound her into a fetal position and blindfolded her. They lowered her, feet first, into the packing case.

The first man, the one Theo thought she had heard answer to "Pano," offered to remove the gag provided she remain quiet. She nodded vigorously and uttered a muffled "Thank you." He inserted plugs in her ears and wrapped her head with an elastic bandage, which held her mouth shut so that, she realized, it was effectively another gag. She felt them placing their loot between her shins and at the end of the crate. A box resting on her feet was, she suspected, the heirloom set of silver passed down through Lyle's family. She guessed by the sound what the rest of the loot was as they packed it: all of her jewelry, tools from Lyle's workshop, and his guns, including the Smith & Wesson revolver. All the while Theo was in agony because the little bit of exercise she got had in no way prepared her muscles and joints to be crammed into this position.

Theo squealed like a stuck pig from the moment she felt the dolly bounce down the first step until she felt the crate slide onto the floor of the van. She wondered where her neighbor Celeste Foyle was. Celeste was the one who almost always came over to satisfy her curiosity and see what new luxury would grace the mansion next door.

One of the men rearranged the bandage so as to free her mouth just after Theo heard the engine start. She felt the van move. That motivated her to renew her efforts to escape. Her efforts to loosen a cord or a knot strained more muscles that weren't already suffering from being bound into a tiny space. Her thigh muscles spasmed in sympathy with the others.

Theo was sure she was going to be raped. She thought back to the woman speaker at the bankers' convention who had rhetorically asked, why are women kidnapped? Theo hadn't taken the lecture seriously because nobody had ever successfully robbed the Goodwin bank. *Will this change me like it did Gloria? OhmyGod, can Gloria be behind this? Is she so determined to get even with her father that she would do this to her own mother?*

Now she was trying to recall every detail from memory. There was that moment when the crate was being loaded onto the dolly. One speaker was close by and shouting. Again she heard that name, only this time it sounded like "Piano."

Theo fought to free herself until she was covered with sweat and exhausted. She accomplished nothing, however, beyond aggravating her discomfort as she was jostled about the box during the bouncy ride. She surmised that they were passing over poorly maintained county and forest service roads.

Then the van stopped and she felt the crate being moved out and into another vehicle. She was grateful to be lifted out by two pairs of hands. She heard a new voice, that of a fourth man. He ordered the other two to walk her around.

Still denied sight and most of her hearing, Theo felt no less helpless after the cords that held her knees against her chest were removed. Her arms remained bound behind her back. She struggled to keep her feet as two of her captors all but carried her to what she surmised was some sort of camping toilet. They demanded her panties, then shut the door and let her relieve the pressure in her bladder, which felt ready to explode now that the wild ride was over.

Unknown hands of an unknown man massaged her legs after she complained of cramps. Then the fourth man walked her up and down an aisle, and she sensed that this new vehicle was an airplane. He massaged her shoulders and upper back, and offered to guide her to her seat. She began shaking, fearful of what would happen next. They hadn't returned her panties after she went to the bathroom.

Theo voiced her fears as if her voice had to carry to the cheap seats in the third balcony, "I suppose you're going to do your worst to me now."

The man laughed. "Mrs. Knight, you're quite an actress. Please speak in a conversational tone. You're safe. I took you to the bathroom and will bed you down for the night. It will probably drop to freezing before dawn."

"Please relax, no one is going to harm you," volunteered another man. "Enjoy your adventure. We'll have you home in time for lunch tomorrow provided your husband doesn't try to be a hero."

"Adventure? Please tell me who you are and what will be my fate?"

The fourth man leaned close so she could hear, "This is a surplus

Air Force C-47, and I am the pilot. You will jump out of this plane tomorrow morning. You will have a parachute … if your husband co-operates."

The last Friday of September nineteen forty-seven was a clear, crisp fall day with the leaves beginning to turn in Goodwin County. Prosecutor Ray Tudbury stood on the second-floor balcony of the courthouse with a hand shading his eyes as he searched the bright blue sky. From the door behind him, Attorney Byron Haskins called out, "Good to see you back in town. How did the Caulfels appeal go?"

Ray waved to his friend, "Hi, By, Joe should be freed. Old Judge Carmichael was well into giving me a good reaming for prosecutorial misconduct until his colleagues reminded him that I wasn't in office last year. The statements by the two deputies serving time at Canon City were devastating. Eventually he apologized to me. Those ACLU attorneys were powerhouses. So much time was spent arguing fine points of constitutional law that I felt Joe Caulfels was a pawn in a much bigger game."

"What are you saying?"

"I'm saying the case should be remanded, but it's no slam dunk because the judiciary never likes to look bad." Ray pointed up toward the zenith. "Look, that's a military C-47. I wonder what he's up to."

"Damned if I know. He appears to be circling. The side door is open."

Ray looked out across the parklike setting of the commons in front of the courthouse. "I wish that guy would either land or move on. He's been buzzing around for almost half an hour. The Jerries used to circle like that."

"So you still don't have enough distance between today and Italy?" asked Byron.

"I've had enough of Italy to last two lifetimes, with too many close calls I still dream about."

Byron pointed at the C-47. "Hey, somebody just jumped out of the plane!"

"There's hardly a breeze," observed Ray. "Whoever that is, he's enjoying a leisurely descent."

Byron watched the parachutist intently. "I don't think that guy knows what he's doing. He isn't even trying to steer himself. He's going to end up in the trees over there."

They watched incredulously as the parachutist grazed the branches and the canopy snagged on a treetop. The lower leafy branches hid the jumper from their view. Ray chortled, "Lordy, Lordy, that's not anyone who trained under Wild Bill Donovan. He could have easily steered clear. Do you think he's trying to impress his girlfriend?"

"Not very impressive, I'm afraid, if she can see him now. Let's go over and see who that is." Byron left the balcony.

Ray ran toward the trees with Byron hobbling along behind. Ahead of him ran a pair of teenage boys. With each puff of the light morning breeze and each gyration of the struggling jumper, the sound of tearing fabric carried across the commons.

Behind him, Ray heard Byron yell, "Call the fire department! Call the fire department!"

One of the teenagers pointed up as he touched the tree trunk with his other hand. "Look, it's a woman up there. And she's all tied up. I'll go up."

A woman? Who'd do a thing like that? And who is she? Ray watched the long bare legs pedaling the air above him. The parachute harness and a bunched skirt protected her modesty. He could see now that her hands were bound behind her and her head was wrapped in a light brown elastic bandage. In the distance came the sound of a fire truck approaching.

Sheriff Larry Shyflinski pulled up in his cruiser about the same time as the fire truck. As Ray shook his hand, Larry looked up at the still-anonymous victim. "This is downright crazy. I was headed over to the bank, and this gets called in."

The answer to his questions suddenly hit Ray. "Could it be? Larry, that looks like the banker's wife, Theo Knight."

"Oh, crap! All this has to be Gloria's doing. I'm disappointed, I thought she was smarter than that. So I guess the appeal blew up in Joe's face, right?"

"Quite the contrary! The judge was outraged by the county's conduct."

Larry said, "Then I don't know why she did it, or how, but Gloria won out. Goodwin National is no more. The Feds shut it down."

"What, could this be a prank?"

"There's an FDIC notice on the door about the bank defaulting. I was on my way over there. There's a crowd gathering."

Ray shook his head. "That can't be. Just the other day Lyle got a request from the FDIC to take control of Hinsdale State Bank right after Labor Day. It's going belly up."

Larry raised his voice. "Aren't you listening? There's a letter on the door stating Goodwin National is now under federal supervision. There's a crowd outside, but no one's inside the bank."

By now the teenager had climbed up to where the parachutist hung suspended. She stopped squirming and remained still with legs straight and crossed at the ankles, so Ray figured the kid must have told her where she was.

While an ambulance came up and volunteer firefighters arrived to flesh out the staff of the engine company, the teenager cut away more of the cords, leaving Theo seemingly suspended only by threads. With all the precision of Keystone Kops, the firemen and townspeople attempted to use a ladder to effect the rescue. Finally, the last of the canopy ripped and she dropped down in jerks. One of the firemen caught her.

As soon as the gag was out of her mouth, Theo spoke in a hoarse voice. "I'm Theo, Theodora Knight. Help me, please! We've been robbed. Please go to the bank. Dear Lord, protect my husband!"

The fireman who unwrapped the bandage exclaimed, "Hello, Mrs. Knight! How are your arms?"

"I'm hurting but I'm okay, now don't worry about me. Save my husband, I beg you! There were three of them, armed with guns." She clapped her hands and stretched her arms above her head to work out the discomfort from being bound overnight.

The radio in the sheriff's car came to life. "Sheriff, like I told you over the phone, the doors to the bank are locked and lights are on, but I can't see anybody inside the bank. It's way past opening time and there's people outside. Should we break the door down?"

"Wait till I get there," answered Larry.

Ray laughed as he studied the letter taped to the inside of the bank's door. "Larry, you got it all wrong. This is actually the letter that put Hinsdale State Bank under the control of Goodwin National Bank. I guess people see what they want to see."

Larry flushed. "Awright, Ray, rub it in. I thought they were talking about this bank." He jimmied the door open and went inside with Ray and two deputies who fanned out and searched. After a few minutes, from behind the teller's booths in the lobby, he said to Ray, "I've got to call the FBI. We've looked everywhere. Nobody is here."

"No, wait," said Ray. "Listen!"

They heard a faint voice that sounded like someone hailing a taxi through a pipe. "Help, help, we can't get out."

"It's coming from the vault!" exclaimed Larry. He motioned everyone to hush and strained to hear the almost-inaudible voice.

This was followed by close to ten minutes of confusing verbal instructions from inside the vault, with much repetition required because the sound was muffled. Finally Larry understood that he should remove a screen from a ventilation tube so he could hear better. Lyle's hoarse voice, still faint but now clear, could be heard through the tube. "We're trapped. Safety handle broken off. To open vault lock requires both a combination and a key. Combination is fifty-five, thirty-four, four. Key is in the left-hand top drawer of my desk in the den at home. Break a window to get in."

Ray checked his watch as the sheriff made the last turn of the dial on the combination lock. *Here it is one twenty-three. It was just after ten when I was talking to Byron on the courthouse balcony and we watched Theo Knight jump. Damn, they have a three-hour head start.*

Larry turned the first lever, then inserted the key in the lock and spun the wheel. The vault door opened. The inside was a mess, with papers strewn all over. The floor was crunchy with gold dust. All inside were soaked in sweat.

A wide-eyed, sweating Lyle was the first to emerge. "Sheriff, they've kidnapped my dear wife! They've stolen my car!"

"Who? I need a description. What's your license number?" The sheriff held his pad and pencil at the ready.

Lyle spat the words like bursts of machine gun fire, "YT 12 ... Forty-seven Lincoln Continental ... That bitch of a daughter of mine ..."

The sheriff ripped the sheet off the pad and handed it to a deputy. "Get the description on the air. Position cars at the passes. Watch for vehicles with two men and a woman."

An employee said, "Correction, there were only two men. Both wore masks. Gloria was not here."

"I don't care," retorted Lyle, "It was too well organized not to be Gloria's work. They've taken my dear wife. She's all I have left. Call the FBI and tell them to sweat the precocious bitch!"

"Lyle, Theo is safe," said the sheriff. "She was taken over to the new doc's office for a quick checkup. Can you give me descriptions?"

"Descriptions? How should I know? I never saw any of them. They were all so damned polite and formal, like they were in the Army. The one in charge ... foreign accent, short, smart." Lyle stopped talking and looked down at the floor. "I'm sorry, Sheriff. Nothing, no one is as important as Theo, my wife. Please, I can't think. I have to talk to her. I've been in that vault all this time with the thought of that dratted airplane in my head ... the fear of identifying her broken body after they threw her out without a parachute. Poor Theo."

After he hung up the phone from talking with his wife, the banker's first words, thundered across the room, were "I told you! Gloria Caulfels, my vengeful daughter, ran the show."

The sheriff's eyebrows shot upward when Lyle turned to the deputies. "Get a warrant, search Gloria's apartment. Her fingerprints are all over this."

He turned back to Lyle. "Your wife mentioned two on the plane. You said there were two here. Now if you never saw them, what makes you so sure Gloria was involved?"

"She tried to destroy me every other way, and she failed. Now they've burgled my home and cleaned out the bank! Who else would think to hang a notice on the door making it look like the bank has failed? Who else would think up such a harebrained scheme to force her mother to jump from an airplane? Last Christmas, she made it clear. She cares nothing for her mother or me."

Larry said, "Dammit, banker Knight, if Gloria was involved, she paid you back in spades. I know I should empathize. But you've been going out of your way to ruin people for many years now."

The phone rang, and Larry picked it up. He listened for a minute, then announced, "This is the airport. Mr. Knight, your car is there, abandoned on the tarmac. The two robbers transferred duffel bags into a twin-engine Beechcraft and were airborne about ten a.m."

Ray pounded his fist on his palm. "Damn it, they could be anywhere by now."

Larry said, "We're alerting federal authorities and will put out an all-points bulletin on the aircraft."

<hr>

Gloria Caulfels wore a blue cotton prisoner's jumpsuit. She squirmed in the chair in the federal interrogation room in Philadelphia. Every few minutes she pulled her left arm back until the handcuff grew tight around her wrist, then leaned forward and resumed tapping the metallic tabletop. She stared at the one-way glass mirror with wide, frightened eyes. *I thought they were coming for me about Four Eff. Instead it's something about a Goodwin bank robbery? That agent Rockwell got downright angry when I told him I'd come in tomorrow with my lawyer. Mister Dadoun doesn't understand why I was arrested. I think it's because I'm a Caulfels now.*

She looked at the calendar on the wall. *Well, here it is four days later. Rockwell said he wanted my cooperation. Hah! Then he arrests me, puts me on a train to New York, and throws me into a cell all by myself. Then in the middle of the night, back to Philadelphia. I don't feel very cooperative.*

As Gloria was musing, FBI Agents "Rocky" Rockwell and Lester Brady came in together. She estimated both were no older than thirty. Dressed in dark blue business suits, they didn't look threatening like Four Eff. She and her attorney Simon Dadoun sat side by side on the opposite side of the table. She saw that one of the agents' folders was labeled JOSEPH CORWIN CAULFELS.

Gloria felt confident sitting with Dadoun, who appeared every inch the wise counselor, with silver sideburns and a mellow bass voice. He had earned her admiration after the ACLU retained him to represent Joe.

Agent Rockwell started. "Mrs. Caulfels, we regret having had to take you into custody, but when you refused to cooperate ...".

Dadoun leaned across the table. "Sir, my client is extremely busy in her own life. She made it perfectly clear that she knows nothing about the bank robbery in Goodwin, Colorado, a place she fled and vowed not to return to. I am shocked that you restricted her freedom when she insisted that she be represented by counsel."

"Counselor, the lady refused to answer questions. We have certain information that she played a role ...."

"Is that source of certain information her father?"

"We feel it is premature to disclose the source. Mrs. Caulfels, we have records to show you have been a regular visitor at the penitentiary at Canon City, Colorado. We need to know who you ...."

The rattle of Gloria's wrist manacle interrupted him as she turned pale and her hand began shaking. "How much power does Mr. Knight have?" she spat out. "Has he bought you too?"

Brady put both elbows on the table and leaned forward. "Mrs. Caulfels, this is absolutely the wrong thing to say to any federal officer. Bank robbery, kidnapping, interstate flight are very serious charges. Your very promising career in high fashion won't be something you could pick up after conviction."

"It may not survive my being arrested in the train station on the way to my New York shoot and not letting me call to explain the situation."

Dadoun said, "Mr. Brady, your people shuffled her around between New York and Philadelphia like a hot potato. She is going through college on scholarship, and even unsubstantiated charges could cause her to lose it. If you have information that implicates my client, produce it."

"Mr. Dadoun, we have too many coincidences. They cleaned out the residence. Mrs. Caulfels had lived there. They came prepared to haul off a windfall from the vault. She had made a report that the bank held too much vault cash. She had faulted the bank for keeping the key to the vault in the cashier's desk."

Dadoun asked, "Wasn't the banker, Mr. Knight, a captive of the robbers all night before the robbery? Wasn't that enough time for them to become acquainted with where valuables were kept in the Knight residence? And how could she have any knowledge of the transfer of gold dust from the Hinsdale bank?"

Gloria whispered in her lawyer's ear. "All I did was follow an American Bankers' Association checklist item by item. I told Daddy--Mr. Knight--he needed to increase his robbery insurance because he hoarded vault cash. Can I ask if he's a suspect?"

Dadoun nodded, and Gloria asked, "Sir, are you sure there was really two hundred sixty-five thousand dollars in the vault? Over the past year and a half, I have cost Mr. Knight a bundle that he spent to get himself off the hook after I disclosed his financial manipulations. What about the gold dust he claimed he was going to ship to the U.S. Treasury? What better way to recoup his losses and get even with me?"

Rockwell replied, "Mrs. Caulfels, I have reviewed the confidential lists that you earlier provided to the IRS. What other documents did you spirit out of your father's bank?"

Dadoun waved a hand. "Don't answer that, Gloria. Be specific, Mr. Rockwell."

"Did you take the ABA checklist? How did you get to be such an expert?"

"Just write the ABA, they'll send you one," Gloria replied.

"You know what I meant. A completed one."

"No, I didn't. I did my homework. I listened. Mr. Knight talked about little else at home. By the way, I worked for the internal auditor at Canon City National last summer." Gloria took a business card from her attorney and handed it to the agent. "Call Mr. Jason Edwards and ask him about my work. Mr. Rockwell, I have no use for Mr. Knight or his money. All I know about the robbery is in the *Goodwin Globe* article. When I saw the picture of the safety deposit boxes broken and empty, it made me angry. Many of the customers are my friends. I'm sorry, I can't help you."

"Every time you refer to your father, it's as 'Mr. Knight.' Why?"

"Thank you for asking that question. I disowned them last Christmas. I don't want their money. I don't want them meddling in my life. I'm never going back to Colorado once my husband is set free."

"What do you tell people when they inquire?" asked Rockwell.

"I tell them I have no parents. They're dead."

"Dead? Is this your reaction to your father when he sought to save his family tree from corruption by placing limits on your libertine lifestyle?"

Dadoun ran a finger under his chin. "Stop, Mr. Rockwell, we fully discussed her husband's conviction over the phone. Taking this young woman into custody on these flimsy grounds is facilitating a continuation of Mr. Knight's vendetta against the Caulfels family."

"Mr. Dadoun, we are just doing our job," volunteered Brady.

"My client has given you insights about her father that I hope you will pursue with the same zeal you have taken toward Mrs. Caulfels. Gentlemen, is there any further reason to hold my client?"

Agent Rockwell went through the motions of reviewing the contents of a folder before he nodded to Agent Brady, who said, "Mrs. Caulfels, I will inform staff you are free for out-processing. Keep our office informed if you move. I hope we didn't come across as too harsh. We have a very tough case with very few leads. Please think back and ask yourself if there were any other people you may have talked to about your father's bank."

To avoid eye contact with Brady, Gloria kept looking down at her wrist well after he released her from the table. Out of the corner of her eye, she watched Mr. Dadoun shake his hand. *This was a good drill. Now I know what to expect when they come for me about the death of Four Eff.*

CHAPTER 25
Freedom

Joe Caulfels drove the white Cadillac nonstop all the way from Canon City to the pass before descending to the canyon above Goodwin. "Ma, a man driving from the Pearly Gates to the biggest mansion in heaven in Pa's luxurious Cadillac couldn't feel better than I do today. Look at the bellies of those beautiful clouds lying on the mountaintops."

Vera Caulfels took her eyes off the road long enough to make an assessment. "Those dark bellies are full of snow. Let's pray we clear the pass before it starts to come down."

Let it snow, I don't care. I'm free, after twenty months seventeen days, to enjoy this day of my rebirth, November 17, 1947! What changes have run roughshod through me over twenty months. I'm married to my high school sweetheart. The last time I sat behind this wheel, all I could think about was leaving Goodwin. Now I have a hunger to stay in the high country ... to look up and see a sky so chock full of stars I can't count 'em.

At last he saw the top of the Caulfels garage ahead, off to the left between the highway and the river. He slowed down, far more cautiously than he had done before he went to prison. After he came to a full stop, he made the turn onto the access road and into the garage. *Well, at least one place hasn't changed while I was inside. The garage looks the same, as does the cable car.*

He stepped from the short path out of the garage onto the cable car. The fatigue of a day on the road disappeared with the first pull on the cable. The track wheels complained loudly about their worn-out bearings. "Ma, I can't count the times I've closed my eyes and imagined that the squeak of the wheels on the outside prison gate was the cable car. Hearing it today makes me want to stay here."

"Son, you have a wife waiting for you back east."

"Do you think if I stayed, she'd come home for Christmas?"

"Don't break her heart. You belong together."

Joe shrugged his shoulders, then paused. He stood by the river and listened to the water working its way downstream. He watched an eagle balance on the air, soaring. The bird dove down and, just out of sight, he heard it hit the water and splash. The raptor flew up again with its prey in its talons. Joe walked into the house with its familiar smells. *Thank you, Lord, for giving me the strength to endure this trial.*

Later, while Vera was fixing dinner, Joe picked up the *Cosmopolitan* magazine with a wallet-size picture of Gloria on the cover as a teaser for the feature within.

Vera called out, "Enjoying Gloria's article in the November *Cosmopolitan*? That girl has everything: brains, beauty, courage, and more drive than most men I know."

Joe studied the picture. "Yes, I can see sadness and more than just a little fear that doesn't match the smile. I worry for her."

"You're the one I worry for. Gloria is tough as nails."

"That's the Gloria she wants you to see. Father Covell told me that Gloria is very insecure in her worth and her womanhood. I'm going to give her all the love and prayers I know how."

Vera came out of the kitchen. She wiped a tear from her eye as she hugged her son. "Joe, I worry for your health, but I feel my buttons almost popping, seeing how you came out of that terrible place a whole man. Let me tell you that I expect her to do some powerful caring for you."

"You're right, Ma, we need to be together now. But that doesn't mean I have to be back there forever."

After a stop for coffee, Joe was at the wheel of the white Cadillac early in the evening on his last Saturday in Goodwin before leaving for the East Coast. He had chosen one last tour of the town on the way to the Foyles' house for a farewell dinner. He intended to arrive from the opposite direction to facilitate parking in front of the Knights' house. *Here it is my last Saturday at home and I haven't seen Mr. Knight.*

Disgusted looks painted Joe's parents' faces when he turned off the engine in front of the Knights'. Orville snapped, "Son, what in tarnation are you doing? There's plenty of room up the street."

"Humor me, please." Joe stepped down from the Cadillac and motioned for them to go to the Foyles'. "This will only take a minute. The two of you go on inside."

"Please, Joe, don't start any trouble. Come with us, please," Vera pleaded.

Joe waved his parents off with a Biblical quote. "I have to ask. The Bible teaches that you must forgive if you are to be forgiven."

Lyle Knight wore an immaculate silk robe over his shirt and tie when he came to the door. Joe smiled and extended his right hand. "Good evening, Mr. Knight. I'm Joe Caulfels, your son-in-law."

Lyle's hand, which had been moving upward toward Joe's, jerked to cup his chin. "Boy, I didn't recognize you with that jailbird haircut. What brings you here? Looking for a handout?"

"No, sir, in a manner of speaking, we're all family. I wanted ..."

With fists clenched, Lyle thrust his hands into the pockets of his robe. "Family! Didn't that hellfire wife of yours give you a copy of her letter?"

"She told me. It was the last thing I wanted."

"Missed your chance at an easy fortune, did you?"

"No, Mr. Knight. The most I will ever accept from you is forgiveness, to end the feuding."

Lyle's face turned red and his voice boomed, "Forgiveness, forgiveness! That ungrateful bitch of a daughter of mine took us to the razor's edge of ruin! Her mother still has nightmares and crying spells from being tossed out of an airplane."

"Mr. Knight, two bouts of heat stroke and over a year in prison weren't exactly a picnic for me either. I didn't come here to fight old wars. I came here for one reason: to ask an end to our families' feuding. To give the children we will someday have, two sets of grandparents."

The sinews in Lyle's neck and jaws stood out as he drew in a deep breath and slowly let it out. "Scrub bastards, you mean. She put you up to this. That bitch! Tell her that … that I won't recognize any of her half-breed litters."

"Keep your money. Do it for yourself. As Mark Twain said, 'Anger is an acid that can do more harm to the vessel in which it is stored than to anything on which it is poured.'"

Lyle slammed the door so hard that the brass knocker tapped the door twice. This left Joe standing on the outside. He heard the sound from within of a chair hitting the floor, followed by a feminine voice asking, "Lyle! What are you mad about? Who was at the door?"

"That half-breed Gloria married. Well, he's made his bed in hell!"

Joe remained at the door of what had become a darkened porch until there was silence. *No doubt about it. The man knows how to hate.*

Joe turned to find his father standing on the sidewalk near the curb. Orville said, "Son, I am so proud of you. Come on, before the man gets a gun. He's so full of hate, he can't see your goodness."

Dinner was over at the Foyles'. Empty dessert dishes remained on the table amid coffee cups that Carole was busy refilling. Joe sat back and luxuriated in the leisure of polite conversation without worry of a time deadline to move on. He told himself he was free. When Carole poured him a refill, he said, "Please tell Andy I changed my mind about staying here a couple of weeks. I missed seeing him before I left."

Celeste said, "I know Andy wanted to be here, but he had exams. It's important that you catch that train Monday so you can spend Thanksgiving with your bride."

Prosecutor Ray Tudbury pulled an envelope from his inside coat pocket. "In case you've thought up another reason to delay departure, Joe, this is my wedding present to the two of you. You let me off with such a cheap wedding, I'm making it up with the honeymoon. These are reservations to the William Penn Hotel in Philadelphia, starting Wednesday through Saturday night. They have been instructed to send me the tab for the whole stay. Enjoy."

"Thanks, Ray. I …"

"I owe it to you both. Here, take it. It's going to be a tough go for the two of you alone. I want you to have some good memories to fall back on. Don't worry about Gloria making conflicting plans. She has the word."

Celeste said, "Joe, I wanted to rent the hall at the church and give you a real sendoff, but everybody here advised against it. The county hasn't been the same since the bank robbery."

"What does the bank robbery have to do with me?" asked Joe.

"They didn't just rob the bank. They looted safety deposit boxes. There was a whole bunch of gold from the Hinsdale Bank too. Mr. Knight keeps telling everyone that Gloria masterminded the whole thing."

"How? She's back in Pennsylvania."

Sheriff Larry Shyflinski, who had been sitting quietly at the table, pulled a sketch from his pocket. "Mrs. Knight was the only one who saw enough of any of them to give a description. This is what the FBI artist drew up. Do you recognize him?"

Joe studied the sketch with an inscrutable expression on his face. "I don't know anybody that has a bushy mustache like that."

Celeste said, "Mrs. Knight told everybody that he had some kind of foreign accent. It wasn't too strong, and all of them were very polite and respectful, like they were military."

Vera leaned in to look at the sketch. She put her hand across it to cover the face below the nose. "Those eyes look a little familiar. Don't you recognize him, son, from when you were in the hospital?"

Joe shrugged his shoulders. "There was a Greek fellow who robbed a bank to keep from being sent to the front. It couldn't be him. They threw him out of the country last year."

Larry pulled his small notepad out of his pocket. "What's his name?"

Joe stared at the sketch. "Can't say I recall. And I can't say this is him. He was a medical orderly, a trusty. He was gone by the time I was in the hospital the second time. I don't want to make trouble for him. What does this have to do with Gloria?"

"This was such a perfectly planned and executed robbery, the FBI feels they had inside help. And everybody knows Gloria has no love for her father."

Vera pointed at the drawing. "I'll never forget the one day they let us visit my sick baby. This fellow shooed us out before I had a chance to really talk to Joe."

Orville asked, "Is there any specific evidence that Gloria was in cahoots with this Greek fellow? Or that the Greek robbed the bank?"

The sheriff, who had finished writing on the pad, put the sketch back in his pocket. "None. Gloria wouldn't cooperate with the FBI. They told me she had some mob lawyer named Dadoun."

"Larry, Simon Dadoun is no mob lawyer—unless you think the ACLU is part of the mob! He represented Joe on appeal," said Ray. "After what happened to Joe, I can understand why she wouldn't meet without counsel. Joe, your mother told me you're leaving for good."

"Yes," Joe replied. *Until someday after her father dies. That man is pure poison.*

"I'm truly sorry that you and Gloria won't be settling here. Goodwin County is the poorer for it."

"I would like to change her mind."

CHAPTER 26

Joe and Gloria Caulfels

Rocky Rockwell, the lead FBI agent on the Goodwin bank robbery, pushed himself to be first in line when the Monday morning train came to a screeching halt on the east end of the Goodwin station platform. He took a deep breath of the clean mountain air in the vain hope it would clear the mental cobwebs of an overnight ride in a coach seat. With both feet on the cold platform, he scanned its length in what he swiftly concluded was a vain attempt to see just one man in uniform. It was empty except for train riders disembarking. *Where is the sheriff?*

Rockwell felt like the proverbial chicken with its head chopped off. He and Agent Brady had flown to Camp Hale with FAA accident investigators to look at the burned-out remains of the rented Beechcraft. Then back to Salt Lake to interview the rental firm. His plans to be home before Thanksgiving were at risk after a personal phone call from the FBI director for him to brief banker Knight because the amount of gold that was reported stolen had stirred Congressional interest.

The agent was peeved to be stood up on a cold, windy platform by back-country law enforcement. The arrival of a classic white Cadillac touring car and four other autos held his attention. The handsome young man who was being seen off was dressed up enough that he concluded this was a rancher's family seeing their son off to college. All the men were wearing cowboy boots except the traveler, who wore well-shined black oxfords and a Stetson hat. Two of the men hefted two heavy footlockers aboard the baggage car.

The agent turned his attention from the Cadillac crowd to the far end of the train, where the sheriff's cruiser had just pulled up. *Criminy, he arrives late and parks on the opposite end of the station. But remember to thank him. Don't forget who got us the lead.*

They met close to halfway down the train. Rockwell extended his right hand. "Sheriff Shyflinski, I'm Rocky Rockwell, FBI. Thank you for meeting my train."

"My apologies for being late, Mr. Rockwell. We have a murder on our hands. I appreciate the serious attention the FBI is giving to the bank robbery. My car is over here."

Rockwell walked beside Larry toward the end of the train. "Call me Rocky. Murder? Does it have anything to do with this case?"

Larry shook his head. "No."

"Good, the lead you phoned in late Saturday has given our investigation real momentum. The director called me and asked that I convey his warm and personal thanks for the Greek lead. I want to let you know that this case has been given the highest priority by the director. We have a total of twenty-six agents on temporary assignment to account for the whereabouts of surplus C-47s on the twenty-fifth of September."

"I'm sure banker Knight will be pleased to know the effort being taken to find this gang."

"I just want to get one thing straight. This Mrs. Caulfels in your report—I understand this is *not* Gloria Caulfels?"

The sheriff put the agent's bags in the trunk before he opened the car door for Rockwell. "No, this is Vera Caulfels, Joe's mother."

"What irony. She may well have inadvertently given us the tip that could lead to her daughter-in-law's arrest."

"It wasn't inadvertent. She doesn't believe Gloria directed this bank robbery. And after my investigation, I don't see any evidence of it either."

The engine's whistle blew. The conductor shouted, "All aboard. All aboard for express to Denver with connections to points east."

Larry raised his voice to ask, "Has the FBI found any direct connection to Gloria, Rocky?"

"In a roundabout way. A Greek citizen, Pano Kargolis, and an Air Force captain, Seth Lawson, trained together at Lowry Air Force Base in nineteen forty. Lawson became a suspect in a string of bank robberies near the base, but there just wasn't enough evidence. Last year Lawson and some others paid cash for a batch of six military model C-47s surplused at Wright-Patterson Field. They were required to fly them out of the country. Five planes were flown to Greece via South America by contract pilots. The sixth flew to Salt Lake City and disappeared. Lawson was the pilot."

"Salt Lake? What does this have to do with Gloria Caulfels?"

"Thanks to the older Mrs. Caulfels, we have established that Gloria knew the Greek. Superintendent Carberry, in Canon City, said her husband has been released. Where can I find young Mr. Caulfels?" Rockwell asked.

The sound of the diesel's increasing engine speed echoed off the canyon's rock walls. White exhaust smoke was carried down the canyon along the length of the train. The engine noise buried all the natural sounds until echoes re-echoed. Larry shouted, "He's on this train on his way to join his wife, Gloria. Joe Caulfels had nothing to do with the bank robbery. He was still in prison then."

Larry pulled the patrol car alongside the white Cadillac just as the train started to roll. Rockwell spotted the same handsome man, waving out the window, whom he had seen on the platform. Larry pointed at him. "That's Joe Caulfels."

"Damn it! I watched him load his luggage. That suit and the Stetson fooled me. I should call the Denver office and intercept him."

They stopped just short of the street's dead end. Both sat in silence as they watched the train pick up speed and disappear up the tracks.

The sheriff turned his cruiser around. "I think you would be wasting your time. Joe was inside long enough to learn not to talk. But you haven't told me what makes you focus on Gloria."

"Experience. I interviewed her in Philadelphia. It wasn't what she said, it was the way she looked and acted. Getting anything out of her was impossible with her attorney there. And does she have motive! I read the appeal file. Her father is a regular SOB. Could you take me to the Goodwin Bank? He's expecting me."

Larry said, "He's had an unforeseen change of plans. Banker Knight is at a spread outside of town with some of my deputies. The people, who are buying the place from his bank found human remains, early this morning, buried under concrete in their barn. I'm not sure why he's so concerned unless he thinks this will somehow affect his mortgage. I'm headed back out there now. Would you like to come along?

"Sure, as long as it's understood that I'm there to meet Knight. This isn't a federal case."

Agent Rockwell sat back in the front passenger seat and took in the spectacular Goodwin scenery. He looked at his watch again to affirm that it was still too early to call the Denver office, then reconsidered the need. *Boy, I'd be pissed if I was hauled off a train on the way to my honeymoon for questioning for something I had no part in. It's better to wait and give Gloria time to involve him. He's had a taste of life inside. He won't want to go back.* Rockwell asked the sheriff. "What do you know about the Caulfels boy?"

"His mother managed my campaign. He's one of the nicest people I've met. Joe didn't deserve to be sent to prison. Worried about him slipping through your fingers? Rest easy, they'll be at the William Penn Hotel through the weekend. It's a honeymoon courtesy of Prosecutor Ray Tudbury. After the disastrous hands dealt them, they've earned this time together."

"That's my thought too," Rockwell agreed. *I'd like to be with my family this Thanksgiving, for a change.*

While the sheriff stocked up on donuts and filled his Thermos with hot coffee, Rockwell learned about Larry's background and how he rose through the ranks to be mustered out as a major. The agent asked, "Were you aware of the extent and depth of corruption in this county when you threw your hat in the ring?"

Larry laughed. "Good question! When Ray Tudbury asked me to run, I was just looking for a job that would pay enough to support my family. When I accepted the call to run for sheriff, I knew there was corruption, but I way underestimated the extent."

"The Denver office said you conducted a purge."

"I didn't start keeping notes until about the end of the first week of the campaign. People came to us, Ray and me. The stories were awful. The first two deputies I interviewed after the election were arrested. They pleaded guilty and are serving time now in Canon City for raping braceros' daughters and wives. The rest of the staff running the jail, except for one officer, resigned and fled town. Ray filed charges."

Rockwell laughed. "Wow, that's a purge. What about the two in the penitentiary, any connection to this Kargolis?"

"Not that I know of.

Rockwell snapped out of his nap to find himself tossed around like a rag doll in an empty five-gallon bucket after Larry turned onto the narrow, ill-kept road into the Blackmon spread. Larry muttered, "The county commissioners raided the road budget, leaving a tremendous backlog of road repairs, and blamed it on wartime shortages."

Rockwell sat with one foot braced against the dash and his hands clinging to the backside of the seat cushion. *Thank God, at last I see a clearing ahead. This is a miserable trail, if I ever saw one.* They came out into the clearing, surrounded by the spectacular view. *Oh my, this is the trade-off for that awful ride. What a beautiful vista.*

Rockwell noted the big barn and a charred brick chimney sticking up where there was once a house. "What happened in the murder investigations of the woman and her baby?"

Larry said, "They've gone nowhere, I'm ashamed to admit. The coroner didn't get the bodies in time to give an accurate time of death. Last December the house burned to the ground. One of the deputies who are now in prison admitted he removed handcuffs that he found locked to the headboard when he found Mae Blackmon and her baby dead from smoke inhalation. He fingered a deputy who turned up missing about the same time as those deaths. That deputy, who was dirty in almost every way, is still missing, along with the last sheriff's wife. She was a sadistic bitch. We tracked her as far as the border. She is a well-educated Mexican national, who speaks good English. There's the crew standing just inside the barn."

"Any connection to today's find?"

"Damned if I know. This morning, before the crack of dawn, I got this phone call from the owner, Calvin Bohl. He told me he found the source of the stink in the barn here. It was a cement-filled gunk tank. The bank had sold off everything else that was movable."

"Now that takes some sophistication. Could this be the killing ground for your local mob?" asked Rockwell.

"Don't know. Mae wouldn't have been in cahoots with them. She was the widow of a man who died in that jail."

The sheriff introduced Rockwell to those present: the undersheriff, two deputies, the coroner, ranch owner Calvin Bohl, banker Lyle Knight, and two of Lyle's attorneys. The FBI agent took an immediate liking to the rawboned sixty-year-old Calvin, who offered the bed of his pickup as a table for the spread of coffee and donuts, then talked about the Blackmon ranch's spicy history.

The coroner invited the sheriff and Rockwell inside the barn. The empty, battered gunk tank lay on its side with the bulldozer parked behind it, the blade still elevated. Just in front of the gunk tank was the upper portion of the plug of cement.

Rockwell saw the bones, with bits of flesh here and there that lay amid clumps of wet, dark gray cement-colored sand. A pair of shiny closed handcuffs were still around the skeleton's wrist bones. The remains of shoes were on the feet. Pieces of a whip stuck out of the block. *This murder case may not be mine, but I'm not going to step back for the time being. What's Lyle Knight's connection to this scene that commands his full attention? Even while he spouted off a couple times about 'that bitch of a daughter,' the man's attention has been on the broken cement plug.*

Rockwell squatted to get a better view of the remains. "I wonder if they buried him alive. What do you think, Mr. Knight?"

"I don't have a clue." Lyle shrugged his shoulders and shook his head without breaking eye contact with the plug. "Who is he?"

The coroner answered, "No identification or clothes. We recovered four thirty-eight-caliber projectiles. One shot got him in the groin, shattering the pelvis. He had to have bled out before he was buried. Don't touch anything, especially the sand. That lye will eat the skin right off your hands."

Rockwell said, "The high lye content all but dissolved the body. Very professional, somebody knew what they were doing. Nobody knows who he is?"

The undersheriff shook his head. "All we have to go on is what's left of the shoes."

"He was a very big man," said Rockwell. "If you're careful in separating the head or upper torso, a plaster mold could be made of the face."

Calvin smiled, displaying front teeth with rotted crowns. "There's one fat feller missing hereabouts for over a year that most people in this county wanted to see dead, just like the judge. Ain't that right, Lyle?"

Lyle Knight scowled at the rancher, then vigorously shook his head. "I ... I don't know who this is."

Calvin spoke as if he enjoyed working a needle. "Hell, he's the feller who made money trails start and stop just short of the bank. He's the feller who liked to teach the kids a lesson by treating the girls real dirty and mean. Like he did your daughter, Gloria."

"John Diamond? Are you sure?" asked Larry.

"Take them shoes out and show 'em to his missus."

Lyle Knight stood tall while he swept imaginary lint from his sleeve. "John fooled many of us. Nonetheless, his misdeeds certainly can't excuse the excesses of others ... and I do regret saying this .... especially of my own daughter. Agent Rockwell, I believe you're here to discuss the progress you're making toward bringing her and her band of jackals to justice."

Rockwell shook his head. "We're making progress, but it's premature to discuss details in public. I am prepared to give you a private briefing in hopes you could help us."

"I'm pleased to hear you've had a breakthrough. I would be glad to give you a ride back to Goodwin. After going through the burned hulk of that abandoned twin-engine plane, I must say my spirits have been very low."

"Mr. Knight, why don't we walk you to your car? I believe I could bring you up to date," offered Rockwell.

Lyle's two attorneys fell in behind him. The banker said, "Calvin Bohl angered me greatly, but there's little I can do. He's only repeating the slanders spread by my own daughter."

The sheriff asked, "Do you still doubt that Deputy Diamond attacked your daughter?"

Larry, Lyle, and Rockwell exited the barn. "Yes, I saw a different man the day he closed his accounts at the bank. If he did ... well, she put herself in jeopardy by willful disobedience," said Lyle.

Rockwell placed a hand on Lyle's shoulder. "Mr. Knight, please thank your wife for us. The description she gave was good enough to allow us to confirm which C-47 they used. And, most importantly, identify the ringleader as someone who served time with Joe Caulfels."

"I just knew the Caulfels were behind this! Then you know where that plane is?"

Rockwell shook his head. "Not exactly. We can place the C-47 in Salt Lake City when the twin Beechcraft was rented by the Greek and the step van was stolen. The last place where we have a firm identification is a small general aviation field outside of Baton Rouge, where they fueled up on the Saturday morning after the robbery. "

"Then, where ...?"

"Abroad, probably South America or Europe. They made a tidy profit, selling six planes plus half a million from your bank."

"How did Gloria get her share?"

"Mr. Knight, the one bit of cooperation I had from her attorney was full disclosure of her finances. I might add that it agrees with her tax returns. She lives modestly. There were no windfalls, and she worked part-time jobs. Her only income now and, I might add, a substantial one, is through her part-time modeling career. You have a remarkably gifted and talented daughter."

"I am too aware of her talents, sir. What direct connection have you made between my daughter and this Greek?"

"In truth, Mr. Knight, we have no evidence, other than what your wife and Vera Caulfels provided our local agents, that Kargolis was involved. We will pursue every lead and if she had a role, she will be prosecuted in federal court."

Lyle opened his car door. There was sadness in his voice. "What a pity. She sowed the wind and now she reaps the whirlwind."

Larry raised his voice. "Pardon me, Mr. Knight, somebody has to say this. You have spent the last year and a half sowing the wind, first encouraging Deputy Diamond to frame Joe, and now you're doing the same thing to your own daughter."

"Sheriff, I was only protecting my underage daughter."

"Cut the bull! Didn't you pay Paul Bixler five hundred dollars to send his buddies the Kilroy cards with the pecker nose?"

Lyle slid into the driver's seat. His face turned red. "It may have been crude, but it snapped her foolish infatuation. How did you find out?"

"We tracked down Bixler. He told me all about the ultimatum and the meeting with your attorney. Lyle, I know both of those kids. Your daughter is a prodigy. She could have taken over your bank. And Joe, what a fine, sober, Christian young man. After all you did to him, his first order of business was to seek peace. You ran him off."

Lyle turned the ignition key. He raced the engine before he drove off. "Sheriff, the very seed of the Caulfels family is evil. I grieve that my only child chose that mongrel to spite me. Good day, gentlemen."

They watched the car turn around and leave. Rockwell said, "I'll be damned. He's driving off without us. Sheriff, I think you have a murder suspect there."

Gloria was in such a state that she required Jenny plus two classmates to help take care of her preparations for her husband's arrival, late on the Wednesday afternoon before Thanksgiving. Somehow they coaxed Gloria past a severe case of butterflies and her secret fear that Joe would reject her when he learned the truth about her. She had been given "the works" at the salon, from shampoo to pedicure. When she left there, she had her hair down and cut to shoulder length, with her front locks combed to the side. To ward off the chill of the fog and the swirling cold, misty rain, Gloria wore a wool suit, a chic fur-trimmed collared coat, and high heels.

She entered the Pennsylvania Station in Upper Darby with Henry Vaughan and his daughter Jenny, bucking the flow of commuters from a train that was departing. She and Jenny were in front, giggling and whispering to one another all the way to the platform.

The trio had been on the platform a few minutes when an eastbound train pulled into the station. Gloria began to jump up and down, and screamed when she saw her husband as he alighted from the train. "There he is! There he is, my darling Joe!"

My husband, bigger than life and even more handsome than I remember. Oh, the look in his eyes. He wants what I want, what we've waited for. How do I tell him? I'm ready. The diaphragm's in. But how do I tell him that my life is wrecked? Why did it happen now? All I'll get is a taste to savor for a lifetime.

Gloria ran the last few yards separating them. Joe dropped his suitcase and swept her into his arms. She pressed against him, inhaled his essence, and hungrily exchanged passionate kisses. Joe whispered, "Thank you, thank you, Lord. Let's always be together. I love you, Gloria."

"Yes ... Yes ...Yes! " Gloria kissed him again and stepped back holding his hand.

Jenny exclaimed, "Gloria, he's gorgeous!"

Gloria beamed. "Joe, this is my roommate Jenny Vaughn and her father ... My husband, Joe Caulfels."

Henry shook Joe's hand. "We'll pick up the trunks you checked. My wife and I would like very much for you and Gloria to join us for Thanksgiving dinner tomorrow. We eat about five. Would you like to come?"

Joe looked at Gloria, who nodded. "You mean home-cooked turkey? Yes, sir. Except I don't know where you live."

"Mr. Vaughan will pick us up at the William Penn and return us there afterwards," Gloria informed him.

Henry put a hand on Joe's shoulder. "There has been a true change since Gloria got the news you were set free, a wonderful change from hiding her beauty to almost exploding like you see on the Fourth of July. Brains, beauty, guts, determination ... She has it all."

"Thank you, sir. I'm free because of her. She means the world to me."

Henry said, "That I know because we've fought in the trenches with her, if only in our hearts. Is that a Stetson you're wearing? We don't see them here except on special order."

Puzzled, he lifted the hat off his head. "Yes sir, this hat, the outfit I'm wearing was a gift from good people, school classmates, veterans, Goodwin folks I hardly knew. One of them, Mr. Kahn, whom I'd only met once when I rented a tuxedo, arranged for everything. When I asked him how I was to pay them back, he told me to find someone else to care for."

Jenny pulled her father's arm. "Come on, Daddy. Let them start their honeymoon." The Vaughans waved goodbye and went off to their waiting car.

The cold, drizzling rain of late November filtered onto the bright rails, and its mist wafted around the two lovers, who stood alone on the platform looking at each other. As Joe watched, he saw a transformation in Gloria that began when the happiness in her eyes turned to fear. This was something, he had come to understand, that some rape victims have to work to overcome. He did the only thing he knew to do. Joe touched her hands, her arms, and ran his fingers through her luxuriant hair. He tried to brighten her up with light conversation. She stood in that same place on the platform with her shoulders set as if in dread. He thought she was coming around, only to feel she was tuning him out when the westbound commuter train stopped.

People flowed around them, rushing toward home. Gloria could have been a statue. The platform emptied until they were alone again. He took a step back from her. She reached out as if she were going to touch his lapel. "Please don't go. I'm so scared about prison."

"There is no reason to worry. All the charges were dropped. Come into my arms." Joe was at a loss as what to do. He saw the anguished look while she bit her lower lip. She held him off with stiff arms while she fussed with his coat buttons and felt his lapels.

"My life of freedom is about to be over. Mrs. Foyle called. They found Four Eff."

Four Eff? Father Covell was right, she has serious problems worrying her. Go slow. Joe held her hands and said, "We may have to go back and testify. He's going to draw a big sentence." Then as he watched, tears flooded her cheeks as she shook her head. The engine of an eastbound train hissed steam from its cylinders as it came into the station. A few commuters went their way. He drew her against him. "Please don't worry." *I know I've said it a dozen times.*

She pulled back from him and gripped his hands hard, as if trying to save herself from a fall. "We can't go back. I killed him. They'll come after me."

"Killed who?"

Tears overflowed both eyes. "Deputy John Diamond."

"You're not joking. How?"

"With Daddy's gun, then I buried him. Maybe it could have been called self-defense. Now that they found him, they'll see I shot him four times."

"Four times, wow! That's making sure. Come into my arms."

"I had no choice. He was going to kill me."

"Where did you leave him, down a mine shaft?" asked Joe.

"No, I buried him in cement just like he was going to do to me." Gloria recounted the evening, from the problems at dinner with her parents to Deputy John's abduction of Gloria and his demise.

Joe felt she was as tense as a jungle cat. At last she finished and he sensed her relaxing. He had wanted to ask the question, yet fearful of her response, "Who else have you told?"

"No one. I shouldn't have told you." Gloria shook her head.

Joe stood still and looked at his bride. He knew he had to say something that would console her. Later he would remember the words he said, but not the mental exercise of putting them together. "To put it in Ma's words, you make me so proud that my buttons keep popping. Thank you, twice. First for the courage to tell me and second, for doing what I should have done. Tell no one else, ever."

She tilted her head and came into his arms. They kissed. Afterward he looked up and down the platform. The station was again empty. He heard the distant sound of a train whistle coming toward the station. Two middle-aged women came onto the platform from the ticket office.

Gloria pressed against him as if she were trying to get inside his overcoat. "I'm scared. They'll figure it out."

Joe whispered into her ear, "Say nothing. The most immediate threat to your freedom is tying you to the bank robbery. Did you meet with Pano Kargolis after he got out?"

Gloria stepped back and poked Joe in the chest. "No! Look at me, please. Like I said to the FBI agents, I forgot I ever talked to him. Those agents scared the socks off me. Darling, what should I do?"

Joe stared at her. *I don't even remember Pano and Gloria talking to one another, but afterward, he asked me lots of questions about the county.* "Please hear me out. In our letters, we agreed that an end to family feuding was our number one wish because Ma and Pa are counting on us to settle in Goodwin. Besides, that high country is home." Joe paused long enough to turn his thoughts into words. "But now that's all changed. The feud won't end. I tried to get through to your father before I left to come here, but he slammed the door in my face. And now, while you told me about what happened to you, I realized all the more that you and I have to forget Goodwin. Our number one priority has to be our freedom and safety. Maybe the Lord is giving us guidance to leave and never return. There have to be other places with cool summers where you can flourish and I can survive. Stay with me, honey, I love you. I need you."

Gloria shivered, but kept him at arm's length.

He asked, "What's wrong?"

The train pulled into the station. "Joe ... Joe, I'm terrified about to-night."

Joe said, "I understand. Let's take one step at a time. Step one is to get on the train where it's warm. And step two is to have dinner and go dancing. Can you go that far?"

Gloria nodded as she looked at the train out of the corner of her eye.

Joe took her right hand in his and in a low, measured voice said, "I take thee, Gloria, to be my wedded wife, to have and to hold from this day forward, for better, for worse, for richer, for poorer, in sickness and health, to love and to cherish, till death us do part, according to God's holy ordinance; and thereto I plight thee my troth. We've lived through the 'worse' and the sickness. Let's give the 'better' and health a chance. I love you, Gloria Caulfels."

The conductor called out, "All aboard. All aboard."

She relaxed against Joe, and he folded his arms around her. "You memorized our vows! Please be gentle with me. Joe, I love you."

They kissed until the train's air brakes hissed, then grabbed their bags and ran to pull themselves aboard the slowly moving car.

Let Him Rot

ALSO BY MARION LONESTAR WELCH

The Wind Whisperer of Edy Swamp
The Menagerie Bar

Let Him Rot

by
Marion Lonestar Welch

Poetic Justice Books
Port St. Lucie, Florida

Published by Poetic Justice Books
Port Saint Lucie, Florida
www.poeticjusticebooks.com

ISBN: 978-1-950433-54-4

FIRST EDITION
10 9 8 7 6 5 4 3 2 1

contents

Let Him Rot

Day After Day

Monotony. Day after day. Detention home ain't no home. A house isn't a home without you, Daddy. Where are you? You tried so hard, working two jobs. Giving your heart, your love, your manly steady strength. Daddy, you are a man who thinks with your heart, you are not always wise but you try. Jim, I love you.

A couple days later a package arrives from South Dakota. It's a Mickey Mouse watch for me from Jim. He always touches my heart.

Wish he was closer.

Breakfasts here are awful. The oatmeal is thin and gooey, the toast is pale and gummy, the juice diluted. Not like the breakfasts Jim made. His were fun adventures. He'd start with a soft Indian chant:

Oh haw oh oh ho! Shame on you, lazy one. I will throw it out to the crows. Ungrateful child.

I of course was the lazy ungrateful child. I'd come giggling down the stairs, trying to sneak up on him. He would attack me, scooping me up, kissing my stomach, putting his ear to my tummy...saying, "Sounds empty to me. Feed this puny child." Pancakes, pancakes.

I miss you, Jim.

Thunder grumbles. The Indian spirit flexes its muscles. I see the angry serpent tongue lash out of the clouds. Oh, a storm is coming. Lightning slashes. The human heart quakes. Mother Earth, Father Sky, they come together in an orgasm of agony.

Where the hell is everybody? The matrons are missing. The girls, such as they are, are sleeping. I am the only one awake and seeing this son of a bitching storm. How many more agonizing years do I have to stay here, in this maggot infested detention home?

Truth and illusion that's what we have here. Faith and fantasy and despair. Doesn't sound like a good mix.

So what can we do? Nothing, just breathe and bear it. And remember something nice.

Just Breathe and Bear It

Terry, thirteen, dark curly hair, soft brown eyes, freckles, funny, sweet. It was a long time ago.

I peddled my bike to girl scout summer camp, seven miles. I was the only Indian kid there. I wanted to earn badges to sew on my sash, show I was as good as those white uppity girl scouts. And I did, tree finder, rock finder, star finder, beader, outdoor cook, and more. Then I got wind of boys' baseball. That did it, I loved sports. I held my own playing with and against guys. So I wandered up the hill to the baseball field.

So I walked on the field and said I want to play. They said no girls. Go to hell I play good. Try me. They did. I threw good, fielded good, ran good, hit good. They let me play. So I biked seven miles in and seven miles home after playing ball for nine hours.

There were wooden stands for people to watch the players. Good back stop, real canvas bases, water fountain. And lots of wonderful hot hours of ball. Some of the guys and I shared ciggies and cigars. I brought my own stolen tobacco and papers, knew how to roll them. By that time I was the shortstop.

Some of the parents and neighborhood kids came to watch. Two girls my age came to watch, me especially cuz I was the only girl on the team. They were my cheer section. Sometimes they brought me jujubes, cookies. They lived right across from the ball field. Patty lived in a big three story house right on the ridge, Terry lived in a white two story house. They were both Catholic and went to Holy Child on Sheridan Road. Patty's dad was a plumber and Terry's dad was the city treasurer. My dad was a lumberjack on the reservation.

Patty didn't always come to watch but Terry did. One really hot day, I ran over to drink from the fountain, threw water on my head and neck. Terry came up and said, "You're so hot, why don't you come to my house for lunch." Sounded great to me.

Her mother was a thin plain Irish lady, very sweet, made good egg salad sandwiches and strawberry Koolaid for Terry and me. Wonderful. Her mother accepted me, a sweaty, shy Indian kid. Terry thought I was some sort of girl hero playing on the boys' team. I thought she was fantastic. So polite and kind and pretty.

Terry asked me upstairs to her room. I had never seen such a girly room. Dolls, pretty pictures, holy cards. Terry was religious. I wasn't, had never been in a church. Terry convinced me to go with her now and then. I continued to go to her house for lunches.

One day it rained out our ball game, Terry invited

me over. It was just as well as I had hurt my leg in a slide. Damn. I was bloody and stiff. Terry was all worried and fussed over me taking me upstairs to fix my cut. The house was airconditioned and cool. I got drowsy on the edge of the bed and lay down.

Terry took a damp wash cloth, wiped my face. I closed my eyes in comfort. Terry touched my cheek with her fingers, then leaned down and kissed my lips, softly.

I was startled as I had never been kissed gently before. She laughed a delightful laugh, kissing me again...longer this time. I opened my eyes and kissed her back.

We spent almost as much time kissing as I did playing ball that summer.

One hot day in June we wondered east from the ball field to the high ridge of the park, found a hill heavy with deep pink wild roses. We sat down, picking and smelling the heady roses. The sun warmed us. Turning to each other we kissed and deeply kissed again. I had an orgasm. I have never been the same since.

That was our summer. I had plenty of sex, unwanted, but never like Terry, unpenetrated.

Terry went on to be valedictorian of her class, married a young handsome sailor.

I went on to kill my rapist and am in detention home for two more years, unless I confess. Then I'll be in prison for life.

Early Morning Duty

Barbara Barnes swings her dark red Jaguar sports car smartly into her assigned parking spot. She grabs her brief case and a brown envelope addressed to her from the county delinquent supervisor. Closes her car door and heads for her office to start a new day. The sky has few clouds, the sun is shining. She thinks it is good, *I'm early and can get a hazelnut coffee.* She goes to the cafeteria, gets her coffee, same as her ex-husband Jeff got her used to.

She hadn't thought about him in a long time. They drank hazelnut coffee while in college. They had started having sex, too. Oh well...time to get to work.

She placed the coffee on the right side of her fruitwood desk, checked the memos in the incoming tray, picked up the letter opener, slit the brown envelope. It was about Francine O'Donnell from her county supervisor. She unfolded the letter, looked at the photo attached. It stated that she had stabbed her brother Robert. *Good Lord!* Francine, her patient, her reticent patient.

She again looked at the photo, an Indian girl, an

angry tom-boy, definitely not a feminine Indian girl. There was nothing feminine or soft about this small child except her name. Yet even with this anger there was something vulnerable. What was it? Was it that she looked so alone?

Yet Barnes knew Francine, or Frankie as she called herself, had deep loyalty and love. She loved her Indian father, great grandmother and cousin. Hated her brother, disliked her mother. Loved animals, outdoors.

Was pleasant...but not open in offering comments in their professional meetings. Frankie is beginning to ask Mrs. Barnes about herself, like her horse and did Barnes like sports. Frankie was curious, but maybe Francine knew more about Barnes than Barnes had gotten from Frankie. But sometimes that's how it is in the beginning of earning trust between patient and psychologist.

Babble Mouth

They all swear not to tell, the used wives, the cuckold husbands, the pressured raped young girls, the backing down boyfriends from challenging the undeclared super-stud. The stud. George the electric company lineman, who by guile, direct penetration by penis, harvests any and all vaginas in sight. His aura is dominantly ugly.

This has gone on for years. there are many layers of emotions at play on the reservation life.

Tribe band members are all related, all two thousand.

That makes it complicated, Indian has married Indian, some Indians have brought in white mates which has resulted in many half-breeds, quarter bloods and even less, but all are tribal.

Sheriff Bannister has parked his squad car at the Community Café.

"Hi, Roy. How's it going?"

"Oh, goddamn mess with that killing on the rez. Have you heard anything? I hate to have to come over here. I'm married to Gail Lonestar. Gail's mother was Rebecca Bearheart from the rez before she married John Lonestar from Clam Lake."

It gets complicated. Married to a reservation member doesn't help.

"You Indians stick together, close ranks, clam up. You look at me as the white cop, forget I'm married to an Indian, rez Indian."

"What can I get ya?"

"Coffee, black coffee. Oh yeah, eggs over easy, couple sausage, biscuits."

Bannister, Sheriff Bannister stares glumly into his cup of coffee. Damn. Well, he's here early to meet up with FBI Anderson who has taken over the reservation murder case. Them goddamn police politics... shit. Why didn't they just take over the whole damn thing instead drag me along like a damn dog on a short leash.

Frankie is sitting out on the side porch, toasting pleasantly in the unseasonal warm sun, watching a fragile yellow butterfly dizzily zigzag in a wild pattern of flight. A whiff of wind boosted it out of control.

Two black cars, one the FBI, the other one Sheriff Bannister's, pull into the circular drive at the O'Donnell farm. Goldie the yellow lab runs out yapping and sounding alarm. She rushes and attacks Bannister's ankles and gets a kick for her bravery. Ridiculous as it seems, the fragile yellow butterfly seems to attack the FBI man's head. He takes a swipe at it in annoyance.

Frankie swings her legs off the porch, looks at the disturbance. Her mother opens the kitchen screen door and greets Roy Bannister. "What are you doing way out in this part of the sticks?"

"Well, Essie. This man is an FBI officer, and we want to ask you some questions about Frankie. If she's seen anything unusual or anyone wandering around down in the southwest end of your land lately. You know someone killed George Walz down there."

A crow rasps a dark babble of gossip.

Feeling Blue

I miss my father, his twinkling eyes and dimples. His touch, his love. I may be in a detention home but he's with Esther. You'd have to have lived with her to know what that means.

There's so much going on in that house of ours that he doesn't know. He works two jobs. Poor Jim. My mother has endless wants, new furniture, rug, clothes. Et cetera. We live on the reservation, no one has all the stuff we do. There is resentment by the Indian women who make do and respect their men.

The worst irritant is me. The kid who sees all, hears all and lucky for her doesn't tell all. I'm ashamed of her doings. Too many men, too many missing hours.

I find it hard to accept being disliked for being her kid. I walk into the tribal general store, women turn their backs, stop their conversation, don't invite me to their kids' birthday parties. It hurts. Especially, these are my classmates. I'm on their baseball teams, their football teams. I play with the boys, they're better competition, more fun. Girls play with dolls and stuff.

My dad sends me little gifts like mittens and wool socks, It's cold in Wisconsin. He writes me notes on what my horses and dogs are doing. How they miss me but not as much as him. They don't know how much I miss them, and being able to be outside. I hate being inside all the time.

My dad is the only good one in my immediate family. Well, Great Aunt Becky and Great Grandma Wabreeze. I adore them. I consider them my mother, my physical mother was my incubator. Then we split company.

Painted With Dark

Mrs. Barnes, the psychologist, asks Francine to share one of Frankie's days out in the swamp. "The swamp seems so important to you. Just relax and talk about it."

Frankie says, "Hmm, okay...

The swamp. Seems to me I was born in Edy Swamp. At least it was where I became aware of life and death. Where I was able to see suggestions of spirit form, not just their presence but also hear their voices. At first it frightened me, then I began to understand. Spirits have lives that travel in time between the past and the present.

I first became aware that I was not alone even though I had gone way out in the Edy Swamp to be alone. I went to get away from aggressive humans in my life. My mother's frustrations came from her stormy mind to her strong hands holding leather belts, rope, and braided riding whips making welts and open cuts in my skin. I never did know what I had done that was so wrong to deserve those beatings.

The marks embarrassed me as I had no good explanations to give my playmates or grownups. My inability to explain put me in a position of being some type of freak.

It was not the red marks that became maroon scabs, but more morbidly, the wounds that wept inside making me feel inferior, different. I went to the swamp for comfort.

The bright sunshine touched my skin in a warm, soothing way. Soft breezes fingered through my thick hair. And my eyes seemed to see in distance forever, blending with horizon, non-violent and quiet. This gave me space to breathe and observe my surroundings.

The smooth bark logs housed green and golden frogs, who stared at me. They were no challenge, just observing. Yellow buttercups calmly rose and fell on water movement. A small kelly-green beetle sat on one leaf sunning. Dainty scorpion flies hover seeking mosquitoes. An eager fish arched its body appearing golden from the early morning sun. Short slough grass bent over, dipping into the glass smooth water, and nature's voice sang a sweet song. This sweet song stayed in my mind and heart for days. At night when preparing to give myself over to sleep, I pulled the memory of this sweet perfect day up to my chin like a soft warm blanket, and securely went to sleep.

There were other days and nights when the swamp mood was not serene. Skies were dark with winds wailing, red willow bushes stripped of their dark green leaves, looking forlorn and frail against the frigid gale. The general glance was sullen and moody.

A bobcat silhouetted against an open space on thin ice, looking for a meal, seeing only sparse tufts of ice.

Where had all the animals gone? I had to learn to look...many had changed the color of their coats, some had gone into hibernation. Many of the birds had flown south, to return in spring. Winter is a different season. The brown weasel with its sharp whistle has turned into an animal with a blazing white coat with a black tail. It was called an ermine.

Flowers and chokecherry bushes fold up, turning to dismal dark foliage for view, giving no hint of their spring and summer glory. Rose petals fall off, no glamorous gift of color or smell, to turn into round solid rose hips.

But not all color is lost from winter's palette. The tops of the evergreen trees remain the first to receive the sun's rays. The orange bittersweet hanging from branches grabs my eye. As do brilliant shafts of scarlet, emerald and bold blue light, reflecting off distant peaks about a quarter mile away. This is dramatic, there are no breaks in these shafts of color. Nature's prism.

Why do I hike out in the swamp? Because it is my escape from my mother's anger and my brother's sexual pursuit of me. I am the youngest and smallest in our family.

I am not willing to be the victim. I will fight back. One way is for me not to be in their range. Outside, be outside, be on the lookout and get a head start. I will outsmart them, outlast them and outlive them.

Popeye

Cornflakes without fruit...

Oh, worse yet? Cheerios...ugh.

And then Eleanore Larsen. If I have to hear how her stepfather did her... And worse yet how she liked it. Hasn't anyone in this place ever read a book? If so, probably that crappy one, *East Indian 100 Sexual Positions*, or romance magazines.

I'd like to play baseball, ride my horse. To hell with these dumb girls. They talk about the rich guys they're gonna marry. Oh boy! Get real.

I wonder how I'm gonna get new shoes; I have a hole in my right one. I wonder if my new friend, Charmaine, is really pregnant and wonder what they do with babies here. I heard some girls have had babies but I don't see any.

Maybe I can write Jim in South Dakota to send me some good shoes instead of mittens. Wonder how he is doing living alone in South Dakota. What really happened between him and Esther? Bob is with Esther. Jim said he had to sell the horses. There is nothing to go back to, never was much. Jim says he gave my dog, Brownie, to Aunt Becky.

One of the matrons comes into the dining room and asks me to go outside and pick flowers for Mrs. Dahlman's office. I'm glad to go outside for any reason. I go to the flower bed with zinnias, big flowers, orange, happy-faced flowers.

I am bending over to pick them when I see an orange furry cat laying there twisted, head separate, blood. It's my stray adopted one-eyed pet Popeye. Who has killed him? Why? Poor little runt, hope he is in cat heaven all healed and happy, playing tag with other kittens.

Shit, so many people are cruel.

Great Grandma

There is a stir in the big room. I hear the girls laughing, shrieking, running. So what's up? I go peek out the window in my door. I see nothing. The angle is wrong.

Mrs. Barnes, the shrink, comes to my room. I'm still in solitary. "Suicide watch."

"Come to my office. You have two visitors. You'll have more privacy there."

I follow her, and there is my great grandmother, Wab, Wabreeze, and my cousin, Manny. I am amazed.

Wab is over a hundred years old, still straight, strong and stern. Her dark black fierce eyes quickly look me over. She comes to me, embraces me. I tear up and nuzzle my face against her, smelling her cigar and good wood smoke smell.

She looks at me a long time, searching my face. Reaches out her brown, gnarled hand, flicks where my braids had been before the detention barbers had hacked them off. Short hair is a sign of mourning in the Ojibwa world. Wab tilts her head sideways...

snorts her disapproval.

Mrs. Barnes moves the maroon upholstered chair for Wab to sit on, smiles. Wab doesn't smile back. Manny laughs, I grin. Wab is Wab.

Wab presses a package wrapped in deerskin containing cooked cold wild rice and venison. She smiles and calls me her little *kush kush*. It means little pig, a private joke between us, I laugh...and cry and hug her waist. She is much taller than I. Great Grandma is a six foot Lakota Sioux who was married to my great grandfather, Chief Ibze.

Wabreeze is a special person in my life. She is my father's grandmother. He is her favorite grandchild. Jim is very loving, so is she. I'm very lucky to have them in my life.

My father asked me if I wanted to make a big hit with Wabreeze. I did. So he told me to go into the tribal store and buy cigars, plug tobacco and snuff and give them to Wab. Her face lit up and I was in. We became pals not just relatives. She even shared her cigars with me. We puffed away into a blissful state of *negaunee* - heaven.

Although I never learned to like the plug tobacco or snuff. I never knew what to do with the spit. I swallowed it once and got sick.

The tribe is proud of Wab's strength and tell the story of an Ojibwa man insulting her by putting his hand on her breast. She turned, took her fist and knocked him down and out! It is said that she was the daughter of Red Cloud's third wife. Red Cloud was a war chief of the Sioux. Guess the genes gone into Wab.

My cousin Manny stands looking around the detention school office. The girls flit by looking at the good looking Indian boy. He grins, lapping it up. He has driven Wabreeze out to the juvenile detention home where I am in. He had to as Wab had threatened to walk the thirty miles. And she would have. She is a determined stubborn woman.

I introduce Mrs. Barnes as my doctor. Wab wants to know if I'm sick. No, I explain that Mrs. Barnes talks to me. Wab looks at Barnes hard.

In our last embrace, Wab whispers in my ear, " Did you do it?"

"Yes."

"Good. Keep quiet. He was a bad man. You are a warrior, they don't understand."

"Take good care of Wab, Manny."

He laughs. "You know I will, but no one can 'take care' of her. She does what she wants."

I say, "Love you both."

After they leave, Mrs. Barnes commented, "You seem to love each other but you didn't say very much."

I laugh. "We don't have to. We already know."

Bang

I was the hunted. I snuck out of the house and headed for the woods and swamp. But this day, the guy with the big red cock was on my trail. I ducked down in the tall yellow swamp grass, cut into the cold creek, stooped down, held my breath.

"Hi, Frankie. Thought you might like to see my new Ithaca shotgun."

Shit!

He came up behind me, wrapped his big hairy arms around me, reached down, whipped his hard cock out, jiggled it in my face saying, "Suck it." I knew the routine. He grabbed my throat, squeezed my mouth open, I gagged, he forced his cock in. "Suck." He lurched, throbbed with orgasm...relaxed. Left me with a cup full of cum. I coughed, gagged. It ran out my nostrils, scalding. I grabbed his gun, lined it up, squeezed the trigger...Bang! Bang again right in his balls.

He screamed, fell down, puking blood. I smacked him on the side of his head with the stock of his gun.

Kicked him in his ribs. "Rot, you S.O.B." Stood staring at his twitching body. Took my knife, cut his prick off, stabbed it. Threw it in the dark water.

An eagle screamed.

Then everything went silent.

These Foolish Things

I remember this, these really... The beautiful yellow and red hard plastic hunting knife you gave me. The Horner harmonica that I played day and night, I only knew three songs. Esther threatened to hang me by my thumbs if I didn't stop playing it in the house. I got on her nerves. The Indian ponies you gave me, the brown paint Raindrop, the circus horse Trixie and Danny the roan beauty. What wonderful horses. What wonderful memories, what a wonderful father, patient and funny, for a young Indian kid.

You taught me to skip stones on water, how to make slings, set almost invisible traps, spear fish. How to respect life and not torture or waste animals. How to make friends of them, study their ways and treasure their babies. You could set me any task, I would do it for you.

We whittled bass wood bears and deer, made flutes of hickory and played duets across from each other on the lake. You taught me to muck my horses' stalls. I remember how proud I was when you gave me an Army McClellan saddle so I wouldn't get too hot riding.

I remember how you let me name every new pet animal. I wasn't very imaginative, Brownie the Great Dane, my pal. Irish, the Irish Setter. Butter, the big orange cat, Tweetie the canary, Momma Duck, obviously the wounded duck I rescued, and Bandit, my racoon, and Patty, my baby deer.

I remember how you made me pick up all the striped ground squirrels I had foolishly shot with the first twenty-two rifle you gave me. You made me clean and cook them and eat them. A hard lesson when the rest of the family ate fried chicken, mashed potatoes and cherry pie. Plus I couldn't sit at the table, I was set at a separate table, sniffling and gagging, totally ashamed.

I didn't shoot at snakes or birds anymore, either. Those carcasses hadn't been found. Hard lesson learned.

Esther and her sisters gave me dolls. I didn't like them.

You brought home a great teddy bear that grunted when he was tipped. I loved him.

I remember the Mickey Mouse watch you sent me from South Dakota. Some damned girl stole it from me at detention home. I saw it on her and broke her finger for being the thief she was. No one steals from me.

The Awakening

Barbara Barnes saw Frankie's shortness, her dark bright eyes intent, saw her frown from sizing her up in contrast to her gentleness in gazing at Aunt Becky, Rebecca Lonestar, tribal holy woman. Frankie on alert, wild, beautiful as a doe. She was not a child anymore but a young Indian woman, with her antenna picking up vibes, her quick mind sorting and evaluating emotions, gleaning reason. The young man, her cousin, black shoulder length hair longer than Frankie's recently institutional cropped hairdo making her look like a young boy, but her body did not. She had strong rounded arms, breasts peeking through her light blue sacky dress. She was short with broad shoulders, athletic, tan skin, tight high cheekbones.

Smiling, Aunt Becky embraced the young girl, stroking her hair, saying, "Soon, you will be released. You shall come stay with me. I have the farm on Clam Lake, you always liked it. It is quiet, pretty. And you will wake every morning seeing the sun shining on the water. Sometimes deer come up to our house from the meadow. Miss Barnes tells me you have learned cooking. That is good. You can help me. I have foster Indian children, the Scotties. And of course, Brownie"

Time Goes By

Time goes by.

It's like the grown ups who are in charge of us hate fresh air. They must know something we don't...like leaves of plants are carnivorous waiting to leap on us suck us dry to die. Maybe the birds are in on the conspiracy too, as if birdsongs touch our eardrums, we'll disintegrate.

Outside my bedroom window I hear the begging of a waif kitten, disfigured, missing one eye and a ripped off ear. Crying to come in. I tell it, it doesn't wanna. It's worse in here. In here they try to break your spirit if the world left ya with any. Run cat! Oh, you're crippled...tough shit.

Time crawls on its stubby legs, looks at its handless watch. Like that painting, with the clock melting, sagging over the edge of a table. That painting by that sad assed guy with the skinny long mustache. That's what our days are like, shitty days.

Nights are nauseating, we girls lie on scratchy over chlorinated sheets, flat skinny pillows and our individual monster thoughts sneer at us.

The End

Three dark sinister gray slender clouds course swiftly, cutting into voluminous soft pink clouds, forerunners of the early evening sunset. An ancient tired green Ford truck lumbering on a two lane road to Pine Ridge Reservation in North Dakota. The father and half-breed daughter are laughing, munching on Fig Newtons, Payday candy bars, smoking flavored cigars and the daughter sipping Diet Pepsi. They're excited, planning on getting an early start the next morning for their long planned trip to Peace River, Saskatchewan, Canada. The father is laughing telling how she will love Frenchie, his pal who tells great stories, mostly lies. Frenchie is a great cook and great hunter.

Frankie says, "Oh, great. Good thing we bought lots of ammunition for our guns." She reaches up and pats the rifles on the gun rack hooked on the back window of the cab of the truck.

Jim laughs. "You're ready for anything, huh yeah, Sport."

"Yep."

There are suddenly squealing tires. Jim glances in the mirror of the pick-up. A garbled message blares out, "Pull over."

Jim knows it can't be him. Frankie looks back. Three shots from the pursuing car zing out the truck's back window. Jim speeds up. More shots. Frankie grabs her rifle, leans back, returns shots. Then a barrage of a tommie gun bursts.

A volley of FBI shots hit her, blowing half of her head off. Brains and blood spew in the air.

Jim screams, "Baby are you alive?" There is no answer.

Jim loses control of the truck, yanking the steering wheel. It lurches as the right rear tire is shot out and leaps a long pine log laying on the side of the road. The truck flips, gasoline spills. More shots but this time the tommie gun hits the truck. It bursts into fire. Jim jumps out, takes his 45 automatic and sends the whole magazine into the FBI. They return fire. Twenty bullets, cutting his body to pieces. He slumps, blood red, dead.

A hawk screams then there is a terrible silence.

They have killed the father and daughter for nothing. They were chasing the wrong truck.

There is no dream, no Peace River. There are only flames, the scorch and scent of death.

Marion Lonestar Welch is an elder of the Band of La Courte Orielles Ojibwa/Chippewa Indian tribe reservation in upper Wisconsin. Known as Lonestar, Marion is a free spirit and a child of nature. She started writing at eighty years old. She lives in Florida, where she is a member of the Morningside Writers Group.

More Titles from Poetic Justice Press

Kentucky Underground [5/2020]
by Paula Martinez

Broken Lines [4/2020]
by Isor Baridakara Deezua

Good Party [3/2020]
by Jeff Weddle

Noemi & Lips of Sweetness
by Ahmad Al-Khatat

Behind the Blue Edge of the Sea
by Judy Shaffer

London Waiting
by Mike Maggiano

Ink
by Lane Mochow

Growing Up Holy and Alone
by Adam Levon Brown

Dear Miss B
by Dominic Albanese

Things Get Weird in Whistlestop
by Julie Carpenter

xenophobicracy
by Ngozi Olivia Osuoha

If It Wasn't for the Earwigs, I'd Be Deaf
by Rose Aiello-Morales

Dead Man's Hand
by Jeff Weddle

Princes & Tides
by Dawn Taggblom

NDN: the words of a little hawk
by Elaine Gerard

Collecting Stars from a Night's Sky
by Clifford Benjamin Oppong

The Black Rose
by Kris Haggblom

The Last Beach Night
by Richard Pruitt

Riding Bareback Backwards
by Christina Quinn

The Death of Disco
by Alicia Young

Break
by Adam Levon Brown

Smile
by Alfred Gremsley

Ten Tiny Tales of Terrible War
by David Teinter

By Some Happenstance
by Dominic Albanese

Tales of Lord Su
by I Kyūu

For Those Who Don't Know Chocolate
by Amirah al Wassif

Hammer of God
by Aria Ligi

available wherever books are sold
Visit https://www.poeticjusticebooks.com/PoeticJusticePress
for information and to order our latest titles